Stalking Throckmorton

A NOVEL

GARY F. JONES

BQB
North Carolina

Published in the United States by BQB Publishing
(an imprint of Boutique of Quality Books Publishing, Inc.)
www.bqbpublishing.com

Printed in the United States of America

978-1-952782-85-5 (p)
978-1-952782-86-2 (e)

Library of Congress Control Number: 2022951143

Book design by Robin Krauss, www.bookformatters.com
Cover design by Rebecca Lown, www.rebeccalowndesign.com
First editor: Caleb Guard
Second editor: Allison Itterly

PRAISE FOR
STALKING THROCKMORTON

AND AUTHOR GARY F. JONES

"Set in a western Wisconsin village near LaCrosse, this memorable novel exudes warmth while delivering an engaging traditional murder mystery connected to the brewery history of this region. Christopher Throckmorton is an admirable three-dimensional amateur sleuth in his thirties. His young son Ben is battling leukemia—an aspect adding emotion and even more urgency to the story. Gary F. Jones has given readers the ingredients for an enjoyable novel: small-town politics and humor, sweet and awkward romance for Chris, a boy we root for, and a wonderful fast pace in a mystery that matters to characters we care about. Highly recommended."

– Christine DeSmet is a mystery author,
writing coach, developmental editor, and member of
Mystery Writers of America and Sisters in Crime.

CHAPTER 1

C arl Kessler was only a shadow in the moonlight as he parted from a tree and slipped through open wrought iron gates on Cass Street, once the preferred address of lumber barons in La Crosse, Wisconsin. The gates to the mansion hadn't been closed in fifty years. The fragrance of roses hung in the cool night air as the shadow blended into the overgrown shrubbery along the drive. He reappeared moments later at the rear of the house.

A credit card in the crease between the door and jamb gained entry. His night-vision goggles, held in front of his eyes by a headset, resembled a small pair of binoculars. In the dark house, the goggles turned the moonlight streaming through the windows into green-tinged day. He worked his way through the dining room and parlor to the library. The library door was locked, as it had been the last time he was in the house. Picking it was child's play.

A coin, the 1804 draped Liberty Bust silver dollar owned by the Kessler cousins, had disappeared between 1900 and 1905. It was worth a fortune today. He guessed that the coin, or information on it, would be in the library or in furniture in use in the master bedroom when the coin disappeared. Drawn curtains blocked the moonlight in the library. He set the night-vision goggles aside and pulled a flashlight from his backpack to search the room. It took two hours to skim through the contents of the desk and an antique wooden filing cabinet. As Carl sorted through a four-generation collection of receipts, invoices, report cards, and letters, he was careful to leave everything as he found it in the desk. By the time he'd finished with the filing cabinet, his patience was exhausted. He threw papers over his shoulder. He pawed books off shelves, flipped through them, tossed them on the floor and checked for hidden cubbyholes behind the shelves. He didn't even find a mention of his quarry.

Next was the master bedroom. He liked to use the goggles and a starlight illuminator when people were around. The sticklike illuminator gave off only as much light as a starry night. With his goggles, he saw everything. They saw nothing. The old lady wouldn't be a problem if she left him alone. He'd cut the phone lines when he entered the house.

The parquet floor creaked as he walked to the grand staircase. The squeaks and groans grew louder as he climbed the stairs and tiptoed down the musty second-floor hallway toward the master bedroom. Traces of lilac perfume reminded him of his grandmother as he approached the door at the end of the hall.

His grandmother had been a shrew. She'd despised him, and he hated her.

A bedroom door opened, and antique electric wall sconces blazed to life. The safety shut-off on his goggles saved his vision. He flipped the goggles up and out of the way. A thin woman with wispy gray hair stood in the open doorway clutching a threadbare blue robe to her bony chest. Thick glasses in tortoiseshell frames magnified her startled eyes.

"Who . . . who are you?" she demanded.

"What does it look like, lady? I'm a thief. Go back to bed. I'll be gone in a few minutes."

Maybe she'd had it with the indignities of growing old, or

perhaps rage at a lifetime of losses overcame fear. She screamed and rushed him, snatched at his goggles and ski mask. Both came off.

"You! You're one of the workmen—"

Her nails were sharp. The bones of her wrist crunched as he grabbed her. Carl pulled her to the stairway, planted one foot, swung her out over the stairs, and let her go. She landed on her back halfway down the staircase, somersaulted onto her head, and landed in a crumpled pile at the foot of the stairs, arms and legs akimbo.

The angle of her neck indicated she was dead. He returned to her bedroom and closed the green velvet drapes. The renter in the old carriage house might be suspicious if he saw lights on at 3:00 a.m.

He ignored the double bed and two dressers. The straight lines and blond wood screamed post-World War II. What he sought would most likely be found in older furniture, something in use around 1900. The other two bedrooms contained more post-war furniture. A door at the end of the hallway opened on the stairway to the attic. The attic air was still broiling from the hot day. He used his light stick to clear spiderwebs from his path as he wended his way around steamer trunks, old floor lamps, dust-covered furniture, and bat droppings. Near the far wall he found what he was looking for: pieces of a dismantled four-poster bed, an ornate dresser with a mirror, and an armoire, all laden with dust-covered spiderwebs.

The dresser drawers were empty. The first two drawers of the armoire held men's clothes so old and moth-eaten they ripped when he pulled them out. Tucked in a thin drawer behind sets of cufflinks was a packet of letters. Another collection of worthless papers? He almost tossed them in frustration but forced himself to read a few.

The first letter he tore open, postmarked 1901, recounted the funeral of a New York Kessler, Carl's great-great-grandfather. His pulse quickened near the end of the second letter, addressed to Joseph Kessler, postmarked 1903. That was around the time the coin disappeared.

"As we agreed," the letter read, "I'll hold the 1804 draped Liberty Bust silver dollar for now. I've entrusted it to my secretary."

His secretary? Who the hell was that? He picked up the envelope and examined the return address. It took only a minute to decipher the script, as the handwriting was clear: "Oscar Kessler, 470 Mound Ave, Rockburg, Wis." Confused, he stuffed the envelope into his backpack. He had a secretary's family to track in Podunk.

CHAPTER 2

C hris Throckmorton turned on the air conditioner in his car on a sweltering Friday. Mid-September in Wisconsin wasn't supposed to be eighty-six degrees and humid. An accountant, he'd shed his suit coat and tie at the end of his meeting for a client at the Federal Trust and Savings. In his early thirties, he hated wearing suits. He'd take business casual any day.

Throckmorton was one inch shy of six feet, lean, and almost rangy. His medium-length brown hair was beginning to recede, but that was covered by a comb-over. There was nothing remarkable about his face. In college, girls found it so forgettable he'd considered growing a beard but never got around to it. He hoped the glasses he'd had to get recently added a little interest to his appearance.

Turning west off Losey Boulevard onto Cass Street, he headed toward the Mississippi and an older part of La Crosse. The dappled shade from the maple and oak trees lining the residential street was welcome but made it more difficult to make out the house numbers, as block by block, the houses became older, grander, and set further from the street. His jaw dropped when he came to the Kessler house. *House? It's a mansion.*

He checked his notes to make sure he hadn't made a mistake, turned into the drive, and drove the two hundred feet to the house. Years ago, his mother had mentioned distant cousins in La Crosse who'd done well in lumber until the white pine ran out in the 1920s. She hadn't exaggerated, but it appeared that the family fortune had gone the way of the pine. The house, a great Victorian pile of red brick, needed tuck-pointing, the woodwork needed paint, and the grounds looked like the gardener had been AWOL for a decade.

Granite steps led him up to a veranda and the front door. He rang the doorbell and waited. Adele Kessler had sounded elderly on the phone. It could take her a while to answer the door in a house this size.

They'd identified each other as fifth cousins through Ancestry DNA, and she'd invited him to drop by at two o'clock. The visit was convenient for him—he was in La Crosse for the meeting, and he'd never met any relatives of his mother's.

He rang the bell again. A car drove up as he waited, and a middle-aged woman dressed in shorts, a white blouse, and carrying grocery bags got out and approached him. "Adele's not answering the bell?"

"Not for the last five minutes," Throckmorton said. "She asked me to drop by this afternoon."

"Oh dear. She tends to nod off after lunch. I'm Eleanor. I shop for Adele, do a little cleaning, help her with the laundry. Here, hold these." She handed him the grocery bags, searched her purse, and brought out a key. "I usually go in the back door—closer to the kitchen—but I saw you here." She opened the door, screamed, and dropped her purse.

Throckmorton peered over her shoulder. He gasped, pulled out his phone, and dialed 911. Judging from the shape of her body on the floor, Adele would never answer a door again.

CHAPTER 3

"Debbie . . . Debbie!" Throckmorton tried to get the clerk's attention for the third time early Monday afternoon. Only a few feet away, eighteen-year-old Debbie didn't respond. He was usually easygoing, but today he drummed his fingers at the checkout counter of Rockburg's drugstore. For a transplant from the Twin Cities, life in the rural Wisconsin village flowed as slowly as the La Crosse River that meandered below it. He'd had two years to get used to it, but today time seemed motionless. Debbie, the cashier, fussed with something on shelves a few feet from him. He couldn't tell whether she was engrossed in her work or ignoring him.

Throckmorton was civil to everyone. What he saw as good manners, his ex-wife Jen had seen as weakness and called him a spineless milquetoast for it. That made waiting for Debbie to do her job a lose-lose situation for him. If he resisted the urge to yell at Debbie, he'd hear Jen's voice question his manhood. If he barked at her, he'd feel like a heel. He set a bottle of aspirin onto the counter with a clatter, cleared his throat, coughed, and waited. He wasn't in a rush, but it was a beautiful day, and damn it, there were limits. "Debbie . . . Debbie!"

"Chris," said a familiar voice, and he felt a tap on his shoulder.

He turned to face a white-haired attorney. "Al, how've you been?"

"Fine, now that I've found you." The wizened old man drew

a letter from the pocket of his his white, short-sleeved shirt. "I have a letter for you from Otto Kessler."

Throckmorton searched Al Huss's face for signs this was a joke. "You can't be serious." He accepted the proffered envelope. Crisp and yellowed, it wasn't addressed or stamped. "Kessler died in 1935. That's what, eighty years ago?"

"Eighty-two. Long story." Al nodded toward Debbie and retrieved the envelope from Throckmorton's hand. "I saw you here as I walked to my office. Perhaps we should go there now to discuss this."

Throckmorton followed Al's gaze. Debbie leaned against the cash register. Her work abandoned and her head buried in a copy of *Teen Vogue*, she had an ear cocked toward him. The magazine was upside down.

Typical. In Rockburg he could pose a question to a friend on the street, stroll three blocks, and have a casual acquaintance volunteer the answer. If humans had developed language to allow them to gossip, as anthropologists speculated, the tradition remained robust in Rockburg. He paid for the aspirin and left the store with Al.

"How's that boy of yours doing?" Al asked as they jay-walked across the street. "Is Mrs. Heath still living in, keeping an eye on him?"

"No. We thought Ben's leukemia was in remission, but the last PET scan found malignant cells. He's on a maintenance dose of chemotherapy. It's enough to slow the replication of the cells, but it wasn't enough to prevent a recurrence. They want to use a new treatment that's been successful in curing cases like Ben's."

Throckmorton turned to look at something on the other side of the street in case he teared up. "The poor kid went through hell on the chemotherapy. He's only nine, and he suffered through oral ulcers, monthly intra-spinal shots, and septicemia. Once he was delirious for a week, jabbered away without making any sense."

"Sounds awful."

"They call the new treatment biotherapeutics. It's like an anti-cancer vaccine. They'll inoculate Ben and let his immune system do the rest—if I can pay for the treatment. My insurance won't cover it. They claim the treatment is experimental."

"Damned insurance companies. How much will it cost you?"

"Two hundred and thirty thousand."

Al let out a whistle. They walked in silence the rest of the way to his office.

A single-story blond brick building, the office was sixty years old according to the date chiseled in a cornerstone. That made it forty years younger than any other commercial building in the three blocks of Rockburg's business district. Al unlocked the front door. "I can't imagine what you're going through."

Throckmorton followed Al into the building. "I've taken out a second mortgage on the house to pay Ben's current medical bills. I don't know where I can dig up another $230,000. The doctors said they have to start the biotherapeutics by December fifteenth or start the hardcore chemotherapy again. I don't think he can go through that again. He'd rather die. I haven't had the heart to tell him about the last lab report."

Al turned on the lights. Empty bookcases against the far wall, an empty wastebasket, and the bare surface of a large walnut desk gave the room a deserted atmosphere. Squares of pale-yellow paint on the cream-colored wall marked where diplomas and bar association memberships had hung.

Al relaxed into a well-padded swivel chair behind the desk.

"I'm retiring, but I'd be happy to do what I can for you. Send me the information on the test, and I'll see if I can lean on the insurance company a little. Odds of success are low, but it's worth a try."

"I'd appreciate that." Throckmorton didn't get his hopes up. It would be a small-town lawyer against a clutch of insurance company attorneys. He took a chair beside the desk.

Al pushed the old envelope across the desk toward Throckmorton. "My grandfather was your great grandfather Otto Kessler's attorney. Otto wrote the letter a week before he died and left instructions to give it to his descendants living in Rockburg after the Depression ended. Gramps gave it to my dad when he started the practice, and he gave it to me when I passed the bar exams. I only learned you were a Kessler when I read the news about your cousin in La Crosse. You have my sympathy."

"I talked to the lady once on the phone. She was a corpse at our first face-to-face meeting. That was a shock. She was the last living relative I knew of." Throckmorton turned the envelope over in his hands. Fine lines spread across its surface with a crackle. A musty smell reminiscent of old books rose from the envelope. "I'm almost afraid to open it."

Al handed him a letter opener. "I hoped you'd do that here. I've wondered what it held for fifty years."

Throckmorton sliced open the envelope, and pulled out a letter. A key, four inches long, dropped on the desk with a clunk. He read the handwritten letter.

MAY 12, 1935

My doctor says my heart is going. The canning factory won't survive long after my death. No one can save it in this economy. You will need resources to restart the brewery when this business slump ends. What remains of my assets are in a foreman's office off tunnel number 4. My attorney can guide you to it. The key to the office is enclosed. The safe combination is 10R-30L-22R.

My prayers are with you, Otto.

"The ink is faded, and Otto's handwriting looks shaky," Throckmorton said. Then he read the letter again, this time out loud. Puzzled, he glanced at Al and back at the letter. "I'm not sure what to make of this. You said Otto died shortly after writing this. Could he have been hallucinating?"

Al shook his head. "According to my grandfather, it sounded like Otto was pretty much aware of things right up to the end."

"To restart a brewery would take a fortune, even back then." Throckmorton estimated it would have taken a chunk of seed money, a hundred thousand or more, to attract investors to restart the brewery in the late thirties. Depending on what they were, assets that were that valuable in 1935 could be worth millions now, or nothing. Millions would save Ben's life—if he could get to it in time.

He wondered how the brewery and canning factory were related and asked Al if they were in the same building.

Al nodded. "Every small town in Wisconsin had a brewery before Prohibition, and they all converted to canning factories in 1920. Most went bust." He turned the key over in his hand. "I would've thrown this letter away if I hadn't misfiled it in the seventies. I found it when I was cleaning out my office. You're the first Kessler descendant I've ever met. Any idea why others haven't returned?"

"There aren't any others. My grandmother and her brother moved to the Twin Cities after Otto died in '35. Mom was an only child, and her uncle Bill died a bachelor in Normandy on D-Day. Mom said we might have distant cousins in upstate New York, but she wasn't sure."

"They'd be irrelevant, vis-à-vis the letter," Al said. "Otto's instructions specified his descendants living here."

"Mom didn't talk about either side of the family." He looked down at the envelope and noticed a logo that said: "Kessler Brewing, Rockburg, Wis.". "I wish I'd seen the brewery."

"You came to town a couple of years too late." Al leaned back in his chair, a faraway look in his eyes. "It looked like a medieval castle at the end of Main Street. I hated to see it go, but it was in bad shape by 2014—bricks were falling off, kids getting in trouble exploring the place. The demolition was the biggest thing to happen in Rockburg in my lifetime. The executive office building and the tunnel under Main Street are all that's left of the Kessler complex."

"Why the tunnels?"

"You can't brew lager beer if the temperature gets over sixty degrees. They had to go underground to brew beer in the summer before refrigeration. There were tunnels and caverns under the brewery, but those weren't supposed to survive the demolition."

"Any idea where tunnel four is?"

"Not a clue. Best guess is that it and the foreman's office were under the brewery and filled in or collapsed when the building dropped."

Throckmorton turned the letter over. "Nothing here, either."

"If they were under the brewery, you'll have less than an acre to search. Gert at the Coffee Cup might know something about it." Al looked at his watch. "It's two. She'll be relaxing after the noon rush. Good time to talk to her—catch her before her afternoon nap."

"She's no older than you, is she? Otto wrote the letter years before she was born."

"Gert's been a waitress since . . ." Al looked at the ceiling and closed his eyes. "About 1965. A few old fossils used to tell her stories about the early days. She's heard more gossip than all the bartenders in town."

"That'd be a lot. Rockburg must hold a record for bars per capita."

"Six bars for nine hundred people should put us in the running." Al stood, pushing off from the chair armrests with his hands. His knees and back creaked as he did. "Gert acts like a grouch. She might give you a hard time, but she's all bark."

"I don't want this all over town," Throckmorton said cautiously.

"You can trust her. She'll bend your ear about the old days, but she can keep a secret. She griped once about feeling like the town's unofficial confessor. In the fifty years I've known her, that's the closest to gossip I've heard from her."

Throckmorton returned the key and letter to the envelope, thanked Al, and walked down the block to the Coffee Cup Café, a single-story, white, wood-frame structure squatting between two brick buildings. The first building he passed used to be a grocery store. It was now a store selling dubious antiques. The building on the other side of the café was the town's beauty parlor. Time hadn't been kind to Rockburg's business district. The windows of empty two-story brick buildings stared across Main Street as he headed to the café. The scene fit Throckmorton's mood.

From the corner of his eye, he saw Wilbur Woodside wave at him from the window of the antique shop. He pretended he didn't notice. Talking to Wilbur, a local horse trader and con artist, could call a man's sanity and integrity into question. A certified public accountant, Throckmorton wouldn't risk his reputation for either.

A breeze pulled at the envelope in his hand, and he tightened his grip. Otto's letter was consistent with a letter he'd found in his mother's things, a letter addressed to his grandmother and postmarked in 1936. The letter claimed substantial assets were missing when Otto's estate went through probate.

But why this treasure hunt? Why didn't Otto leave his assets to his son and daughter? Was resurrecting the brewery that important to him?

A bell above the door jingled as he walked into the Coffee Cup. He stood next to a jukebox from the 1960s and looked down the length of the café. It wasn't far. The place could feel cozy or cramped depending on how many people were there. A row of four booths sat on the right behind the jukebox. A white Formica counter and eight red vinyl and chrome stools stretched along the wall to his left. Beyond the counter and booths were the kitchen and a single restroom. A white-haired gnome of a woman relaxed in the third booth, stirring a cup of coffee and reading a newspaper.

She looked up from her paper. "Chris Throckmorton. My heavens, what brings you here to disturb an old woman's rest?"

"Mind if I join you?" he asked.

Gert motioned him to sit while she got another cup of coffee. He slid onto the cracked vinyl seat across from her. The brown vinyl shaded to purple and the original red around the edges.

"How's your son doing?"

He didn't want to go through that again. "He's doing well,

for now. Al Huss suggested I talk to you. He had a letter for me from Otto Kessler."

"A letter for you?" Gert's eyebrows rose. "You're pretty well preserved if Otto wrote you a letter."

Throckmorton explained the letter's history and its contents.

"Why'd you move back to Rockburg?" she asked. "Couldn't you stand living with sensible people?" She sipped her coffee. "If you were looking for the eccentric and peculiar, Rockburg is the mother lode."

It took effort for Throckmorton to keep a straight face. "Aren't you a little hard on Rockburg?"

"Do you know any other town that's had an attempted armed deposit?"

"Ah, what?"

"An attempted armed deposit. Back in the eighties, a young guy kept his stash of pot in his safe deposit box. He made a big purchase one night and was the first one through the door when the bank opened the next morning. The time lock on the bank's vault wasn't working, and nobody could get to the boxes."

Throckmorton leaned back and prepared for a story. He hoped it would be short.

"The kid got paranoid—thought it was a plot to steal his marijuana. Got so worked up he pulled out a gun. They talked him down, told him to come back later, but by then some idiot had hit the silent alarm."

"Isn't that what they're supposed to do?" he asked.

"Not if you want to keep it quiet that you can't get into your own vault."

That would be Rockburg. "Every town has somebody who's a little goofy," he said.

Gert relaxed into the booth's padding. "You weren't here

the year the townspeople got into a fight over whether to shut down the whistle that blows three times a day. Any idea what that whistle's for?"

"Nope. Farmers tell me they can hear it two miles from town."

"You can hear the damned thing in every bedroom in town too. It marks the shift changes at the canning factory that closed eighty-two years ago." Gert looked at him over her glasses. "Still think this town is normal?"

He had to agree. Commonplace events took absurd twists in Rockburg.

"Now, what about the letter?"

"If the canning factory went bankrupt, would Otto have had any assets left?"

Gert rubbed her forehead. "The canning factory declared bankruptcy months after Otto died. I heard wild tales when I started waitressing, mostly from old river rats and layabouts who met here to swap stories and nurse a cup of coffee. A couple of 'em claimed the Kesslers bought jewelry as an investment when the brewery was in its heyday. I wouldn't have believed those old fools if it weren't for one story they all agreed on. Kessler's daughter lost a diamond brooch at a church picnic in the park in '32 or '33. Half the church helped her look for it."

"Then the assets in the safe might be jewelry?"

Gert shook her head. "I doubt it. It would take a lot of jewelry to rebuild a brewery, and what a sick, old bird thought was valuable in 1935 might not be worth a leaky spittoon today. Whatever it is, it won't be easy to get your hands on it. The tunnels were supposed to collapse when they dropped the brewery, and the village owns the site."

"Think the mayor would let me search for the office?"

"Unlikely." She shook her head again. "The mayor doesn't

want people exploring. Big liability for the town if somebody gets hurt. Mucking around in what's left of the tunnels might make your son an orphan." She raised her eyebrows and looked him in the eye. "You know, the assets might not be jewelry. Mice or mold could have turned cash or bonds into confetti by now."

Throckmorton rested his chin in his hands and considered the word *orphan*. The thought of Jen getting her hands on Ben turned his stomach. He and Jen had been married for seven years, but neither he nor Ben had heard a word from her since she walked out three years ago. He'd tried to reach her through her attorney, but he hadn't been able to do even that once the divorce was finalized. She would ignore Ben and have her claws on the life insurance payout within a week. But this treasure hunt might be Ben's last chance.

"Do you think the Kessler murder in La Crosse is connected with the assets you're after?" Gert asked.

"I doubt it. We were fifth cousins. I looked it up: our last common ancestor would have been six generations ago. Any ideas where I can get information on the tunnels?"

Gert sipped her coffee. "Your best bet is the Rockburg Historical Society. They're only open on Tuesdays, and they're shorthanded. The staff is all volunteers, most over sixty-five. Try it Tuesday, and bang on the door if it's locked."

"Is there anyone I can contact to get in earlier?"

"Alice, but don't press your luck. Best not to start off by irritating her. The town constable thinks that's his job. And you may have bigger problems. The town board wants to get rid of the brewery lot, and Wilbur Woodside is sniffing around, looking to buy it cheap."

Throckmorton leaned back in his seat, a knot in his gut twisting. "Wilbur buys and sells farms and livestock. What would he want with an empty lot in a dying town?"

"We're talking about Wilbur, remember? Do you know anyone else who'd have the balls to sell a gelding for breeding or forty acres of swamp for farming? The buyers were blowhards who bragged all over town how they'd screwed Wilbur on the deals. When they realized he'd taken them, both of 'em kept quiet rather than admit they'd been played for fools."

"I've heard rumors about Wilbur but never details. I won't associate with a character like that."

"Rockburg doesn't have enough angels to be that picky. You'll get farther working with what good you find in people. I don't think you'll be a target for Wilbur, though. Buying, selling, and trading is a game for him. Pros don't play amateurs."

He glanced at his watch. "Time to pick up Ben. Thanks for the information."

Throckmorton left the café, got into his car, pulled onto the street, and swore. He was in Rockburg's daily traffic jam. School was out, and every bus the school district owned was on Main Street. Buses loaded with students celebrating the end of the school day bracketed him.

He Googled "Kessler" on his phone as he waited for the traffic to clear. There were thousands of hits. He added "New York" as a search term. There were still hundreds of hits. Near the top of the list was an unsolved burglary last month in Utica. Someone stole the letters and papers of Wolfgang Kessler and his heirs from a local historical museum. Wolfgang had made his fortune in brewing after the Civil War and died in 1891.

So there were Kesslers in upstate New York, and there'd been a break-in and theft of their papers. Rooms in the Kessler mansion in La Crosse had been ransacked the night of Adele Kessler's murder. There were thousands of Kesslers. Two break-ins might have been a coincidence. Otto wrote the letter in 1935, long after Wolfgang Kessler died. Still, whoever killed Adele was looking for something, maybe the same thing as the Utica theft.

The hunt for Otto's assets was loaded with unknowns. No one alive knew where the office or tunnel four were, but Throckmorton would never forgive himself if he didn't try to find it for Ben.

CHAPTER 4

Wilbur Woodside was dusting a display case in the old grocery store Monday afternoon when he saw Throckmorton walk by and head toward the Coffee Cup Café. Kind of late for lunch. That made it seem mighty odd. So was the display case—it'd been a freezer, but it hadn't worked in decades. It didn't need to, not since he'd turned the place into an antique store. It hadn't been much of a grocery store. He'd seen 7-Elevens with more floor space.

He rubbed his chin as Throckmorton entered the café. Everybody in town knew Gert would be settling down for her afternoon nap. Locals with any sense didn't interrupt her beauty sleep just to chit-chat.

Throckmorton was carrying an envelope. His hands had been empty when he'd crossed the street with Al. Put it all together, and Wilbur had a little mystery.

A short, bald, high-school dropout, Wilbur had a talent for turning little mysteries into tidy profits. It was especially gratifying when he extracted those profits from the hides of men who thought themselves his betters. Toward that end, he always wore dusty green work pants and worn work shoes. Together with his customary bland expression, it gave people the impression they were talking to a friendly dullard, someone easily fleeced.

Although he sold anything from cattle and farms to antiques, the natives called him a horse trader. In rural-speak, that meant he could've been a used car salesman if he ever turned honest. No one held their breath.

A dollar was a dollar, so locals scoured garages, attics, and abandoned barns for anything covered by cobwebs, dust, and bird crap. They'd haul in whatever they found for Wilbur's inspection. He'd attach a price tag and an antique, collectible, or *objet d'art* was born. The locals gathered that *objet d'art* was French for junk.

A bell jingled, the door closed, and Marty Schmidt, a tall, skinny guy with a weathered face leaned on the display case. He wore patched jeans, a short-sleeved shirt that had seen better days, and had a long stem of bromegrass in his mouth. "Mornin', Wilbur. I got a load of antiques in my pickup out front."

Wilbur followed him out the door. They stopped at a beat-up 1989 Dodge Ram parked in front of the store.

Hands on his hips, Wilbur frowned and shook his head. He hoped Marty hadn't noticed that he'd glanced at the truck but inspected its cargo. "I don't buy old trucks. Park this piece of junk somewhere else. It'll give my store a bad name."

"The truck's cherry, but I'm selling what's in the back."

Wilbur stepped closer to the back of the truck. If Marty could call this rolling piece of crap cherry, it'd be interesting to see what he'd call an antique. He pretended to ignore the white porcelain crown and an empty wooden crate next to it in the pickup's bed. "12 4oz Lith Tins, Standard Oil of New Jersey" was stamped on the crate. The crown was an ornament from a Standard Oil gas pump of the 1930s. A phone call would get him three hundred for the crown and the old crate. Four harness hames sat buried under other stuff. Hames were curved wooden and brass parts of a harness that buckled onto the collar. The wood was weathered, and the brass balls tarnished to a blue green. Probably came from old show harnesses. Slap "antique" and "verdigris" on the tags, and he'd get fifty a pair. He looked up *verdigris* on the internet the first time he heard the term. It struck him as a damned fancy word for brass that needed polishing.

The rest of the stuff in the truck should bring a hundred dollars. Two hundred if he called it *objet d'art*. Some fools would buy anything if it had a name that sounded French.

He turned to Marty, shook his head, and tried to look disappointed. "Marty, Marty, everything with cobwebs on it ain't an antique. A layer 'a dust don't mean somethin's valuable, and I'm not gonna buy everything you bring me that's covered with bird shit, even if ya squeezed it out of your pet rooster yourself. Now move your truck."

"Okay. Whatever you want," Marty said with a shrug and acted as though he was searching the front pockets of his jeans for the truck's keys.

Damn, Marty, Wilbur cursed to himself. Marty was getting too good at this. Wilbur had seen the key in the truck's ignition switch. "Ya don't deserve it, but I'll take the whole load off your hands for fifty bucks if you move the truck pronto."

"Seven hundred."

Wilbur pretended to stagger backwards. "Good God Almighty! Do I look like I was born yesterday?" Wilbur looked up and down the block. The sidewalks were empty, but what the hell. "People are lookin' at your truck. I want it outta here. I'll give you two-fifty if you move it quick."

"Five-fifty."

They settled on $450 for the load.

"Bring the stuff in," said Wilbur. "I ain't cartin' it in myself for that price." He stalked into his store, trying to look angry. Best guess? He'd profit $350 to $400 on the deal. Not bad for five minutes of work, plus another hour on the phone later.

With Marty's load tucked in his storeroom, Wilbur got back to Throckmorton. Why the devil was he dropping in on Gert in the afternoon? Throckmorton opened his office in Rockburg two years ago. That made him a newcomer by Rockburg standards. Maybe he didn't know Gert's habits, but he'd been in there quite a while.

He'd never done business with Throckmorton; in fact, he was sure Throckmorton avoided him. That wasn't unusual. Some people acted as though they'd soil their precious reputations if they got near him.

The way the locals responded to the guy's name amused Wilbur. Most of the town called him Throckmorton, not Chris. It was a point of civic pride. Every town had a Chris, maybe three or four, but damned if anybody knew of another town around here with a Throckmorton. Rockburg had little going for it, so the natives clung to anything unique about the town. That pretty much limited them to the abandoned brewery, that blasted whistle, and Throckmorton.

Wilbur had been in a bar in Westland when a local blowhard went on a rant about its wonderful new high school. Had a swimming pool and room for four hundred students. When the jerk called Rockburg High a dilapidated antique with room for only two hundred, Art Schroeder, a guy from Rockburg sitting next to the braggart, took offense. He stood straight, raised his eyebrows, and jabbed a finger in the bastard's chest. "Yeah, every two-bit town has a school, but Rockburg's got a Throckmorton. Ya got one of those in this pissant burg?"

Art had finished his beer in a gulp, slammed the empty glass onto the bar, and stomped out of the tavern before anybody could ask him what in hell a Throckmorton was. Wilbur stayed put on his stool and nursed his beer while the Westland locals bickered over who'd won the argument. He had made a point to remember the incident because he'd have to be careful if he ever traded horses with Art.

He scratched the stubble on his chin. Good chance he could make a profit keeping an eye on Throckmorton. He'd talked to Al, picked up an envelope, and hustled down to the Coffee Cup where he spent quite a while with Gert before driving off in his car. Whatever they talked about was important. Gert wouldn't have put up with anything else during her nap hour. He'd done it once and the old buzzard had ordered him out, cussing like a marine.

CHAPTER 5

Throckmorton pulled into the parking lot beside the Rockburg elementary school. Ben waved from the steps at the school entrance and walked to the car. His hair had grown back, but he still wore a stocking cap whenever he was outside. Anyone who'd gone through rigorous chemotherapy was exquisitely susceptible to infections.

Nine-year-old Ben took his time, frequently turning back to watch mothers picking up their children. Throckmorton cringed; he was lonely himself and felt helpless to fill the hole in Ben's life. The more the mothers hugged their kids, the more depressed Ben seemed. Jen had walked out on them three years ago. She'd texted Throckmorton to tell him to pick Ben up at school, and she was gone when they got home. A note she left made it clear their marriage was over and she was filing for divorce. It took a while to internalize the note, but after reading it, Throckmorton felt more relief than jealousy or betrayal.

The first years of their marriage hadn't been bad. Jen criticized him about small things, but she'd lightened the critiques with humor. Her appraisals took on a sharp edge after Ben was born. She lit into Throckmorton once about the way he'd opened a plastic sack from a grocery store. He suspected undiagnosed depression magnified their problems, but she refused to talk to a professional. Her criticisms of him had become more pointed, more frequent, and more sarcastic. He found himself editing everything he said to avoid her remarks. And their sex life? That never recovered from Ben's birth. By the time she walked out, they resembled roommates who barely tolerated each other. Hell, after she filed for divorce, she'd insisted he communicate with her only through her lawyer. He didn't even know if she knew about Ben's leukemia.

Ben climbed into the passenger seat, and Throckmorton checked to make sure he was strapped in. He noticed the seat belt was a little tight. Good. Ben had gained weight. "How'd your day go, kiddo?" It took all Throckmorton's strength to shove the doctor's report out of his mind and avoid crying.

"Okay," Ben said, not taking his eyes off the other kids and their mothers.

Throckmorton pulled into traffic and eased past a line of cars loading kids. "Did your teacher comment on your project?"

"No."

"Did you get tired today? Still able to handle a whole day of school?"

"Dad, I'm okay. I'm keeping up with the work, and Mrs. Jones said everybody's had their vaccinations, so you don't need to worry about that either."

Throckmorton adjusted the rearview mirror to watch Ben. *He knows my questions before I ask them.* He saw Ben crane his head toward the waiting cars, his attention glued to his classmates and their parents. Ben was usually chatty after school, but today his lower lip trembled. Something must have happened in school.

"How was the math test you studied for last night?"

"Okay."

He tried again. "Did the tutor help?"

"Uh-huh."

"Anything happen in class?"

"No."

Throckmorton gave up trying to start a conversation and

the car remained quiet for most of their drive. A block from home, Ben murmured, "I wish I had a mother. A brother would be nice too."

Throckmorton took a slow breath before answering. He'd do anything for Ben, but how could he explain the intricacies of marriage to a kid? He'd tried, repeatedly, but he always came back to some variation of "it's complex." The comment had become routine since the divorce. Sometimes Ben would suggest a woman, any age, married or single, as a possible new mother. He wasn't sure whether Ben missed Jen or missed a mother figure. She'd been a hands-off mother. Whatever her problems, it was he and Ben that had to make a go of his family.

"Things like that take time," he said. He felt more sympathy than optimism. The last years of his marriage had left him with little self-confidence with women, not that he'd had a surplus before. In high school, he was a thin, gangly nerd in a school that exalted jocks. In college, he studied physics and math, then switched to business and accounting. Not many coeds in those majors. It was only in the required humanities courses that he'd met many women. They thought him so clueless about fashion and color coordination that one of his dates assumed he was color-blind—a discussion he preferred to forget. His forays into small talk had been awkward. He tried too hard to impress, and his lack of confidence had been crippling. Worse, according to his roommates, he hadn't recognized it when girls had shown an interest in him.

Dinner of ham, baked potatoes, and green beans was quiet. Ben did his homework while Throckmorton cleaned up in the kitchen. He read to Ben before bedtime, a habit they'd gotten into when Ben was hospitalized. Tonight he read for longer than usual. Whatever happened at school that day had brought fresh urgency to the hole in Ben's heart. Throckmorton wished he knew how to deal with that, but until he figured it out, cuddling and closeness were all he could provide.

When Ben dropped off to sleep, Throckmorton carefully eased off the bed and tiptoed out of the room. A few minutes later he buried himself in work until *The Late Show*. Work helped keep loneliness at bay.

He thought of Otto's letter again. Even with health insurance, Ben had racked up eighty-five thousand in medical bills. That had taken every cent Throckmorton could lay hold of. The new treatment was out of reach unless Otto or Al came through for him. It could take a month to turn whatever was in the safe into cash. He'd better be in the safe by mid-November. That gave him two months to get around Mayor Earl's control of the lot, find the tunnel, and excavate to the office. He couldn't afford to give up his accounting practice. Any work he did on Otto's letter would have to be in his spare time, and he'd have to do it before Wilbur bought the lot.

Thinking about a medical system that balanced Ben's life against how much money he could raise often made him so furious he couldn't think, but he couldn't afford that. He had to stay clear-eyed and calculating, even scheming, to save Ben's life. On his way to bed, he snuck into Ben's room. Ben was sound asleep. Throckmorton watched him for a moment before tucking him in and kissing his forehead.

CHAPTER 6

Carl Kessler sat on the edge of his bed and pulled on his socks. Killing the old lady at the Kessler mansion had been a mistake. Cops paid attention to murders. His search for the 1804 draped Liberty Bust silver dollar had dragged him from Utica, New York, to La Crosse, Wisconsin, and now to a jerkwater hole named after rocks. It was sucking up time, but finding the coin would be worth it. Traveling with his girlfriend JP wasn't cheap, and he didn't want to leave a paper trail. He'd applied for credit cards under stolen identities before leaving Utica. The address he used was an apartment he kept in St. Paul under a false name.

After murdering Adele and searching the mansion, he'd driven from La Crosse to his St. Paul apartment to wait for the credit cards. Once in his St. Paul apartment, he'd taken time to stretch and do his normal fifty pushups each morning. He had to stay supple and in shape, but he couldn't look so muscular that people noticed. He was six feet tall, but average looks and medium build made him forgettable.

After a romp in the sack with JP, he'd suggested she stay in St. Paul while he searched for the coin in Rockburg. That idea crashed before he'd completed the sentence.

JP was built, and she kept herself in shape. Unfortunately, working out was about the only work she did while he was around to pick up the tab.

"So what am I supposed to do while you're whooping it up in Wisconsin?" she'd asked.

"Whooping it up in Rockburg?" He'd given her an amused stare. "Really? Rockburg?" He'd read her his notes. "Population 912. I hear the social life is frenetic—drinking beer and watching reruns on TV until the sidewalks roll up at eight o'clock."

"I can read Wikipedia too. Rockburg is nineteen miles from La Crosse. 'La Crosse, population 52,000, population of the metropolitan area is 132,500, with many fine restaurants and shopping opportunities.'"

"Peterson, you can't eat and shop all day. Three days, and you'll be broke and complaining you're bored." He only called her Peterson when she irritated him.

She'd slid her arms around his neck and laid her head on his shoulder. "It's a lovely drive to La Crosse, the nights will be fun, and we can sleep in most of the time. I can help you on this job. I've got contacts in Rockburg. Good ones."

She'd been right. Knowledgeable contacts were valuable.

The new credit cards were in his mailbox Monday morning. They drove south from St. Paul on US 52, looped around Rochester, and picked up I-90 at Marion. The rich, rolling farmland above the glacial moraines of the Rochester Plateau transitioned to the unglaciated Driftless Area as they neared the Mississippi River.

The interstate descended through a narrow valley carved through sedimentary rock of the Paleozoic Era. Fish, amphibians, reptiles, ferns, coniferous plants—all put in their first appearance during the two hundred fifty million years the sediments were laid down. Their drive through the valley took ten minutes. Carl hadn't gotten a degree after five years of college—never paid attention to what courses were required, just took the ones he enjoyed, like geology.

The day was sunny and ninety degrees—hot for September. The road turned south along the Mississippi, past limestone bluffs looming hundreds of feet above them. They turned east again and crossed the Mississippi to La Crosse, Wisconsin. He took the first exit for La Crosse and found a nice motel. He didn't want JP bellyaching about a cheap room, bad food, and inadequate air-conditioning while he planned his moves in Rockburg and read the *La Crosse Tribune's* account of the Kessler murder. He stuck with old-fashioned hard copies of the newspaper—no chance of leaving an electronic trail.

He used one of the public computers at the city library to examine air and ground views of Rockburg and 470 Mound Avenue, Oscar Kessler's home in 1903. An online search found that Oscar's son, Otto Kessler, inherited the house and brewery in 1904 and had lived in the house until he died in 1935. The current owner was Maude Jones. Nobody named Maude could be less than seventy.

Over lunch, JP said they had to change his New York license plates. "Everybody knows everybody in Rockburg. Drive down a street twice and half the town will be talking about the strange car with New York plates."

Monday afternoon he stole a pair of Wisconsin plates in the parking lot of a mall on the east side of La Crosse while JP stood watch. She stayed to shop while he drove to Rockburg to get familiar with the town.

Rockburg was thirteen miles east of the shopping mall. I-90 ran along the southern edge of the broad La Crosse River valley. Forested hills on either side of the valley were bisected by steep, narrow valleys branching from the central valley—*coulees*, the locals called them.

Mature fields of corn and tracts of grain and hay stubble covered both sides of the river bottom.

Rockburg hugged the lower slopes of hills on the southern edge of the valley. The village looked tiny to a New York native. Seven blocks long and nine blocks wide, the town was bordered by farmland on three sides and wetlands and the river on the north. The Kessler house was on a corner, close to the sidewalk. Overgrown shrubs screened most of the house from the sidewalks. A clump of lilacs would provide limited cover in the backyard, but a neighbor's house had a view of the rear entrance. He'd have to be careful.

The Rockburg Historical Society was closed until Tuesday. Carl collected JP at the mall, rented a panel truck in La Crosse, visited a Menards, and picked up pamphlets about windows and doors. Tiresome sales pitches by door-to-door salesmen were so common that nobody would question his act.

On Tuesday morning, he parked around the corner from the historical society. Within an hour he learned that Oscar Kessler was so cheap it was mentioned in the paper, although the paper said he was "thrifty" instead of cheap. He retired in 1899 because of poor health and died in 1904. *A retired cheapskate wouldn't have had a secretary in 1903 when he wrote the letter. Was he deranged or lying? Could "secretary" have been a code word between the cousins?*

A stout, gray-haired battle-ax ran the historical society. Carl asked her about Oscar Kessler.

"You want information on Oscar Kessler? Otto's father?"

"Yes. He was a cousin of Joseph Kessler, the lumber baron. I'm doing genealogical work for a friend. I picked up some information on Oscar from the materials you have on display. Do you have anything more on him?"

She looked him over and went back to her romance novel. "We have a box of letters and documents from 1855 to 1935 that haven't been inventoried yet. They aren't available to the public."

Carl gritted his teeth and thanked her for her time. *She'd better have a good security system if she thinks that's the end of the subject.*

He parked in front of the Kessler house at 1:30 that afternoon. The air-conditioner in the rental, a white panel truck, couldn't handle the heat, and his shirt, soaked in sweat, stuck to his back.

The house needed paint and a new roof. A frail, white-haired woman answered the door when he knocked. He told her he was a dealer for Pillar Windows and Doors and handed her one of the four-color pamphlets he'd picked up at Menards. "We have a crew in the area and a sale on windows. Replace all your windows and we'll knock off thirty percent on the windows and installation. You'll never get a better deal," Carl said and gave her a figure he thought was low.

"I can't afford that." She handed the pamphlet back to him.

"We need advertising in the area, and just for you, we'll replace three of your windows at no cost if you'll let us make a video of the work. A before-and-after sort of thing. How about that?"

She swallowed his story and invited him in. He put on latex gloves—told her they were to keep oil from his hands off her walls. The windows she chose to replace were on the second floor. There, he thumped and probed around the windows, measured them, and made notes on his clipboard. The window frames were rotten. The windows stayed in the walls by force of habit more than anything else. From the condition of the house, Carl was sure Maude's family had never stumbled on the 1804 silver dollar.

Her parents had done little except remodeling the bathrooms and kitchen in 1953, she said. Those were the last updates made since Otto Kessler died. "My father used the library as a den, but he didn't even rearrange Otto's furniture," she said.

There'd been no evidence that Otto Kessler or his family

knew that Oscar had a valuable coin. He must have stored it in a private place—his library or bedroom—and it might still be there. Carl asked Maude questions as though scheduling the work. She mentioned that she had no relatives in town and rarely left the house.

He glanced at his watch. It was 2:30. There'd been no traffic on the street in the hour he'd been there. Mid-afternoon, most people were at work. No witnesses. *She'll tell the neighbors about her free windows if I don't do it now.*

They chatted about scheduling the work as they walked to the second-floor landing. He was finding staircases useful. It didn't take much of a push to send the old girl flying down the staircase. Although her head hit the steps hard four times as she rolled down the stairs, she was still moaning at the bottom. A kick to her temple with a steel-toed boot ended that.

Knocks on the back door interrupted him as he checked her for a pulse. He overreacted. In the quiet neighborhood, the knocks sounded louder than gunshots. Carl's heart thundered against his ribs as he hustled through the kitchen to the back door. He spotted a rolling pin on the kitchen counter. It was better than nothing. He grabbed it and pressed himself against the wall by the door. On a peek out a window he saw a middle-aged blonde at the door. She banged on the door three more times and left.

He waited ten minutes and scanned the backyard from the kitchen windows. *Nobody in sight. I'll search the place later. Probate will tie the house up for months, anyway.*

The phone rang as he grabbed his clipboard. He ignored it, walked to the panel truck parked in front of the house, and took the interstate to the main library in La Crosse. There, Carl searched on the library's computer for rental ground-penetrating radar and metal detectors. He found that equipment mounted on a two-wheeled cart, all available for rent at a Madison business. He liked to play with electronic gadgets, and the old geezer might have buried the coin or stashed it in one of those damned tunnels he'd heard about.

Back at the motel he had another romp with JP and afterwards thought while she napped. He needed sophisticated equipment, metal detection and ground penetrating radar, but he didn't want a local clerk to remember him. That made the company in Madison perfect. It was only a bit over a hundred miles away; easy to reach but unlikely to be included in a local police search if things came to that. Wednesday morning, he and JP would check out and find a motel near Tomah, a small town near the interstate. It was forty miles east of Rockburg and about fifty-five miles east of La Crosse. That would put him out of town when Maude's body was discovered.

CHAPTER 7

When Throckmorton opened the door to the drugstore on Tuesday morning, a thin woman barged past him, spitting and hissing under her breath. She shouldered him out of her way, though she looked to be over seventy, and he must have outweighed her by eighty pounds. The few people on the sidewalk scampered out of her path as she marched down the block.

An attractive honey-blonde was at the cash register. He nodded toward the front door. "Looks like somebody needs their medication adjusted," he said.

"That was Agnes," the blonde said. She was easy on the eyes. Her smile glowed, but he figured anyone who'd gotten rid of a customer like Agnes would be happy.

"You're new here, aren't you? I'm Chris Throckmorton."

"I'm Nancy Twittle. First day on the job," she said.

He pulled a prescription from his shirt pocket. "I'd like to have this filled for my son."

"Certainly. Mr. Wilson can have it ready in fifteen minutes." She nodded toward the old-fashioned soda fountain. "We've modernized. We serve espresso, cappuccinos, and lattes now if you'd like to wait."

Throckmorton considered the offer. "I . . . I'll pick it up later." His schedule was tight, no time to socialize. With her looks, he wouldn't stand much of a chance anyway.

She smiled again, cocked her head to the side, and leaned

toward him. "Are you sure? I'll give you the first one as a free sample."

"Nah, maybe tomorrow." He turned and walked out of the store.

Throckmorton dropped by the Rockburg Historical Society at two o'clock. The old shoe store had been built in the 1890s of rust-colored brick with a wood-framed display window that covered most of its narrow front. The building backed up to the tracks that paralleled Main Street. Sand and dirt ground into the worn wooden floor gave it a gritty feel. Along the walls, pictures and implements from early Rockburg perched on shelves that once held boxes of shoes.

A stout, gray-haired woman sat in a wooden armchair, feet resting on a stool, her ankles crossed. Glasses were perched halfway down her nose as she read a paperback. She peered at Throckmorton over the top of her glasses. "Can I help you?"

"I hope so. Do you have information on the old Kessler brewery?"

She took her feet off the chair and sat upright. "Kessler, Kessler, Kessler. You're the third person today to ask about the Kesslers and the brewery. Doesn't anybody want to read about something else in Rockburg?" She stood and advanced toward him. Barely five feet tall, she carried something of the bulldog in her appearance.

"There were stores and churches and bars and a livery stable." She punctuated each type of establishment by hitting the glass top of a display case with her index finger. "The whole damned town wasn't defined by that brewery. There's still a lumberyard here, and we used to have two newspapers, one published in English, the other in Welsh. Rockburg had—"

He took a step back. "Whoa. My grandmother was Otto

Kessler's daughter. I'm trying to dig up information on my family history."

The woman's shoulders sagged; she searched a pocket of her blouse. "You wouldn't happen to have a cigarette on you?"

He shook his head. "I don't smoke."

"I'm not supposed to either, but it's getting to me. I hid cigarettes around here, but one of those goody-two-shoes on the morning shift must have tossed 'em out. My name's Alice, by the way."

"Pleasure to meet you, Alice. Do you have—?"

"Yes, we've got pictures of the Kessler family and the brewery. Some go back to 1854. It's a good collection up to 1935 when the canning factory closed. Most of our pictures are on display over here." She walked to a wood-and-glass display case and waved at the wall behind it. "Shelves there have old bottles and Kessler beer signs. We even have a few letters between Kessler family members. Those—"

The floor started to vibrate and she held a hand up, as if to say, "Hold it." The display cases and shelves rattled. A pulsing roar from the rear of the store made conversation impossible. Through a back window, Throckmorton watched the cars of a freight train race by in a blur, a thrumming click sounding as each steel wheel rolled over a joint in the rails.

"I hate those trains," she said as the noise faded into the distance. "They weren't a problem in the old days when they stopped down the block, but they just roar through town now. Anyway, those letters aren't on display, but I can let you look at them if you're careful. We haven't inventoried a couple boxes of Kessler memorabilia, so they aren't for public view until that's done."

Throckmorton glanced at his watch. Talking about what he

couldn't see was a waste of time. "Can I look at the documents that you have inventoried?"

"Sure. You can work over there." Alice nodded toward an antique library table against the far wall. "And we do accept donations. You can make the check out to the Rockburg Historical Society."

Throckmorton set his briefcase by the table. The old wooden armchair was surprisingly comfortable. Alice brought him a group of Kessler pictures and copies of old newspaper stories. A 1935 newspaper on the top of the pile announced the bankruptcy of the canning factory. That was encouraging. It was the company, not the family, that went bankrupt.

He scanned through the articles about the Kessler family. Every man in the pictures, even those in taverns, wore a suit coat and tie. They must have had rivers of sweat running down their backs. *Thank God I can get by with jeans and a polo.* The pictures were interesting, but not what he needed now. The clock was ticking. Whatever was in the buried office might be out of his reach if he didn't get to it before Wilbur bought the lot.

He found a copy of the *Rockburg Independent* from 1862. He caught his breath when he read the headline: "Kessler Imports Stonemasons to Build Tunnels." The text announced Italian stonemasons had arrived to carve tunnels and caverns from the rock under the brewery and build stone arches to support the building above them. In Chamber of Commerce hyperbole, the article claimed the addition of the underground spaces would allow the company to brew Rockburg Lager beer all year long.

His heart rate upped a notch. He checked other copies of the *Independent* from that era. The papers reported the length of the tunnels, the cavern space available for brewing, and endless commercial hype about the brewery, but nothing about the underground office or tunnel number four.

An hour later, Throckmorton leaned back in his chair and rubbed his eyes. He stretched, glanced at Alice in her chair, and weighed the risks of asking her about the tunnels. She was an intimidating old bird.

Alice looked up from her book as he approached.

"Sorry to disturb you. Does the historical society have details on the brewery's construction or information about the tunnels under the brewery?"

She frowned and rested her book in her lap. "And how would tunnels relate to your family history?" She returned to her book.

He felt like a sixth grader explaining why he hadn't finished his homework. "I'm, ah, I'm also writing a book about breweries in small towns in Wisconsin at the close of the nineteenth century."

Alice stared at him over her glasses. It was a look that slowed time. Seconds turned to minutes. She seemed to look right through him.

She tapped an arm of the chair with one finger. "Tunnels? I've heard about a couple of 'em. The one under Main Street is the only one people have explored. Other tunnels they found were partially filled with sand and water. Nobody thought it worth the effort to go farther." Alice's brows knitted together. "Who's your publisher?"

"Publisher? I . . . I don't have one yet." Throckmorton swallowed hard. "Is there any chance there's something about tunnels in the documents that aren't on display?"

Alice rubbed her face with her hands. "I suppose I can inventory the stuff in the boxes. If I go at it in my spare time, I might get 'em done in . . ." She leaned back in her chair. "Make a donation to the historical society, something over fifty dollars, and I'll have them ready for you by next Tuesday."

"Deal!" He pulled his checkbook from his briefcase and wrote the check. He considered asking her to keep his search confidential but decided against it. In Rockburg that might ensure everyone in town would hear about it. Instead, he gave Alice his business card. "Call me when you've completed the inventory, would you, please?"

Alice used his card as a bookmark in her novel. A bare-chested man embraced a nubile brunette on the cover. The book could be research—a historical romance? Maybe those were period costumes strewn across a bedroom floor in the background.

"You should talk to Maude Jones. She lives in the Kessler house. Her dad bought it from Otto's estate. As I recall, the Joneses didn't do much to the house. Maude hasn't even put in air conditioning. There might be documents in the attic or Otto's library that would help you." Alice handed him a note with a phone number.

Just then, the front door of the historical society opened and Wilbur walked in. Throckmorton thanked Alice, nodded to Wilbur in passing, and left. Alice had mentioned two other men asking about the Kesslers. That couldn't be common—not that many people stopped at the historical society. He headed to his car, pulled out his cell phone, and called Maude Jones. She didn't answer.

CHAPTER 8

"What can you tell me about Chris Throckmorton?" Nancy asked.

Nancy and Frieda Olson were having coffee at Frieda's home on Tuesday. The house was on a farm at the edge of Rockburg, a farm too small to be anything but a hobby now.

The women sat at Frieda's kitchen table, sampling her latest excursion into baking. The room was square, with counters along three walls and a small hardwood table in the center. Off-white cabinets, pale-green Formica counters, and bright yellow paint made the kitchen seem cheerful and spacious.

Nancy nibbled tentatively on a piece of chocolate cake. She'd eaten at Frieda's before.

"Throckmorton?" Frieda's eyes lit up. "Ya know, I meant to introduce you two. You'd be perfect for each other."

Throckmorton had been friendly when Nancy met him at the drugstore, and she'd seen him at the library with his son. That made him the opposite of Gary, her ex-husband. Frieda's husband John was a nice guy. Maybe Frieda's taste in people was better than her baking.

"He has a son. Is he divorced? Widowed?" Nancy asked.

"Throckmorton's wife left him a year before he came to town. They lived in St. Paul. A cousin of mine lived in the same subdivision. She said his wife just up and walked out one day. Story has it she didn't even say goodbye to their little boy. The kid was only five or six."

"Did he abuse his wife?"

"Oh, gosh no. My cousin told me it was the other way around. His wife complained to everybody about him, even when he was standing right behind her. Poor guy couldn't do anything to please her."

"Do you know him well?"

"Sure. He's John's accountant, and I see him at the library when I work there on Tuesday and Friday evenings. His little boy is usually with him. Throckmorton's a nice guy but kinda bookish."

Bookish. That piqued Nancy's interest. Gary hadn't read a book since high school. She'd been a freshman, an English major, when she met him. He was a few years older than her and had a good job. Easily impressed, she was pregnant two months later. She finished the semester, dropped out of school, and married him. In their four-year marriage, since their daughter's birth, his interests had been limited to beer, sex, and fishing, and she wasn't sure about the fishing. He rarely caught anything on his trips to the lake—always claimed they weren't biting. It'd been such a frequent refrain she wondered if anorexia was common among perch. It would be refreshing to talk to a man who had broader interests and read widely.

It was after one of Gary's fishing trips that she'd discovered what an S.O.B. he was. She found a woman's panties in the back seat of his car. A lifelong resident of Rockburg, she'd decided she and Amanda, her now six-year-old daughter, would have a better life without Gary and filed for divorce. They were better off without the jerk, but eligible men were scarce in Rockburg for a twenty-eight-year-old woman. But no matter what, she'd promised herself she'd never get tied to another lothario, with roving eyes, roving hands, and a wandering dick. Her new job at the drug store had been a major stroke of luck after subsisting on part-time jobs since the divorce. Mr. Wilson, the pharmacist, provided medical insurance and flexible hours that allowed her to be home when Amanda got out of school.

"Would you like another piece of cake?" Frieda asked.

That question had a definite answer. One piece of Frida's cake was all she could handle. "No, I shouldn't," Nancy said.

"Ya know, I'll bet I can arrange an accidental meeting with Throckmorton for you at the library. How about it?"

Nancy hesitated. This could turn into a debacle if Frieda arranged accidental meetings as well as she baked. "You're sure it won't seem brazen?"

"Oh, don't worry. I've set up library encounters for a couple of my friends. There isn't anything to it. He'll be there tonight. Let's give it a shot."

———

The library was next to Foster's barbershop. Foster died sixty years ago, but his empty barbershop still stood like a memorial to the old man. Nancy arrived at the library at seven o'clock, four hours after she'd left Frieda's house. Like most of the other buildings on Main Street, the long, narrow library was an old red brick building. Its bookshelves were tall and made of darkly stained wood. She met Frieda at the help desk. Although no one was near, Frieda whispered, "He's in the history stacks. I'll help you find him."

Nancy wavered. She appreciated Frieda's enthusiasm, but still. "Are you sure this will work?"

Frieda came around to the front of the counter. "It's perfect. Don't worry, just follow me."

That sounded ominous. Nancy hesitated but followed. As they neared the stacks, Frieda lowered her voice to a barely audible whisper. "He's a decent guy, kind of boring sometimes, but you'll get along great."

Communicating by hand signals, Frieda crept toward her quarry. Nancy's courage faltered as they approached the history section. She clutched her purse and stood by the biography aisle. Frieda looked back and with a nod beckoned her forward.

Frieda tiptoed past rows of bookshelves, peeked into an aisle, and motioned Nancy to her side. "Shh—this row, ancient history. The aisle is narrow. He'll have to say something as you walk past him."

Nancy flicked a piece of lint off her sweater, patted her hair, glanced at Frieda for encouragement, and rounded the corner into the aisle between Alexander the Great to her left and Egypt, Old Kingdom to Sparta, and the Peloponnesian Wars on her right. From the colorful dust jacket on the book Throckmorton was holding, she saw he was reading about the breweries of early Wisconsin.

A twinge of cowardice made her pause. He hadn't looked up from his book. She could still back out.

A pair of hands pushed her forward. *Frieda!* Startled, Nancy careened into Throckmorton like an out of control truck.

"Oof. What . . . ?" Throckmorton exclaimed.

"Oh, excuse me." Nancy cringed and silently cursed Frieda. "I am so sorry. Let me pick that up." Her face flushed as she knelt to recover the book she'd knocked from his hand. As she stood, the back of her head struck his chin as he'd bent down to get the book. His glasses took flight, and he stumbled backward into the bookshelves as Nancy staggered forward. She felt a crunch under her foot. A glance verified she'd stepped on his glasses.

He rubbed the back of his skull where it had hit a shelf. "Excuse me . . . where are my glasses?"

"Oh, I am sorry," Nancy repeated. Hair hung in her face, and tears welled in her eyes. Her head hurt. She'd almost sprained her ankle when the heel of her right shoe landed on the instep of his left foot.

Frieda's plan had sounded simple; he would recognize her from the drugstore and say hello. She'd smile demurely, ask what he was reading, and after a few minutes of badinage, they'd go out for coffee. She wished she'd stayed home and cleaned the oven or organized the jumble under the kitchen sink.

Throckmorton knelt and picked up his glasses. He bent the frames into a semblance of their proper shape. One lens remained. "Ah, hello, Miss . . ."

"Twittle, Nancy Twittle. We met in the drugstore the other day." She pushed her hair out of her face and looked at his glasses. "I'm so sorry about your glasses." She knew she should have cut the story off there, but she couldn't stop herself. "One of my heels must have caught on something." She handed him the book he'd dropped.

"Thank you." He looked at the polished floor behind her. His frown expressed doubt that anything could have caught on her shoe. "Are you all right?" he asked. "You aren't hurt, are you?"

"No. I'm so sorry. Are you okay?"

"It was nothing, but I'd better pick this glass up before someone gets cut." He picked up the shards of the shattered lens and excused himself.

"Can I at least pay for the glasses?" Nancy asked.

"Not necessary. Nice to meet you again," Throckmorton said, and with a nod, he turned and walked out of the aisle.

She saw him dump the glass into a wastebasket, collect Ben from the children's reading area, and limp out of the library. With a wave to Frieda, she left the library before tears began running down her face.

CHAPTER 9

Sticking to his plan, Carl drove with JP through Tomah on their way to Madison on Wednesday. There, Carl rented the equipment he needed and drove back to a motel outside of Tomah. The confluence of 1-90 and I-94 a couple miles east of Tomah made it a busy place, a place where it was unlikely anyone would remember Carl or JP, at least if JP behaved herself and didn't throw a public fit about something.

Carl used credit cards and a phony driver's license he'd gotten under a different name. He considered dyeing his hair but figured it wouldn't be necessary. Their motel didn't have surveillance cameras. At least that was working for him.

Over dinner that evening, JP complained about the quality and choices in the free breakfast and the truck-stop menu in front of her. She whined that he'd dragged her out of bed early for the trip to Madison, and she nearly had a conniption when he told her she might have to help him push the equipment cart back and forth over the old brewery site. She made such a stink about it her life expectancy would have been damned short if he hadn't been seen with her by so many people, and if he didn't need the information she promised to get him.

Back in their room, he put his hands on her shoulders, turned her to him, and looked her in the eye. "We need the information this equipment can provide. It could tip us off about what Throckmorton is looking for—a room, a safe, a cabinet—and it could show us how to get it first or be ready to nab it after Throckmorton does the heavy work."

JP glared at him. "And when do I have to get out of bed to help you with this?"

"Daybreak tomorrow is five-forty five. We'll be up and on the road shortly after four tomorrow morning and unloaded in Rockburg by five. I want to be done and on my way out of town by six-fifteen. My computer will record all the data and I'll work out the results when we get back."

JP's eyes were wide and her mouth hung open as though she were going to scream, but the only sound that came out was a hoarse rasp. She gasped a couple more times, stood up, and demanded, "If I'm going to put up with this shit, I want to know exactly how much this damned coin is supposed to be worth." She glared at Carl and crossed her arms over her chest. "I'm not budging until you cough up a figure."

"It will be $850,000 tax-free dollars. Is that enough to keep your interest?"

JP's eyebrows stretched toward her hairline and her snarl turned into a beatific smile. She took a step toward Carl, wrapped her arms around his neck, and kissed him deeply. When she came up for air, she smiled and rubbed noses with him. "Carl, lover," she murmured as she undid his belt buckle. "If that's what we have to do to get it, we'd better get to bed. Three o'clock Thursday morning will come awfully early."

—————

After talking to Alice on Tuesday, Throckmorton spent the rest of the week working to free up time for the search for Otto's assets. He called Helen Heath, a widowed grandmother, and arranged for her to pick Ben up at school and keep him through dinner three times a week. She'd been almost a mother to Ben during his recoveries from the intense chemo. She was familiar with his meds and knew the problems to watch for. With that settled, he talked his housekeeper into making dinner for them twice a week through December. He spent the rest of the week catching up on work and creating macros in his Excel files to automate more of his work.

During breaks in his work, Throckmorton tried to set up an appointment to go through Otto's old house. He called Maude on Tuesday, twice on Wednesday, and again on Thursday and Friday. She never answered. On Saturday he called from the Coffee Cup where he'd stopped for lunch with Ben. As they ordered, he asked Gert if Maude might be vacationing.

"Maude has never taken a vacation," Gert said. "She can't afford it, but there's something odd going on. Elvira Hanson mentioned Maude this morning. She missed their Wednesday Bible Study group. Maude has never missed that before. She rarely drives anywhere but to church, and you can't miss it when she does."

"Is she the lady who putts around town in the 1942 Studebaker?"

"Yup. It was her father's car. She only drives to church. A neighbor takes her when she needs to go shopping."

Throckmorton told Gert of his failed attempts to call Maude. As he finished his coffee, Gert called Suzy Wentworth, Maude's neighbor, and handed the phone to Throckmorton. Suzy said she hadn't seen Maude since Tuesday morning. She worried that Maude may have had a fall or a medical emergency. Throckmorton thought of Adele's body lying at the bottom of the staircase. He didn't want Ben to see anything like that. He called Mrs. Heath.

"I have to drop Ben off at Mrs. Heath's," he told Suzy. "Meet me at Maude's in half an hour."

He turned to Ben. "Hey, kiddo, how'd you like to finish that hotdog off while you watch Saturday cartoons at Mrs. Heath's?"

Ben grinned and nodded. Throckmorton thanked Gert and paid for their meals. He dropped Ben off at Mrs. Heath's home, and drove to meet Suzy.

Otto's old house, now Maude's, sat on a rise three blocks south of Main Street. A large, two-story, white building, it was almost square, a common design in houses built before World War I. A dilapidated garage, once a stable, stood twenty feet from it. The garage only had one car but was large enough for three.

Suzy, a slightly built woman with gray roots, met him at Maude's back door. Dressed in old slacks and a patched shirt, she looked like she'd been cleaning her house. She preceded Throckmorton to the rear porch, knocked on the door, and called Maude's name. When there was no answer, she tried the door. It opened.

A wave of hot air, heavy with a sweet, putrescine odor, swept over them as the door opened. Suzy turned aside and vomited; Throckmorton struggled to hold his lunch down.

"Would you call 911 please?" Throckmorton gasped. He held his handkerchief over his nose, grateful his mother had insisted he always carry one. "I'll take a quick peek inside." He walked through the kitchen to a doorway on the other side of the room. Maude's bloated corpse was lying at the bottom of the staircase in the front room. A glance was enough. He gagged and hurried out the back door.

Suzy was waiting at the property line between her house and Maude's, cell phone in hand. Throckmorton took several deep breaths in the fresh air before he could speak. "There's a dead body at the bottom of the staircase. Did you call 911?"

Suzy put her phone on speaker, and he heard the 911 operator ask what the problem was. She explained the situation, and they were told to wait outside until a sheriff's deputy arrived.

"Fine with me. No way would I wait inside that house," Throckmorton said.

The light breeze shifted. They were now downwind of Maude's house, and her back door was open. The house was thirty feet away, but Suzy looked green. Throckmorton said he'd wait in his car for the sheriff if she wanted to wait in her house. She scurried to her back door without answering.

The sheriff's deputy arrived first, followed by the coroner and a forensics team with a body bag. Throckmorton stepped from his car and suggested to the deputy that they go to Suzy's house to talk. There, Suzy explained how they'd found Maude, and the deputy got their names and phone numbers.

"Officer," Throckmorton asked, "was this an accident?"

"It's too early for me to comment," the deputy said. "But that's probable."

"God, I hope it was," Throckmorton said. *Theft of Kessler documents in Utica, NY, Adele died at the bottom of her stairs and her house, a Kessler mansion was ransacked, and now Maude has died in an old Kessler home. This can't be a coincidence, but what the devil is going on? If someone is behind all three, they've now come to Rockburg.*

CHAPTER 10

After lunch Saturday, Frieda and Nancy gathered in Frieda's kitchen. Frieda pointed at a colorful green carton on the counter next to her new coffee maker. "Take your pick," she said. "There's an assortment of cups for four different flavors."

Nancy chose one, put a cup under the spout, and pushed the appropriate buttons. She smiled at the first taste of the coffee. "Oh, I wish I could afford one of these. It almost makes me forget that disaster at the library."

Frieda sipped her coffee and sat at the table. "Things could have gone better. We'll do better next time."

Nancy shuddered at the thought as she took a seat across from Frieda. "Next time? How can I make a good impression on Throckmorton now?"

Frieda waved her hand. "It can't be that bad. You looked lovely. He isn't worth chasing if he can't overlook a silly accident." Frieda tapped a finger on her table, then took a cookie from the plate and slid it across the table to Nancy. "We just have to make him think he's chasing you."

Elbows on the table, Nancy ignored the cookies and rested her chin in her hands. It was tempting to credit Frieda for the debacle in the library, but Nancy wasn't one to blame others. She'd agreed to it. "Cripes. The one good-looking, educated, single man in town, and I've blown it. He must think I'm a klutz."

"Oh, it can't be that bad." Frieda casually sipped her coffee.

"Life of a single parent in a small town is lonely, Frieda. I just wanted to meet someone nice, someone who reads, who values things other than sports. But where do I go from here? Half a dozen men have propositioned me since I threw Gary out, and every one of them was an arrogant jerk worse than Gary. There wasn't one I'd have coffee with, let alone go to bed with." She looked at Frieda. "Do I look desperate? Is there something wrong with me?"

"Those guys are bottom-feeders, honey. I could probably name 'em. Don't let 'em get to you."

"But why do they think I'm on the bottom, and how do I get Throckmorton's attention without scaring him away?" Tears welled in her eyes as she thought of how long it had been since she'd had anyone to talk to in the evening.

"How about a blind date?"

Dumbfounded, Nancy stared at Frieda.

"Throckmorton comes over to review John's books every quarter. He works late and stays for dinner."

"How do you set up a blind date when he already knows me?"

Frieda smacked the tabletop with her hand. "That's the beauty of this. Amanda can visit my Emma for a playdate. They're the same age, both are in Mrs. Wilson's first grade class, and they get along well together. You drop by to pick her up half an hour before dinner, and I'll think of a reason the girls should play a little longer. You'll have to stay for dinner with Throckmorton." Frieda looked triumphant. "What do you think?"

"John will go along with this?"

"John will go along with whatever I ask. He doesn't question me about playdates, and I don't ask him about the price of shelled corn or pork bellies. We'll feed the girls early when Throckmorton's here. That way dinner will be just for the adults."

"How should I handle Tuesday and Friday at the library? I told him I'd see him there."

"Smile, wave, show a little leg if you want to, but let him come to you like you would a puppy. Make him think he's chasing you."

"Chase me? You've got to be kidding. More likely he'll avoid me, and I wouldn't blame him."

"Don't worry about it, honey. Most men are so simple they'll fall into your lap if you feed 'em on time, keep their beer cold, and hint they might get lucky." Frieda thought a moment and frowned. "Throckmorton's a little different. He'll talk all night about politics, history, books, or half a dozen topics that'll put you to sleep before dessert. Stay awake, pretend you're interested, and he'll be yours."

"You think so?" Widely read and a history buff, Nancy was intrigued by Frieda's description of Throckmorton, but it raised further concerns about Frieda's tactics.

"He seems kinda shy around women. You might have to be more forward than normal, just to get him to notice you're female." Frieda smiled and leaned back in her chair. "It's a plan, then. I'll ask John when he'll be here for dinner and give you a buzz."

Frieda got up and collected their cups. "Here, let me get you a refill. Then try one of the cookies. It's a new recipe."

Nancy examined the cookies as Frieda put the coffee maker through its paces. "What are they?" she asked cautiously.

"Double chocolate. I altered the recipe a little. Didn't have enough cocoa powder, and I wanted to cut back on the calories, so l substituted tomato paste for some of the cocoa. I read about that trick in a magazine. Think anyone will notice?"

Nancy felt Frieda's eyes on her. She took a small bite of a cookie, chewed thoughtfully, and searched for an honest but noncommittal statement. "You must have used the tomato paste that comes with the pizza spices already in it."

Frieda beamed. "I knew you'd like them. I'll make another batch for dessert when Throckmorton is here."

Nancy took a sip of coffee to wash the taste from her mouth and cover her expression. She couldn't let her future depend on Frieda's cooking, not after that sample. "I can't expect you to do all that work for me. Let me help you in the kitchen that night."

Frieda waved a hand. "Oh, you don't need—"

"Please," Nancy said as she thought of ways to keep Frieda out of the kitchen without hurting her feelings. "I'd feel guilty if I didn't help you out. You've already done too much for me."

CHAPTER 11

Throckmorton had lunch on Monday at the Coffee Cup. Gert was busy in the kitchen. She waved to him but didn't have time to talk. As he left, he looked toward the end of the street where it dead-ended in the gap where the Kessler brewery once stood. Somewhere under that lot were tunnels and the underground office, or what was left of them. With luck, he might find evidence of the tunnels on the surface. That could shave weeks off his timeline.

He zipped up his jacket against the wind and cool air and walked the two blocks to the brewery site. He would have felt silly using his car to go two blocks. The Kessler office building, now the last building at the edge of town, was a hundred feet east of the site of the former brewery and once the terminus of a tunnel.

The two-story brick building was the only commercial building in town that had double-hung rather than large display windows on the first floor and a steep hip-roof instead of a false front facing the street. It looked like a substantial home except it lacked a yard and curtains in the windows. Plywood covered two second-floor windows, and the windows on the first floor were filthy. The leaden sky, empty street, and deserted building evoked a sense of brooding desolation.

He surveyed the barren lots that formed a shallow U around the end of the street. He took out his phone, brought up shots he'd taken of photographs at the historical society, and compared them to the space before him. The small lots flanking the site had held the bottling plant and brewmaster's house. He walked to the edge of the brewery lot and dug the toe of his shoe into the dirt. It was packed solid. Sand, dirt, and broken concrete would have been used to fill cavities after demolition. Large chunks of broken concrete would make a search for the tunnels difficult—might even require dynamite to get through. Way too dangerous without hiring experts. He paced across the lot, searching for a depression, discoloration, or a variation in soil texture—anything to indicate where a tunnel had been.

Nothing. Odd tracks in the dirt caught his attention. They looked as though a kid had dragged a toy wagon or cart back and forth over the lot, but the tracks were precise, covering the entire lot in a grid pattern. He didn't know of anyone or anything that left tracks like that.

The hair on the back of his neck stood on end as he examined the tracks. He had a creepy sensation that he was being watched. *Oh, for Pete's sake. Get a grip. You're scaring yourself in broad daylight. Must have been the sight of Maude's body.* He ignored the feeling and continued exploring.

The brewery had been built on the shoulder of a low hill. Railroad tracks on the south edge of the site swept past, headed east and west. He pictured a short spur line with loading docks attached to the brewery on that side and towering malt silos on the north end.

From the site of the malt silos, the hill sloped down to a plain crossed by a county highway north of the brewery site. The back of the brewery, facing west, had overlooked a creek at the bottom of a broad ravine. Both creek and ravine appeared to be untouched. He used the exposed edges of broken concrete for footing in the ravine wall to climb down. Halfway down, he began to slip and slide toward the bottom. He pawed at dirt, grass, and gravel with his hands, scraping his shoes against crumbling dirt. By sheer will and grasping a few well-rooted weeds, he scrambled back to the top.

He caught his breath and cleaned the dirt from under his broken fingernails. His shoes were scuffed, his pants were torn and filthy, and even the elbows of his windbreaker were coated with dirt. He wouldn't try that again without a rope.

Maps of the village from 1955 had shown a gravel road running between the brewery and the brewmaster's house, downward along the edge of the ravine to the county road, a hundred yards away. He followed a narrow, graveled strip between the lots until waist-high brush blocked his path. From there, between bushes and tall weeds, he made out parallel tracks of gravel and dirt headed down the slope to the county road. An abandoned gravel road, rough but passable.

He looked over the edge of the ravine. Along the bottom of the ravine wall, half-hidden by tall grass and brush, a path started at the county road and headed back to an area behind where the brewery had stood. Parallel ruts visible in a few places suggested the path had once been another road, possibly a back entrance to the brewery.

A picture of the rear of the brewery taken before Prohibition showed a large arch in a brick façade, low in the building's center. It opened on the ravine. It was below ground level but several feet above the bottom of the ravine. It must have opened into a basement—or something deeper.

Trees and brush obscured the arch in pictures taken in the late twenties and early thirties, implying Prohibition had ended traffic to the rear of the building. The arch must have been an entrance to the cavern and tunnel system where the brewing took place. Prohibition would have ended that activity.

From where he stood on top of the brewery lot, there was nothing to indicate where the arch had been. Frustrated, he walked back to where Main Street dead-ended at the site and mentally drew a line from the office building to where the bottling plant had stood across the street. A tunnel had gone beneath the street along that line, but nothing on the surface hinted at a tunnel below.

His gut was tying itself into a knot. Finding the tunnel and getting to the safe had sounded uncomplicated in the abstract. But now, standing on the lot, it looked like an impossible task . . . unless there was still an entrance to the tunnel complex in the basement of the Kessler office building. Gert said the village owned the lots and the empty office building. He'd have to talk to the mayor—and do it before Wilbur bought the land.

He pulled his cell phone out to call Mayor Earl Stevens at his home but thought better of it. Earl could be prickly, according to Gert. He put his phone away and walked back to the Coffee Cup.

The lunch rush over, Gert was wiping up the counter when Throckmorton walked in. He eased onto a stool.

"Coffee, please."

"Back already?" she asked.

He looked around the empty café. "There were things I wanted to ask you when you were alone."

"I didn't think it was my wonderful coffee that brought you back." Gert poured him a cup. "Alice told me you didn't find what you were looking for at the historical society."

Throckmorton frowned. "How much did she tell you?"

"She said you wanted information on the brewery tunnels, you were a lousy liar, and you didn't have your story straight before you asked questions."

Throckmorton winced. "Cripes. I didn't think I'd said that much to her."

Gert shook her head. "Don't worry. She didn't say a thing to Wilbur."

"Good. We crossed paths as I left."

"Alice said he cornered her before the door closed behind you. Tried to pump her for information on what you'd been up to."

Throckmorton sat bolt upright. "Good Lord! Why would Wilbur be trying to find out what I'm doing?"

"That's Wilbur. If there's a dollar loose in the county, he'll try to get half of it. Alice kept her mouth shut. She doesn't approve of his shenanigans. I don't worry too much about him, but I haven't known him as long as she has."

Throckmorton wrapped his hands around the warm coffee cup. "But if she told you I was asking about the tunnels, who else did she tell?"

Gert limped around the end of the counter, took a stool next to him, and stretched her legs. "Oh, that feels good. Alice and I are old buddies. She won't say a thing to anyone else. She knows Wilbur will grill half the people in town about what you're doing. He was a troublemaker when she had him in middle school, and his oldest daughter wasn't any better."

"Alice was a teacher?"

"Retired fifteen years ago. She was a good teacher. Tough, too."

Throckmorton remembered his meeting with Alice. "I can believe that." He told Gert he wanted to rent the Kessler building to gain access to the tunnels. "Rent will be cheap in Rockburg, and remodeling for an office shouldn't cost too much," he explained. "It's the least complicated way I can think of to get into the tunnels. Any advice on how to approach Earl?"

"Call him Mayor Stevens or Mr. Mayor. Keep the conversation on the office building and what you want. Don't disagree with him if he brags about his investments. It won't be easy to play that stupid, but that's the cost of doing business with Earl. Lord help you if he starts on his survival nonsense."

"Survival what?"

"He thinks he's an expert on surviving nuclear winter, World War III, a meteor hit, or, what did he call it . . . ? An extinction-level event. Yup, that's what he calls it. He doesn't bring it up often, but he'll talk all day if he does." She massaged her brow. "And if his wife answers when you call, stick to making an appointment with Earl. She gets chatty."

"Anything else?"

"Talk to Alice about him tomorrow if you want more background. She had Earl in school and watched him grow up."

———

Throckmorton glanced down the street toward the historical society as he left the Coffee Cup. The society wasn't supposed to be open, but Clarence, a paunchy retired plumber and the town constable, was standing in the Society's open doorway. Throckmorton walked over, curious why the society was open on a Monday.

Clarence was talking to Alice. He leaned against the door-jamb, pen and notebook in hand, his badge pinned to a white T-shirt a size too small for his girth. His wife loved to cook, and Clarence wasn't the sort to exercise if he could avoid it.

"Why do you think there was foul play?" he asked Alice.

Hands on her hips, fists clenched, she didn't seem to notice Throckmorton as she glared at Clarence. "I told you, a friend called to tell me that the society's door was open. When I got here, I found the door ajar. The drawers of a bureau from the Kessler house were pulled opened, and boxes of Kessler letters were dumped on that table." She pointed at an antique library table, papers scattered over and under it. "These boxes were in the storeroom last night. We've had them for years but haven't had time or staff to inventory them."

Throckmorton's interest piqued. *Another theft related to the Kesslers?*

"What was in 'em?" Clarence asked.

"They contained documents, primarily letters between Kessler family members."

Clarence hitched his belt a little higher under his gut. "What were the letters about?"

Alice's face looked like a thundercloud. "I don't know. We haven't inventoried them yet."

Clarence wrote something, looked at his notebook, and asked, "Ah, anything missing?"

Throckmorton saw the muscles of Alice's jaw flexing, her brows furrowed. She growled, "The boxes have not been inventoried, Clarence. We don't have a list of what was in the boxes, and I haven't touched anything on that table."

Clarence jotted in his notebook. "Were the letters valuable?"

Throckmorton looked away, covered a smile with his hand, and pretended to cough as Alice erupted. "How the devil would I know, Clarence? The goddamned documents haven't been inventoried." She gave Clarence a glare that would have withered grass.

Throckmorton stepped forward. Alice didn't suffer fools, and she'd clobber Clarence if he asked another inane question. It'd be best to separate them before he asked Alice what happened. "Sorry, I couldn't help overhearing," he said. "I'll call the sheriff's department, Clarence. They'll want to take over the investigation, anyway, and that would mean Alice would have to answer a bunch of questions twice."

"Yeah. Good idea. Better call a locksmith, too, Alice."
Clarence bent to examine the lock on the front door. "This thing
must be the 1894 original."

Throckmorton's jaw dropped as he watched Clarence brush
his fingers across the lock plate.

"Could be scratched here." Clarence passed his fingers over
the plate again before Throckmorton could stop him. "Yup,
scratches."

"Might even have been fingerprints on it, Clarence," Alice
hissed. "Please leave the lock alone and go back to your card
game. Mr. Throckmorton and I will handle this."

Clarence put the notebook back in his empty holster. "Well,
let me know if I can help. You've got my number."

Alice glared at him. "Yes, Clarence. I have your number." As
Clarence walked away, she growled, "Boy, do I." She turned to
Throckmorton. "Thanks for the help. I assume you didn't come
down here just to rescue me. What can I do for you?"

Throckmorton swallowed. Alice was a challenge to talk
to when she was in a good mood. "I saw the open door and
thought I'd drop by to tell you how much I appreciate your
work. I really—"

"And the society appreciated your check but spare me the
treatment. I believe the missing documents are from 1890 to
1910. Meet me at Gert's at three, and I'll let you know if I have
more information by then."

Throckmorton agreed and mulled over the information as
he walked back to his car in front of Gert's. Otto died in 1935,
a generation removed from 1910. The Kessler-related crimes
had moved from Utica to La Crosse to Rockburg. Did Otto hide
valuables he bought during the brewery's heyday, or was the
perp looking for something unrelated to Otto's letter?

Throckmorton worked on his client's accounts until three and drove back to the Coffee Cup. It was nearly empty. He slid into a booth across from Alice. "Everybody must be down at the historical society watching the sheriff's deputies."

"Too many people with nothing good to occupy them," huffed Alice. "The deputies haven't let me get near the documents. It may be a week or more before I can estimate what's missing. How else can I help you?"

"When we first met, you said I was the third person to ask about the Kesslers that day. Do you remember who the other two were?"

"The first one was a stranger, mid-thirties, muscular. The other is the fiancé of Gloria, Agnes Throttlebottom's grand-daughter. I don't know much about him, but he's spent days pouring over pictures and articles about the brewery and Kessler family."

"Did you know that someone stole Kessler letters from the 1890s and later from a museum in Utica, New York?"

"No, but how would that be connected to the theft here?"

"Adele was murdered during a search of the mansion library. That's two, maybe three thefts and a murder in just two months, all connected to the Kessler family. Each crime has been closer to Rockburg. I suspect they're related. Someone is searching for something, and they're playing hardball."

Alice didn't look convinced. "Possibly, but more likely a coincidence. Lots of people named Kessler. I'll keep my eyes and ears open, though. What else can I help you with?"

"Gert said you could give me some background on Earl Stevens."

Alice removed her glasses and rubbed her eyes. "The day

is depressing enough without talking about our mayor. Why would you want information about that arrogant prick?"

"I'd like to rent the old Kessler building. My office at home isn't—"

"Your house doesn't connect to the brewery tunnels, right? Save the bullshit for Earl."

Throckmorton glanced about. There was no one close enough to overhear their conversation. "Man, you get right to the point." He frowned. If Alice made the connection, how long would it take Wilbur or Earl? He told her how Gert had suggested he approach the mayor. "She said I should talk to you if I wanted to know more."

"Sounds like Gert. She doesn't think any more of Earl than I do, but she won't say much. You'll understand Earl if you remember that the difference between pride and arrogance is knowledge. He tries to skate by on native intelligence, and he is bright, but he doesn't put the work into learning a subject in depth. On most topics his knowledge is superficial. He can be charming, but at heart, he's self-centered and greedy."

She explained that being mayor of Rockburg was an elective position a normal person got if he wasn't present to decline the honor. Earl didn't see it that way. The job suited him. It allowed him to do almost nothing, complain about all the work, and brag about the brilliant job he was doing. Alice and others had figured an imaginary job was the safest place to park Earl after he retired and had time on his hands.

He'd been on the school board at the time of his election, but he didn't play well with others. Before Earl could whine about his new workload as mayor, the school board gave him a certificate expressing their thanks for his service. It was framed and signed by the entire board.

"They would have cast it in bronze and mounted it at the

steps of the high school if it would have gotten him off the board faster," said Alice with just the hint of a smile. "Stroke his ego to get along with him. Do that, and you'll see his chest puff out and his chin point a little higher—looks like a bantam rooster strutting around a farmyard. Nose gets so stuck in the air he'd drown in a good rain. He sees the world in black and white, and white is whatever's good for Earl. Above all, he'll never admit he was wrong. If a project of his goes belly-up, it was your fault."

"Sounds like a gem."

Alice sat back in her chair. "Those are his good points. Keep the conversation away from taxes, survival crap, and the evils of big government or he'll be off chasing squirrels."

"Chase what?"

"Running off on his favorite topics. His guff can be hard to swallow, but if you can listen to the gasbag and nod in agreement now and then, he'll spend the rest of the day telling anyone who'll stand still how he proved what a genius he is. It's been his favorite topic since he was in high school."

Throckmorton thanked her and asked when she might know what was missing from the historical society. She promised to call him when she did.

As he walked out, he realized Alice probably knew who Earl dated in high school, what his in-laws thought of him, and how his kids did in school. In a town with few secrets, everybody would know what Throckmorton was up to the day he bought a shovel.

CHAPTER 12

T he mayor's house was large for Rockburg. Like other old homes in town, it was a rambling white clapboard house built over several generations. The original two-story structure was nearly square, typical of homes built in the late 1800s. Sometime around World War I, when the agricultural economy boomed, a rectangular addition was added on. Indoor plumbing and electric lights were available in town. A porch added during the same era wrapped around two sides of the house. Windows and screens that enclosed the porch were more modern, early 1950s, Throckmorton guessed.

Throckmorton parked in the shade of maple trees in front of the house Tuesday morning. Earl met him at the door and showed him to the den, a large room with dark wood paneling and a hardwood floor. He motioned Throckmorton to a wooden armchair in front of a mahogany desk large enough to satisfy a Napoleonic ego. Behind it, Earl sat in a swivel chair with a leather-upholstered back so tall it made Throckmorton think of a throne. Recessed lighting in the ceiling made Earl's chair the focal point of the room.

After a few pleasantries, Throckmorton got down to business. "Mr. Mayor, my home office is no longer adequate for my business. I could build a new office, of course, but the old Kessler building might fulfill my needs if it's structurally sound."

Earl leaned back in his chair, turned to the side, and crossed his legs at the knees. "The Elks used the first floor as a clubhouse until last January. You'd have to upgrade the electrical service and remodel the interior." He paused, and gave Throckmorton an appraising look. "You're an accountant, aren't you?"

"Yes. I do the accounting for the co-op, the cheese factory, and several large dairy farms."

"That's what I'd heard." Earl leaned forward. "I don't let everybody in on this," he said in a low voice, "but I've found an offshore investment fund with an incredible profit record, simply incredible. The dividends are tax-free." Earl seemed to search Throckmorton's face for signs he was impressed. "That's a big advantage for men with our incomes. Damned government taxes the hell out of people like us—people who make the economy run—and gives it to fools and loafers." Earl brought his fist down on his desk for emphasis.

Throckmorton kept his mouth shut and nodded agreement. He had a feeling his morning was shot.

Earl sat up straight. "I can show you the last two annual reports and a brochure about the fund."

"I'm interested, but I don't have free cash to invest at the moment. My son had leukemia and racked up major medical bills." He looked at his watch. "Mr. Mayor, I only budgeted enough time for this meeting to talk about the office building. Can you give me copies of the reports to read later?"

Earl shook his head. "I don't let copies leave the office. I don't want this information spread around. It would be a good investment for your successful clients, the smart ones. Minimum initial investment is two hundred thousand, but the fund manager might make exceptions if I talk to him or if I invest it for them under my name. You can't wait too long, though. The manager plans to close the fund to new investors soon."

Throckmorton kept his expression bland and attentive. He wondered whether Earl was a con man or a sucker duped by one.

He looked at his watch. "Okay, I'm interested. Can you explain it in about five minutes? I'm eager to look over the Kessler building."

Earl pulled two flashy pamphlets from a drawer and slid them across the desk to Throckmorton. "I've invested my life savings in this fund. The returns have blown past anything I bought through my stockbroker. Eighty percent interest last year, and the fund guarantees fifty percent. That's fifty percent of your investment in profit every year, and it's tax-free! It's like having a license to print money." He looked beatific. His voice was reverential. "Been in it two years, and I've ordered a BMW for the wife; my Jag XJ comes in next week. Extended wheelbase for eighty-three thousand bucks." Earl leaned back. "I'm paying cash."

Earl's claims dumbfounded Throckmorton. How could a man run a business and yet be gullible enough to believe any fund could guarantee fifty percent interest? He paged through the fund's brochure as Earl went through his sales pitch.

Throckmorton couldn't think of a way to speed Earl through his sales pitch, but he might be able to prove this investment was a scam. "Mind if I write down the name of the fund and the manager?" he asked. "I'll check them out later, but I'll keep the information to myself."

"I guess that would be okay," Earl said, "but don't take too long to make up your mind. If you're like me, it's worth it just to screw the federal government out of taxes."

Throckmorton wrote down the manager's name, the name of the fund, and its principal holdings. "It looks impressive, Mr. Mayor, but I don't see any information on the fees the fund charges."

"I charge two percent of your initial investment to cover my time to help you make the purchase. The fund charges half of a percent per year. You can see it had a fantastic performance, even in years that were bad for the markets. And remember, all the interest is tax-free."

"So the fund is back-loaded?" Throckmorton asked.

Earl frowned. "What?"

Throckmorton revised his opinion. If Earl didn't know what a back-loaded fund was, he didn't know enough about investments to be a con artist. "If a fund doesn't charge a fee to buy in, it usually charges a fee when you sell. You said the fund isn't front-loaded. Is there a fee for selling shares?"

Earl shook his head. "Nope. The only fees are mine for setting you up and the half percent per year to the management. See what a deal this is?"

Throckmorton leaned back in his chair and wondered if Earl shouldn't give power of attorney to a sane person. "How long have you been a broker?"

Earl grinned and made a dismissive gesture with his right hand. "Oh, I'm not a broker. I just help to smooth the way."

Earl's grin reminded Throckmorton of the mythical Alfred E. Neuman who'd graced the covers of *Mad* magazine he'd read as a kid. He dropped any doubts about the fund being a scam. The manager's first name was probably Bernie. "Almost too good to be true, isn't it? How did you find this fund?"

"I searched the web for offshore investment opportunities," Earl said. "One day I got a call from the manager. I guess you could say he found me."

That sounded right to Throckmorton. It surprised him that Earl had gotten only one call. The Nigerian princes must have taken the week off.

Earl reached into a drawer, pulled out a sheaf of papers, and slid them across the polished desk to Throckmorton. "The manager described the fund and emailed me these reports."

"Did you ask your financial advisor about it?"

Earl shook his head. "That shyster and I parted ways years ago. Every time I found a promising offshore investment, he'd give me a load of horsepucky about unregulated markets and risk. He only wanted me to buy the funds he was selling."

Throckmorton pretended to consider the fund. Odds were good he wouldn't get a lease for the Kessler building if he didn't. "I'll be in touch if one of my clients is interested. Now, about the office building. Can I have access to it? I need to see if it's suitable and get an estimate from a contractor for the remodeling."

Earl seemed satisfied with his evasions, and a few minutes later Throckmorton left Earl's house with the key to the Kessler building in his pocket.

———

Throckmorton parked by the fire station a block from the Kessler office building at eight, an hour after sunset. Closer might attract attention, even at that hour, since the only buildings on the block were the Kessler office, a closed Ford dealership, and an empty house. A parked car on the block would stick out like a Democrat in Oklahoma. Wilbur would be on it faster than a fly on garbage.

A small roof protected a concrete pad at the front entrance to the building. The door was in good shape. The key turned easily and the hinges didn't squeak. That seemed odd, considering the second-floor windows were covered by plywood, until he remembered it was recently used as a clubhouse for the Elks. Inside, he flicked a light switch. Nothing happened. Of course—the village had turned the electricity off.

He pulled out a flashlight, but the windows on the front and east side of the building and a nearby streetlight provided adequate light. A small foyer opened on a big, rectangular room. The floor was covered with worn carpeting, probably the dining room.

To his right was an entrance to a long, narrow room. The worn linoleum was faded except for a broad strip that ran the length of the room five feet from the interior wall. There was no wear on that, and the colors, yellow and brown, were bright. Throckmorton guessed it was where the bar had been. Any club for men in Wisconsin had to have a bar.

Toward the rear of the building, he came to a hallway with two doors marked Kings and Queens. *Talk about juvenile humor. Maybe proximity to the bar explains it.*

The light faded as he walked down the hallway. It didn't have windows, and the dark paneling on the walls sucked up what light there was. He fumbled with his flashlight. "Great move, Einstein," he mumbled. It was new, and he hadn't looked to see how to turn it on before he was in the dark.

The beam of the LED flashlight startled him when he found the button. It took a moment for his eyes to adjust. He was close to the end of the hallway. There were unmarked doors on each side and a door marked Exit a few feet in front of him. He took a guess. The unmarked door on the right opened to wooden stairs that descended to a landing and disappeared into the basement's gloom. This was what he was looking for.

The flashlight beam played over the dingy white walls of the stairwell and highlighted fine cracks in the paint. *Plaster, not drywall. It's the original finish.*

The stair risers were worn, save one—probably a recent repair. He gingerly put weight on the first step. The wood felt solid. The step didn't give or creak. He followed the stairway down, testing each step until he was sure it would hold his weight.

His flashlight augmented the murky light from two dirty windows high in the wall at the front of the building. He swept the beam of the flashlight across the basement. It was a single large room with a bare concrete floor. He had a clear view of the whole space.

In the room's center was a modern oil furnace with air ducts radiating from it—modern and rectangular in cross-section. A few curved metal straps dangled from the floor joists above him. He'd seen straps like that in an abandoned building—a building with a rusted coal furnace. Curved straps would have supported the original round air ducts from a coal furnace.

The plastered finish of the stairwell continued from the stairs to the corner under the front of the building and along the wall facing the brewery site. The plaster stopped twelve feet before reaching the next corner. That section was whitewashed concrete blocks.

The mortar at the seam of the plastered wall and the painted concrete blocks was rough and uneven, the workmanship sloppy. Kessler wouldn't have stood for that. The initials "JB" were stamped into two blocks that were cut to fit small gaps at the seam. Throckmorton's first job out of college was at Johnson Brothers Concrete, the first company in the area to produce concrete blocks. They'd started business in 1940. He'd worked there as a bookkeeper for two years.

"Finally, I get a break," he said as he ran a finger along the initials. The JB blocks used in the patched wall were made at least five years after Kessler died, and the corner was the closest part of the basement to the brewery. He knew the entrance to the tunnel complex was behind this patch.

The stairway creaked behind him. Throckmorton whirled around, his heart pounding and his flashlight aimed at the stairway. He remembered he hadn't locked the door behind him when he'd entered the building.

The flashlight's beam illuminated only empty stairs. He swept the beam over the rest of the basement. Nothing, but he couldn't see under the stairway or behind the furnace. He picked up a three-foot piece of two-by-four at his feet. It wasn't as good as a baseball bat, but it was better than nothing.

Pulse racing, he was alert and observant, adrenaline coursing through his veins. The only noise was the sound of his footsteps as he walked back to the stairway. He noticed nailheads surrounded by bits of plaster protruding from the floor joists above him. They ran in two lines that converged to form a large L, from the stairs to the front wall and along that wall to the remodeled section. That made sense to him. There had once been a hallway with finished walls along those lines.

He pictured the basement as it had been eighty years ago, the coal furnace on one side of the plastered walls, a bright, clean hallway leading to the patched wall on the other. Management hadn't wanted coal dust on their white shirts when they took the tunnel to the brewery.

A soft scraping came from the first floor toward the middle of the building. Throckmorton was wired, prepared to swing at anything as he came to the top of the stairway. If he turned left, the way he'd come in, he'd have to pass three doors. His back would be exposed to each of them as he walked past. He stepped into the hallway and turned right. He hit the panic bar of the rear exit at a run and barged through the door to the outside.

Despite the cool night air, he was sweating as he rounded the corner of the building and leaned against the wall until his breathing returned to normal. The front door of the office building slammed shut. Footsteps echoed off the sidewalk, running east toward the center of town. *What the hell have I gotten myself into?*

———

Carl hoofed it away from the old Kessler building. He'd followed a guy about his age, some guy by the name of Throckmorton who apparently had gotten the keys to the building. Carl recognized Throckmorton; he'd seen him looking over the site of the old brewery a few days earlier. If the guy was looking through the Kessler building, maybe he was on the hunt for the 1804 silver dollar, too. He followed Throckmorton into the building, but twice he'd screwed up and spooked the guy. Throckmorton had bolted out the back of the building and Carl did the same from the front door.

Throckmorton went to a car parked down the street and tore out of there. Carl hid in the shadows of an abandoned car dealership across the street for an hour and waited to see if anyone else showed up. Nobody did. That meant Throckmorton hadn't called the cops or anyone else. The front door to the Kessler building was still open. He returned to the building and examined the basement. That was where Throckmorton had concentrated his search.

Carl found a wall that had been rebuilt on the cheap. He'd read enough about the tunnels to figure out what Throckmorton was up to. *I'll let him do the excavation, and I'll collect the goods.*

CHAPTER 13

T hrockmorton called a company that sold home security systems Wednesday morning after his scare at the Kessler building. He didn't ask for a quote—just told them to install their best system in his house as soon as they could. He still had credit cards that weren't maxed out. *Quality and speed on this could save Ben's life and mine.*

That afternoon with Ben in school, he stopped by the Coffee Cup Café. It was empty except for two older women chatting in the third booth. Throckmorton took a seat at the counter and ordered coffee and a chicken sandwich.

"Taking time off?" Gert asked as she brought his order.

He glanced at the two ladies again. It wouldn't make any difference who overheard him if he kept the conversation to remodeling. By now, everybody in town knew he wanted to rent the Kessler building. "I need your advice. Can you recommend a local contractor?"

Gert pulled out her notepad and wrote "Eric Brown" and "discreet." The bell over the door rang as she tore off the page and handed it to him.

"Afternoon, Gert, Throckmorton," Wilbur said, taking a stool next to Throckmorton. "Just a cup o' coffee for me, Gert." He turned to Throckmorton. "I seen ya was lookin' over the old brewery office. Lookin' to see where your great-grandpappy worked or searchin' for buried treasure?" Wilbur laughed and slapped Throckmorton on the back.

Throckmorton flinched at the mention of buried treasure.

He discarded the notion that Wilbur had followed him through the office building last night. Whoever was there last night took off in a run; overweight, middle-aged Wilbur wasn't a candidate.

"Jeez, I didn't mean to scare ya. Are ya always this jumpy?"

"Sorry, my mind was on something else," he lied. "I need to expand my office. The old office building looked like a good place to expand." Throckmorton took a bite of his sandwich and washed it down with coffee. "Where did you hear I'm related to the Kesslers?"

"Well, aren't ya?"

"On my mother's side. But it's a long way back. How did you know?"

"Somebody mentioned that some time ago. Can't remember where, but I talk to people all over the county. I get a little info here, a little there. What d'ya think of the old place?"

Throckmorton chewed another bite of his sandwich to give himself time to think. "It looked solid. It'll need work, but it's cheaper than putting up a new building." He glanced at his watch. "Whoops. Later than I thought. Appointment with a client—sorry, I have to go." He motioned to Gert, dropped a ten-dollar bill on the counter, and excused himself.

———

Wilbur had never thought of himself as a student of people, but he was a keen observer. He rubbed his chin as he watched Throckmorton walk out. *Old Throck paused before answering a simple question. Probably thinkin' up a lie, and the way he checked his watch? Does he think I'm a moron?*

Wilbur caught Gert's attention as she walked by. He glanced toward Throckmorton, still visible across the street. "Our friend sure was jumpy, wasn't he?"

"Not particularly." She handed him his bill and went back to the kitchen.

It didn't surprise him. Gert was often tight-lipped with him—always seemed to have something else that needed her attention when he asked questions. This time he knew that whatever was going on, she'd been in at the start.

He left his payment on the counter and crossed the street to the drugstore. His best sources in Rockburg were store clerks and bartenders. He used bartenders sparingly; those who had information were circumspect or expensive. Teenage checkout clerks were a different matter. They were often bored, and they weren't as suspicious as bartenders. They hadn't learned to charge for gossip. Show a bit of interest, offer a little praise or a modest tip, and the dam would break.

Wilbur was a great dam buster. There was an art to the process. He had to be careful as he guided the conversation into the proper channel. Some kids had mouths that worked faster than a whip-poor-will's ass in chokecherry time. They'd talk to anybody. Damned fools might tell everyone they saw what he'd been asking about. The whole town could know about it before dinner if he wasn't careful.

He took a stool at the counter of the drugstore's old-fashioned soda fountain. It hadn't changed since he was a kid, except for a chalkboard behind the counter listing lattes, iced coffees, and flavored espresso drinks.

"How's your day going, Debbie?"

Debbie looked up from her iPhone. She was the chattiest of his contacts as long as he kept her happy with a little attention and regular tips. "Kinda quiet today," she said. "How's by you?"

"Oh, a slow day," Wilbur said. "I was lookin' at the end of Main Street, and there was that big, open spot. Strange not to see the old brewery there. It was there all my life, not as a brewery—I ain't that old. I always knew it as Clayton's feed mill."

"Yeah." Debbie put her iPhone on the counter. "My older sister said that after they closed the feed mill in 2010, kids used to sneak in and have beer parties in the cavern and a couple of the tunnels . . . not that I ever did. My girlfriends told me about them." She smirked. Her focus seemed to wander somewhere beyond Wilbur. "A couple guys kept sleeping bags in rooms that were out of the way. Candles made it real romantic. Jimmy had a sleeping bag with an air mattress . . ." Her eyes took on a dreamy look until they strayed back to Wilbur. "Uh, I never saw those things myself, but girlfriends told me about 'em."

The conversation lapsed until Wilbur gave Debbie another prod. "That's right. There was a regular baby boom in town for a few years. Earl's granddaughter got caught there with Billy Petersen, didn't she? Neither one had a stitch on. Earl had a fit. Demanded they tear the building down when the story got around. That was 2014, wasn't it?" When Debbie didn't respond, he added, "Pretty lonesome on that end of town now."

Debbie smiled, her eyebrows shot up, and she leaned closer to Wilbur. She lowered her voice. "Elmer Johnson told me old Mrs. Schmidt saw Throckmorton walking around the site one morning. Real early, too, like he didn't want people watchin' him. Did you know that Throckmorton is related to the Kesslers?" Debbie leaned back, as though to see how Wilbur took her pronouncement.

Wilbur arched his eyebrows in mock surprise. "No! You don't say!"

Debbie beamed. "Yup. Al Huss came in with an old letter from Otto Kessler for Throckmorton. Al didn't want him to read it here. They didn't want me to hear what they was sayin', so they went to Al's office."

"Well, I'll be darned," Wilbur said with a smile. He dropped a five on the counter. "Can I get a black coffee to go? You can keep the change."

Pleased with his new information, Wilbur sauntered out of the store and crossed the street to his antique shop. He was back in his store when his cell phone vibrated. He looked at the caller ID. *Shit.* Sarah, his oldest daughter. She only called to complain about whatever he'd done lately.

He answered the phone and wished he hadn't. She'd heard about him selling a gelding as a stallion. Damn! He knew the buyer hadn't talked about it. He'd been too ashamed to admit he'd been fooled. Must have been somebody else.

"Damn it, Dad! Can't you even behave yourself for a couple of months in an election year? Give me a break, will ya? I got an uphill battle as it is."

She was a pistol, all right. He figured she'd hang him from a flagpole by his balls if she thought it'd get her another hundred votes.

"That was just a little misunderstanding, sort of, but it wasn't much."

"Dad, if I grabbed you by your nuts and cut 'em off, would you call that a little misunderstanding?"

"The buyer didn't complain about it." He ended the call rather than take more guff. *Damned politicians. She got herself appointed interim sheriff, and now she wants the job permanent. Seems to think making my life hell is the easiest way to win the election.*

The way things were going, it was time to find an excuse to talk to Earl about that brewery lot again. But if he showed too much interest in it, Earl would jack up the price. He'd have to be cagey and wait for the right moment to bring up the subject.

CHAPTER 14

Thursday morning, Carl relaxed on the bed of their motel room near the Tomah interstate exit. Modern and clean, it was decorated in shades of brown and cream. A flat-screen TV on the dresser, a decent bed, and a refrigerator and microwave made it darn comfortable.

"Did ya get a La Crosse newspaper like I wanted?" he asked as JP walked into the room. A slim brunette, she'd spent money from a divorce settlement on breast implants. They gave her quite a figure.

"Sure. Ya think I'm an idiot?" She tossed three thin newspapers at him.

"What the hell are all these, Peterson? I asked ya for the *La Crosse Tribune*.

"That's what I'm giving ya, Carl, the last two issues of the *La Crosse Tribune* and Monday's issue of the *Coulee Courier*."

"What the hell is the *Courier*?"

"It's a weekly with the news from the little burgs in the area. Or do you think Rockburg qualifies as a metropolis?"

The news he wanted was in the second paper he scanned. "Here it is, 'Ms. Maude Jones of Rockburg suffered a fatal fall in her home last week. Neighbors discovered the body several days after the mishap. The coroner estimated the date of death to have been September nineteenth or twentieth. She is survived by' blah, blah, blah."

"What's the date on the paper?" she asked.

"Monday, September twenty-fifth."

"And the paper?" Her voice had an irritatingly arch tone.

"All right, it's the damned *Courier*. Are ya happy now?"

"Ecstatic. So, when are you going back to the house?"

"I'll drive by the house a couple times for a few days to see if the sheriff and clean-up crew are gone."

He left at noon and came back with KFC chicken. She glared at the bags. "Jesus, Carl. How long we gotta hole up in this dump? Like, when can we go out for a decent meal?"

"If you don't mind being"—he looked through his fraudulent driver's licenses on top of the dresser—"Mrs. Hank Rosseter tomorrow, we'll move back to La Crosse. More choices for restaurants, maybe a Victoria's Secret to get you ready for Friday. It'll look like we got into town after the old biddy croaked."

———

It was past ten the following Monday, and Carl looked over the new motel room he and JP shared in La Crosse. It was a mess. JP was a great lay, but she was incapable of picking up wet towels or tidying up a room, and she'd bitch like hell if he asked her to do some laundry. He had to put up with it for a while yet because he needed her contacts in Rockburg.

Carl's analysis of his electronic data indicated it wouldn't be easy to get to the most likely target buried in the brewery lot. That made hunting through Maude's house for information on the 1804 draped Liberty silver dollar critical.

"Want me to come with you?" JP asked.

He continued to dress: black shoes, black pants, black sweatshirt, a black ski mask, and night-vision goggles. It had been another ninety-degree day, but the nights were chilly. "Too risky. We got one pair of night goggles, Peterson," he said. "I work alone at night."

"I could drop by a shop that sells hunting equipment, pick up a pair for a couple hundred bucks?"

He looked over his goggles. "Don't."

"Why not?" she pouted.

He turned and glared at her but was careful not to let his irritation show in his voice. "Because you'd get what you paid for—infrared goggles that see warm bodies, nothing else, and you won't have an emergency cut-off if somebody shines a light in your face."

"So what kinda goggles do you have?"

He held the goggles in one hand, as though offering them to her. "Light-amplifying goggles with a safety cut-off. I can see my way around with nothing more than starlight or this light stick." He held up a black metal rod about eighteen inches long. "This puts out less light than you'd have on a starry night. With it, I see everything. Others see nothing."

She crossed her arms over her chest. "Why can't I get goggles like yours?"

"'Cause you don't have $850, and I don't want to draw attention to us. Few people will pay for this quality. Clerks working on commission remember those who buy these, and that's a risk we won't take. Besides, you've got other work to do. Practice making cow eyes at your ex-hubby. Get clothes that look sexy without being slutty. We need to know what he's up to and what he knows."

He carried three twelve packs of beer into the bathroom. "Put on gloves, get your butt in here, and help me empty these."

She groaned but joined him in emptying the cans in the sink and tossing the empties in two garbage bags. When they got down to the last six cans, he told her that was enough and tossed the six full cans in the bags with the empties. He threw his backpack over his shoulder, grabbed the garbage bags, and headed to their car.

At midnight in Rockburg, he turned his lights off two blocks from the Kessler house. The narrow field of vision of the night goggles hampered driving, but they got him to the house and up the driveway that circled to the back. He parked behind the clump of lilacs. The house and shrubbery screened the car from the view of all except one of Maude's neighbors. That house was dark.

Rather than pick the lock, he kicked the back door in. It would look like the work of teenagers. Inside, he put on gloves and lowered the curtains in Otto's old library in case he needed to turn on the lights. He searched the room, pulling books from their shelves and papers from the desk. Thumping the walls and flooring, he identified four areas that sounded odd. A hammer easily broke into those, but he found nothing. On the second floor, he repeated the procedure in the master bedroom and the second largest bedroom with the same results. Before he left each room, he poured a couple cans of beer on the floor and tossed empty beer cans around as he left. He messed up the bed in the master bedroom and dropped a used condom on the floor. The condom had been stuck to the inside of a wastebasket in their motel room when they checked in. *Let them try to identify me with that.*

After searching the house, Carl hadn't found a damned thing. He left Rockburg headed east on County U. The route was longer, and he had to double back to get to La Crosse, but there were fewer houses and no speed traps on the road. It was four o'clock Tuesday morning when he pulled into the motel's parking lot.

CHAPTER 15

B y Saturday morning, Throckmorton's new security system was installed and tested. Throckmorton looked at the invoice and prayed there would be something valuable in Otto's safe.

Ben watched cartoons before lunch while Throckmorton talked to Eric, the contractor Gert had recommended. Eric was tall and dressed in worn blue jeans, work boots, and a denim shirt, the sleeves rolled to his elbows. They bent over a blueprint of the Kessler office building spread on Throckmorton's dining room table.

"Looks nice, but what'll it cost?" Throckmoron asked.

Eric stretched and massaged his lower back with both hands. He put a contract on the table. "Figured you'd ask." He pointed to the contract. "That's the total above your signature line."

Throckmorton had hoped for something lower, but he trusted Eric, was comfortable with him, and Gert had vouched for his discretion. It was time to broach a touchy subject. "If I get a lease that includes the basement, there's a section of the basement wall that needs work. I don't know how extensive the work will be, and I'd like to keep it confidential."

Eric folded his arms. "If you're looking for something in the old tunnel complex, you're going about it the wrong way."

"Damn! Am I that transparent? Is everybody in town talking about me and those tunnels?"

"It's not you. It's the combination of the Kessler basement and confidential work."

Throckmorton relaxed. This project was making him feel paranoid. "That's a relief."

"People think there are old beer barrels or artifacts in the tunnels. What are you looking for?"

"There was a small office off a tunnel. Nobody alive knows where it is. A safe in the office holds something valuable. It could be anything from stock certificates to gold. Gert thinks anything there is worthless by now."

"If you're looking for a sizeable chunk of iron or steel, use a metal detector. It will take a good one to find an open route, something more sophisticated than those made for hobbyists."

"How can a metal detector find an open route?"

"High-end metal detectors find a lot more than metal. They can find open spaces—tunnels—under thirty feet of dirt, and stone walls and large metal objects sixty feet deep. The right detector could find the safe, map the tunnels, and tell you which ones are passable."

That was good news. "Where would I find something like that?"

"You might find...nah. You won't find anything that so-phisticated locally. You'd have to go to the Twin Cities or Madison to get one, or I've seen 'em for sale on the internet."

"Got a couple minutes? I'll check the web now. It would help if you'd point me in the right direction and tell me what I'm looking at."

It took three minutes on Google for them to find the OKM eXp 6000 detector. It used electromagnetic pulse, ultrasound, and Visualizer 3D software to assemble 3D multicolored diagrams of soil layers, rocks, voids, and metal objects deep under the surface. All components communicated by Wi-Fi, including the Android video eyeglasses that allowed the operator to see the probe results in real time. Eric helped him translate that into English.

Throckmorton stared at his laptop. "I like the idea of the metal detector, but the pictures of the read-outs look like a chimp threw paint at a canvas. Do you have a plan B?"

"Sure. A friend works for Subsurface Imaging and Mapping. Tell SIM what area you want them to examine, what you're looking for, and have a check ready. They'll use magnetometry, VLF metal detection, and GPR."

Throckmorton snorted, shook his head, and looked at Eric. "Mind interpreting that for me?"

"Very low-frequency metal detection and ground-penetrating radar. They normally charge $7,500 per acre. The brewery lot is about half an acre. They'll probably charge you four to five grand."

A brick made itself comfortable in Throckmorton's stomach. Following up on Otto's letter was expensive. "Pricey, aren't they?"

"Not much more than buying a high-end detector," Eric said, "and you'll know what's down there when they're done. Do it yourself, and you could be left scratching your head wondering how to read the results."

Eric's logic was sound. Throckmorton wondered why sound logic was always expensive. There was another hitch too. "I can't hide what I'm doing if I have a crew traipsing back and forth over the brewery lot." He pictured a crowd, cell phones taking pictures as they watched men wearing weird glasses move strange equipment over the ground. That would put the gossips in high gear. There was something worse. "And Earl. Contracting it out means I'll have to get permission from him."

"Can't help you there. Earl and I don't get along well. He's a pain in the ass generally, and a suspicious pain in the ass if you want approval for anything. It's damned near as bad as when he gets going on his survivalist crap."

"Yeah, I've heard he's interested in that."

"'Obsessed' is a better word for it." Eric paused. "It might help to blow a little smoke up his ass—tell him you want to clean out the tunnels; stockpile 'em with dehydrated food, survival equipment, and guns to survive whatever catastrophe has his attention today. You'll have to listen to an hour of delusional bullshit, but that's easier than trying to talk sense to him."

"To keep my options open, I'll still lease and remodel the Kessler building."

After Erick left that afternoon, Throckmorton called SIM and asked for a bid on finding the safe under the site of the brewery.

After finishing with SIM, he took a deep breath, crossed his fingers for luck, and called the mayor. "Earl, this is Chris Throckmorton. Remodeling the Kessler building looks doable. It'll work out if I can get a five-year lease."

"Five years, huh? Do you want to lease both floors?"

"I'll only need the first floor and basement."

There was silence on the line.

"Earl, are you still there?" Throckmorton asked.

"Why do you want the basement? What are you going to do with that?"

"Ah, if I'm the sole tenant, I'd like to have control of the heating plant. I was thinking . . . I um . . . could use the basement for storage space, and I might want to add central air."

Silence. He was about to say something—anything—when Earl spoke. "Say, were any of your clients interested in the offshore fund?"

At least he was ready for that question. "If I recall, you said the minimum investment was two hundred thousand?"

"Yup. They'd better get in fast before the fund closes."

"None of my clients have that kind of money to invest. If they did, they'd rather invest in their farms."

"Just between us, I could make an exception," Earl said. "How about a minimum of a hundred thousand?"

Throckmorton chose not to answer. The fund sounded shadier every time Earl mentioned it.

Earl coughed. "Well, maybe, I mean . . . I might be able to strike a deal with the fund manager. He might accept fifty thousand if three or four of your clients would each invest that much."

"Earl, none of my clients showed the slightest interest in the fund." He hadn't mentioned it to his clients and had no intention to.

Earl was quiet, apparently chewing that over in his mind. "Well . . . what about you? Do you want to kick in on this? For advertising, I could let you in for fifty thousand."

"Any spare cash I have is for medical bills or will be used on my new office."

"Well, have you set up a college fund for your boy? If it's a 529 plan, you could cash it out, pay the penalties, and buy shares of the offshore. The way this sucker pays off, it'll cover his medical bills, his college education, and let you spend your summers on the Riviera. How about that?"

Throckmorton didn't want to admit that he'd already emptied Ben's educational fund. "No, Ben's mother made me put his college fund in trust," he lied. Earl made Wilbur look like a pillar of the church. *Wilbur* . . .

Throckmorton had an idea that seemed downright inspired.

It made him feel giddy. "You might want to talk to Wilbur, though. He mentioned something about treasure when he came into the Coffee Cup the other day. If I were you, I'd drop by his store and give him your sales pitch," he said.

"Did I hear right? You think Wilbur might be interested?"

"Absolutely. An offshore fund free of IRS oversight would appeal to Wilbur. He's much more financially—he searched for the right word—"sophisticated than my clients." Throckmorton grinned. It wasn't a lie. Worst case, maybe a fib. Taking money from the arrogant and greedy could count as sophistication.

"I've heard Wilbur gets audited by the IRS every few years." Earl chuckled. "He might be just the person for this fund. I have to see him about other things, anyway."

Good. Earl was off his favorite topic. But would he be talking to Wilbur about purchasing the brewery lot? Throckmorton was screwed if Wilbur bought it. He had to get to Otto's assets as quickly as he could. "What about the lease for the office building?"

"You said you wanted the basement too?"

"Yeah. Then I won't have to call you at night or on a weekend if the furnace goes out," Throckmorton said.

"Good point," Earl said. "This wouldn't have anything to do with the old brewery tunnels, would it?"

Throckmorton jerked as though he'd touched a live electrical wire. "Tunnels? What tunnels?"

"How long have you lived in Rockburg?" Earl asked. "I thought everybody over five knew about those tunnels."

Throckmorton realized his mistake. "Oh, well I knew about the tunnel under Main Street. I didn't know there were others. I just need the lease to include the basement, Mr. Mayor."

"Hmm. Maybe. I'll have to think that over." Earl's voice had an edge. It had gone from jocular to suspicious.

Throckmorton hit his forehead with the palm of his hand. *Shut up! Get off this phone before you start babbling.* He told Earl he had a call waiting and hung up.

———

Earl put his phone down. There'd been a sudden change in the tone of Throckmorton's voice. He sounded scared. *That son of a bitch is up to something. It seems to have something to do with the tunnels that he wants to keep secret.* Earl headed to Main Street. He didn't believe in investigating on an empty belly, so he stopped at the Coffee Cup for a cheese Danish. Gert always marked them down in the afternoon.

Throckmorton had tripped all over his tongue about the tunnels, seemed desperate to keep it a secret. Earl pondered as he chewed. *There must be something valuable stashed in the tunnels. I've got him by the short hairs. He can't put a shovel to that lot without my permission.*

It was a short stroll from Gert's to Wilbur's emporium of dubious antiques. He let the door close behind him and looked over the store. The wooden floor was a worn, dingy gray.

He picked up a lamp marked "style popular in the 1930s, $50."

"Wilbur wording," Earl scoffed. He'd seen it on the side of the most suspicious artifacts Wilbur had for sale. It implied much, guaranteed nothing. He noticed "Made in China" on the ceramic hardware that held the light bulb. Earl snorted. The only antique in this place was probably the store itself.

Another glance around the store, its dozen tables of ceramics, light fixtures, old tools, picture frames, and assorted junk found no sign of Wilbur. "Hey, Wilbur! Are ya here?" Earl bellowed.

"Just a minute," came from a back room.

Wilbur appeared, rubbing and clapping his hands together,

knocking off dirt and dust. "Earl, I'll be damned. What brings you here?"

"Throckmorton suggested I talk to you about an offshore, tax-free investment opportunity. I'd also like to talk to you about our friend Throckmorton."

Wilbur scowled. "Investment? Did he say why he thought you should talk to me?"

"He said he figured you were flush, mentioned something about treasure—that you might want to invest money in a sweet deal. At least fifty percent interest per year, guaranteed."

Hands in his back pockets, Wilbur said, "I ain't got no idea why he'd think that."

"I stopped by Gert's for a snack. Since you're so close—"

"Gert's? Yeah, I teased Throckmorton about walking over the brewery site lookin' for old Otto's . . ." Wilbur rubbed his chin. "Ah, I asked him if he was lookin' over the old family business."

Earl caught Wilbur's hesitation and fixed him with a glare. "You know damned well that's not it. This has something to do with the old brewery tunnels. I've never heard anybody over the legal drinking age getting a hard-on about those. I figure he's looking for something valuable enough to rent and remodel the office building as a cover story to dig into the tunnels."

Wilbur's face remained a mask. "Do tell."

"Nothing happens in this town without you hearing about it, so I figured you'd know what he's up to."

"I might have my suspicions."

Almost a head taller than Wilbur, Earl moved close enough to loom over him. "The village owns the Kessler building and those lots, and I'm the mayor. With your contacts and my office, we got Throckmorton's nuts in a vise. He can't get squat unless we say so. You with me or against me?"

"Oh, I'd never do anything against you, Mr. Mayor."

Earl hated it when Wilbur put on his simpleton act. "Cut the shit, Wilbur. Are you in or out? I can twist Throckmorton by the balls over this, with you or without you, but I'll bet this rundown excuse for a store lets you move money without a paper trail. The IRS hasn't been able to lay a finger on you, and I know damned well they've tried. I'll cut you in just to launder whatever money we get out of Throckmorton."

"Since you put it like that, Mr. Mayor, I'm in."

CHAPTER 16

T
hrockmorton parked under a tree in front of the mayor's house on Monday. He took his time getting out of his car. Early in October, the lawns were still green, the trees were turning colors, and it was a beautiful sunny day. It was a shame to ruin it talking to Earl.

Subsurface Imaging and Mapping, or SIM, hadn't sent him a bid yet. Until they did, he wouldn't know if they'd do the work or if he could afford them. There wouldn't be a reason to meet with Earl if either of those was a problem, but Earl had called and demanded he meet him at 1:15 today. According to his watch, it was 1:13.

Earl had refused to give him a reason for the meeting and insisted he be on time, neither early nor late. He didn't have a clue what had gotten under Earl's skin, but the man was angry about something.

He flinched as he recalled his response to Earl's question about the tunnels. Damn, he'd sounded stupid. In the weeks since Al gave him the letter, he'd learned that every native of Rockburg old enough to be out of diapers knew the stories about the brewery tunnels. To a suspicious guy like Earl, his request to lease the basement and pretended ignorance of the tunnels was as good as announcing he wanted access to them.

He picked up his pace when he realized Earl might be watching him. Dragging his butt as he walked to the house would only make him look guilty.

Earl didn't answer the doorbell on the first ring.

Throckmorton waited and rang the bell again. He waited a reasonable period and knocked loudly on the door. There were footsteps inside. Earl opened the door, invited him in, and led him back to his office in silence.

Throckmorton was wary. Was Earl playing mind games with him, or was the doorbell out of order? He'd demanded the meeting and insisted on punctuality, but he was slow to open the door. They made it all the way to the office without Earl asking him to buy shares in the offshore fund. That was so out of character it seemed creepy.

Earl opened the office door and ushered Throckmorton in. "I believe you know Wilbur. I've asked him to sit in on our little confab."

Wilbur's presence hit Throckmorton like a bucket of ice water. Earl gestured toward a chair, but he continued to stand. "What's going on? I thought this was a meeting between you and me about the Kessler building."

"That's what we wanted to talk to you about. Wilbur tells me you got a letter from your great-grandpappy Otto, then got jumpy as a goosed squirrel when Wilbur teased you about hunting for treasure. When—"

"What kind of inquisition is this? I came here to finalize the lease for the office building."

"Sit down and hear me out," Earl said in a firm voice. Throckmorton didn't move, but Earl continued. "As I was about to say, when I mentioned the brewery tunnels, you pretended you'd never heard of 'em. The kids in town hear about 'em before they're old enough to think about sex, and they get to that too damned young. I figure your office project is a cover story to hide what you're up to while you hunt for something in those tunnels."

Throckmorton had no good answers. Maybe bluster would

work. He put his hands on his hips and remained standing. "I came here to lease the Kessler building, not listen to conspiracy theories. Do we have a deal on the lease? If not, I'm out of here."

Wilbur shifted in his chair. "Aw, come on, Chris. Sit down. Take a load off. Relax. Earl and I can help you for, oh, say half of whatever it is you're lookin' for. After all, you're the one who got Earl and me thinking about this."

They had him. The two people in town he most wanted to avoid working with, and he was at their mercy. He looked at Wilbur and took the proffered chair before they noticed how shaky his knees were. "I brought you together?"

Wilbur chuckled, leaned forward, and made eye contact with Throckmorton. "You told Earl I came into a treasure. Now, that there is pure bullshit."

Throckmorton would have kicked himself if he were alone. He wondered how often he'd heard a plaintive, "But it seemed like a good idea at the time." He understood it now.

"It was clear you were after the tunnels," Wilbur continued, "when you got all hot to lease the basement of the office building. We figure you're looking for something under the brewery lot. Wouldn't be worth that much work unless it's valuable. Earl and I haven't worked together before, but he thought helping you is a good place to start." Wilbur leaned back in his chair. "Earl, why don't ya get us all a drink?"

Earl had watched Throckmorton park and take his time getting to the house. He'd ignored the doorbell to make Throckmorton stew, and he was curt to the point of rudeness when he led him to the office. Throckmorton damned near turned white when he saw Wilbur. That was good. They had him off balance.

But then Wilbur told him to get drinks. Jesus! Wilbur was

playing his part, but the son of a bitch didn't have to order him around like a servant in his own home.

"No beer for me," Throckmorton said. "Coffee, tea, or diet soda."

"Coffee for me," Wilbur said.

Earl went for the drinks only because standing there glaring at Wilbur and Throckmorton made him feel foolish.

Wilbur was lecturing Throckmorton when he returned with the coffee. "The way I see it, we can help you—smooth the path, so to speak. If we gotta dig to get to the office, I know a couple of guys as strong as bulls and dumb as rocks. They'll do the heavy work and won't ask questions."

Wilbur accepted the coffee. "Earl here can get you whatever permission ya need to work on the village property, can't you, Earl?"

Earl left Wilbur's question hanging in the air. Sitting on the edge of his desk, Earl loomed over Throckmorton and watched him in silence. Most people didn't handle silence well. He figured that after a few minutes of the silent treatment, Throckmorton would talk just to break the silence. With luck, he'd talk about what he was up to with those tunnels.

It didn't take long. Throckmorton turned to Wilbur. "Okay. If you want to be my partners, I'll show you the letter from Kessler, but you'll have to share my costs."

Wilbur shrugged. It offended Earl. It was as though a pigeon he was hunting had crapped in his eye. He'd planned on holding out a hand and letting Throckmorton give him money, not ask him to ante up to join the game.

"Can ya be more specific on these costs you want us to share?" Wilbur asked.

Throckmorton's expression relaxed. "I'm searching for a safe Kessler claimed was in an office off tunnel number four.

No one knows where or how deep under the brewery it is. I've asked a subsurface imaging company for a bid to locate the safe and identify open tunnels leading to it."

Earl fidgeted as he listened to Throckmorton. Sitting on the desk put him above Throckmorton, but damn, his desk was hard, and the corner poked him right in the ass.

"After we get whatever assets Otto put there, you can use the tunnels for stockpiling dried food and survival gear. Guns, ammo, that sort of thing."

Earl's head jerked up at the word "survival." He hadn't realized Throckmorton was a survivalist. By golly, Throckmorton had something there. Pictures of crates of supplies in the tunnels could push sales of his book, *After the Big One*. He wouldn't need to spell out how he advised surviving nuclear war or an oppressive government. Tunnels. Anyone would understand their value; keep your stuff safe from starving mobs and government spies in black helicopters. Pictures would increase his sales of survival gear too.

He glanced at Wilbur, who seemed to be ignoring Throckmorton's last remarks. He'd tried to warn Wilbur about the calamities sure to happen someday, but the stubborn ass had walked out on him. Said he didn't have time to listen to bullshit.

That still frosted Earl. *Riots, starvation, and big government aren't bullshit.*

"How much is that underground mapping gonna cost?" Wilbur asked.

"I haven't heard yet. Based on the company's standard fees, it will be four to five thousand."

Wilbur whistled. "Ya couldn't find anybody with a dousing rod? Those guys worked for a bottle of booze and a few bucks."

Throckmorton snorted. "And you got what you paid for."

To hell with this, Earl thought. *Cut the shit. Get to what's important.* "How much is in the safe?"

Throckmorton shrugged. "I don't even know what is in the safe. It could be family jewelry, cash, stocks, bonds, or something moldy and worthless. In the context of Kessler's letter, the current value of what he called the family fortune could be from zero to fifty million."

Earl's jaw clenched. "That's a damned big range."

Throckmorton shrugged. "Life is stochastic."

Earl felt his face flush. The smart-assed bastard was showing off, trying to make him and Wilbur feel like hicks. "What the hell does that mean?"

"Everything in life is based on probabilities. We fish and take our chances, or we cut bait and let someone else take the risk. You don't like it, I'll go it alone."

"Gettin' back to questions that got answers, can this company tell which tunnels are open?" Wilbur asked.

"That's what they claim. They can tell the difference between dirt, water, and stone plugging a tunnel too."

Wilber tilted his head. "When will they send a bid?"

"They emailed me a list of questions. I sent the answers back this morning. They said it'd be a few days to a week before I get a bid."

Wilbur slapped his hands on his knees and stood. "Then there's no use talkin' further until ya get that bid. Let Earl know when ya do, and we'll get together again."

Earl showed the men out. Wilbur got into Throckmorton's car and the two of them drove off. That gave him a start. Perhaps Wilbur simply didn't want to walk back to his store. It was uphill all the way. Still, if Earl didn't keep an eye on those two, he could find himself the odd man out.

His biggest problem was he had no free cash. Every cent he

had was in the offshore fund, but to get a share of fifty million? He'd find the money for that.

———

"Can ya give me a lift back to my store?" Wilbur asked.

Throckmorton paused. He didn't want to spend any more time than he had to with Wilbur, but he had to drive past Wilbur's store. It would be churlish not to give him a ride. "Yeah. Get in the car," he said without enthusiasm.

Wilbur turned to him as he started the car. "Ya had to bring up that survivalist shit, didn't ya? We'll be lucky to get Earl to think of anything else."

Wilbur was quiet and looked straight ahead until they got to Main Street. "You know what he'll want to do, doncha?"

Throckmorton parked in front of Wilbur's antique shop. Wilbur continued, "He'll want to turn those damned tunnels into an armory, a little fortress, play soldier like a six-year-old. Damn! I had plans for that lot if I could get it cheap enough. Now I'll have to pry Earl out of there."

It improved Throckmorton's 'mood, knowing he'd found something Wilbur and Earl didn't agree on. "Sorry about that, Wilbur. Things are tough all over."

One of his clients had told him that "things are tough all over" was Wilbur's pet phrase when his customers complained.

A smile crossed Wilbur's face. "Thanks for the ride."

At home that night with Ben safely tucked into bed, Throckmorton poured a slosh of Amaretto, neat, in a brandy snifter. His mouth burned when he took a breath after swallowing a sip of the almond liqueur. It wasn't quite as bad on the second glass. It would take two to get to sleep after his afternoon with Earl and Wilbur.

The email from SIM arrived in Throckmorton's inbox at noon the next day. He called Earl, and they met with Wilbur at two o'clock. The three took chairs around Earl's desk, and Throckmorton passed out copies of Otto's letter and the email from SIM. They grabbed their copies and read in silence.

"SIM, Inc. What the hell's that?" Earl asked.

Throckmorton leaned back in his chair. "Subsurface Imaging and Mapping, Inc."

"Forty-two hundred. At least it wasn't on the high end of your estimate," Wilbur said. "How'd they get a bid that quick?"

"SIM charges by the acre," Throckmorton said. "They calculated the size of the brewery lot from Google satellite images."

"What's this black streak at the end of Otto's letter?" Earl asked.

"That's the combination to the safe. We won't need it until we get into the office. This is my guarantee that you guys won't raid the safe when my back is turned."

Earl glared at Throckmorton. "What? You don't trust us? That's no way—"

Wilbur laid his copy of the letter on the desk. "Cut the bullshit, Earl. We'd do the same if we were him. What we need is an agreement on how much you and I have to pay, how much we get, and do we get anything back if this turns into a snipe hunt."

Straightforward, rational, and to the point—that surprised Throckmorton. Wilbur might be easier to work with than he thought. Splitting up the work would help when they hit problems. Throckmorton didn't know anything about excavation, and he had no contacts among men who'd be interested in digging out a tunnel. It was easy to back away from the unfamiliar by delegating it to Wilbur. He told himself it would give him more time for Ben and his clients if Wilbur hired and managed the crew. Trust would be another matter. As Gert said, he'd have to take advantage of what good qualities Wilbur had and guard against the rest.

"Okay," Earl said. "What's the ante and how big is our cut?"

Throckmorton shrugged, stretched his legs, and tried to appear comfortable. "Parts of the tunnel may have been collapsed or filled in. Cost will depend on how much we have to excavate and whether it will be simple enough for Wilbur's men to do."

Earl glowered on his high-backed throne, and Wilbur slouched comfortably in his chair. "The village pays for the underground whatchacallit," Wilbur said.

Throckmorton held up his hand. "Hold it. I won't be a party to fraud. We can't stick the town for the mapping."

"Hear me out before ya get your shorts in a twist," Wilbur said. "I'm negotiating with the village to buy the property. I'll ask for information on the stability of the site. Any other buyer would do the same. The village will have to pay for the underground map no matter who they sell it to."

"I can push it through the village board," Earl said. "They'll do what I want 'em to."

"We do this project in stages," Wilbur continued. "We'll start step two, clearin' out the tunnels if the tech guy's report looks good."

They argued over how to split the project's costs and rewards for half an hour until Wilbur proposed they split the costs equally. If they located the safe, Throckmorton would get sixty percent of whatever they found—ten percent as a finder's fee, plus fifty percent as his share.

Earl proposed he split the remainder with Wilbur sixty/forty: sixty percent for himself, and forty percent for Wilbur.

Wilbur got his hackles up over that, but Throckmorton didn't care how they split their share. He told them to have fun and walked out. Anything that got those two fighting between themselves was good for him. With the SIM bid in hand, they were finally making progress, but he had to be careful. Wilbur's plan to stick the village with the bill could be fraud.

The theft of Kessler documents in Utica, Adele Kessler's murder in La Crosse, and the break-in and theft at the historical society were like an arrow pointed at Rockburg. That, coupled with the two men who asked Alice questions about the Kessler family and Maude's death, kept him awake at night. The information he had scared him. It proved there was danger, and what he knew wasn't sufficient to protect Ben or him.

CHAPTER 17

TUESDAY, OCTOBER 3

Throckmorton was sitting in his home office staring out the window. Piles of paperwork sat on the desk around and between two computer screens. The bookshelves were filled with notebooks containing printouts of his client's financial data. Through a partly open window, he could hear Ben playing with a friend in the backyard. It sounded like the kids were having a great day.

The phone rang, pulling him from his thoughts. It was John Olson, Frieda's husband.

"Hey, Chris," John said. "It's about dinner tomorrow night. Frieda—"

Throckmorton smiled at the thought of Frieda's cooking. A reprieve was welcome. "I can skip dinner if you and Frieda have something else going on. I'll go over the books with you and eat at Gert's."

"I'd join you if Frieda would let us off that easy. She has plans for the dinner. Have you met Nancy Twittle?"

Throckmorton thought of his last encounter with Nancy at the library. "Yes . . . we've bumped into each other once or twice."

"Well, you're going to meet her again. Nancy told Frieda she's interested in you. Frieda's in full-bore matchmaking mode."

Throckmorton was speechless.

"Are you still there?" John asked.

"Yes. I wasn't sure I'd heard right. I have a hard time believing a woman as attractive as Nancy is interested in me."

"Believe it."

Throckmorton remembered Jen's constant complaints about his appearance, his conversations, even his lack of sex appeal. "Are you sure Nancy was talking about me?"

"Yup, you're their target. Frieda will make up an excuse for Nancy to be here for dinner. Nancy even volunteered to help in the kitchen. I'm all for having someone else cook, but I thought it only fair to warn you."

"Thanks. I'm not good at reading women—probably would have been oblivious without the heads-up." Throckmorton considered his options. He'd been on blind dates, years ago. All were best forgotten, but he was interested in Nancy. "Okay, I'll go along with it, but only if you'll step in and end the socializing if I tell you we should get back to work. If things are going south, it'll give me an easy way out."

Amanda and Emma were on the floor of the family room finishing a game of Chutes and Ladders when Nancy arrived at the Olson house. Emma, a little brunet in slacks and a sweater, scrambled to her feet as soon as she saw the grease-stained fast-food sacks Nancy carried. "I smell chicken and"—she sniffed a bag—"French fries."

The girls grabbed folding chairs at a card table and squirmed in their seats as Nancy distributed their dinners.

Even John looked envious as he walked past on the way to his office. She wondered how much Frieda had shared with him. As John took her coat, Nancy said, "Good evening, John. Frieda said Amanda and Emma's project wasn't finished. She suggested I stay for dinner. You don't mind, do you?"

He leaned toward her and whispered, "Throckmorton is in the office working. You've got thirty minutes to salvage what you can of dinner."

"You're a dear," Nancy said. "Can you keep Frieda occupied if I send her out here to relax?"

"I can, if Throckmorton doesn't have too many questions about the accounts. I think he's being picky just to stall." John lowered his voice. "He's eaten here before. I know he'd rather eat at Gert's, but he's afraid it will insult Frieda if he doesn't have dinner with us."

Nancy took a deep breath, gathered her bags of groceries, straightened her back, and marched into the kitchen. "Hello, Frieda. Can I help with anything?"

"Oh, good. You're here. Could you put the broccoli in the microwave? The package says heat three minutes, stir, and heat again. I give it ten minutes straight. It's done when it comes out. The steaks are ready to go under the broiler."

"I'll get right to it." Nancy set the package of broccoli aside. "You look like you could use a few minutes off your feet. Why don't you sit down, talk to John, and have a glass of wine? I can take care of things here."

"Thanks. Wine sounds good." Frieda pulled a bottle of cabernet from the refrigerator and poured two glasses, one for herself, one for Nancy. "I'm going to duck up to my room for a minute. Call John if you need anything."

Nancy tasted the cold wine as Frieda left. She grimaced. The wine had oxidized to vinegar. Although tempted, she didn't pour it down the drain. *Wouldn't want her to pour me another when she comes back.* She set the glass aside and pulled the ingredients from her grocery bags. "Tournedos Henri IV coming up."

Twenty-five minutes later, she opened the door to the living room and signaled to John. "Is Throckmorton ready to break for dinner?"

"Almost. Give him another ten minutes."

That gave her just enough time to finish the salad. She heard Throckmorton's voice in the living room as she opened the cabernet she'd brought.

Frieda returned to the kitchen and held the kitchen door open as Nancy carried the salad to the table. Frieda seated her across the table from Throckmorton and explained that Nancy was there because of the extended play date. Throckmorton pushed a small portion of salad around his plate until John elbowed him in the ribs and bent toward his ear. He glanced at Nancy, smiled, and tried the salad.

"This is fantastic. What is it?"

"A variation on Frieda's tossed salad," Nancy said. "It's a classic orange and onion salad with raspberry vinaigrette layered over lettuce."

"It's delicious. Did you do the cooking this evening?" he asked.

Score one for the good guys, Nancy thought. "Frieda did all the hard work. I popped in when it was time to dish things up." She knew the lie was transparent. "How would everyone like their steaks?"

Nancy took the orders and returned to the kitchen, Frieda right behind her. "You didn't have to do all this fancy stuff," Frieda said. "They're used to my cooking. And this, 'how do you want your steaks?' I just give it to 'em as it comes out from under the broiler. That's good enough for me."

"You're feeding them, Frieda. I'm trying to erase the bad

impression I left with Throckmorton at the library. I hope you don't mind if I tweaked the menu a bit this evening."

"Go to it, as long as you're doing the work. Need any help?"

Nancy put the steaks in a hot frying pan. "I'll fry the steaks and make the sauce Madeira. Would you dice a few scallions for me, put the *haricots verts* in a covered casserole, and set them on the table?"

"What in the world are 'hairy cots very' and scallions?"

Nancy gave Frieda a sharp look. "*Haricots verts au maître d'hôtel* is blanched green beans tossed in melted butter. Scallions are green onions. Do you have any?"

"Oh, sure. Should-a called 'em green onions in the first place." Frieda got the scallions from the refrigerator. "Just don't spoil John. I don't want him thinking he can eat this way every night." Frieda looked over Nancy's shoulder. "What are you doing in the pan?"

"Making the sauce: scallions, garlic, and butter, fried in the meat juices then simmered in Madeira. It's sauce Madeiraise. I'll add sliced mushrooms at the end." She nodded toward a platter of bread fried in butter. "We'll put the steaks on toast points, pour a little sauce Madeiraise over them, top the steaks with artichoke hearts, and add a couple tablespoons of béarnaise sauce to each."

"Mercy, that'll ruin John for my cooking."

Nancy assembled the steaks on plates. "Don't worry. John knows this is a special night. He won't expect you to duplicate it." Hands full, she nodded toward the open bottle of wine. "I brought a wine tonight. It shot my budget for the next month. If you'll take it out to the table, I'll bring the steaks."

Frieda picked up the bottle. "Are ya sure you want to serve this? It isn't even cold. Should I put it in the freezer for a few minutes?"

"No . . . let's go with it as it is. We wouldn't want to spoil John." She nodded at Frieda's bottle of wine. "How long ago did you open that?"

"Last week, or . . ." Frieda paused. "Or was it the week before that? Can't remember. Nobody drank any, so the next day I corked it and stuck it in the fridge. It's been out a while, but it should be cold yet." Frieda placed Nancy's bottle of wine back on the counter and reached for the cold cabernet.

Nancy thought fast. "No, let's wait. You can bring it out if anyone wants a cold drink." She carried the plates into the dining room before Frieda could come up with more ideas.

Throckmorton leaned over his plate, closed his eyes, and sniffed. "This is wonderful," he said. "There is Madeira, the charred notes of beef, piquant garlic, earthy mushrooms, and hints of anise. That must be from the tarragon. The aroma is extraordinary, Nancy."

Nancy was impressed. "You have a discriminating nose, Mr. Throckmorton."

Throckmorton nodded. "Sometimes it's too sensitive, but please, call me Chris."

Frieda looked puzzled. "I didn't see ya put any tarragon in this. Where did that come from?"

"The béarnaise sauce is seasoned with it, Frieda," Throckmorton explained. He twirled his wineglass and sniffed. "Marvelous!" He picked up the wine bottle to read the label. "Frieda, you shouldn't have. A Bravante 2009 cabernet! A Howell Valley cabernet this old must have cost . . . I feel guilty drinking it."

"Sorry we didn't have time to chill it," Frieda said. "Nancy brought it, but I've got a cold bottle in the kitchen if you'd rather have that."

Nancy saw Throckmorton shoot Frieda a questioning

glance. Frieda didn't seem to notice. He tried the meat and closed his eyes as he chewed. "The steak is marvelous, Nancy, and the green beans are just right."

She watched him tuck into the steak. He looked pleased, but the conversation floundered. She caught Frieda staring at John and twice jerking her head toward Throckmorton. John didn't get it. Frieda glared at him, turned to Nancy, and asked if she'd seen any good movies lately.

"*Frozen*, an old *Pete's Dragon*, the *Toy Story* movies, *Snow White and the Seven Dwarves*," Nancy said. "I've seen most of them five or six times. I may see the same movie two or three times on the same day."

Frieda looked at Throckmorton. When he didn't pick up the conversation, she said, "Same favorites as Emma. What about your son, Throckmorton?"

"That's close to Ben's list," he admitted, "Since he turned nine, I have a rule that he can't watch the same movie more than twice a week." He looked at Nancy. "I don't think I've watched a first-run movie since my wife . . . um, I mean, well, since we split."

Nancy noticed Throckmorton wince after bringing up his divorce. "Same here. I haven't been to a movie since I tossed Gary out. Everything Amanda and I see comes on a disk. I wasn't sure movie theaters were still in business."

"Do you have time to read?" Throckmorton asked.

"Do children's books count? Except for a half hour before I fall asleep at night, I only get to read books to my six-year-old. The last adult book I read was Barbara Tuchman's *The March of Folly*, which was published in the eighties."

"That book was depressing," Throckmorton said. "Tuchman is one of my favorite authors, but the chapters about Vietnam were painful to read."

Nancy and Throckmorton compared current US policies to the self-destructive activities of governments described in Tuchman's book, from Solomon's block-headed son Rehoboam to the morass of the Vietnam War. John limited himself to nodding agreement, and Frieda's head swiveled from Nancy to Throckmorton as though she were watching a tennis match.

Nancy wasn't sure she could trust her impression that things were going well, but Throckmorton smiled at her when Frieda asked if the green beans were too crunchy, if anyone else wanted a cold glass of wine, and if steaks were supposed to be that pink on the inside. With no response from her queries, Frieda fetched a plate of her chocolate cookies from the kitchen and passed them around the table.

Nancy almost choked on her coffee at sight of the cookies. *Oh, no! Not those chocolate, tomato, and garlic monstrosities.* Before she could warn him, Throckmorton took a large bite of one. He chewed quickly, swallowed, leaned back in his chair, and stared at the rest of the cookie.

"Frieda baked the cookies this afternoon," said Nancy. She picked up the coffee pot. "Care for more coffee?"

Throckmorton held his cup up for a refill, took a sip, and swished it around in his mouth. Nancy saw Frieda frowning at him. Apparently, he saw it too. "Ah . . . great coffee, Frieda. I was rolling it around my tongue to get the full flavor. Do you have your own mix of coffee beans?"

"Just the usual." Frieda looked at him suspiciously and sipped her coffee. "Tastes normal to me."

"Perhaps it was the freshly baked cookie with the coffee," Nancy offered.

Frieda perked up. "Care for another? I got lots of them."

"No . . . thanks, but I'm full," Throckmorton said. A flush

crept up his neck, and he asked John if they could start work on the taxes.

The corners of John's eyes crinkled, and he put a hand over his mouth. He delayed answering as he chewed. At least it looked like he was chewing, although the cookie Frieda had given him was untouched on his plate. "It may be a little early for that, Chris. Frieda, let me help you clear the table." He suggested Nancy and Throckmorton relax in the living room. "We'll only be a minute."

"Thanks. The coffee was a lifesaver," Throckmorton said, as he escorted Nancy into the living room.

Nancy saw the kitchen door swing shut behind Frieda. She turned to Throckmorton. "You looked like you needed it."

"Was it that obvious? I thought I'd learned to control my expressions when eating here. Thank you, from the bottom of my heart, for a fabulous meal."

He sat close to her on the couch. Nancy had to keep the conversation going at first, but that improved when the discussion turned to daycare, sitters, and other problems they shared as single parents.

The conversation didn't last long after Frieda and John returned from the kitchen. Nancy mentioned it was a school night, and Amanda had to be home in bed soon. As Throckmorton escorted her to the door, she remembered Frieda's comments. Maybe she was right about men and food, but how could she have learned that the way she cooked?

While Throckmorton held her coat for her, he asked, "Would you care to go to a show and dinner on Saturday? A musical I love will be playing in La Crosse."

"I'd love to," she said.

As he drove to Mrs. Heath's to pick up Ben, Throckmorton sang what he could remember of Celine Dion hits, "Because You Loved Me" and "The Power of Love," off key, off tempo, and garbling the words. He didn't care until he missed a turn and took the wrong street. That brought him down to earth.

After he put Ben to bed, he went to his office and played Rod Stewart's album, *It Had to Be You*, and danced around the room. He hadn't felt this lighthearted in years. Maybe Christopher Marlowe got it right: "Where both deliberate, the love is slight, Who ever lov'd, that lov'd not at first sight."

A red light glowed on his answering machine. Still humming along with Stewart, he picked up a pen and hit Play.

"Hello, Chris." It was Jen's voice. He dropped into a chair next to the desk, the music forgotten and a hollow in his chest where there'd been a warm, expansive feeling.

"I'm traveling to Minneapolis on Friday the sixth. I'll be driving right past Rockburg, probably in the late afternoon. Is it okay if I drop by to see Ben? We can spend more time together, for Ben's sake, if I sleep over." Her voice took on a sultry note. "For old time's sake, darling? I miss you both so much, honey. See you Friday evening."

He sat looking at the answering machine for several minutes, trying to bring order to his feelings. How would Ben respond? Throckmorton had informed Jen's attorney of Ben's leukemia and the treatments, but he had no idea if the attorney had been able to contact her. How would the poor kid take it when she drove away on Saturday—if she stayed that long? Should he let her spend the night, for Ben's sake, invent a reason why the guest bedroom wasn't available, or flat-out tell her no?

Or should he pretend he hadn't listened to the message, take Ben to the movies on Friday, and to a UW football game in Madison on Saturday? That would work if Ben didn't have an appointment for bloodwork at the oncology clinic. He could leave a note addressed to Frieda and John on the door saying where they'd gone. That'd guarantee she wouldn't hang around.

But refusing to let her see her son? Could she drag him into court for that?

The last years of their marriage had been hell, but they'd had a few good years. Her "darling" and "relive old times" had created a warm glow—not for long, but it had been there. Whether it originated in his heart or his crotch, he wasn't sure. He wasn't sure what to do about his date with Nancy either.

CHAPTER 18

Suzy Wentworth waited at the back door of Maude's house with her hands in the pockets of her jacket Friday morning, the sixth of October. She'd called Throckmorton concerned about something suspicious at Maude's house.

"I was cleaning dead plants out of my garden and saw Maude's back door hanging open. The sheriff and the cleaning people are done with the house . Nobody else is around. Should I call the police?" she'd said over the phone.

"Stay put," he'd said. "I'll be right there."

Within a few minutes, Throckmorton had driven over to Maude's house to find Suzy waiting for him. This might be his last chance to look through the house. The sheriff would declare it a crime scene if anything was out of place. That could put the house off limits for weeks, and it might be months before they'd make the details public.

"Hello, Mr. Throckmorton," Suzy greeted him. "Do you think we should go in?" Her voice had a conspiratorial tone.

Throckmorton nodded. "I'd hate to call the sheriff if the cleaning crew simply forgot to lock the door."

"Absolutely." Suzy's expression suggested she didn't believe a word of that.

"There shouldn't be any problem if we walk through and don't touch anything."

Suzy pulled her hands out of her pockets. She was wearing latex gloves.

"Don't touch anything, even with gloves," he said. "You might move something important."

Throckmorton watched Suzy hustle ahead of him toward Maude's door. Obviously, Suzy was excited about this. She bounced up the three steps to the door and entered the house before Throckmorton put a foot on the first step. *Spry old girl.* The doorframe was splintered. Even he could see someone had kicked it in.

The house was still warm from the recent hot weather. Throckmorton kept his hands in his pockets. Whenever he saw Suzy reach for something, he admonished her to leave it alone. The smell of chlorine disinfectant and old beer permeated the kitchen. It grew stronger as they moved to the front of the house and the library.

Pieces of broken plaster hung from holes in the wall of the library, and splinters surrounded gaps in the floor. Papers, books, and empty beer cans lay scattered about the room. Other rooms on the first floor were untouched. Two bedrooms on the second floor were ransacked. Throckmorton couldn't help himself. He counted the empty beer cans—not even aware he'd done it at first. He chalked it up to being an accountant.

Suzy muttered, "Teenagers and a beer party."

"Strange teenagers. They left exactly twelve empty beer cans in each of the rooms they searched, none in the other rooms. It smelled the same for the spilled beer. All those books and papers tossed around? Someone was searching for something, and they wanted us to think this was a beer party."

"Good point. The cops didn't clear all their gear out of here until last Saturday. This stuff must have been done since then. That doesn't make sense. Kids would have partied tonight, after the football game. I'll call 911."

They hurried down the stairs and left the house. Throckmorton pointed to the splintered doorjamb as they left the house. "Be sure to mention somebody kicked the door in.

Throckmorton didn't want to be at the house when the sheriff's deputy arrived, but he didn't have much choice. He didn't think it safe to leave Suzy alone, while she waited for the cops. If someone ransacked the house and disguised it as a beer party, Maude's death was another murder, and he had competition for Otto's treasure.

Throckmorton approached the deputy when he arrived. He had the impression the deputy only pretended to believe his story about going through the house to avoid a needless 911 call. The deputy's attitude changed when Throckmorton mentioned his concern about the beer party theory and reminded him of the theft of Kessler documents at the historical society. He gave Throckmorton a piercing look. "You know disturbing a crime scene is a felony, don't you?"

"We didn't touch anything—kept our hands in our pockets and barely stepped into the rooms," Throckmorton babbled. He turned to Suzy for support.

"He's right, Jim. We didn't touch anything, and we were only in each room a few seconds." The corner of one of her gloves stuck out of a jacket pocket.

The deputy glared at Throckmorton. "I'll let it go this time, Throckmorton, but get it through your head that amateur sleuths who muck up crime scenes will find their asses in jail." He turned toward Suzy. In a conversational tone, he said, "And that goes for you too, Aunt Suzy. Did you move anything when you went through the house?"

She shook her head.

"That better be true. This is a murder case, not a garage

break-in. I can't protect you this time if you've tampered with evidence. Now, both of you get out of here. The sheriff will call you if we need more information."

Suzy nodded; Throckmorton relaxed. The deputy walked to his car as he radioed his office.

"*Aunt* Suzy?" Throckmorton asked.

"Yeah. He's my sister's boy. Did you see the condom under the bed?"

"No. You didn't move it, did you?"

"Nah, I wouldn't touch it, even with gloves on. But did you notice there was only one? That'd be a pretty lame teenage beer party."

On the way back to his car, he passed the squad car where the deputy was still talking to his office. Throckmorton slowed his pace. "Yeah," he overheard the deputy say. "The Westland librarian said it was a young guy from La Crosse, about twenty-two. She'd never seen him before. He used the library's computer to search for night-vision goggles. She assumed it was for hunting."

Night-vision goggles? Hunting at night is illegal, but that's for game wardens to worry about it. Why did the deputy report that from a murder scene?

It only took him a few minutes to drive the eight miles to Westland. He caught the attention of a woman behind the library Information Desk and introduced himself as an amateur photographer. "I'd like to get night pictures of wildlife. Do you have information on night-vision or infrared goggles?"

"Why would you need the goggles? It's your camera that will take the pictures, right?"

"Ah . . . I'll spend a couple nights in the woods to select the right places to put the camera traps."

She asked for his county library card and wrote down his

name and address. "Sorry I have to do this, but the Sheriff's Department has asked about anybody interested in night-vision equipment. Deputy came in here this morning, but he wouldn't tell me anything about it. Do you know why they're doing this?"

Throckmorton had an answer for that—not a good one, but he hoped it would pass muster with a librarian. "Deer season. Local kids might be planning to hunt at night. It's dangerous and illegal, but effective."

"Hmm. Maybe that's why a young guy from La Crosse drove all the way out here to do his research. He was in last week looking for infrared and something called Starlight night vision. Probably thought we were far enough away from his home the cops wouldn't trace it back to him."

"What was the kid's name?"

"Can't tell you. Privacy laws."

"Do you remember when the sheriff asked about the goggles?"

The woman screwed up her face and looked at the floor. "It was about the time that lady got killed in La Crosse—the one who fell down the steps. Ya know, Myrtle, she's busy shelving books, has a cousin who works in the Army Surplus store in La Crosse. She said the cops told her they wanted to know pronto if anybody buys night-vision stuff. I've never seen the deputies in such a lather to protect deer. We got too many if you ask me. Nearly hit one last night. It'd be a blessing if those night hunters thinned the herd."

Throckmorton thanked her and headed to his car. *Why the devil is law enforcement so excited about night-vision goggles? They must be sitting on information they've picked up.*

On his way back to his office, he called Wilbur and Earl and left voice messages about the break-in at Maude's. They need-

ed security for their excavation. He didn't want to move a
shovel of dirt until he was sure they were safe—surveillance,
an officer or rent-a-cop at the dig, whatever it took. And
Ben? Were he and Ben at risk even with his new security
system?

He'd hardly put the phone down when it rang. It was Suzy
Wentworth. "Mr. Throckmorton, Thelma Jones—she lives
across the street from Maude. She dropped by, and we got to
talking about the last day anyone saw Maude."

"That would be September nineteenth, the Tuesday I first
called her."

"She said a strange panel truck parked on the street outside
Maude's house. Stayed quite a while."

"Strange?"

"Yeah. It was white. Nobody in town has a white panel
truck. Thelma saw a guy walking around the house taking
pictures. He knocked on the front door. Maude didn't answer.
That's when he got out his camera. Well, Thelma had baked
cookies and took a tray over to Maude's, probably to see why
the truck was there. I've had her cookies, and they're not great.
Anyway, she banged on the back door three times and didn't
get an answer. Thelma's kind of heavy, and you hear it when
she knocks."

"Did she recognize the man taking pictures?"

"Yeah. He looked a lot like Agnes's future son-in-law."

"Agnes?" Throckmorton asked.

"Ya, she's the old spitfire I heard you ran into at the drug
store."

Throckmorton remembered the incident. It was the first day
he'd met Nancy. *So we've got a white panel truck from out of town
and Agnes's son-in-law taking pictures.* Throckmorton was certain

it was one of the men who'd visited the historical society to gather information on the Kesslers.

Throckmorton tried to work on a client's books, but his mind kept turning back to what he learned about the police interest in night-vision goggles and what had happened at Maude's house. He couldn't make sense of it. Too much information was missing. Alice called an hour after Suzy called.

"You asked me to call you when we knew what was missing at the historical society," Alice said. "There's now a gap in our collection. We have no letters from 1890 to 1904. I read a few of the letters when we first got them. The Utica, La Crosse, and Rockburg branches of the family had a steady correspondence between 1860 and 1904. Letters from La Crosse fell off after 1904 and even more so after 1933 when Otto became ill. Letters from the New York branch of the family were less common after 1904 and stopped entirely in 1921. Some kind of nasty argument. The last letters from them indicated they were searching for the 'Kessler 1804.' No one in the La Crosse or Rockburg branches of the family admitted to knowing where it was or even what it was."

"What was the 'Kessler 1804'?"

"No idea," Alice said. "It might be a stamp, a coin, a painting, or something else."

"And you believe the stolen letters were those between 1890 and 1904?"

"There are no other gaps in our collection."

For God's sake, why? The dates of the stolen letters didn't fit his theory that the killer was after Otto's assets. Otto didn't hide them until 1935. "Were there gaps in the letters from 1933 until Otto's death?"

"Hard to say. Otto took sick in 1933. Old, sick guys don't write many letters, and the Wisconsin Kesslers didn't communicate with the New York Kesslers after 1921. The letters between La Crosse and Rockburg didn't stop completely until Otto's children moved out of town. That was months after his death."

Throckmorton thanked Alice and ended the call. Telling her that Maude's death now looked like murder could get him into trouble. The cops would publicize that soon enough. *What would letters from 1890 to 1904 have to do with assets Otto hid in 1935? Nothing makes sense.* Sitting at his desk, he started to bounce his right knee. It was an old habit he had when he was nervous or frustrated. He knew he was in a fight—maybe a fight to the death—but he didn't know who he was fighting or what they were fighting over.

CHAPTER 19

T hrockmorton spent Friday afternoon focused on his date with Nancy tomorrow night. Maybe he wouldn't do anything stupid with Jen this evening if he kept that in mind. A plan emerged. He'd cancel his late afternoon appointment and pick Ben up early at school in case Jen went there first. That would be like her. If she didn't show up at school, on the way home he'd tell Ben that there'd be a surprise—just in case she didn't show up at all, which was also like her. A trip to Rockburg's new ice cream shop would be an alternate "surprise" if that happened.

He drove past the row of parked school buses and checked the other end of the line. Jen wasn't in any of the parked cars, nor on the sidewalk. Good, so far. He parked his car and waited for the kids to come out.

He collected Ben and cleared the traffic around the school before asking him how his day had gone. Ben was chatty. He'd aced the reading test, got all his math problems right, and yes, Mrs. Jones had given him his meds at noon.

Throckmorton's mind wandered. What the hell was Jen up to? Why was she here now?

They were halfway home before he slipped in his announcement. "There'll be a surprise for dinner this evening."

"We're going to get pizza? You're not cooking?"

Throckmorton glanced sideways at him. *Was that sarcasm? From a nine-year-old? He must be feeling better.* "That's not the surprise. You'll see when . . ." He couldn't think of a story that would cover both a trip to the ice cream shop or Jen showing up. He went with the parental standby, "You'll see later."

Ben rattled on about his day at school, apparently not too interested in what the surprise was going to be. As they neared home, Throckmorton saw a strange car in his driveway. It had to be Jen.

Ben didn't see her until they turned into the driveway. "Mommy," he screamed, jumped out of the car, and ran to her.

Jen was leaning against the front fender of her car, a sporty blue Honda with a scratch on the right fender and Wisconsin license plates. Probably a rental. Cigarette smoke curled away from her.

Back to that, huh? I wonder what other bad habits she's revived.

He noticed, couldn't help it, that she looked good in a gray, clingy sweater, fitted skirt, and stiletto heels. Her figure was even better than he remembered. Maybe she'd been working out. She was the picture of a woman with taste—something new for her—dressed for the hunt.

Stiletto heels to visit a nine-year-old? Memories he couldn't control flitted through his mind. Those memories made him careful and her sudden interest in Ben after three years made him suspicious.

She flicked her cigarette to the pavement and leaned down to embrace Ben. "I missed you so much, honey." She stood, stepped back, and examined him. "My, you've grown. Are you starting second grade this year?"

"Third grade," Ben said. "My teacher, Mrs. Jones, said we'll start using a keyboard next week."

Throckmorton stood back. He wasn't in a rush to talk to her, nor was he sure how the conversation would go. He'd have to keep his guard up. Wishful thinking could be as dangerous as any plans she had.

She turned to him at a pause in her conversation with Ben. "Hello, Chris. You're looking well."

That ticked him off. *She walks out without a word, shows up after three years, and acts as though things are normal. She hasn't even asked about Ben's health.* He acknowledged her with a nod and turned back to the car for his cell phone that was still attached to the charger. It gave him a few seconds to get a grip on his anger. When he turned back toward her, she was only two feet from him.

She embraced him and cooed, "Chris, I'm so sorry. You have every right to hate me, but I'm a new person now. I've gotten my life back together, with time and a lot of professional help. Can you forgive me?"

He didn't answer.

She took a step back, her hands still on his arms. "You're looking so fit."

He caught a faint whiff of her perfume. His anger dissipated before he recognized the fragrance as the one she'd worn their first night together. The scent aroused an intense emotional memory

Shaken, he took a half step backward. He remained stiff and aloof with an effort. "You're looking . . . well. How was the drive? Are you still living with Steve what's-his-name?"

"Steve and I split up two years ago. I was in Milwaukee this morning. I live there now. It was a long drive, but I didn't mind. Wisconsin is beautiful in autumn."

That's a first. He remembered a few of their drives together. She'd criticized his driving, bitched about the weather, and harped about why they were making "this godforsaken trip." Another whiff of her perfume tamped down his anger.

She stooped to pick up Ben but didn't get him off the ground. "*You* have gained weight. Your dad's cooking must have improved." Ben asked and she released him to look her car over. Turning to Throckmorton, she whispered, "He looks thin. Is anything wrong?"

"He's had seven months of chemotherapy. Or didn't you know? He has acute lymphoblastic leukemia. Ben is lucky to be alive."

Jen's mouth opened and her eyes grew large. She turned to look at Ben for a moment. When she turned back to Throckmorton, she whispered, "Oh my God! Why didn't anyone tell me?"

"I told your attorney about Ben. It would have helped to know where you were. Why didn't you call before?"

"I . . . I told you, I was in therapy, trying to get my head straight." She looked back at Ben again. "But he's okay now, isn't he?" she asked quietly.

How much should he tell her, a mother who forgot she had a son for three years? He wasn't sure he'd dare tell her Ben's leukemia was back. She might blurt it to Ben before Throckmorton could explain it to him. He had yet to summon the courage to tell Ben. "He's in remission, for now. They're keeping him on a low dose of chemo. He still goes in for checkups every other week, but the leukemia could return any time."

"Thank God he's okay." She glanced at Ben again, watched him a moment, and turned to Throckmorton. "What are your plans for dinner? Should we eat at home or the Carriage Inn?"

As she talked, Ben came up and took her hand.

Gall rose in Throckmorton's throat as he considered her last question. *Home? You've never lived here. We haven't been under the same roof for three years.* "Carriage Inn. We'll meet you there." *Neutral ground. Less likely I'll do something stupid.* He nodded to Ben. "Get in the car, Ben. Your mother doesn't have a safety seat for you."

The smile left Jen's face for an instant as Ben let go of her hand and got in Throckmorton's car. *Keeping her temper under control. Has she changed, or does she want something?*

He got in the car, backed out of the driveway before she could object, and drove toward Main Street. She seemed to recover quickly from the news of Ben's illness. He wondered if she'd make a scene at the restaurant because she had to drive there alone or if she would remain gushy and friendly.

He and Ben waited outside the restaurant while she parked her car. The three wove their way through the restaurant's bar to a small table in the dinning room.

"Where do you live now, Mom?" Ben asked. "How long are you going to stay? Are you going to move to Rockburg?"

The rapid questions didn't give her a chance to answer. When he stopped to breathe, she asked questions instead of answering.

"How are you doing now, Ben?" she asked. That was followed by questions about how he'd spent his summer, and where he and his dad had gone for vacations. Ben didn't bring up the big question until they were finishing their meal. "Are you going to stay, Mom?"

Jen started to answer, but Throckmorton cut her off. "Your mother is on her way to Minneapolis. It's a long drive, and she must leave early tonight."

Jen shot him a quick glance. He couldn't tell whether it was a look of surprise, a glare, or both.

"I'm leaving tonight?"

"I've been using the guest bedroom to store client records. I took the spare bed apart and put in shelving." He gave Ben a sideways glance and hoped the kid hadn't been in the room recently. He'd lock the guest room door, to be safe, when they got home.

Jen put her napkin next to her empty plate. "I'm sorry to hear that."

She and Ben talked over dessert. He told her how nice the nurses had been and how Mrs. Heath had stayed with him for three weeks each month while he recuperated from the chemo. "She picks me up at school three times a week. Sometimes I get to stay overnight when Dad's working."

Jen looked at her watch. "I have a long way to drive tonight, honey, so I have to leave. But the next time I'm here, I'll make sure I arrive in the morning, and we can spend all day together." She looked at Throckmorton. "I'd hoped we'd have time to talk about us, about what you've been doing for the last three years. I have a lot of apologizing to do. I can be back in two weeks. Will that be okay with you? Can you set time aside for us to talk?"

Common sense told him to say no, but with Ben there he couldn't refuse.

He avoided her eyes for as long as he could. "We'll see you then."

She rose, gave Ben a hug and a kiss on the cheek, and told him she heard he'd been so brave during his treatments. Standing next to Throckmorton, she put her hand on his back and leaned against him. "I hope you can forgive me," she whispered, and kissed him on the lips. He tried to resist, but her perfume brought too many pleasant memories.

Damned perfume! What the hell is she up to, and why does she get to me like this? Does celibacy cause insanity? He watched her walk to the door. Lord, but she was in great shape. Watching her walk had always been one of his favorite views, something about the way her hips rolled with each step. *Get a grip!*

Throckmorton was watching Jen maneuver through the bar when Ben tugged on his sleeve. "Dad?" The kid sounded distraught. "Is Mom leaving again? Isn't she staying?"

Under his breath, he muttered, "We couldn't be that lucky." As Jen disappeared from the restaurant, he told Ben, "She can't stay tonight, but don't worry. She'll be back in two weeks. You'll see her again soon, and she will be able to stay longer then."

Ben dropped his hand and looked at the floor. "But it's been so long, Dad. Will she stay with us next time she comes?"

Throckmorton couldn't think of a decent answer for Ben, so he struck up a short conversation with one of his clients. He didn't want to get out of the restaurant before Jen had time to drive off. As soon as the conversation was over, he felt Ben's hand in his.

"Dad, will she stay longer next time?" Ben asked. There wasn't much hope in the kid's voice.

"She'll stay overnight next time," he said, striving for non-committal. "Maybe sometime later she'll stay a bit longer. We'll have to wait and see."

CHAPTER 20

B en was reading a comic book in his room when Throckmorton knocked on the door frame and entered. "Pack a change of underwear and your jammies in your backpack, Ben. You'll have dinner at Mrs. Heath's tonight. I'll be at dinner with a . . . friend."

"Can I stay the night?"

"That's why you're packing your jammies, kiddo. It'll be late by the time I get back. You don't mind staying overnight, do you?"

Ben shook his head emphatically. "Mrs. Heath makes great breakfasts, and she's got boxes and boxes of her son's old toys."

Throckmorton dropped him off at Mrs. Heath's Saturday afternoon, washed his car, and cleaned the interior. He'd never been a neatnik about his car—a friend had called it a rolling landfill—but tonight he wanted to make a good impression.

Nancy showered and dried her hair. Tonight would be her first date since she'd married Gary six years ago.

The scene at the Carriage Inn last night bothered her. She was crossing the street near the inn on her way home when she saw Throckmorton, his son, and another woman. From where she'd been standing, it sure looked like that woman kissed Throckmorton on the lips. Maybe she hadn't. Maybe the whole thing *was* innocent. The way the woman had hugged Ben, she could have been an aunt, Throckmorton's cousin—or his ex-wife. If that was his ex, he might have been innocent, but she wasn't.

Her hairbrush wasn't in the drawer where she kept it or on any of the flat surfaces near her vanity. She went to Amanda's room where Amanda was playing with her golden retriever, Rolf. "Amanda, did you brush your hair with Mommy's hairbrush?"

Amanda put her hands in her lap, shrugged her shoulders, and shook her head. She didn't look at her mother.

"Do you know where Mommy's brush is?"

"Uh-huh." She left the dog, ran to her dresser, reached behind a framed picture of her with Rolf, and produced the missing brush.

The doorbell rang as Nancy returned to Amanda's room to give her a lecture about leaving Mommy's things alone. No time for that. Amanda's sitter was at the door. Nancy gave her instructions for the evening and returned to her bathroom to finish getting ready.

She noticed long strands of blonde hair on the brush. *These can't be Amanda's, so . . . great, now I'm losing hair.* Remembering Throckmorton's sensitive nose, she used her favorite perfume sparingly.

"Mommy, a man is coming to the door," Amanda called out.

The first thing Nancy saw as she entered the living room was Rolf on the couch, lying on her coat. He'd rearranged it into a comfortable bed and looked quite pleased with himself. "Rolf, get down. Off. Shoo!" She brushed a blizzard of dog hair from her coat before she opened the door for Throckmorton.

She motioned Throckmorton inside. "Come in, Chris. I'll be ready in just a moment." She glanced at the carpet and couch and prayed that the dog hair wasn't too noticeable. "Have a seat while I talk to the sitter."

Throckmorton took a step toward the couch. Nancy panicked. "Oh, no. Not there. Better avoid the couch. It has dog hair all over it. Excuse me," she said, and hustled up to Amanda's room where she gave last-minute instructions to the sitter and collected herself. This was a hell of a way to start a first date.

On the way to the restaurant, Nancy asked, "Who was the woman you were having dinner with last night."

Throckmorton sat straighter and seemed a bit tense. "Dinner?" he asked.

"Yes, at the Carriage Inn."

"That was Jen, my ex. She showed up out of the blue, fussed over Ben, and asked to stay the night. I told her that wasn't possible. She's headed for the Twin Cities. Said she'd drop by in two weeks to spend more time with Ben." Throckmorton paused for a moment. "We rarely spoke after she moved out and filed for divorce. She hasn't spoken to me since the divorce was final. I'm not sure if she's up to anything, but my attorney explained during our divorce that I'd have to let her spend time with Ben. I'll not let them out of my sight, though."

That reassured Nancy, and the conversation moved to safer topics until they arrived at the Waterfront Restaurant and Tavern in La Crosse. On Front Street, it seemed only feet from the Mississippi. A mile to the north, the Black and La Crosse rivers joined the Mississippi. The backwaters on either side of the main channel made the river look more than a mile wide.

Nancy noticed what looked like hair falling out of her coat when Throckmorton handed it to the coat check staff. The area around the coat check counter was dark. No one seemed to notice the dog's hair. She put it out of her mind and walked with Throckmorton to the dining room.

Their table overlooked the river. Pale blue and pink clouds floated in an orange and crimson sky as the sun slipped behind the bluffs across the river. Shadows enveloped the valley as twilight drifted into dusk. Lights blinked on along the river and on boats underway in the main channel. Bow waves from small craft and ripples from the current made the reflections shimmer and twinkle. She squeezed Throckmorton's hand. "Oh, Chris, it's so beautiful. We couldn't ask for a more romantic scene."

Dinner wasn't adventurous—aged rib eye steaks and a California cabernet. They weren't rushed. Keeping their meal simple allowed them to concentrate on the view and each other. A full moon completed the scene as their steaks arrived. The tender medium-rare steaks had a robust beefy flavor with a touch of smoke, complemented by the dry, full-bodied cabernet with hints of currants, bell pepper, and oak flavors.

Throckmorton told her about Ben's leukemia and hinted at a new and troubling prognosis. Nancy told him about her love of literature and her hopes to return to college, finish her education, and teach English literature in high school. Throckmorton seemed to be familiar with the Cavalier and Restoration poets. As they talked, Nancy realized what she'd missed when she married Gary. For years before her divorce there'd been few nights out, conversations only about sports, and little affection. Throckmorton filled a need she'd buried so deeply she'd forgotten it was there.

The Weber Center for the Performing Arts was a block south. They considered walking to the theater, but clouds obscured the moon. A cool breeze suggested rain, and Throckmorton drove to the Center. He found a parking place, and they walked hand-in-hand to the entrance. It surprised her how comfortable she felt with him.

While Throckmorton picked up their tickets, she watched the river from the glass-paneled bay of the lobby. Lights on a truss bridge spanning the Mississippi turned the bridge into an illuminated steel spiderweb; under it, running lights outlined a barge pushing its tow upriver.

The coat check counter at the theater was well lit. A cloud-burst of reddish-blond dog hair enveloped the counter when Throckmorton handed her coat to the attendant. Nancy held her breath as she watched the faces clustered around the counter. No conversations faltered. No one's expression changed. No one stared at her coat, and the overworked girl checking the coat seemed too harried to notice. She cautiously exhaled. Her nerves must have made it appear worse than it was.

She allowed herself to relax as the usher guided them to their seats in the small Lyche Theater. It was an intimate theater, well suited to *The Fantasticks*, a two-act musical with imaginary scenery and a three-musician orchestra. Their seats were in the first-row center of the balcony. Nancy was sniffling five minutes into Act II, and Throckmorton looked like he was fighting tears by the middle of the act. They held hands and leaned against each other, their heads touching, as Luisa and Matt reconciled on stage.

The musical ended with more tears and the reprise of the song "Try to Remember." Throckmorton didn't seem embar-rassed. What the heck—the song was about passion, loss, and the "fires of September." She was twenty-eight; he was in his early thirties—they weren't old but no longer kids. They'd each suffered through an unhappy marriage and the song struck an emotional chord.

The cast took their final bows, the lights came up, and Nancy dabbed at her eyes with a tissue. "I'm sorry," she sniffled. "I love that song, but it always leaves me blubbering."

Throckmorton sniffed and looked pensive, nothing like Gary. That jerk would have been looking at his watch, fidgeting in his seat, and whispering crude jokes through most of the musical.

It felt right when Throckmorton put his arm around her waist as they joined the crowd shuffling out of the hall. She leaned against him when the crush of people halted forward progress. He reached for her hand as they descended the carpeted stairway to the lobby, picked up their coats, and made their way through the crowd to the exit. A cool mist engulfed them outside the theater, and Throckmorton offered to bring the car up.

"Don't bother. I'd rather walk with you than wait." She feared that separating, even briefly, would break the enchantment of a magical night. The mist felt so good against her face, she didn't use her jacket's hood. They walked to the car together, dodged cars and puddles, and at the car he opened the door for her.

Throckmorton turned on the heater. Nancy reached for his hand and squeezed it. "It's been ages since I've enjoyed myself so much."

"Same here."

Moisture condensed on the inside of the windshield. Throckmorton turned the heater to defrost and waited for the windshield to clear before backing out of the parking space.

"Care to drop by Jimmy's for a nightcap?" he asked. "It's on our way back to Rockburg."

"I'd love to, but we can't stay long. I have to relieve the babysitter before midnight."

"Shouldn't be a problem, we . . ." He sniffed. "Do you smell anything?"

Nancy thought about the dog hair on her coat and Amanda's evasive answers about her brush. It dawned on her. *The hair on the brush was Rolf's.*

She opened her window a little. "No, No . . . I don't smell anything."

"Are you sure? Why did you open your window?"

"I . . . I've always liked the smell of rain—well, not the rain, but the clean smell of the air and, ah, the earthy smell of the . . . earth." Even in the dark car, she could tell Throckmorton hadn't swallowed that one.

"Never really noticed the smell of rain."

Was he being sarcastic? She knew she should shut up, but she was desperate and couldn't stop. "I read somewhere—maybe *Scientific American*—that scientists have discovered that bacteria in the soil cause the odor."

"You subscribe to *Scientific American*?"

He sounded impressed, which made her feel better.

"What did you think of last month's cover article?"

"Cover article?" she asked, hoping for a hint.

"Yeah, of *Scientific American*. The article on *Australopithecus afarensis* and whether it was a dead-end or one of our ancestors."

Oh, crap! Time for a little truth. Not the whole truth—a soupcon, a smidgeon. "I didn't see it. I don't have a subscription, really. I read the article in a copy I picked up while waiting at the beauty shop." She cringed as it struck her how stupid that sounded.

Throckmorton turned to look at her so quickly the car swerved into the wrong lane. "Wow! That's pretty rarified reading for the beauty shop in Rockburg."

"Maybe it was at the doctor's office. Yes, that's where I saw it."

"The GP in Rockburg? Sam Galen's office? Boy, you were

lucky. I've never seen anything deeper than *Sports Illustrated* and the *Ladies' Home Journal* there, and those copies were ancient."

Why can't I just shut up, she thought. "It was probably at the Gunderson Clinic in La Crosse. I had to take Amanda to an allergist."

"Is Amanda having prob—?" Throckmorton sniffed again in mid-sentence. "Are you sure you don't smell anything? It smells to me like . . ." He inhaled a long breath. "Dog. It smells like a wet dog."

Nancy winced. She felt the air coming in through her window, flowing over her, heading toward Throckmorton. She closed the window.

Throckmorton cracked his window open. *The smell must really get to him*, she thought.

"Ben must have let his babysitter's dog in the car," Throckmorton said. "Or maybe it was the neighbor's collie."

Nancy gulped. How long would it take Throckmorton's sensitive nose to isolate the source of the smell? What about when he walked her to the door? He'd at least expect a goodnight kiss. She considered telling him about Rolf, but it was one thing to own a dog but quite another to smell like your dog. Throckmorton had said that his sensitive nose created problems sometimes, but she hadn't thought they'd be her problems. With her luck, Rolf had probably parked his butt on her hood. Did her hair smell like a wet dog too? She thought about Throckmorton's ex-wife. *No way would that woman have smelled like a wet dog even if she owned a kennel.*

Mortified, she panicked. *First the library, now this. What will he think of me?* She put her hood up and cinched the drawstring around her face. After years of criticism from Gary, she didn't have the self-confidence or courage to tell him the truth and hope they could laugh over it, especially after that stupid reference to *Scientific American*.

I've lied a little. Might as well go whole hog. "On second thought, I'd better go home. The sitter has to be home early because she's in the church choir." Nancy moved as far away from Throckmorton as she could. "She sings in the choir for the early service."

———

Throckmorton felt the air in the car grow tense, but he was clueless why. At a red light, he glanced at Nancy. All he could see was her hood, her eyes, and her nose. She looked like a big bird with a small beak—a nervous bird that watched him closely but quickly turned away whenever he looked toward her. She clung to the door as though she might jump out.

Her stories were as odd as her behavior. None of the churches in Rockburg had a congregation large enough to justify two services, and all the services started at ten to give dairy farmers time to finish milking and their morning chores.

He felt sick. Everything had been going so well. "What's the matter? Did I say some—?"

"It isn't you," she whimpered. "I . . . I have to get home."

"But—"

"Please, just take me home."

It took only ten minutes to reach Nancy's house, but it was a silent and uncomfortable ten minutes. She opened the car door as he pulled up to her house, scrambled out, and said, "I had a wonderful time, wonderful. I'm . . . I'm sorry." She slammed the door and bolted for her porch.

Throckmorton drove home bewildered. Was it something he'd said? Maybe it had something to do with seeing him with

Jen. That woman had made his life hell. It would be just his luck for her to screw up his relationship with Nancy.

CHAPTER 21

Throckmorton took Ben to the park on Sunday. As he pushed Ben on the swings and then on a merry-go-round, his date with Nancy intruded on his thoughts. Why had their date ended so ignominiously? He couldn't stop thinking about her and the wretched ending of their date.

He thought they'd had fun, that things went well. They'd been so comfortable, so right together. It'd been such a contrast to the daily criticism of his looks, intelligence, and social skills Jen had ground into him during their marriage. Nancy was the first woman who was interested in him and seemed genuine. He felt like a fish on a line; he'd taken the bait, and like the fish, had a hook in his gut.

Monday morning, he paced around his home office and chewed antacid tablets between client appointments. To keep his mind off Nancy, he plugged depreciation, interest rates, and tax breaks into computer models to calculate how far in the hole his new office would put him if Otto's assets were worthless.

That afternoon, he scrolled through his emails. SIM had sent an email with two files: the contract and the invoice. They would do the survey within seven days after the return of the signed contract and receipt of the first payment.

He forwarded the attachments to Earl and phoned Al Huss. After asking him if he was enjoying retirement, he moved on to why he'd called. "Al, I'd like to send you a letter. Don't open it when you get it. Put it in your safety deposit box for me. Are you okay with that?"

"What's going on?"

"Earl and Wilbur figured out what I was up to at the brewery. Earl said he'd block access to the brewery lot unless I took them on as partners."

"Sounds like extortion. I'd walk away from it. Wilbur can be an honest partner or pull nonsense that'll drive you nuts, and Earl . . . Lord! He's greedy, arrogant, and delusional about that offshore fund."

"You forgot to add he's bat-shit crazy about the survivalist stuff."

"Then why are you working with them?"

"I'm trapped. I have to work with them if I want to find out what Otto stashed. They want to talk the village board into paying for the subsurface mapping of the lot, supposedly to guarantee that it's safe to build on. They claimed any buyer would require it, so it was a legitimate cost for the town to pick up."

The phone was silent for a minute before Al cleared his throat. "It's still fishy if they're silent partners with you on a treasure hunt no one else knows about. I wouldn't touch this project if Earl hasn't disclosed that to the board."

"I'm sure he didn't. Will I be culpable if a court rules Earl is defrauding the village because of his interest in this?"

"Probably. It's a good reason for you to get out of it."

Throckmorton leaned back into his chair and felt like a deflated balloon. Things were as bad as he feared they'd be. He thought of a way out. "Will I be in the clear legally if I give the village treasurer a check to cover the cost of the subsurface mapping? He'll keep it quiet for a couple of months if I tell him I'm letting Earl dig a legal hole for himself. The whole board would go along with that. They're sick of him."

"You'll be in the clear if you pay for the mapping, but I still advise you not to work on anything with those two."

Throckmorton had never realized how depressing good advice often was. "Normally I'd take your advice, but I've got an itch to see what Otto left me. It might be Ben's only chance, and whatever information I find on my family will be more than I have now. I'd like to mail you a copy of the contract and invoice from SIM and an explanation of what's going on. Would the sealed letter and postmark be evidence of what my understanding of this mess is in case those two pull something worse than sticking the village for SIM's bill?"

The phone was quiet. The silence continued until Throckmorton asked, "Al, is there a problem?"

"Just thinking. This is off the cuff. I didn't do much work as a defense attorney. What you describe might give you some cover. Send it certified mail so I have to sign for it. Do not lose the receipt. Promise me you'll go straight to the authorities if you see those two pulling anything illegal."

"Absolutely. Thanks, Al."

"Don't mention it. I'd pay to see Earl squirming on a witness stand. Wilbur always finds a way to weasel out of trouble. Be careful, Chris."

Throckmorton's next call was to Jack Weber, a friend and stockbroker. Jack agreed to dig into the background of Earl's offshore fund. Throckmorton's last call was to the town treasurer. He told him what Earl was going to ask for at the village board meeting that night. The old man was indignant that Earl would ask the village pay SIM's invoice. He calmed down when Throckmorton said he'd drop off a check for the first payment. The old guy sounded chipper when he added that Earl might get in legal trouble if he asked the village to pay the invoice.

That evening, the town board met, as usual, in the bank's conference room. Earl sat at the head of the conference table next to Arly Petersen, the village clerk. Arly wrote the meeting minutes by hand. His gnarled, arthritic fingers made it a laborious and likely painful process. That kept the minutes short and their approval quick.

Six members of the town board sat around the oval table studying the papers before them. Their furrowed brows looked like plowed fields. Earl had never been good at reading faces, but even he could see the board members were suspicious.

Marty Knudson, a bald guy in his fifties, fidgeted in his chair. Both elbows on the table, he looked over the top of the papers Earl had distributed. "Let me get this straight. You want us to pay forty-two hundred dollars to have a contractor come in to do a subsurface map of the brewery lot?" He put the paper down, leaned back in his chair, and crossed his arms over his chest. "Remind me, why are we going to do this?"

Earl held Marty's gaze. "As I explained, Wilbur's bid on the lot is contingent on proof that the lot is safe to build on. We know there were tunnels and a cavern under the brewery. We *think* we filled them in or collapsed them when we dropped the building in 2014, but we don't have proof. Any buyer will ask for a guarantee that the lot is stable enough to build on."

With brows knitted and eyes narrowed, the board members sure as hell didn't look happy. Could be they just didn't want to spend the money. They suspected Wilbur's bid for the lot would be less than forty-two hundred. Probably right, too. There wasn't a damned thing Earl could do to change that.

He brought up what he hoped would be the clincher. "I was walking over the lot yesterday and heard something under me—sounded like a gush of water. The ground turned kinda rubber-like when I took a few steps," he lied. "The village will be liable if we sell the lot and a building erected on it collapses. We need to know about any problems and at least inform the buyer."

The board members exchanged glances, but expressions around the table didn't change. *So much for my clincher*. He tried again. "We might even be liable as individuals if we don't do this." He didn't believe that was true, but it sounded ominous.

He stared at the board members around the table, daring them to disagree. He'd never lied outright to the board before, despite what people thought. His lies tonight, recorded in the meeting minutes, could get him indicted if anybody started snooping around. He'd skated close to the line that separated exaggeration from fraud before, but this was the first time he'd stepped over it. Well, maybe not the first time, but the first time there'd be a written record and half a dozen witnesses.

No point in doing things halfway. If he was going to cross the line, he might as well pole vault over it and do handstands on the other side. He looked the board members in their eyes, one at a time. "Last month was abnormally wet for this region. I'm afraid something funny is going on in what's left of the tunnels under the site—maybe even in the tunnel under Main Street." He shook his head, trying to imitate the mechanic who'd repaired his car last year. "Best we check on it before a sinkhole opens under somebody's kid walking across the lot. We're getting a deal from this company because they usually charge twice that much."

He saw no reason to add that the higher charge was for twice the work.

George Albrecht shook his head. "That's the same rigmarole the contractors give me every other summer. It's never been a deal." He tapped his pen on the table and looked at the other board members. "Has anybody looked into this company?"

Earl stood. He'd done his homework. "I checked these guys out with the state and a couple of their past clients. They do good work." He paused. Time for the handstands. "And we are getting a deal. Their regular *minimum* fee is over seven thousand."

He figured he could claim Arly was half deaf or had forgotten to add "per acre" if any lawyers called him on it. Any jury would believe that once they saw Arly's swollen and twisted knuckles. Earl was amazed the old coot could still hold a pencil, but Arly was well-liked and insisted on remaining the board's secretary.

Skinny Petersen, the youngest member of the board, raised his hand. "Will they give us a written report we can understand, or will we have to hire another group to interpret the report and a third company to tell us what corrective action is required?"

Earl hadn't thought of this, but from what Throckmorton had said, SIM would answer questions about their report. He didn't give a shit about corrective action. He'd get somebody to forge a report if he had to. "This is a turn-key deal. SIM will provide a report and answer any questions." Earl talked fast enough he didn't think Arly could write down what he said.

The village board members grumbled, but Earl knew he had them. "We don't need to rush this. We can discuss it all night if we need to," he said. The Packers were playing, and the game would be televised locally. None of these guys wanted to miss that. His motion to hire SIM passed unanimously on the first vote.

———

Earl and Wilbur met in Earl's office the next day. "You gave 'em the contract and invoice?" Wilbur asked.

Earl pushed himself away from his desk. His chair rolled smoothly on the hardwood floor. Levers under his seat controlled the height, tilt, lumbar support, and even the height of his armrests. The other chairs were simple and wooden. Everything in Earl's office was calculated to intimidate visitors.

It never seemed to work on Wilbur.

Earl leaned back in his chair. "Yeah, I gave them the papers."

"And?"

"They fussed a little about the price, but I told them I'd checked around and we're getting a deal. The differences in the technical shit each company promises will be gibberish to anybody but a mining engineer if any of the board members double-check." Earl smiled. "You gotta understand, Wilbur, I have the board in the palm of my hand. They argue some, but they always do what I want in the end. They agreed to the SIM mapping once I showed 'em I had everything nailed down."

"So the village treasurer will cut the check?"

"Cut it this morning. Delivered it to my office himself. You know, I've never seen the old coot happier to hand out a check. I underestimated my powers of persuasion."

"When will SIM do the survey?"

"Throckmorton said seven to ten days." Earl thought about the board. "We can't have board members dropping by and asking questions. The SIM crew might start blabbing about an old safe. Board members would get suspicious, maybe call the DA."

Wilbur stroked his chin and looked pensive. "Tell 'em that SIM pays the crew by the hour. It will cost extra if they take up the crew's time asking questions. The crew isn't supposed to speculate about the results. The data has to be jiggered or something by a computer."

"Analyzed?"

"Yeah, that's the word. Tell 'em management doesn't want the crew making guesses and misleading clients."

Earl smiled and nodded. "That should do it. We got this thing nailed down tight. Care for a beer to celebrate?"

CHAPTER 22

TUESDAY, OCTOBER 10

E d Wilson stepped out of his drugstore for a few minutes and left Nancy in charge. It was a slow day, so she would stock the shelves, clean the soda fountain, and straighten up the comic book displays kids had pawed through. None of those kept her mind occupied. She relived the final fifteen minutes of her date with Throckmorton and obsessed about the woman she'd seen him with at the Carriage Inn.

The few customers who came were picking up pictures, either printed from film rolls or from digital cameras. Ed hadn't invested in new technology, so they were all sent out. Older women picking up family photos were the hardest. When Mrs. Elmwood collected hers, she insisted on showing Nancy every picture taken at the Elmwood family reunion. Nancy oohed and aahed over baby pictures of Mrs. Elmwood's new grandson, gushed over pictures of the older grandchildren, and, with a catch in her throat, congratulated her on her handsome new son-in-law. At least her day wasn't as bad as the time Thelma Peterson trapped her into looking at four hundred pictures of her trip to Indiana.

Then Ada Jones walked in. Ada was there for the photos of her daughter's wedding. The store was empty except for Ada and Nancy. She couldn't think of an excuse to avoid looking at all of Ada's pictures, and Ada was on a roll. Nancy stopped listening to Ada's running commentary after the fourth picture.

All she saw after that was Throckmorton's mournful expression as she scrambled out of his car.

Noon brought more customers, but an hour later the store was empty again. She had time to think, time to review her life in Rockburg. Hope had been too perishable a commodity to survive four years with Gary and two years as a single mother in a small town. Social ties with most of her married friends had withered after the divorce. Hope died in isolation, but she didn't know how to face the future without it.

Tears rolled down her cheeks; she sniffled and blew her nose. She'd expected too much from one date. She knew that, but since her marriage to Gary, everything she touched turned to heartache and self-recrimination. Bleary-eyed, she hid in the cosmetics aisle, wiped away her tears, and checked her makeup in a small mirror mounted on the counter.

She heard Ed behind her. "You okay? Customer get to you? Agnes wasn't in again, was she?"

"No, no. I'm ... fine." A catch in her throat betrayed her. She turned back to the mirror to avoid looking at Ed. "Couldn't be better. I'm just ... checking my makeup."

Ed looked uncomfortable. He glanced around the store and seemed to fix his gaze on a clock above the soda fountain. An electric clock with a phony pendulum, it was a black and chrome monstrosity with "Drink Coca-Cola" written in small red lights across the clock's face. She asked him once why he kept something that butt-ugly. He said it was to remind him that there were well-paid people in big cities who had less sense and taste than anyone he knew in Rockburg.

"I can hold the fort this afternoon," he said. "Why don't you go to Gert's and have a cup of coffee? Catch the old grizzly before she starts her afternoon nap."

"Okay," Nancy sniffled. "If you're sure you don't need me."

"I'm fine. Go complain about Gert's coffee. Tell her I called her an old grouch who ought to be ashamed to serve that bitter stuff. See what she says."

—

The old stool squeaked as Nancy sat at the counter. "Hi, Gert." It was more a moan than a greeting. "Can I get a cup of coffee, cream, no sugar?"

"Sure." Gert looked at Nancy and glanced across the street toward Ed's as she set a cup in front of Nancy. "Ed send you over here to tell me I have rotten coffee?"

"How did—"

"Was I a grizzly or an old grouch this time?" Gert smiled and sat on a stool next to her.

Nancy hesitated, sniffled. "I think he called you both."

"He did, did he? He's in a rut. No imagination anymore. I'll have to get him a thesaurus for Christmas." Gert sipped her coffee. "Looks like you've had a tough day. Would you like to tell me about it?"

Nancy's explanation started under control, but Gert's comfort and understanding pushed her to go further than she'd planned. Gert didn't say much. Her sympathetic expression and nods brought out the tale, and an occasional pat on the back was sufficient to buck Nancy up.

"Too many shy couples break up because one or both of 'em can't muster up the courage to tell the other how they feel," Gert said. "They dance around a problem until one of 'em gives up and gets out."

Nancy had calmed down by the time her phone rang. She glanced at the phone and her eyes grew wide. She showed the screen to Gert.

Gert took one glance. "For gosh sakes, answer it."

With a tentative smile, she answered, "This is Nancy."

"Hello, this is Chris. How . . . um . . . how are you?"

"Oh, Chris, I . . . I'm well." Something in Nancy told her that if she didn't go for it now, she never would. "Chris, I have to explain my behavior the other night."

There was no stopping once she started. She told Throckmorton about the dog using her coat as a bed, her daughter using her hairbrush on the dog, and her panic when she realized that she was the one who smelled like a wet dog. She struggled to hold herself together by the time she completed the story. Her rapid, disjointed explanation couldn't have been easy to understand, but he seemed to get the gist of it, or at least pretended to. "I'm so sorry. I should have explained that night, but I was mortified. Can you forgive—"

"You don't need to apologize. I'm just glad we got it straightened out. Can we try again? Would you like to have dinner on Friday night?"

Before she could think, she asked, "Ah, what about your ex? Are you really free, or is there a chance you'll be getting back together?" The line went quiet and Nancy swore silently at herself for blurting that out so suddenly.

Throckmorton spoke a moment later. "Jen wants to get back together, but I doubt if it'll work. I don't trust her. I remember too many nasty comments and wretched nights. It's hard to get past that, but I'll try for Ben's sake. We can put dinner off a few weeks, but I'd like to stay in touch. Can we meet at Gert's for coffee tomorrow?"

That answer was more honest than anything she'd ever gotten out of Gary. Best to roll with it and see how things turned out. "I'd be happy to. How about ten tomorrow morning?"

CHAPTER 23

Throckmorton and Earl stood on the sidewalk by the Kessler building on a bleary, overcast Thursday as the three-man SIM crew arrived for the subsurface mapping. He watched as two of the men pulled a cart loaded with instruments over the brewery lot while the third man sat at a computer in their van. Ten minutes of that was enough for him. Rain looked imminent. Something about the tracks the technicians' cart left on the lot nudged a memory. He was uneasy but couldn't identify why. When he felt a few raindrops, he walked to the SIM van, followed by Earl.

Throckmorton asked the technician a couple of questions, gave him his cell phone number, and turned to walk to his car. He almost collided with Earl. "He said it'll take another two hours," he told Earl. "I'm going home." He nodded toward the tech. "They don't need us. It's sprinkling, and I've got work I should be doing. I imagine you do too. The tech said they can't say anything until their boss has written the report."

"I'll, ah, I'll stick around." Earl's eyes darted about the site, avoiding Throckmorton's. "Somebody has to keep gawkers from interfering or asking questions."

Throckmorton looked around. Except for himself, Earl, and the SIM team, there wasn't a soul visible for two blocks. "Have it your way. Give me a call if the crowd gets out of control."

He headed back to his car. Why would Earl volunteer to stand in the rain watching something as boring as two guys push and pull a cart back and forth over the same ground? Earl hadn't shown interest in the technology. He might ask the crew to do something, but the contract specified precisely what SIM would do.

Maybe Earl thought he could get a step ahead of Wilbur and Throckmorton by looking at the computer display in the truck as the data came in. That would fit his character. Throckmorton wasn't worried—Earl wouldn't understand the data if they printed it out and handed it to him. The drizzle looked like it would be a downpour in another five minutes. Earl was welcome to stand in it.

━━━

Throckmorton was working in his home Thursday afternoon when a client called.

"Hey, Throckmorton, Greg here. How come ya didn't tell me about Mayor Steven's investment fund? He said I could make more money with less work if I sold the farm and put my money in an offshore fund he knows about. Said I could make fifty percent interest and wouldn't have to pay any income taxes on it."

What the hell? Throckmorton sat up, his shoulders tense. "What did Earl say about that fund?"

"The mayor talked to my dad, said he had a great investment opportunity. He tried to get me to sell a forty-acre lot we're renting out, claimed we could make a bundle by letting him invest the proceeds. He said we'd make enough in five years to pay off the whole farm. Dad's about bouncing off the walls thinking about it."

Throckmorton seethed. *Earl, that son of a bitch! Going to my clients behind my back.* "I have a friend checking on Earl's fund. I'll let you know what he says, but put the brakes on your dad. Fifty percent interest, tax free, sounds like fairy dust."

"That bothered me too. Oh, I almost forgot to tell you, but I was delivering a yearling bull to a farm outside of Neillsville a couple weeks ago and stopped at the Tomah truck stop for lunch. Guess who I saw?"

"No idea."

"A woman who sure looked like your ex-wife was at a table with a guy. She was fawning all over him. My waitress pointed them out because they'd been eating there for days and hadn't left a tip yet."

Throckmorton stared at his phone. It took him a moment to recover. "I didn't know you'd met Jen. You're sure it was her?"

"I saw you at dinner with her the other night. One of the guys told me who she was. The waitress at the truck stop told me her name when I asked."

Throckmorton thanked Greg, promised to get back to him, and called Jack, his stockbroker buddy.

Jack answered on the first ring. "Chris, glad you called. You won't believe what I dug up on that offshore fund you mentioned. It's headquartered in St. Croix. You were right—it's a scam. The returns it claims are extraordinary, but none of the big investment houses have put a nickel in it. I ran a search on the manager. He was indicted for fraud in New York, Florida, and Arkansas. Never convicted, though."

"Wow!"

"Yeah. That's the good news. The fund has no stock in any of the companies it lists as its largest investments. I couldn't find a record the fund has ever purchased stock in those companies or any other companies on the New York exchange."

"It's a Ponzi scheme?"

"You nailed it. Your friend better get his money out pronto before the bubble bursts or the FBI nails the manager. Anyone who's taken profits out and hasn't paid income taxes will be up to their ass in trouble with the IRS. There's nothing tax free about this thing."

"How can we shut it down?" Throckmorton asked. "I've got clients putting money into it."

"Want me to send the information I collected to the SEC? They might be faster to act after the Bernie Madoff fiasco."

"Do that. I'll call an old friend at the IRS. That'll double the chance that somebody in authority will get their butt moving."

Throckmorton called his contact at the IRS and told him about the fund. He promised to send the details in an email. Then he called Earl to warn him that the fund wasn't legit. Earl was a delusional prick, but Throckmorton didn't think he was a scam artist. He wasn't smart enough.

"Throckmorton, I was just about to call you," Earl said. "Have you decided how much to put in the fund? Time's wasting."

How clueless can the man be? "No, Earl. I'm afraid I have bad news. That fund has never purchased shares in the companies it claims are its biggest holdings. There's no record that it's purchased shares in any stock traded on Wall Street, and the manager has been indicted for fraud in several states."

"What kind of shit is this?" Earl snarled. "How'd you happen to hear it, or are you working with somebody to smear me?"

"I called a stockbroker who looked into the fund for me. It's a flat-out Ponzi scheme. You're legally obligated to contact everyone you talked into investing in that turkey and help them pull their money out."

"Why? 'Cause a snot-nosed, small-town bean-counter doesn't know anything about finance? You've got a lot of nerve going behind my back, you bastard. I saw you and Wilbur drive off together the other day. I don't know what kinda deal you struck with him, but the two of you can whistle for permission to dig on the brewery lot," Earl sneered. There was a crash and the line was dead.

Throckmorton looked at his phone. *My God, Earl hung up hard enough to make that noise.* He shook his head and looked up Greg's number in his client list and called him. "Earl's fund is a Ponzi scheme. Don't touch it. If you have any neighbors who've invested in it, tell them to get their money out fast. It could collapse any day."

Greg said he thought it might be something like that and thanked Throckmorton for checking it out.

Throckmorton had barely put his phone down when Wilbur called. "What did you do to piss off Earl? He called me mad as hell. Accused me of trying to screw him over on this treasure hunt. As for excavating to get to the safe, he told me I could piss up a rope as far as he's concerned. Said he told the town constable to arrest anybody found on the brewery lot, 'specially if they're holding a shovel."

"Oh, for God's sake. Is Earl a complete idiot? I discovered his pet investment is a scam, and I called to warn him."

There was a long silence before Wilbur answered. "Haven't ya figured out that if a sixty-eight-year-old believes in Santa, it's 'cause he wants to? Earl was livin' in his own little world, just waitin' for Santa to make him rich as hell, then you showed up and declared open season on reindeer. Shit, I may have to buy the lot before we can do anything, and then that ornery son of a bitch will probably try to block the deal."

"Do you think he might cool down in a couple of days? Maybe we can talk to him then?"

Wilbur sighed. "Earl don't get over things real quick. Better give him a week. And what's this 'we' stuff? This'll be your call. When ya call him, it'll have to be, 'Good morning, Mr. Mayor. How ya been, Mr. Mayor?'"

"You've known him longer. Wouldn't it be better if you called him?"

"Nah. I've had a belly full of Earl, and you ain't gonna learn to keep your mouth shut if I clean up this mess for ya. You call him. Maybe the lesson will stick. Do it in about a week, maybe two. I'll tell my crew to take it easy until then."

Throckmorton put the phone down and thought about what Greg had said about seeing Jen in Tomah. It didn't seem possible, but he wondered if she had a hand in everything going to hell for him. He couldn't see a connecton, but what the devil was she up to?

————

Unable to work on the project until Earl cooled down, Throckmorton concentrated on catching up with his accounting work and spending time with Ben. They took a walk in the park on Sunday afternoon. The gold-tinted autumn sunlight picked out the yellows and reds of dead leaves strewn across the green of the park's grass. The hazy, autumnal sunlight and bare branches lent an elegiac quality to the scene, heightening his sense of foreboding.

"Want to sit and rest a minute?" He sat close to Ben and put an arm around him to keep him warm. "The clinic called this morning."

He felt Ben stiffen.

"It's nothing serious. Your liver enzymes are still high. They're coming down, so that's nothing to worry about, but your white cell and platelet counts are low again."

"Do I have to have another transfusion?"

"They said they'd be ready for you by the time we finished our walk. You didn't have anything else planned for this afternoon, did you?" He gave Ben's shoulders what he hoped was a reassuring squeeze. "It's no fun, but it'll only take a couple hours, tops. You're a tough kid. You can handle it. The PA said they've got a new Disney movie you can watch."

"Can I watch the whole thing? Last time the transfusion ended before the movie."

They stood, and Throckmorton took Ben's hand. "We'll buy a copy on the way home if you don't get to see the whole thing. How's that?"

There was a buzzing in his jacket pocket as they headed to the car. He dug his phone out and answered. "Chris Throckmorton."

"Chris, this is Jen. How's Ben doing?"

Throckmorton grimaced. *Should've checked caller ID.* "Ben's fine. He's looking forward to your next visit. Can I give him a date?"

"Ah . . . let me check my schedule. I'll be there next Saturday, that's the twenty-first. We can spend Saturday afternoon and most of Sunday together—if I can stay over at your place."

He clenched his teeth and glanced at Ben. "Do you want me to make motel reservations for you?"

The line was silent. "Um . . . I'm not sure I can afford that again so soon. Can't I sleep on the couch?"

He looked at Ben again and squeezed his hand. "Okay." He motioned Ben to stay where he was, stepped a few feet away, and lowered his voice. "There isn't going to be any funny business. Understand?"

"Geez, you don't need to be so rude. I'll behave . . . but it's difficult when you're so close."

He rolled his eyes.

"How've you been?" she asked. "Is this time of year still your slow period?"

"I can't talk for long. Ben has to go in for another transfusion in a few minutes."

"Oh my gosh. Is it serious?"

He took Ben's hand, and they walked toward his car. "No. It's gotten to be routine. They do this as a precaution."

"That's good. How is your project going?"

Throckmorton's pulse picked up. "Where did you hear that I've got a project?"

"I have friends in the area who keep me up to date. They said it involved your grandfather's brewery."

"It was my great-grandfather's brewery. I do have a project, but I haven't done anything on it yet."

"Well, good luck with it, whatever it is. I'll see you next Saturday."

On Monday morning, Throckmorton looked at the calendar. It was mid-October and they hadn't moved a shovel of dirt yet. He still had to call Earl and eat crow. The idea of apologizing to Earl disgusted him. No way in hell could he take the stress of a week thinking about making that phone call. He sat at his desk and called Earl's cell phone.

There was no answer. He called Earl's home phone, but there wasn't an answer there, either. He tried again an hour later. Neither phone answered. He called Earl's former company, thinking someone there might know how to reach him.

"Hi, I'm trying to reach Earl Stevens. He used to own your company," Throckmorton told the receptionist. "Would you know where I can reach him?"

"You'll have to get in line behind a whole bunch of guys

with warrants and badges," she said with a sigh. "They just seized all our financial records from the years Earl owned the company. I've never seen anything like it—just barged in, shoved the warrant under my nose, and started going through the files."

Throckmorton was speechless. He'd hoped the IRS would move, but he'd never heard of them moving this fast before. A raid like that required planning and warrants. They must have had the warrants before Throckmorton even called his friend at the IRS.

"Do you have any idea what this is all about?" the receptionist asked.

"Ah, maybe." He hung up, torn between feeling sorry for Earl and relief that he'd disappeared.

CHAPTER 24

E arl sat at his desk, and with shaky hands, he called Wilbur.
"Christ, Wilbur, I'm in trouble. Do you know a good tax
lawyer?"

"I heard ya got rousted by the tax boys," said Wilbur.
"Nobody in the bank or your old company was supposed to
talk about it, so it's all over town. Did they freeze your accounts
too?"

"Yeah. They got me trussed and gutted like a pig. I have
some money in—"

"Shut up, Earl," Wilbur growled. "I don't want to know. The
less I know about your affairs, the better off we'll both be. If
they got warrants for your financial records, maybe they got
warrants for surveillance too."

"Damn. How—"

"Drop by the store tomorrow. I got an . . . antique vase I
think your wife would like. I'll give ya a deal on it."

Earl sorted through what Wilbur had said. Surveillance—
did he mean wiretaps? Earl cringed as he tried to remember
how much he'd said on the phone with people when he sold
them shares in the offshore fund.

"Are ya still there, Earl?"

"Yeah." Earl's hands trembled again. He gripped the phone
with both hands and pressed it against his temple to steady
them. He needed to answer Wilbur with an innocent-sounding
comment. "Ah, see you tomorrow, then. I've been looking for

a gift for our . . . anniversary. An antique vase sounds like just the thing."

Earl hung up and took a deep breath. He hoped the IRS didn't know his wedding anniversary was three months ago, but that wasn't likely. He forgot it most years.

When Earl walked into the antique store the next morning, he found Wilbur whistling as he polished a silver-plated coffee pot. He put the coffee pot down, grabbed Earl firmly by the elbow, and headed him toward the door. "Let's go for a walk. Shame to stay inside on a sunny morning like we got today."

"Huh?" It was fifty-five degrees and overcast.

Wilbur held a finger to his lips. "Let's take a walk."

Earl still didn't understand what Wilbur was up to when he grabbed his jacket and guided him out of the store and down the block. Wilbur didn't say a word until they'd crossed Main Street.

"I'd rather be too careful than sloppy," Wilbur explained. "They may have my store bugged if they know we're working together on Throckmorton's project. From what I hear, you've got bigger problems than anything buried under the old brewery. I don't want your problems spreading to me."

With his mind on the IRS, Earl was barely aware of his surroundings. He would have stumbled into a lamppost if Wilbur hadn't grabbed him by the elbow. As they passed the Sportsman's Tap, Earl bellyached about his troubles.

"Damn, Wilbur, the offshore fund is a fraud. I put my life savings in that sucker; I'll be lucky to get my money out before the whole thing collapses. The IRS claims I owe over half a million in back taxes, penalties, and interest on the profits I took out. They gave me thirty days to pay up or face twenty years in prison. I need a sharp attorney."

Wilbur dug into the pocket of his jacket, pulled out a folded piece of paper, and handed it to Earl. "Give this guy a call, but we gotta talk about our project with Throckmorton. You have more on your plate than you can handle. Safer for all of us if you drop out."

They turned into a wide, unpaved alley that ran along a bowling alley and behind several stores. Wilbur said nothing. He marched on, hands thrust into his pockets, head bowed, eyes on the ground. Earl saw expressions play across Wilbur's face as though he was holding an animated conversation with himself. The crunch of their feet on gravel was the only sound as they trudged past the bowling alley.

Earl wore gloves. His hands weren't cold, but he kept them in his coat pockets. He could feel a tremor in his right hand. It would start to twitch any minute, maybe the left hand too. He needed a tranquilizer or a drink. Maybe both, and quick. They'd walked another thirty feet before Wilbur's last comment sank in.

Earl stopped and grabbed Wilbur's arm, forcing Wilbur to turn toward him. "What do you mean when you said I needed to 'drop out' of this project?"

"How many problems do you think you can handle at once? Didn't ya learn that when your ma was mad as hell and getting out the belt, the first thing you had to do was get your hand out of the damned cookie jar? Think, man, think."

Earl did a slow burn. He hated it when Wilbur treated him like a fool. He'd like to tell this uneducated son of a bitch what he thought of him, but he kept his mouth shut and sulked until they came to the end of the alley. As Wilbur turned right and took the sidewalk toward Main Street, Earl said, "Okay. I'll stay away from the brewery for you, but I'm the one who brought you into this. I expect my share of what you find. I'll hold up my end of the deal. Send me the bill for my part of the excavation costs as that goes along."

"You'll get your share," Wilbur muttered. "Just be damned sure you stay out of it for now. After you pick out something for your wife, we don't talk on the phone, we don't nod to each other on the street, we don't even say hello until you're straight with the IRS. Understood?"

Earl nodded, frustrated that Wilbur was in control, and worse, that he made sense.

They crossed Main Street and headed toward Wilbur's store. "Let's find something for your anniversary," Wilbur said. "What colors does your wife like?"

———

Wilbur watched Earl leave his store. The vase Earl selected was the ugliest piece of junk ever to cross Wilbur's threshold. Wilbur couldn't decide whether Earl's troubles had distracted him or the jerk couldn't tell the difference between attractive and hideous. Maybe Earl didn't like his wife. That was his problem, not Wilbur's.

He looked at a calendar hanging on the wall and estimated when SIM would send the report and second invoice. He assumed they'd be sent to the village board or Earl. Two problems faced him. The first was that SIM might mail the report to Throckmorton, as he was the person who'd first made contact. That wouldn't look right if the village was paying for the mapping. His other problem was that the calendar was from 1952.

No matter when the report arrived, it would be best if it went to the secretary of the village board. He pulled out his cell phone and called Throckmorton.

"Throckmorton, this is Wilbur. I'd like to talk to you about . . ." He paused. He should have thought of a safe topic to justify the call. "About working on my taxes for next year." Wilbur heard a gasp and coughing. It sounded like Throckmorton was shocked by the request. Understandable, since Throckmorton had avoided him until he and Earl forced him into this partnership. "Can you meet me at Gert's around one, right after lunch?"

"Okay. What's going on? Are you in—"

"We'll talk at Gert's at one," Wilbur said, and ended the call.

The last of the lunch crowd was gone, and Gert was wiping down the counters when Wilbur arrived. He ordered a cup of coffee, took a booth, and waited. Throckmorton arrived soon after. "What did you want to talk about?" Throckmorton asked, as he slid into the booth.

"You've heard about Earl's problems?"

"I got the impression Earl's in trouble, but I'm not tuned in to the local grapevine."

Throckmorton was frowning and avoiding eye contact. Wilbur couldn't decide if it was because Throckmorton didn't like him, didn't like to be seen with him, or if he wasn't telling the truth. Didn't matter either way to Wilbur.

"The greedy bastard is up to his neck in trouble with the IRS. Financial records seized, bank accounts frozen, the works. He might be broke. He put all his money in a fraudulent fund."

"I knew about that, but I don't see how that affects our project," Throckmorton said. This time he looked Wilbur in the eyes.

So he was lying. "I don't want Earl's troubles bringing the IRS to my door," Wilbur said, "and I'm damn sure you don't want that kind of attention either. Having the IRS investigate you can't be good for an accountant's reputation."

Throckmorton leaned back in the booth and nodded. "Point taken."

"Earl agreed that I should handle things for him on our project. He stays away from us until the IRS is off his ass. I promised him he'd get his share of any treasure. Normally, I'd kick him out, but I don't want to piss him off right now. All he'd have to do is point at me and the IRS could tie me in legal knots for a year. They don't seem to trust me."

"Really? I wonder why."

Throckmorton's smile irritated the hell out of Wilbur. "I don't give a shit what you think about me. I got three things I want you to understand. The first is that you don't have to worry about me on this project. I'll play straight with you 'cause I can't afford angry partners. The second thing is that you should call SIM and make sure they send the report to the village board. The village is paying for the work, and the report belongs to them. And in the future, you don't call Earl for anything except your lease."

The smile left Throckmorton's face. "I told you before, I won't be a party to anything illegal or unethical. I—"

"I'm not asking you to break any laws or cover up for me. Everything we're gonna do will be squeaky clean. I don't even want to see flyspecks on it. From today, you only deal with Earl as the mayor of this here burg. Talk to him about your lease, about garbage pickup, or whatever your neighbor is doing that pisses you off, but you talk to me about anything with our little project."

Throckmorton nodded. "Understood."

Wilbur stood and tossed a five on the table by his empty coffee cup. "Good. If we're gonna be partners, we gotta be honest with each other. Ya can't claim you're honest and lie to me like you was when I asked if ya knew about Earl's problems."

Wilbur stalked out of the Coffee Cup, his mind already on other deals he'd have to polish up if the IRS came calling.

———

Throckmorton was stunned. How did Wilbur know he'd heard that the IRS had pounced on Earl? Throckmorton moved from the booth toward a stool at the counter. Gert waved him back. "Might as well stay there. I'll bring coffee."

She put a cup of coffee in front of him and joined him in the booth. "Gosh, my feet hurt. I'm getting too old for this work." She rested her right leg along the length of the seat. "That's better. Now, what did you say to poor Wilbur? I haven't seen him that worried since his wife found out his girlfriend was pregnant."

Throckmorton snorted, almost spewing a mouthful of coffee. "Do you know everything that happens in town? Doesn't anybody here have any secrets?"

"There must be a lot of things I don't know about. That scares me, 'cause I've heard about too many stupid and mean things. What I haven't heard about is probably worse."

"If you want to hear something strange, Wilbur just gave me a lesson in honesty, and the old reprobate was right."

Throckmorton told Gert about how Earl and Wilbur had made themselves partners on his treasure hunt. "Once the IRS showed up, Wilbur went from shady to Puritan overnight. I can't figure out what he's up to."

"He's probably worried about the IRS expanding their investigation. They've audited him three, maybe four times.

They haven't clipped him for anything major, but that must take a toll on a man. As worried as he looked, I'd say Wilbur will be on his best behavior until Earl is clear with the IRS."

"That's comforting, but I don't think I can let my guard down. He's still Wilbur."

"Wilbur will play it straight with you if that's what he said. He doesn't usually lie outright. He just doesn't tell anybody everything he knows. Business is a game for him. You're neither an arrogant pain in the ass nor a player. It wouldn't be any fun for him to put something over on you."

"I'm not enough of a challenge, eh? That's comforting."

"Don't be fooled by his dumb hayseed act," Gert said. "He's about the sharpest man in town."

On Wednesday morning, Throckmorton received an email from SIM. Glancing through it, he learned that the safe, the office, and a nearly clear path to it were intact and easily accessible. He relaxed back in his chair. He felt as though a great weight had been lifted from his shoulders. They could get to the safe and Otto's treasure, although he had to remind himself that the treasure still might be worthless.

He picked up the phone and called Wilbur. "The report is in." He held the phone with his left hand as he scrolled through the report again on his desktop monitor. "SIM sent the report to the village board and copied me." Throckmorton forced himself to relax. Talking to Wilbur put him on edge. This was some partnership. "I'll email it to you now."

"I'd rather wait to get an official copy from the village board," Wilbur replied.

"Okay with me. We can set up a teleconference to discuss it with an SIM rep after you've read it."

"No teleconference," Wilbur said. "I'll join you in your office. Put it on speakerphone. You got time later this week for us to go over it together?"

Crap. Throckmorton had hoped to avoid extra meetings with Wilbur. He tried to think of a way out of it, but it was a reasonable request. Irritating Wilbur would only complicate working with him. "I'm free on Thursday and Friday after four o'clock."

Throckmorton was sliding a roast into the oven for dinner when Wilbur knocked on the door late Thursday afternoon. Throckmorton showed him into his office and handed him a twenty-page report.

Wilbur talked as he read the summary on the first page. "If I understood the email ya sent, they identified the safe, the office, and two tunnels we'll have to use to get to it." He looked up from the report. "How come ya don't look happy about it?"

"I'm pleased with the results," said Throckmorton, "but the tunnels are partially filled with dirt, sand, and water." A surface map of the site was on a computer monitor. With a few clicks, the other monitor came to life. The track of the equipment cart overlaid the surface map on the left screen and the subterranean structures and artifacts were shown on the screen to the right.

Throckmorton watched grid lines move across the site. It triggered the memory that had made him uneasy when he watched the SIM crew at work. "Holy shit," he whispered.

"What's that?"

"We're not alone on this hunt." He beckoned Wilbur to look at his monitor. "These grid lines on the surface map? Those look like the tracks their cart left at the site."

"So?"

"I saw identical tracks on the site almost a month ago. Someone else did subterranean mapping, and they're way ahead of us."

Wilbur watched the tracks cross the screen. "Damn. At least nobody can dig on the site without everybody in town knowing about it."

Anxiously, Throckmorton turned to Wilbur. "There have been thefts of Kessler letters and murders connected to Kessler homes, and the homes have been searched. All of these things happened around the time I got the letter from Otto. Now this. I think whoever committed the murders and ransacked the Kessler homes is the one who left those tracks. We're in a race with somebody who plays hardball."

"I'd hoped we wouldn't need to," Wilbur said, "but it's time to let the sheriff know about the letter."

They watched in silence as the grid diagram covered the brewery site on the monitor. Throckmorton felt sick. This was more than he'd bargained for. Ben could be in danger. "You call the sheriff. I have to have a security system installed for the lady who takes care of Ben. Ask the sheriff if the department will provide security or at least surveillance when we start to dig. This could be their chance to catch the murderer and our chance for professional security."

Wilbur put the report down. "We got to learn to trust each other or somebody will get hurt." He offered his hand to Throckmorton. "We got a deal, partner?"

Throckmorton shook Wilbur's hand. "Deal." At that moment he trusted Wilbur as much as any man he knew. That felt strange.

"Good." Wilbur dug a check out of his shirt pocket. "I heard about your little deal with the village treasurer. Here's a check for my share of the SIM payments. Now, as I read this report, they drew us a map to get to the office, but they weren't exact about the tunnel dimensions or how stable they are—same for the office. We gotta pin 'em down on that."

Throckmorton's mind was reeling from Wilbur's check and his knowledge of his secret deal with the town treasurer. He forced himself to concentrate. "What if they can't tell us anything about the stability of the walls?"

"Then we'll have to dig down from above or contract with an engineering company. That'd be another expense I hadn't planned on. Set up the call with SIM and let me know when." Wilbur stood. "I can let myself out."

CHAPTER 25

People under stress could be as stupid as those in love, but they were geniuses compared to multitaskers. Throckmorton didn't think of the obvious until noon on Friday. He was finishing lunch at the Coffee Cup when it hit him.

"Crap! Gert, I need my check. I have to get home."

"What's the rush?" she asked, pulling out a pad and handing him his tab. She eyed the food left on his plate. "Was the chicken that bad?"

He glanced at the check and tossed several bills on the counter. "Chicken was fine. Jen is coming tomorrow. Keep the change," he said, and rushed out.

Visions of Jen arriving a day early, prowling outside his house, squeezing between shrubs and peeking through windows, galloped through his mind as he drove home. She'd see that the guest bedroom was empty, not full of records as he said. That would be like her—just to throw him off, just to have the advantage for herself. His lie about the guest room being filled with shelving and records was the only thing that had kept her from wheedling permission to spend the night on her last visit. He needed that excuse.

What could have happened that night played out in his imagination. She would have driven home with them—maybe "to put Ben to bed like I used to." With Ben safely stashed, they'd have a nightcap. She'd give him a goodbye kiss and press against him with her arms around his neck. Guest bedroom, hell, he would've carried her luggage right into his bedroom. He wouldn't have been a fish on a hook; he would've been netted, gutted, and mounted over the fireplace, right under her former stud, Steve what's-his-name.

He breathed a sigh of relief as he drove up his driveway. There wasn't a strange car in sight.

In the guest bedroom, he stripped and dismantled the bed and leaned the headboard and rails against the wall where they'd be conspicuous from the door or the window. He moved boxes of records off two sets of metal shelving in the basement. A quick look at all the bolts holding the shelving together convinced him to move each unit to the bedroom without taking them apart. They were big and a major pain in the butt to get up the stairs and down the hall. He managed to negotiate the turn into the bedroom without gouging the woodwork or wall with the first unit.

He pulled the second set of shelves out of the stairwell, put slides under the legs, and glanced at the kitchen clock. Bad move. In a rush, he scraped the woodwork and gouged the drywall as he dragged the unit down the hallway.

Smooth move, Sherlock. She can't miss that if she looks down the hall. Why not just say that I moved them today?

The alarm went off on his cell phone as he hefted the last box of records from the basement back onto the shelves. It was time to pick up Ben at school. He'd gotten hot from the work. Sweat ran down his forehead, neck, and back. Even the waistband of his pants felt soggy as he stood back and examined his work. Four boxes on shelves that could hold eighteen—not impressive, but it would do.

He checked the time again. It wouldn't matter if she beat him to the school to pick up Ben today. He had time for a quick shower. The doorbell rang as he was toweling off. *Damn! Did*

I forget to cancel Fred's appointment? He scrambled out of the shower, grabbed his robe off a hook, and trotted toward the door.

He skidded to a halt as he rounded the corner from the hallway to the entrance. *Shit! Think for once.*

Jen stood in the entryway wearing the same tight sweater she'd worn two weeks ago, and a smile that covered almost as much as her short skirt. "Hi, Chris. The door was unlocked. I let myself in. Hope you don't mind." She looked him over, arched her eyebrows, and cocked her head. "Were you getting ready for me? Does this mean I'm forgiven?"

He felt his face flush. The belt of his robe was loose, and it was obvious he was naked under it. "No . . . just cleaning up, that is, I'm getting ready to pick up Ben at school."

This was it, his nightmare. Alone in the house with Jen, his memories, his hormones, damned near naked, and aroused, despite himself.

She pressed herself against him and whispered in his ear, "I know I've been a fool. Please forgive me." She kissed him.

He tried to draw back, but she had one hand behind his head while her other slowly slid down his chest and abdomen. There was that perfume again. *My God, how stupid can I . . . Does a nerve go directly from my nose to . . .*

He pushed her away, or tried to. She didn't let go—with either hand. "Ben, I have to pick up Ben. He'll be waiting . . . school." He tried dislodging her hands. It didn't work. It only increased the firmness of her grip and that played hob with his determination to break loose.

"Don't worry. I called Mrs. Heath this morning. She's going to pick him up. She'll feed him dinner and breakfast tomorrow." She kissed him again and nibbled on his earlobe. "We have the rest of the night to ourselves."

She wrapped an arm around his neck and pulled him in for another kiss. He felt lost. Ben had been his safety net, the last dependable barrier between himself, temptation, and stupidity, and she'd blown it away. And that damned perfume. He tried again when he got his lips free. "This is not a good idea. It's too late for . . . too much, don't do that. Water has gone under the bridge."

She guided his hand with hers. Their hands slipped under elastic. She leaned against the wall and drew him to her. His self-control crumbled. "Stop it, Jen. Get a grip. Don't . . ."

He wasn't sure whether he was talking to himself or to Jen. It didn't matter. She wasn't listening. It was clear she remembered all the right buttons to stroke, and she was busy.

He clung to reason, only to find himself in the quicksand of rationalization. *We're adults. We were married . . . water, bridge, wet . . . Oh, that feels good.*

⸻

He awoke with a tongue in his ear. This was not how his day was supposed to go. He tried to think of a worse direction it could have taken, but nothing remotely approached the screwed-up stupidity of what he'd done. He was naked. So was Jen. *Now I've done it. Life was complicated before, now . . .* Her arms and legs wrapped around him like an octopus, her tongue wriggled in his ear. He moved his head an inch away.

"Oh, that was good," she murmured. "I've missed you so much."

So much for original dialogue. He opened one eye and looked at her. Her eyes were closed. She was smiling, a demure, self-satisfied smile. *How much was she acting? Is there a* Method Acting for Dummies *or* How to Seduce Imbeciles? *Maybe a* Treatise on

Manipulating Morons: Mastering the Fake Orgasm? *Damnit, but I'm an idiot. I didn't even think to use protection.*

He moved to disentangle himself from her arms.

"I'm hungry," she said. "The Carriage Inn still has Friday night fish fries, doesn't it? Or we could go someplace more romantic to celebrate our reunion. Get a bottle of wine? You'd like that, wouldn't you?"

No. Idiot isn't strong enough: blithering idiot, brainless dolt, dickhead? Yeah, dickhead. That's close, but none of 'em do me justice.

"This shouldn't have happened. It only complicates a bad situation," he told the ceiling, unwilling to look at her. He moved a few more inches away. "The Carriage Inn is quiet, and we have things to talk about."

It'll get us out of the house and away from this bed. His brain registered what she was doing with her left hand. *Not again, and I'm not even drunk. Don't any nerves run from my brain to my dick?*

"We could shower together," she whispered. "It's been a long time since we did that."

Long time, yeah. Not since our honeymoon, not even the few times I suggested it after that. He rolled off the bed and grabbed his robe. *Has she listened to a thing I said?*

"Go ahead, shower. I have some phone calls to make. I'll shower after you."

He stood in his living room berating himself. From there he could see Jen's car parked in his driveway. It looked like the same car she was driving on her first visit, the same scratch on the right fender. *So it wasn't a rental—maybe her Tomah friend. Another guy with more balls than brains.* He looked at the license plates again. This time he noticed the plastic frame around the plates. "New York" was stamped on top, "The Empire State" on the bottom. He didn't remember seeing that before, but he hadn't looked closely either. He thought of the New York branch of the Kessler family and the theft of Kessler letters in Utica. That was the start of the thefts, murders and searches connected to Kessler properties, and the car suggested Jen was involved with that. Now he was convinced she was playing him for a fool. *Was Jen's new man responsible for the Kessler related crimes? If so, he could be one dangerous dude.*

———

At the Carriage Inn, people looked at them and whispered to each other. *Crap,* Throckmorton thought. *Should've gone someplace out of town—far out of town. Everybody in Rockburg will be talking about us.*

"It was so nice to have your arms around me again, lover," she said.

He put down his menu. For Ben's sake, he had to keep relations civil, but it wouldn't be easy. "What happened this afternoon was a mistake. If you want us to get back together, we have to take it slowly. We have to think about it, not get wrapped up in sex."

She did a phony pout. "Maybe, but lying next to you naked with our arms around each other was wonderful."

He changed the subject to Ben and his hospitalization. Over dinner, he suggested counseling again. She tried to change the subject. When that didn't work, she said they didn't need it.

"You're dreaming," he said. "We were both miserable the last two years we were together."

"But I was depressed and had anxiety issues. I'm seeing Dr. Brownell now. He's wonderful. I'm a new person."

Probably banging him too. But give it a chance, for Ben's sake. "Then we shouldn't rush it. I don't know the new you, and I'm sure I've changed, too."

She smirked. "You haven't changed that much."

He put his napkin next to his plate. "You're sure. I'm not. We take time to work this out, or we don't do it at all."

She reached across the table and put a hand on his. "If I spend the night, I'll prove I can make you happy."

He trembled and thought of how much temptation and trouble would happen if she stayed a night with him. "That's not a good idea."

"But we've already bounced all over the bed. We'd have done it twice if you hadn't gotten so stuffy when I woke you." She slipped off a shoe and ran a toe up his thigh. "Once more for old time's sake?"

He moved her toe off. "You're staying at your motel. Come back tomorrow morning at ten. Ben will be home by then."

She sighed and looked at her plate. "Don't you want dessert?"

"I'm full."

She assumed an innocent look. "I wasn't thinking about that kind of dessert."

"Good Lord, Jen. We made a mistake. A second one will only complicate—"

Her toe was back against his thigh. He looked at her plate. It was empty. "Time to go." He grabbed the check and stood before her toe got any further and his willpower cratered again. "We'll drive to the house; then you go to your motel. That's it."

She sniffed and looked away. "I feel so used."

He choked back a derisive snort.

The drive home was silent. He parked his car and nodded toward hers.

"Can I come in for a nightcap?"

"No. I'll see you tomorrow."

He kissed her goodnight—would have felt like a cad if he hadn't.

———

At nine the next morning he collected Ben from Mrs. Heath's. Jen showed up at ten. She talked and played with Ben until lunch. Throckmorton stayed out of their way. He didn't want Ben to see his mother in action. Common sense told him to stay away from her, her warm touch, and her subtle scent. The cool and rational front he projected was a sign of weakness, not strength.

Ben took his mother on a tour of the house. His chatter kept Jen's attention when they passed the gouged drywall, and he kept her busy talking about his friends at school when they opened the guest bedroom for her review. She didn't say anything about the nearly empty shelving. Throckmorton was so relieved that she didn't question his lie about the guest bedroom being unavailable that he let himself be drawn into teaching Ben how to play Hearts until noon. The three lunched at the Coffee Cup. Gert gave him a questioning glance, a frown, rolled her eyes, and took their orders. He was sure she'd wanted him to see the eye roll.

Back at the house, Jen roped him into playing board games on a card table with her and Ben. She followed when he went to the kitchen for soft drinks and tried to trap him in a corner by the sink. He dodged her, got back to the card table, and avoided serious discussion until Ben went to the bathroom.

"So?" she asked. "How do you feel about us today?"

"This is great for Ben. I haven't seen him this happy in the last year, but don't get his hopes up. Don't lead him on unless you plan on making regular visits. He went through hell when you walked out. He stopped eating, stopped playing, just moped around and cried. Don't put him through that again. He went through more than any kid should have to during his chemo. I can't imagine what one intra-spinal treatment would feel like. He had seven."

"I—"

"Let's talk on the phone once a week. Ben would like that too. We can see each other in a month."

"I had a hard time getting to sleep last night thinking of you and yesterday afternoon. What can be wrong with enjoying ourselves again?"

"Give it a rest. Scratching every itch isn't how healthy people live."

She was quiet until Ben returned. "How has life been treating you, otherwise, Chris?" she asked.

He blathered away for a minute about work, taking care of Ben, talking about the weather.

"How's your project going? When will you start excavating?"

His mind froze; he struggled to come up with an answer. "It's too early to say." *She wants a timeline for the excavation. Is this why she's back? To get information for her new boyfriend?*

He changed the topic to Ben's tutoring during the summer to catch up with his classmates after missing months of school, and Ben told her about his first month back in school this fall. While Ben chattered, Throckmorton dropped out of the conversation. His reprieve lasted only a couple of minutes.

"So, what's it like, working with Earl and Wilbur? How long will it take you to get to the safe?"

He glared at her. "I didn't say anything about a safe. Where did you hear that, and how did you know I was working with them?"

"I hear a little from friends, a little from relatives."

How much digging into his project had she done? A lot

more than could be ascribed to casual curiosity, that was clear. Greg had said she was at a motel in Tomah with an unsavory-looking character. She was driving a car from New York, the place where the first Kessler letters were stolen, and she showed up here shortly after the murders. The car probably belonged to her boyfriend. The connection between Jen, her boyfriend, and the murders was now even stronger. He'd have to be careful what he said.

"Wilbur said he can hire a couple guys cheap. We split the costs and whatever we find in the safe, if anything. That way nobody will be out much if there's nothing there."

She stayed away from the subject for the rest of the afternoon and returned to her motel. Ben waved enthusiastically as she drove off. *She hasn't changed at all if she's here to check on my project. I didn't use protection.*

—————

He called the local clinic first thing Monday morning. It was a small medical office with a receptionist and a physician present three days a week. He got past Sylvia, the receptionist, and was able to speak to Sam, his doctor. "Jen, my ex was here, and I did something stupid. We—"

"Yeah, I heard about that. It was the topic of discussion at the coffee klatch at Gert's."

"Oh, crap! Anyhow, I didn't use protection, and I don't trust Jen. When and where can I be checked for STDs?"

"Unless you have symptoms—tingling in your penis, a burning sensation when you urinate, a rash, a chancre—wait at least a week after the incident. Have Sylvia set up an appointment for you—tell her it's for a checkup. She doesn't need to know the specifics."

Throckmorton walked to his office, his mind racing. Damn!

It would be a week before he could be tested and probably a couple more days before he could get the results. He couldn't take a chance of infecting Nancy. Nope. They couldn't even kiss until he was sure he hadn't picked up an STD.

That afternoon he met Nancy for lunch at Gert's. He'd tried to keep Jen in the dark on what he was doing, but he wanted Nancy to understand what he was up to and why it would be taking up a lot of his time. "I may not have much free time for the next month. I'm looking for a safe under the old brewery site. Wilbur and Earl forced me to accept them as partners. Wilbur's sharper and more reasonable than I gave him credit for. We agreed to be honest with each other and shook hands on it. I know this sounds crazy, but I trust him."

"That's good news. What's in the safe?"

He explained that he wasn't sure and that strange things related to the Kessler family had been happening. "I'm counting on this to provide enough money for a new treatment for Ben. It's experimental, the insurance company claims, and they won't cover it."

"Oh, my lord. How sick is Ben?"

"He's not too bad now." Throckmorton avoided looking Nancy in the eyes, afraid he might break down. "Mild chemo is keeping things in check, but he needs the new treatment or a return to rigorous chemo to be cured. I'd . . ." Throckmorton paused, pulled out a handkerchief, and blew his nose. "I'd rather not go into it now."

"I understand," Nancy said, and put her hand on his. "How did things go with Jen's visit?"

He gave her a redacted summary of the visit. "A client told me she may have moved in with another guy. I don't think her interest in me extends past what's in that safe. It's a relief to know what she's up to, but how do I prepare Ben?"

"I can't help you there," Nancy said. "Gary was such a rotter it wasn't hard to break the news to Amanda. She's never looked back. He hasn't poked his nose into our lives again either." She pushed the remains of a salad around her plate. "Let Ben and his mother have another weekend together when she shows up. Amanda and I'll drop by your place with a pizza on Thursday after school."

Throckmorton agreed with alacrity. It was a great idea, and it meant Nancy was still interested in him.

CHAPTER 26

The Monday afternoon teleconference in Throckmorton's home office was short. Broken concrete blocked the tunnel from the Kessler office building to the brewery. Most of the other tunnels didn't connect to the office that was their target. Two of the tunnels they could use to get to the office were six feet wide by seven feet tall and connected to the cavern under the brewery. The cavern looked like it connected to what had been a rear entrance to the brewery. Ceilings of the cavern were higher, from eight to twelve feet. SIM agreed to determine how stable the office, tunnels, and entrance cavern were for an extra five hundred dollars.

Wilbur frowned. "Those other tunnels and caverns, how much will it cost to get this here engineer's opinion on them?"

Puzzled, Throckmorton looked at Wilbur and mouthed the word "why?" They heard the click of keys on a calculator as the SIM engineer put together an estimate for the added work. "That will cost an extra twelve hundred. Would you like me to proceed with that too?"

Throckmorton shook his head. Wilbur said, "Go ahead. Send us the information on the cavern and what we need to get to the office as soon as you've got it. You can send the rest later."

Throckmorton reached for the mute button, but Wilbur blocked his hand. "Route the invoice to me. I'll write a check for the twelve hundred." He gave the engineer his email address and ended the teleconference.

Throckmorton was flabbergasted. Wilbur had volunteered

to pay for work they didn't need. He hadn't even haggled over it. "Why in the blazes did you ask for all that analysis, and why didn't you try to get a better deal? I thought you were a horse trader."

"We're not big enough to dicker with SIM. That was a take-it-or-leave-it offer."

"But why all the extra information on tunnels we don't need to go through?"

Wilbur paused and gave him what looked like an appraising glance. "I'm buying the lot, and I want to know how stable it is." He broke eye contact with Throckmorton and stretched in his chair. "We can use sump pumps to get rid of the water in the tunnels, but we gotta figure out how we're going to shift all that sand out. He said there was up to five feet of it in places."

So, he doesn't want to share his plans. It wasn't worth arguing over. "Any ideas how to move the sand?"

"We'll start small. Shovels, picks, and a wheelbarrow. I got a couple guys lined up who work cheap."

Throckmorton thought of asking what "cheap" would get but put that conversation on hold. He didn't have anyone to replace Wilbur's crew; they were stuck with them. Besides, Wilbur's ability to line up workers was one reason Throckmorton had agreed to their partnership.

＊

On Tuesday morning, Wilbur sat at his desk in the back of his store. He didn't want to do it, but he picked up his phone and called his daughter. "Sarah, I need some help. It'll help you too."

"Ya moving out of Wisconsin?" she said. "I'll pay the movers if you get it done before the election."

Smartass. She's been ragging my ass ever since she got herself appointed interim sheriff. "No. This is law enforcement stuff. I—"

"I'm not going to look the other way or cut you any slack, Dad."

Typical. She always assumed the worst. He tried to sound conciliatory. "And I'm not asking you to. Remember them murders in the old Kessler homes?"

The line was silent for a moment. "How did you know that Maude Jones's death was a murder?"

"My partner, Throckmorton—"

"He's the guy who found the body? I thought he was a straight-arrow CPA?"

"Yeah, he is, a straight arrow, I mean. He and a neighbor lady called it in. Throckmorton said there were twelve empty beer cans in each room. He didn't think that could have been a coincidence."

There was a pause before Sarah answered. "I won't ask how he knew about the empty cans. The count could have been a coincidence, but there weren't any fingerprints or DNA on the cans. Teenage drunks aren't that careful. There was a planted used condom too."

That was something Wilbur hadn't heard about. "How'd ya know it was planted?"

"The forensics people said it was a month old. How does all this involve you?"

"The murders were in Kessler homes, only Kessler documents were stolen from the historical society, the Kessler mansion burglary, and a museum in Utica, New York. Throckmorton and I are looking for valuables his great-grandpappy, Otto Kessler, hid under the brewery in 1935. Somebody tailed Throckmorton when he was at the brewery site and in the Kessler office. We think it's the killer. He might be lookin' for the same thing we are."

"Jesus," Sarah exploded. "Then drop your damned search

and let my department take over. Are you guys trying to get killed?"

"You know me better'n that. How about we keep on lookin' for the goodies. We'll be bait for the killer. Put surveillance cameras in, monitor our dig, and keep an eye on Throckmorton's house and kid."

"This is a first," she said.

"What?" Wilbur wasn't sure if he should take offense, but knowing Sarah, it was probably an insult. "Is it a first that I'll work with your deputies?"

"No. It's the first time you've had a good idea that was honest."

———

Lousy day to start a project, Throckmorton thought. It was overcast and fifty degrees. He shivered in a light jacket as he stood in the ravine behind the brewery lot matching points on SIM's diagrams with wooden stakes along the top of the ravine thirty feet above him. They'ed been placed by the SIM crew to mark the entrance to the cavern and tunnels. He turned when he heard his name. It was Wilbur and two men in their mid-thirties coming up the path from the county road.

"Throckmorton, I got some guys you should meet." He nodded to a wiry man about six feet tall on his right. "This is Johnny, and"—he jabbed a thumb toward a short, muscular man on his left—"this is Adam. I've hired them to dig us a path to the office."

Both men had scruffy beards and wore scuffed work boots, patched jeans, and denim jackets. Their stocking caps needed a visit to the laundry.

Throckmorton asked Wilbur if they could talk privately. Wilbur told the men to get the shovels, picks, and wheelbarrow out of their pickup. When they'd left, he turned to Throckmorton, his hands in his pockets. "You got a problem with something?"

Throckmorton crossed his arms over his chest. He felt kind of defensive, but this was a sore point. "Yeah. I thought we were going to talk to the sheriff before we started digging, and can we depend on these guys not to tell everybody in town what they're doing?"

"A sheriff's deputy will meet us at your house tonight. Don't worry, Johnny and Adam will try to tell everybody they see what they're doing, but nobody—"

Holy shit. This was exactly what Throckmorton had feared. Hands on his hips, he demanded, "What? I thought we agreed to keep this quiet?"

Wilbur spread his arms and assumed a wounded expression. "If ya wouldn't interrupt, I'd tell ya that's exactly what I'm doing. Johnny's the most boring guy you'll ever meet—takes all day to tell a knock-knock joke—and Adam is worse than my wife when it comes to ruining a good story. He starts in the middle and goes both ways. You'll never see a bar empty out faster than when one of these two tries to tell somebody what they been doing all day."

Throckmorton raised his hands in defeat. "That's the strangest story I've ever heard, but you're the one who knows them."

"Ya don't believe me, come back at five tomorrow afternoon and ask 'em how much of the tunnels they cleared." Wilbur raised a finger in warning. "Don't do it a minute before five, though. We gotta get a full day's work out of 'em."

"I'll do that," Throckmorton said. "What time will the deputy show up tonight?"

"About eight. He'll be in an unmarked car. The sheriff wants their involvement quiet," Wilbur said, lowering his hands, palms down and open in the universal "quiet" gesture. "By the way, you were right about Maude's death. A source I got says it was murder. You got Mrs. Heath's security system put in?"

Throckmorton nodded. "She was a little nervous when I told her why, but she loves Ben and will go along with anything to keep him safe. Technicians will be there tomorrow morning to install it. In the meantime, we've got to get started on this excavation. We've spent a month and haven't turned a shovelful of dirt yet."

He handed Wilbur a picture from 1918 and pointed to a leafless bush clinging to the slope at eye level with them. "The floor of the entrance appears to be where that bush is. Top of the arch looks like it was about ten feet above the floor."

Wilbur nodded, motioned to Johnny and Adam as they returned with their gear, and told them where to dig. Throckmorton walked back to his car, shaking his head and muttering to himself about Wilbur and his hiring rationale.

That night he showed Wilbur and the sheriff's deputy into his office after he'd put Ben to bed. The officer, dressed for undercover, could have passed for Johnny's brother. Looking like Adam and Johnny didn't increase Throckmorton's confidence in him.

The department had watched the historical society and the brewery lot for several days already. Technicians dressed to look like laborers would install security cameras around the dig once Adam and Johnny had cleared a path into the first cavern. Infrared cameras would record activity at night, and deputies in a van outside the closed Ford dealership across the street from the Kessler office building would monitor the feed in real-time. They'd have to use Constable Clarence to monitor the feed occasionally because of manpower constraints. Throckmorton cringed and asked them to keep that to a minimum and to check Mrs. Heath's home periodically when she was taking care of Ben.

Throckmorton had considered the dangers they faced in the abstract as an intellectual problem. The officer's description of the security measures made the risks to Ben and him almost palpable.

He was still mulling over security and Wilbur's crew when he met Nancy for lunch the next day at Gert's. Few others were in the café. In hushed tones, he told her about the sheriff's involvement in his project and Wilbur's workmen. "Hiring two blabbermouths is the dumbest thing I've ever heard of."

"Is it important to keep the dig quiet?"

"We can't hide the dig. I'd like to keep our progress quiet, though. A thief who knows when we're close to the office would know when to strike."

The corners of her mouth twitched. "Are you going to take Wilbur up on his offer?"

"What offer?"

"Are you going to drop by the dig this evening and ask how things are going?"

Throckmorton jerked his head up. "You're damned right I am. His story is the most cockamamie thing I've ever heard."

She smirked. "Is our date for pizza at your place still on for tonight?"

Throckmorton nodded. "Sure."

"Warn the deputies I'll be at your house, email me your security code, and drop a key off at the drug store. I'll pick Ben up at school and have the pizza ready when you come home."

———

Throckmorton stopped by the Kessler building late Thursday afternoon, to check on the remodeling. From there, he eased his car down the abandoned dirt track to the county road and walked back to the excavation. Above him, the stone arch was cleared of sand. The setting sun lit the cavern entrance like a spotlight.

Excavated sand lay in a wide mound below the arch, covering all but the top rung of the stepladder Johnny and Adam had used to climb to the entrance. Johnny gave Throckmorton a hand as he clambered up the mound and walked along a short path scooped out of the three to four feet of sand they'd encountered on the floor of the main cavern. Deeper in the cavern, Adam was pushing a wheelbarrow toward him between thick, squat stone pillars that supported the low barrel vaults that once kept the brewery from collapsing into the cavern.

Throckmorton stood to the side as Adam squeezed by with the load of sand. He dumped it on the mound Throckmorton had just climbed. "Did you have some visitors today?" Throckmorton asked.

"Yeah. They said you knew about 'em. They told us to take a break while they worked in here."

Throckmorton looked around but couldn't see any cameras. He hoped no one else would either. "Looks like you guys moved a lot of dirt today."

Johnny, one boot on his shovel, clasped the top of the handle with both hands, and leaned into it. It was a position Throckmorton thought of as County Road Crew Parade Rest. "Well, it could have been more. I got here early this morning to get a good start, but Adam came in later. He thought I'd said to be here at eight."

Adam tilted the handles of the empty wheelbarrow against a stone wall and left it leaning there. "That's when ya said we'd start. I was here on time. Say so if ya want me here at seven."

"Tomorrow, let's start . . ." Johnny studied the sandy stone floor and ran the toe of his boot over a clean patch in front of him. "This is pretty rough in places." He glanced along the path cleared through the sand. "Ya know, it's rough in most places except for a few that aren't, ya understand? That rough surface catches my shovel, spoils my follow-through. A broom might work better close to the floor." He nodded toward a smooth section of floor they'd uncovered. "The smooth places, like that one there, they ain't no problem."

"So what time am I 'sposed ta be here?" Adam asked. "And Mr. Throckmorton, are we to keep dumping the sand out the front? We can't dump it there much longer. The ladder's damned near covered and—"

"That's where Wilbur told us to dump it, Mr. Throckmorton," Johnny said, "but we'll have to move that mound of sand tomorrow or it'll plug up the entrance. I'm a little taller, so I could still get in, but Adam here would be too short. Think we can get a skid steer for that?"

Throckmorton frowned. "You'd like a skid steer to—"

"What do ya mean, I'm too short?" Adam objected.

Johnny's face lit up. "My brother has a Bobcat. It's kinda old, but it'll work. We could rent it cheap once he's cleaned his barns."

Throckmorton held a hand up to silence Johnny before the conversation wandered further afield. He tried to keep his voice level. "It looks like you've cleared a path through the first six feet or so. How far is it to the first tunnel, and how long will it take you to get there?"

Johnny hitched up his blue jeans. "Oh, about . . . ya know, it would have gone faster, but Adam forgot his work gloves this morning." And he was off on another round of changing topics in mid-sentence and arguing with Adam.

Throckmorton bit his cheek, clenched and unclenched his

fists. This was more than a man should have to put up with. "How many days will it take to get to the second tunnel?"

"It all depends, Mr. Throckmorton," Johnny said.

The dialogue between Johnny and Adam segued to the need for a generator and lights and Adam's talent for electrical work. Throckmorton tapped the toe of a shoe and wondered what it would take to get a straight answer from these two.

They were discussing where they could get the wheelbarrow tire repaired when Throckmorton barked, "Quiet." He had a powerful urge to shake each of them by their shoulders. "I want a number of days. One number—no explanations, no excuses, just a simple number."

Johnny looked at Adam. "What do you think? Four, five days?"

Adam considered the question before he launched into a complaint about the blisters on his hand, the ointment Johnny had given him, and the stains it left on his gloves. He was warming to problems with the wheelbarrow tire when Throckmorton cut him off. "No more talking. Take care of your blisters and the damned tire. Forget I asked anything. When you see Wilbur tomorrow, tell him I understand."

Throckmorton stormed to the entrance, scrambled down the mound of dirt, swearing under his breath all the way to his car. He hoped the killer would find Johnny and Adam at a bar and try to pump them for information. It would be poetic justice.

At home, he slammed the door as he entered, wiped sand and dirt off his shoes and pants, and stomped into the kitchen. Even the smell of hot pizza didn't mollify him. "You wouldn't believe—"

Nancy handed him a drink. "Have this. I fed the kids earlier. They're doing their homework."

Throckmorton held the drink up. "What the hell is this?"

let 'em hang battery-operated lamps and run a cord along the ceiling to the sump pumps, but that's it."

Throckmorton found that reassuring.

———

Throckmorton met Wilbur below the excavation site in the late afternoon of a windy, overcast Monday in the low forties. Hands in the pockets of his jacket, Wilbur looked apprehensively at the cavern entrance. "Johnny call you too?"

Throckmorton nodded. "He was excited, said he had an idea." He gave Wilbur a sidelong glance. "I didn't have the stomach to ask any questions."

"You're learning. He told me the same thing." Wilbur kept his eyes on the cavern entrance. "I couldn't make out what the hell he was talking about, but I told him to stop it until I checked it out. Fool was so excited he hung up on me before I finished."

Adam's grinning face appeared at the entrance. "Almost ready! We'll see how it works in a minute." He disappeared back into the cavern.

"Oh, for Pete's sake," Wilbur took a few steps toward the entrance. "Stop," he barked. "Whatever you're doing, stop." Hands on his hips, he yelled, "Don't do anything until I've looked at it."

"Looked at what?" Throckmorton asked.

"How the hell should I know? Whatever those two idiots have cooked up."

Throckmorton noticed a large hose snaking from the edge of the brewery lot above them and down the slope of the ravine to the cavern entrance. Small bushes and dead grass had hidden it from his notice earlier. The flat hose swelled as he watched.

Pointing at the hose, Throckmorton asked, "Any idea what that hose is for?"

"I was going to ask you." Wilbur cupped his hands around his mouth and shouted, "Adam, Johnny, get down here, now, both of you."

Adam's head reappeared around the edge of the arch. He smiled broadly and put his index finger and thumb together in the "okay" symbol. "All set," he yelled and disappeared again.

Wilbur hung his head. "God help us. He's either trying to cast rabbit shadows on the cavern wall or they've started."

"Started what?"

Wilbur shuddered, looked at Throckmorton, and nodded toward the hose. "Johnny's in the volunteer fire department. My guess is they've 'borrowed' a fire hose from the department, hooked it to a hydrant on the street, and plan to flush the sand out of the tunnels."

Throckmorton looked at the opening under the stone arch. "Think it's safe to go up there?"

"Don't let me stop ya. When you've managed to collar those idiots, haul their asses down here. But I'm not going anywhere near that entrance till you've got both of them under control and out of the cavern."

Water trickled out of the entrance. The trickle turned into a stream as Wilbur and Throckmorton hastily backed away from the entrance. The water soaked into the sand packed beneath the entrance until the top three feet washed away in a gush. The stream turned into a river. The pounding hiss of water spraying under high pressure echoed from the cavern.

Adam appeared in the entrance. His back to Wilbur and Throckmorton, he waved his arms and yelled at Johnny, who was somewhere back in the cavern. A jet of water caught him in the chest and blew him out of the entrance. He did a summersault, landing in the pike position, upside down and backward, his butt buried in wet sand.

"What was that?" Throckmorton asked Wilbur.

"A seven. I'd give it a three for difficulty and an extra four for sheer stupidity." Wilbur shook his head. "I wonder if Johnny is still in control of the nozzle, or is it loose and whipping around? I'll get up to the street and turn the water off. Can you check on Adam?"

Wilbur trotted back down the path to the county road in the waning light. A moment later, his car rocketed up the abandoned road to the brewery lot, tires throwing a rooster tail of dirt and gravel behind him.

Throckmorton waded toward Adam through water and sand. His loafers and pant legs soaked up the cold water. The mud got deeper the closer he got to Adam. It pulled his shoes and socks off. He was wet, freezing, barefoot, and standing in two feet of frigid muck when he reached Adam, who was lying on his back in the sand with his head pointed down-hill.

"Can you move?" Throckmorton asked.

Adam rolled over and tried to get up. His knees and hands sank into the mud when he tried to stand. "Can ya help pull me out of this?" he whimpered.

With Throckmorton pulling and lifting on his upper arms, Adam managed to draw his limbs free of the sucking muck. He looked like a drowned dog when Throckmorton got him to his feet.

They both had to work to get back to dry ground. Panting from the exertion, Adam bent at the waist, hands on his knees. "Just . . . let me catch my breath."

Throckmorton glanced back at where his shoes had slipped off. They weren't worth fighting through the mud to find them. The sound of spraying water stopped, and the swollen firehose collapsed as the water drained from it. "Wilbur's got the water turned off." He looked up at the cavern entrance. "Any idea what shape Johnny's in?"

"Last I saw, he was fighting to control the nozzle. The lantern went flyin', the light went out, and I caught a blast of water in the chest." Adam shivered. "Damn, I'm cold," he whispered.

They walked down the path to where Throckmorton's car was parked. He wrapped Adam in a blanket from his trunk and drove the route Wilbur had taken to the street above. His feet had warmed up enough to be comfortable by the time he parked next to Wilbur's car. Wilbur paced beside his car, talking on his cell phone. Throckmorton left his car's engine running and the heat on for Adam.

"Adam okay?" Wilbur asked.

"Cold, but he's all right other than that." Throckmorton shook a leg to rid himself of sand and water. "My shoes are somewhere in the mud, and my pants are soaked."

"I got a guy bringing blankets, lighting, and a ladder to get Johnny out. Afraid I haven't got extra shoes."

Twenty minutes later, Wilbur and Throckmorton entered the cavern; each held a flashlight and carried a blanket. Fog enveloped them at the cavern entrance but dissipated as they moved farther into the cavern. Shadows cast by their lights and the thick stone arches supporting the ceiling made Throckmorton think of a medieval dungeon. The four-foot-high banks of sand lining the recently cleared trail had collapsed. What had been a cleared path looked like a creek bed with stretches of rippled sand interspersed with pools of water. Walking was reduced to a lurch, as with each step their feet sank into sand the consistency of pancake batter. Their feet pulled out of the mud with a slurp with every step.

Throckmorton's wet feet were numb. He swept the cavern

with his flashlight and nudged Wilbur. "Over there." Light glinted off polished brass to their right. "Looks like the nozzle."

"Yeah, but that ain't where they should have been working," Wilbur said. "It must have whipped over there after our genius lost control." He played his flashlight on a tunnel entrance ahead and to their left. "That's the tunnel they were working in."

Lifting his feet to clear the mud, Wilbur splashed toward the tunnel through a shallow pool. He looked like a kid playing in a puddle.

They waded through the sand up the slight grade of the tunnel. The sand was firm and the going easier, as most of the water had drained into the cavern. Wilbur's flashlight picked up a strip of torn, pale-blue fabric. He lifted it, shook it to remove clinging sand, and held it up to the light.

Throckmorton, glad to have an excuse to rest for a moment, panted from the exertion of wading through the muck of the cavern. "What do you make of it?" he asked.

Wilbur held the center of the strip close to his flashlight. "Feels like denim, and it looks like a buttonhole on the edge. If it weren't so clean, I'd guess it was a piece of the shirt Johnny wore all week." He turned his flashlight into the black tunnel. "Johnny?"

A low moan answered. He called Johnny's name again. Motionless, both men listened intently.

A quiet groan, "Over here," came from the shadows ahead.

They found Johnny half naked, soaked, and shivering a few yards farther up the tunnel. He huddled behind a stone pillar, his head bleeding. What clothes still clung to his body hung in shreds.

"Sweet Jesus. Can you move?" Wilbur asked.

Johnny moved each limb a few inches. "Yeah. Hurts like hell, though."

"What the devil happened to your clothes?"

"I kinda lost control of the nozzle."

Wilbur helped him up. "Kinda?" he snorted.

"Yeah. The water threw me against the wall, tore up my clothes, and tossed me around. It felt like getting skinned with a dull knife."

Wilbur wrapped a blanket around him. "Lucky it didn't kill ya, ya damned fool. Two men are supposed to be on that nozzle. Come on. I'll take ya back to my place for a hot bath and coffee."

When he got back to his car, Adam joined Johnny in Wilbur's car. Throckmorton ignored a big wet spot left by Adam on the passenger seat. As he drove away, he passed a rusty van in front of the deserted Ford garage. An antenna stuck out if it, wobbling. He rolled down his window to get a better look. No lights were visible, but he thought he heard muffled laughter coming from the van.

Tomorrow he'd have to consider how badly the night's work would delay getting to the safe, but tonight the cold and damp forced everything but dreams of a hot bath from his mind as he drove home.

To top off the perfect day, he had a message from Jen waiting for him on his answering machine. She'd visit on Friday, Saturday, and Sunday.

He had lunch with Nancy the next afternoon. Their lunches helped him cope with the stress of the excavation and worries about the phantom footsteps he'd heard at the Kessler building. He told her of Jen's visit and how he dreaded its effect on Ben.

"Let Ben and his mother have their weekend together," she said. "The kids have a day off from school next Friday.

Thursday won't be a school night. You and Ben come to my place for dinner Thursday. Six o'clock, okay?"

Anything that helped take his mind off Johnny, Adam, and Jen was a godsend. "Thanks. I look forward to having dinner with you and the kids."

CHAPTER 28

Wilbur paced back and forth in front of Throckmorton's desk late Tuesday afternoon. "We gotta get moving on this dig. It'll be November tomorrow, and I'd like to know what's in the safe before I make a bid on the lot."

Throckmorton gestured widely with his hands. "You don't have to remind me." He didn't know what Wilbur planned for his share of the safe's contents, nor did he tell Wilbur why he was in a hurry.

"How long will Adam and Johnny be laid up?" Throckmorton asked.

Wilbur stopped his pacing and sat in the chair in front of the desk. "They didn't break anything. They can be back on the job by tomorrow." Wilbur leaned forward in his chair and looked at the subsurface map from SIM.

Throckmorton silently cursed the time lost. He pointed to a dark area on the map. "I think this is where we are. We still have twenty feet of tunnel with two to five feet of sand in it to clear before we get to tunnel four and several yards after that to get to the office. The tunnels slope down to the cavern, so we'll be digging uphill."

"Damn." Wilbur stood and leaned over the map. He tapped a finger on a blue square. "That's the office, right?"

Throckmorton nodded. "The red square inside it is the safe."

"I've hired a couple guys to do some construction at the cavern entrance. The sheriff has a man in the crew to make sure the cameras cover where we're working and the entrance to tunnel four. The construction won't be much. If you'll go half on it, it'll cost us four hundred each."

"What's the construction for?"

"I figure the geniuses set us back a week with their last stunt. The construction is for sump pumps, lights, stuff to get the sand hauled out faster."

"How will the construction speed things up?"

Wilbur remained sitting, hands on his knees. "Hauling the sand out is our bottleneck, that and our two chuckleheads. We can't haul sand with the Bobcat. It'll fit in the cavern but won't have room to maneuver. The tunnels will be worse. It's a straight shot from the entrance, through the cavern, and up the first tunnel leading to the office. We'll run a rope through a pulley at the entrance to a wagon in the tunnel. The Bobcat can sit outside and pull the wagon out by the rope. I'll have to hire another hand to drive it, but it's worth it to speed things up."

The plan seemed too complicated and still depended on Johnny and Adam, but Throckmorton didn't have an alternative to offer.

"A couple guys are at it now," Wilbur said. "It'll be ready tomorrow when the boys are back."

———

Throckmorton walked up the path to the excavation site the next day. Wilbur had called and asked him to check on Johnny and Adam. "Try not to give 'em an excuse to ramble on, and don't ask 'em how they feel. I did that last night and wasted an hour listening to 'em describe their aches and pains."

Clouds hung in a leaden sky, and the temperature had dipped into the mid-forties. Throckmorton looked over Wilbur's construction project: a used telephone pole planted in the ground in front of the entrance was braced with timbers on two sides. A pulley was bolted to the pole slightly higher than the floor of the entrance. A small platform projected from the entrance to the pole. A rope ran from the tongue of a short wagon in the tunnel, through the pulley, and down to the base of the pole where a couple hundred feet of rope lay in a coil. Adam tied one end of the rope to a hitch on the Bobcat.

"Hi, Mr. Throckmorton," Adam called. "Come to see us use the cart and Bobcat?" He waved at a teenager in the Bobcat. "That's my nephew."

Throckmorton nodded and kept his mouth shut. His conversation with Johnny and Adam was still fresh in his mind. He had to give Adam credit—he couldn't imagine how the guy could be so unfailingly cheerful despite what he put himself through.

The Bobcat idled a few feet from the pole. Adam's nephew pumped the clutch, revved the engine, raised and lowered the bucket, and adjusted a truck side mirror that was mounted to the right of the cab.

"All set?" Adam called to his nephew. "We'll push the wagon in and load it. When I come out and wave, put the Bobcat in first gear and drive slowly toward the creek."

"How'll I know when to stop?" the kid asked.

"Keep an eye on the mirror. I'll wave to stop you, but you'll see the wagon too."

"Will you be to the left or right of it?" the kid asked.

Throckmorton glanced from Adam to the kid. *Nephew, huh? The inability to end a conversation must be genetic.*

Then Johnny called from the entrance, "Adam, are ya gonna help me push the wagon in, or are ya gonna spend the whole damned day yapping with your nephew?"

The rope fed out as the wagon trundled back into the cavern. Several coils of rope remained at the bottom of the telephone pole, even with the cart backed into the tunnel. That didn't seem right, but Throckmorton didn't want to get into a never-ending conversation with the kid. He thought of the work piling up in his office and waited to see if Wilbur's new procedure worked. With hands stuffed into his coat pockets, he stamped his feet to stay warm. Adam appeared in the entrance five minutes later and waved.

The kid had earbuds in, and his head was down. He was focused on his phone, playing a video game. Adam yelled to him, but nothing happened. The kid didn't seem to hear him over the idling Bobcat. Throckmorton approached the Bobcat and tapped the kid on the shoulder.

The tap startled the kid. He jerked, let out the clutch, and the machine lurched forward a foot. The engine died. A rear wheel narrowly missed Throckmorton's foot.

"Pay attention, will you?" Throckmorton yelled. "Take the earbuds out, turn off the music and games, and pay attention. Adam's telling you to pull the cart out."

The kid nodded and eased the Bobcat toward the stream. Throckmorton backed away. He didn't want to be near the jerry-rigged supports or the rope if something broke.

The kid's eyes were fixed on the side-mounted mirror. The extra coils played out. The rope tightened and stretched under the load. The kid's eyes remained riveted on the mirror.

As the Bobcat approached the creek, Adam appeared in the entrance waving his arms and yelling, although the wagon wasn't visible. The kid waved back, but his eyes were glued to the mirror. The Bobcat continued to crawl forward. Throckmorton saw another disaster looming when the Bobcat was five feet from the creek bank. He ran toward the Bobcat, waving his arms. The kid stopped the machine when the front wheels were inches from the stream bank.

The stream, sixteen feet wide and with a strong current, had cut a channel through the bottom of the ravine. The tree-lined banks were nearly vertical and four to five feet high on the bend in front of the Cat.

The kid stared at the mirror as the creek bank collapsed under him. The Bobcat did a slow swan dive into the water. The dive jolted to a halt when the Bobcat's bucket dug into the sandy bottom of the creek. The startled kid sailed over the bucket into the creek. He sputtered in the frigid knee-deep water and floundered toward the bank.

"Get your skinny ass back in there and turn the damned engine off," Adam bellowed. "If'n the motor sucks water, it'll have to be rebuilt."

"I'm freezing!" the kid whined.

"If ya didn't want to freeze, ya shouldn't have gone swimming!"

Throckmorton held his breath as the kid splashed to the Bobcat. The bank had collapsed unevenly, and the Bobcat canted heavily to one side. The kid headed to the lower side to turn off the engine. The ignition switch was within easy reach from there, but the boy would be crushed or drowned if the skid steer toppled onto its side. Throckmorton exhaled as the engine sputtered and died and the kid crawled up the bank.

"Why the hell didn't ya stop the Bobcat when I waved?" Adam asked the kid after he'd climbed out of the creek.

The kid wrapped his arms around himself and shivered. "I th–thought you was excited about how g–good everything was goin'."

"Are ya deaf, boy? I told ya to stop when I waved."

"But you said you'd wave from the right side of the cart. The cart wasn't at the entrance."

Throckmorton told Adam to get the kid in a warm car and

find him some dry clothes. The two headed down the path to the county road, still arguing. It promised to be a long conversation.

Throckmorton telephoned Wilbur. "Do you have a preference for tow trucks?"

"Huh?"

"What tow truck company would you like me to call?"

"Oh shit, what's happened now?"

"The Bobcat is in the creek." Throckmorton peered over the bank at the skid steer. "It's still right-side up, sitting on its rear wheels and the bucket, but it's listing heavily." The nautical term seemed appropriate, given the setting. "The bucket dug into the creek bed and kept it from going all in. A tow truck might be able to get it out if they get here soon."

"What the hell? What happened? No, don't tell me. It'll just piss me off even more."

Throckmorton held the phone away from his ear. He heard a crash like a chair tipping over.

"Goddamn it all!" Wilbur roared. There was another crash. He got testy after that. He calmed down after a loud and innovative string of profanity. "You don't have to call the tow truck. I'll do it."

"Ask them to hurry. The current hitting the bucket is causing turbulence, and the bank is eroding. It might tip on its side any minute."

Twenty minutes later, the tow truck parked on the county road and the driver walked in. A tall, lanky guy with an easy smile and a twinkle in his eye nodded to Throckmorton. "What's Wilbur got today?"

"Think you can get the truck in here?" Throckmorton pointed at the Bobcat.

"No problem, but how in hell did you get a skid steer in the creek? That must have taken special talent."

Johnny came out of the cavern and headed toward the Bobcat.

"You got Johnny and Adam working for ya?" the driver asked.

Throckmorton shook his head. "They work for Wilbur, not me. The kid who drove it into the creek is Adam's nephew."

"That explains it. I'll bring the truck up. The ground must be solid if you guys got the cat to the water." The driver's face broke into a smile. "Mind if I take a couple pictures for Facebook? My son would love to put 'em on his wall."

"Ask Wilbur. I'm just an observer."

"It'd serve Wilbur right for trying to get by on the cheap again." Still smiling, the driver shook his head. "I shouldn't complain. Wouldn't be enough work in town for two tow trucks if it weren't for Wilbur and his geniuses."

Throckmorton glanced around to make sure none of Wilbur's crew was within earshot. "Why does Wilbur put up with these guys? They're friendly and cheerful, but they drive him nuts. I couldn't stay sane if they worked for me."

The driver looked toward the stream where Johnny and Adam fussed around the Bobcat. "They're Wilbur's third or fourth cousins. It goes way back, but Wilbur kinda looks after 'em, keeps 'em employed and out of too much trouble."

It took careful work and a couple heavy timbers to keep the Bobcat upright, but it was back on the path in an hour. Another hour of tinkering and the engine started.

Wilbur gave Johnny and Adam the week off. He told Throckmorton it would take him that long to cool off enough to talk to them.

Throckmorton was tense whenever he thought of the delays at the dig. He'd let Wilbur run the excavation because Wilbur knew everybody in the county, and Throckmorton didn't know anything about excavating. He'd hoped Wilbur did, but he'd been wrong. Wilbur knew how to get by on the cheap. It was time for Throckmorton to take control.

CHAPTER 29

Nancy started cooking Wednesday, as soon as she got home from work. She'd chosen to keep Thursday's meal simple. According to the weatherman, the temperature would be in the low thirties. A stew would be great on a chilly evening. Slow cooking overnight would make the meat tender and tasty and it would improve with reheating tomorrow.

Her kitchen filled with the sweet, smoky aroma of fried bacon. In an old cast-iron frying pan, Nancy browned cubes of chuck roast in bacon fat. Amanda sat at the kitchen table and watched her mother work. She moved to a stool next to the stove where she could observe more closely. "What are you doing, Mommy?"

"Making beef stew. Don't get too close, honey. This pan is hot. The fat might spatter."

Then followed five minutes of "why" about everything Nancy did. She explained the stew was for dinner tomorrow, the bacon bits would give the stew extra flavor, the meat would be cooked slowly in wine to make it tender, and the wine was called burgundy. Nancy rummaged through spice bottles in a cabinet next to the stove. "I'm sure I have some thyme," she muttered. In frustration, she pulled a dozen small bottles out, several at a time, read the labels, and put the bottles on the counter.

She found the thyme and a bay leaf in the back of the cupboard, added them to the beef, and answered another round of "why." As she answered Amanda's questions, she picked up a bottle of marjoram. That always tasted good in beef stews. She gave the marjoram three shakes over the pot. She stirred, sampled the liquid around the beef, and added another shake of marjoram.

"Why did you do that, Mommy?"

"It wasn't in the recipe, but I like the flavor and smell of that spice," Nancy said. She put the marjoram and other bottles back in the cupboard.

The kitchen was redolent with frying bacon, beef, bay, and thyme. Amanda jabbered away, but Nancy was busy and missed what she'd said. At least it wasn't another "why."

The muffled chime of her cell phone came from another room. Nancy gave the braising beef a stir and followed the sound through the living room to a closet by the front door. The phone stopped ringing before she could dig it out of her coat pocket. She'd missed a call from Throckmorton. She quickly called him back, and he was immediately complaining about Wilbur's crew.

Nancy sat in an easy chair. "I'd rather talk about tomorrow night than Wilbur. Can you be here by six?"

They talked about little things until she realized how long Amanda had been alone. When she returned to the kitchen, Amanda was moving her little chair away from the stove. It hadn't been there earlier, but Nancy didn't ask about it. There was a lot of work to do, and she'd spent too much time cleaning the house. She peeled potatoes and carrots, trimmed small onions, and sautéed mushrooms in butter as the beef braised. She sniffed tentatively at a sharp aroma floating from the stove as the mushrooms sizzled next to the braising meat. Puzzled, she sniffed around until she isolated the meat as the source. The odor hadn't been there earlier.

She was about to taste the braising liquid again when she

noticed the clock on the stove. "Oh my gosh! Amanda, it's late. You should've been in bed an hour ago." Nancy moved the mushrooms off the burner, picked Amanda up from her stool, and hustled her to her bedroom.

———

Late getting home from work Thursday, Nancy launched into a frenzy of picking up after Amanda, setting the table, and completing the beef bourguignon. Nothing was going to go wrong on their date this time. She added the vegetables to the crockpot with the beef and turned the heat up. She smelled the same spicy odor she'd detected the previous night. Puzzled, she picked a wooden spoon from the jar to sample the stew.

A crash came from upstairs. Amanda screamed. Nancy dropped the spoon, hastily plopped the lid back on the crockpot, and ran to see what had happened. Amanda wailed like a cat with its tail caught in a door as Nancy took the stairs two at a time. She found Amanda on the floor of her bedroom next to an overturned stool, holding her elbow and sobbing, stopping only to gasp for air.

Amanda was bruised, scared, and wanted attention, but she wasn't seriously injured. Nancy soothed her, and between sniffles, Amanda admitted that she'd stood on the stool to reach a board game in the closet.

Nancy gave the elbow the obligatory kiss, stroked Amanda's hair, and rocked her. By the time the sobs were under control, there was barely time to dress and put on her makeup before Throckmorton arrived. She was checking herself in the mirror when the doorbell rang.

Nancy met Throckmorton at the door. "You look lovely tonight, Nancy," he said. He gave her a peck on the cheek and presented a bottle of wine as the kids wandered off to play a game. "You said you were cooking with burgundy. A burgundy should go well with whatever you're making. I picked this up a year ago but haven't had a good excuse to open it."

He sniffed the air. "The food smells wonderful. Something spicy tonight? Should I have gotten a German wine, a Kabinett or Spätlese, something sweet instead of the burgundy?"

The stew's tangy aroma was sharper than when Nancy had added the vegetables. "We can taste the stew before you open the burgundy, and yes, it's a new recipe I found, a variation on beef bourguignon," she lied.

The edgy aroma couldn't be from the marjoram she'd added; she knew what marjoram smelled like. Whatever it was, it was too late to make changes. "I've never made it before. I hope you don't mind being guinea pigs tonight."

She excused herself, collected Amanda, and headed for the kitchen. "Back in a minute," she told Throckmorton.

Nancy lifted the lid on the crockpot. The steam from the stew opened her nasal passages, abruptly cleared her sinuses, and filled her eyes with tears. She replaced the lid and turned to Amanda.

"Did you help Mommy cook last night?"

Amanda nodded.

"Did you put something in the stew while Mommy was talking on the phone?"

Amanda shrugged, looked at her shoes, and fidgeted. She was clearly taking the fifth.

"Can you show Mommy what you added to the meat?"

Amanda glanced toward the jar holding the wooden spoons and acted as though she hadn't heard her mother.

Nancy followed the glance. A spice bottle was lying on its side behind the spoons. The label wasn't visible, but at least it was a spice and not dish soap, furniture polish, or bug spray.

She sent Amanda to play with Ben before she picked up the bottle and examined its label: cayenne pepper.

That explained the aroma. From deep in her memory, she retrieved a picture of sweet iced tea and hot peppers from an article she'd read months ago in *Bon Appetit*. The article claimed that high concentrations of carbohydrates soothed the effects of capsicum, the active ingredient in hot peppers. *What the heck*, she thought. *Sugar is a carbohydrate. Sweet iced tea might help. If we can't eat the stew, I'll order pizza.*

She carried the casserole containing the stew into her small dining room. Her dining table was just large enough for four people. A phone book was put on Ben's chair to give him a little boost, and a thick dictionary was put on Amanda's chair. Nancy called everyone around the table and said a prayer. "Before we begin," she said, "you should know that when we were on the phone last night, Amanda helped Mommy cook. She added cayenne pepper for me. She's getting to be quite the little chef. I'm brewing iced tea to go with the stew. We'll order out for pizza if it's too spicy to eat."

"I like hot food," Throckmorton said with a smile. "Let's give it a try." He turned to Ben. "You like spicy food, right?" Ben shook his head and giggled.

Nancy made the kids peanut butter and jelly sandwiches which they were happy with. Throckmorton sampled the stew. He gasped, took a swig of iced tea, swallowed, and panted. Tears ran down his cheeks. "It's good, just a bit warmer than I'm used to. Delicious . . . in its own way." He swallowed more of the sweet iced tea. "I've never eaten a potato with more flavor," he gasped.

Nancy forced a smile. She selected a small piece of beef and chewed tentatively. Her reaction was the same as Throckmorton's: chew, swallow, and gulp several glugs of the tea. "I *think* we can eat it." She panted for a bit, pushed back her chair, and stood. "I'll make more iced tea."

They ate the stew, gushed tears, and bolted down iced tea. There was enough panting during the meal to dub a soundtrack for one of the porn flicks she'd found on Gary's computer. Communication with Throckmorton was primarily desperate pointing at the pitcher of iced tea. When Throckmorton finished the stew on his plate, Nancy managed to ask, "Care for seconds?" without breaking into giggles.

Throckmorton choked, swallowed hard, and laughed. Nancy wasn't sure whether the tears running down his cheeks were from the cayenne or laughter. He didn't try to speak. He held his right hand over his plate and pointed at the iced tea with his left.

Ice cream for dessert soothed their irritated mucous membranes. The kids built towers, castles, and bridges after dinner with Amanda's wooden blocks and watched Disney movies on television. They were asleep on the floor, and Throckmorton and Nancy were cuddling on the couch by the middle of the second movie.

Nancy nodded toward the kids. "They're zonked."

"Shame to wake them up," Throckmorton said. "I'd better get Ben home. I didn't explain before, but he's had a relapse of his leukemia. Ben has to start the hardcore chemo or a new, gentler treatment by mid-December." Throckmorton told her about the cost and why he'd have to pay for it.

"That's a world of pressure on you to find something in Otto's safe and find it soon." Nancy kissed him and leaned on his shoulder. She felt so sorry for Throckmorton and Ben, she toyed with the idea of suggesting they stay the night, but it was too early for that. She'd rushed into a relationship before. Once was enough. She nodded toward the kids, sleeping close to each other. "They played well together. I was worried how that would go given the difference in ages, and neither has had to share their parent with anyone else for years."

Throckmorton kissed her. "I had a marvelous time tonight. Jen will be here to see Ben Saturday, but how about dinner again next week? If you like fish, every restaurant in the area will have a fish fry Friday evening."

"Mmmm. Should we take the kids or stick them with a sitter?"

"Let's make it just the two of us." He gave her another gentle kiss.

Nancy nibbled on his ear. "I can bring the cayenne if you think the fish will be too bland."

Throckmoton snorted. "I think we should give the cayenne a rest for a while. My intestines may demand it."

CHAPTER 30

J en pulled into Throckmorton's driveway Friday afternoon. Throckmorton took her aside while Ben changed into clean clothes. "I got a phone call a week ago about something you should know. I called you, but you didn't answer."

Her smile disappeared when she looked into his eyes. "What's it about?"

"You need to talk to your doctor. I had myself checked at an STD clinic after our tryst. I was positive for chlamydia. The only person I could have gotten it from is you. You should notify your other partners."

"You couldn't have picked it up from me," she hissed. "You must have gotten it from some local bitch you're banging."

Still the same old Jen, always blames her victim. "I haven't had any other partners, Jen. I've been celibate—something you should try. Chlamydia isn't a big deal. One dose of Azithromycin and a couple of weeks of celibacy and you can go back to your old habits. I got my shot last week."

He heard Ben's bedroom door close and footsteps in the hallway. "Here he comes. Be civil; be a mother to him. You can sack out on the couch, as we agreed."

Jen talked to Ben for an hour, looked through his school assignments, played his favorite board game with him, and took him to the Carriage Inn for dinner. Throckmorton didn't take part in the dinner or conversation that night. Jen slept on the couch, watched Saturday morning cartoons with Ben, and left before noon.

Ben looked forlorn as she drove off. Throckmorton didn't bother to wave. *After three years, she shows up right after the Kessler murders, quizzes me about my project, and is working with some guy from New York state. That's too many coincidences.*

By dinner Ben was sulking in his bedroom. The door was open. Throckmorton knocked on the doorframe. "Hey, kiddo, time to eat."

"Not hungry."

Throckmorton sat on the bed next to him, wrapped an arm around his shoulders, and gave him a hug. "Upset because Mom didn't spend more time with you?"

"She said we'd have all weekend. Why'd she leave so early?"

Man, kids ask tough questions. "Your mother . . . your mother has a lot of things on her mind. She has a bunch of problems to solve, and she'll be distracted until she does. You know what distracted means, don't you?"

"Like when I talk to you but you keep working and don't listen?"

Ouch. "Yeah. Grown-ups do that, but so do you when you're reading a favorite book or watching a good movie, right? Well, we can't depend on your mother to remember everything she promised. Big problems can do that to people."

Ben leaned against him. "But why doesn't she have time for me?"

If I knew that, I wouldn't have asked her out for our first date, and you wouldn't be here. "I don't know, honey, I don't know."

They sat in silence. "You have all your homework done?" Throckmorton asked.

"Didn't have any."

He gave Ben a squeeze. "How about a movie? I'll see what's playing in La Crosse. We'll go tomorrow, I promise."

CHAPTER 31

Throckmorton did a search on his computer on Monday, looking for small skid steers or suitable substitutes. He found two and located a dealer that had them for rent. The smallest could work in the cavern and the tunnels without the use of a cart or wheelbarrow. So far, the cart and wheelbarrow had been the problem. He called Wilbur. "I've got a way to do it."

"Do what?"

"Move the sand." Throckmorton told him he'd found a dealership that would rent a subcompact tractor with a front-end loader. Even with a bucket on the front, the tractor was small enough to fit in the most cramped tunnel they had to clear, and it had lights aimed forward and back. "We'll have to clear an area in the cavern for it to turn around, but Johnny and Adam can do that with shovels. With a tractor in the cavern, we'll need fans for ventilation."

"And?"

"What do you mean, and?"

"Nothing on this goddamned project has been simple. How much will it cost?" Wilbur paused. "Does the price include insurance?"

"Yeah. The bid includes insurance. It'll cost us five hundred a day for the first three days, three hundred a day after that." Renting the tractor would push every one of Throckmorton's credit cards to the limit if they split the cost.

The phone was silent for a moment. "More than I wanted to spend," Wilbur said, "but it's better'n any idea I've had."

Throckmorton tackled the hard part. "There's one condition the dealer stipulated."

"Yeah, what's that?"

"Johnny and Adam aren't to touch the tractor or anything connected to it. Neither are any of their nephews. Seems your boys have a reputation."

———

The next morning Throckmorton was fooled by the weather again, and only wore a fall jacket when he went to the excavation. It was a typical November day in Rockburg—a dazzling sun in a cloudless sky and air so cold it cut through Throckmorton like a knife. A jerry-rigged ramp of packed sand, dirt, and rock five feet high reached from the floor of the ravine to the cavern entrance. A truck carrying the subcompact John Deere arrived mid-morning. Throckmorton signed the rental and insurance papers. Wilbur reached for the keys when the truck driver held them out.

The driver closed his fist around the keys. "I was told not to give you the keys until you tell me who'll be operating the tractor."

Wilbur withdrew his hand. "Oh for God's sake. It'll be my nephew, Roger, here." He nodded toward a dumpy guy in his mid-twenties. "Will that suit you?"

"Anybody but two guys named Johnny or Adam." The driver smiled. "Sorry, Wilbur. Those were my orders." He handed Wilbur the keys.

Wilbur turned on a big exhaust fan near the cavern entrance as Roger drove the tractor up the ramp and into the cavern. He cleared a path to the first tunnel and from there to its junction with tunnel number four by four-thirty. The angle between the two tunnels was too sharp for the tractor to negotiate in the restricted space of the tunnels.

Throckmorton played his flashlight on the walls of tunnel four ahead of him. A wooden door—the door to the office—was twenty feet ahead on the right. He thought of trying to wade through the sand to the door, but memories of the struggle to help Adam out of the muck dissuaded him.

The sand in tunnel four was one to two feet deep, and it was wet and heavy. Without thinking, he asked Johnny how long it would take them to clear the way to the door with shovels.

Johnny picked up a handful of sand. "This here's heavy stuff, Mr. Throckmorton. It'll take . . . well, let's see, if—"

Throckmorton didn't think he could stand another disquisition on a simple question. "Give me a rough estimate. Yes or no, will it take all day tomorrow?"

"Yeah, at least—"

"Will it take two days?"

"No. The sand's too heavy, but if'n we use shovels to fill the bucket and Roger takes it out with—"

"Okay. Call it a day. Get an early start tomorrow."

Throckmorton walked back to his car. *We're nearly there.* The week was going well, but he couldn't shake a sense of foreboding.

⸺

Carl woke from his nap, rolled over in the motel bed, and checked his watch. It was ten p.m. Time to get into his black clothes, black coat, and black ski mask. He prodded Jen and woke her up. "Get up. We have to get going if we're going to check up on your ex-husband tonight."

She groaned, sat up, and looked at the alarm clock on the

nightstand. "Okay. Just give me a minute," she said as she rolled up to sit on the edge of the bed.

Carl noticed that she hadn't whined, insisted on going shopping, or asked to eat at an expensive restaurant since they'd moved back to La Crosse. She'd told him about the chlamydia. He'd tested positive too. Jen claimed she got it from Throckmorton when she'd seduced him as Carl had told her to. Carl figured that was bullshit, but he didn't press the issue. Hell, she probably got it from him. He was just happy she no longer argued with him every time he asked her to do something.

As she dressed, she asked him, "Remind me, what are we going to do?" She yawned and stretched expansively. "I want to be sure I have my part right."

"We're going to wait until late. We'll park a few blocks from where they are digging, maybe down by the Presbyterian church. You stay in the car ready to pick me up, and I'll go through backyards and alleys to get to the excavation. I can avoid the cops in that van they have sitting at the Ford dealership and any cameras they might have on the path in from the county road. I'll use the night-vision goggles to take a quick look to see how far they are from the office and safe."

As she put on her coat, she asked, "Didn't you say they might have security cameras in there?"

"I'll be in and out fast, just in case. No cop will get near me. The security your husband has put around his house is more dangerous."

—

Throckmorton woke from a nightmare about tolling bells. It was 2:00 a.m. and his phone was ringing. Half asleep, he answered it.

"Mr. Throckmorton, this is Deputy Johnson. I was monitoring the surveillance cameras in the van. We had a bite."

"Ah, what?" Throckmorton didn't think he was fishing. He turned on the light on his nightstand. Nope, he wasn't fishing.

"The infrared cameras picked up someone entering your excavation. He was in, out, and gone when we got here. The guy moved fast."

Throckmorton sat upright, wide awake. "Do you want me to come down there?"

"No. Better if you meet us at the excavation tomorrow morning. We don't want to draw attention to ourselves."

Five hours later, Wilbur and Throckmorton followed an undercover officer into the excavation. Nothing was out of place, and no one had attempted to wade through the sand to the office. Throckmorton hadn't been able to sleep after the phone call, and with the adrenaline rush over, he was having trouble keeping his eyes open. "Was it a false alarm?" he asked.

"No. We have it on videotape. Someone entered the cavern. He didn't have a flashlight, and no lights were on. We suspect he had night-vision goggles, probably 'star-light goggles.' They can work with small amounts of light, maybe from a light stick, a special one that wouldn't be brighter than a couple of stars."

"I'd heard you guys were checking on purchases of night-vision goggles," Throckmorton said.

The officer looked at him suspiciously. "Where'd you hear that? It's not supposed to be public knowledge."

"A librarian told me. She was in a chatty mood."

The cop shook his head. "It's near impossible to keep something quiet when we canvass a bunch of people. An elderly gentleman was renting an apartment in the old carriage house at the Kessler mansion in La Crosse. He was up late making a trip to the can when he saw the lights in Adele's room flash on for thirty or so seconds. There were no more lights, but we found a man's footprints in the attic. That room has big dormer windows, so any light should have been visible. Our new sheriff insisted we check on night vision. I thought she was nuts. If the killer is using something like that, it would explain why no one saw lights at the historical society or Maude Jones's home, assuming it was the same guy."

"Could you tell what he looked like from the video you got tonight?" Wilbur asked.

"No, but he was about six feet tall and looked muscular. His movements were fluid, like an athlete." The officer looked at Wilbur, then Throckmorton. "If you see him, or if you think you know who he is, do not take him on yourself. Call us. If he confronts you, get to some place safe and call us."

That sounded great to Throckmorton. He'd never fought anything more dangerous than figures on a spreadsheet. He'd defend himself if cornered, but it would be a last resort.

Throckmorton went home for a nap before noon. Sleep was elusive. Wilbur called him a few hours later to tell him they'd reached the office door. He said it was so rotten he could push it in, but he knew Throckmorton would want to be there when they opened the office.

Throckmorton was in the tunnel within ten minutes. He tried the key in the office door, but rust had frozen the lock. The door buckled with a hard kick. A solid bank of cobwebs, opaque with accumulated dust, blocked the entrance. Throckmorton swept the cobwebs away with a piece of wood from the door. He played an LED flashlight over the office interior. Dust motes stirred up by the first fresh air in eighty years danced in the beam of the flashlight.

"Amazing," Throckmorton said. "The room is dry."

Wilbur tapped a stone step with his boot. "The room is eight inches above the tunnel floor, and the tunnel slopes down to the cavern."

They entered the room and stood in front of a black safe, four feet wide and six feet tall. The word "Yale" in gold letters, barely visible through a thick layer of dust, arced across the upper third of its double doors. Rust marred its finish in a few scattered areas. Dust prevented close examination.

To the right of the safe sat a wooden chair and a table, both covered in cobwebs and dust. Shelves on the wall to the far right held papers, dust, and more cobwebs. A tall cabinet or armoire covered with dust stood in the shadows against the wall to the left of the safe.

Throckmorton blew the dust off the dial on the right door of the safe and wiped it clean with his handkerchief. "Should I try opening it here, or do you want to move it into the cavern? It's on steel wheels."

Wilbur held a battery-powered lantern over the safe. "Push it anywhere you'd like if you got a yen for a hernia. I'd open it right where it sits. That sucker must weigh a thousand pounds. It'll take four strong men to bull it around a corner. What did Otto say about opening it?"

Throckmorton brought a copy of the letter from his pocket. "The combination of the safe is 10R-30L-22R," he read.

"Did he say how many times we have to turn the dial before we stop at each number?" Wilbur asked.

Damn. Throckmorton had no idea how many turns, and his brain was fried from lack of sleep. He placed his fingers nervously around the dial. He moved the dial to zero, turned it three times clockwise, stopped at ten, twice counterclockwise to thirty, and once clockwise back to twenty-two. "If it's like a modern lock, that should do it," Throckmorton said. He grasped the brass handle to the left of the dial and twisted.

It didn't budge.

They tried starting with four turns to the right with variations on the number of turns to the left. After forty minutes of trying different combinations, Throckmorton couldn't remember what combination of turns they'd tried and which one he wanted to try next. Frustration and sleep deprivation were a toxic mix.

"It's late. I'm exhausted and making mistakes. I'll search the web tonight for information on old Yale safes, get a good night's sleep, and try again tomorrow morning. That okay with you?"

Wilbur stared at the safe. "Okay. But if we got a thief around, tonight could be the night. I'll call the sheriff and ask for an extra deputy."

Throckmorton shrugged, too tired to worry about competition. "I'll be here at eight tomorrow morning," he said, and walked out.

———

That evening, Nancy and Amanda brought four frozen cartons of General Tso's chicken to Throckmorton's house and nuked them in the microwave. As they waited for dinner, a crestfallen Throckmorton told them about his day. "We got into the office this afternoon. It was miserable in there. Dust and cobwebs covered everything. I couldn't even open the safe with the combination in my hand. We don't know how many times we have to turn the dial on the safe past zero when we go from one number to the next."

The microwave dinged and Nancy removed the chicken

and nuked a bowl of instant rice. Throckmorton collapsed into a chair at the end of the table. Nancy massaged his shoulders. "You'll find a way. Is it anything you can look up on the internet?"

The microwave dinged again and she removed the rice. "Time to eat. Have some tea with dinner and you'll feel more like working." She dished up meals for herself, Throckmorton, Ben, and Amanda. Throckmorton was abnormally quiet as they ate. He excused himself and went to the computer in his home office as soon as he'd finished eating.

Nancy cleaned up after dinner, gave the kids a couple scoops of ice cream each, and wandered into Throckmorton's office. "Any success?" she asked as she looked over his shoulder at the screen. He leaned back in his chair, stretched, and yawned. "I've been searching for instructions on opening nineteenth-century Yale combination locks. I think I've got it. We didn't think to turn the dial back to zero after dialing in the last numbers. That was standard with Yale locks back then."

"What else was in the office?"

"Not sure. We concentrated on the safe." He thought for a moment. "I believe there was a chair, a table, a tall bureau or something, and shelves on a wall. Everything was dusty, and I was beat. Why?"

"Any furniture in the office has to be antique, maybe valuable. You've said you didn't know much about your family. There might be information on your family on the shelves, in the bureau, or in the safe."

"Good point. I hadn't thought of that. It's something we can look into after I get the safe open."

The printer hummed and a copy of the instructions for opening Yale safes chugged out of the printer. Throckmorton picked the pages up and moved them to his desk without reading them. "I have to get to bed. I'll go over these in the morning."

CHAPTER 32

The next morning, Throckmorton leaned against one of the pillars supporting the vaulted ceiling and waited inside the cavern for Wilbur. He'd dressed better today—long insulated underwear, a sweater, and a warm coat. Fog blanketed the entrance where the warmer, humid air of the interior met the freezing outside air. The fog swirled, and Wilbur walked in with Earl on his heels.

Earl didn't look Throckmorton in the eyes. His morose expression and slouch reminded Throckmorton of a whipped dog. Throckmorton glanced from Wilbur to Earl. "Resolve your problems with the IRS?"

Wilbur nodded to Earl. "Go ahead. Might as well tell him."

"Sort of."

"What does that mean?" Throckmorton asked.

Earl didn't look at Throckmorton. "It means I'll testify so they can nail the son of a bitch who ran that crooked fund."

Throckmorton looked at Wilbur and raised his eyebrows.

Wilbur handed the tractor keys and a battery-powered lantern to Earl. "Here. Go up that tunnel until you come to a small John Deere. You'll have to back the tractor out a couple yards to get to the office. The tractor is rented, so don't ding anything against the walls."

Earl disappeared up the tunnel, and Wilbur turned toward the cavern entrance. He spoke in a low voice, "Don't push him. He won't go to prison, but the IRS took the title to his house, his new Jag, and a vacation cabin he has on a lake up north. He got most of his money out of the fund in time, but the state may hit him up for back taxes. With penalties and fines, that'll be over a hundred grand. He'll have more than half of his cash left, but cars, homes, the big assets—they're already gone."

"That bad, is it?"

"Yeah. He's an arrogant prick, but I feel sorry for the bastard. He's depending on what he gets out of the safe for his retirement. That ain't a recipe for mental health the way this project has gone."

The rumble of the tractor rolled from the tunnel and echoed around the cavern. It coughed once and died. Wilbur nodded toward the tunnel. "He's got the tractor out of the way. You got a safe to open."

They found Earl holding a battery-powered lantern and looking at the safe. Throckmorton pulled out a notepad, a pencil, and the instructions he'd printed. He asked Earl to step aside and direct the light to the dial on the safe.

Earl glared at Throckmorton. He moved, but he put the light on the table to the right of the safe. When Throckmorton squatted in front of the safe, Earl stood behind him, peering over his shoulder. His shadow blocked most of the light.

"Damn, Earl," Wilbur growled and moved to Throckmorton's left with a flashlight.

The flashlight provided plenty of light, but Throckmorton felt uneasy with Earl leaning over him. Working with Earl for ten minutes was more irritating than working all month with Wilbur.

"What's the notebook and paper for?" Earl asked. "I thought you knew the combination?"

Throckmorton bit his tongue. Provided everything went well, he'd only have to work with the ass for a few more minutes. "I have the numbers, but I don't know how many times I have to rotate the dial past zero before going to the next number. A record of what's been tried and failed will help."

"Well, get on with it. I don't want to stay in this dungeon all day."

Throckmorton wondered if he could take Earl's attitude for another fifteen minutes without blowing up. "I'll start with four clockwise turns past zero before the first number, then vary the number of turns for the other numbers."

He'd only made it to the third number when Earl asked, "Can't you do this faster?" Complaints that the room was too small, too dark, too humid, and too stuffy followed. Nothing was too minor for Earl to ignore. Throckmorton went through the first two combinations of turns before twisting to look at Earl. "Would you like to help me get this done faster?"

"Why? You're the big . . ." Earl stopped in mid-gripe. "Sure. Whatever you want."

"Good," Throckmorton said. "Step back. Give me a little breathing room." He was about to demand that Earl shut the fuck up, but he controlled himself. "Silence would help too. I might be able to hear the tumblers move if people stop talking."

Throckmorton repeated the combination of turns he'd used for the first number. He felt more than heard a faint click on the number ten, but not on the following numbers. The lock didn't open on either try. It took half an hour to work through the possible number of turns following two turns to the left before stopping at thirty, the second number.

There were no further clicks, and the safe didn't open.

Maybe Yale safes used an easily remembered pattern. Four turns past zero to start and one less turn for each following number. It's nearly the only thing I haven't tried.

Throckmorton stayed with four turns to the right and stopped at the first number. He spun the dial to the left, passed zero three times and stopped at thirty, the second number. He felt a slight resistance when he reached thirty. He spun the dial to the right, passed zero twice and stopped at twenty-two, the third number. A subtle increase in pressure was needed to hit twenty-two, as though a tumbler had to move. It was so slight he thought he might have imagined it, but he stopped there.

Throckmorton's knees ached as he came to the last number. He worried he might turn the dial too far or jiggle it if he adjusted his position to relieve the pain in his knees. He reversed the dial again and stopped at zero.

There was no change in the resistance in the dial, no click. He tried the handle of the safe.

It didn't budge. Sweat trickled down his forehead. In frustration, he almost spun the dial to start the process over again. His right leg started to cramp; he stood and hobbled back and forth until the pain subsided.

"Did you get it?" Earl asked.

Throckmorton knelt in front of the safe again. His hands were clammy. He wiped them on his pants and turned the dial to the left until it came to zero again. There wasn't any change in resistance. Perhaps he was too tense or his knees and thighs too sore for him to feel minute changes.

He released the dial to avoid accidental movement and put gentle pressure on the handle. It gave a quarter inch. His heart pounded as he increased the pressure. With a scraping sensation, the handle moved an inch. He twisted the handle with all the force he could muster. Metal grated against metal, and the handle turned ninety degrees. He pulled. The great steel doors of the safe opened with a bone-jarring creak. Throckmorton felt a surge of relief. His shoulders and legs relaxed—he hadn't been aware of how tense he'd been.

Behind the exterior doors were two steel inner doors—

substantial, but nothing like the four-inch-thick outer doors, and without a lock. The inner doors were decorated with a landscape painting, like the pictures of the Yale safes Throckmorton had found on Google. He ignored the artwork and tried the doors. They swung open without effort. Earl grabbed the lantern and held it close to the open safe. A wooden door covered a box a foot wide and two feet tall mounted in the center of the safe. Three wooden shelves flanked it on each side. The lower left shelf held a small pile of assorted papers. The middle shelf to the right of the cabinet held a paper bundle that was wrapped in twine dark brown with age.

Earl reached over Throckmorton's shoulder, hooked the twine with one finger, and pulled it. The bundle hit Throckmorton in the head as it slid from the safe, and the eighty-year-old twine snapped. The package burst open and documents scattered over the dusty floor.

Throckmorton seethed, but it was Wilbur who spoke. "Watch what you're doing, Earl. Now pick up the damned mess you made."

Earl, Wilbur, and Throckmorton scrambled on their knees in the dust and gloom to pick up the papers. Earl collected a fistful of documents and rushed to the table to examine them in the lantern light. Throckmorton and Wilbur continued to collect papers in the shadowy recesses of the room.

Earl groaned. Turning toward the table, Throckmorton watched Earl inspect the documents he'd collected. The scrawny mayor's hands shook as he flipped through the papers. His face looked pale in the dim light. With each new page, he moaned, "No, no."

"Every one, every one of them. Oh, God . . . goddamn it," he whispered. He picked up the yellowed papers on the table and threw them at the wall. "Not a goddamned one is worth shit," he yelled. He pointed at Throckmorton. "You! You're the one who sucked me into this. It's all your fault."

He turned to Wilbur. "And you . . . you can go to hell if you think I'm going to pay for excavating this worthless hole." He looked back and forth from Wilbur to Throckmorton. "The two of you worked together. You set me up to ruin me." He wheeled and stormed out of the office. Seconds later Throckmorton heard him cursing at someone in the tunnel.

Johnny poked his head into the office. "The mayor looked kinda' peeved. He grabbed a lantern right outta my hands." He turned and peered down the gloomy hallway toward indistinct echoes of rage before asking Wilbur, "Ya got anything you want me to do?"

Throckmorton ignored him. He gathered the papers he had, went to the table, and scanned through them in the light of the lantern. As he scanned the pages, he thought he might be sick. How would he tell Ben? That would be something to do later. Now he had to explain this to his partner. "Wilbur," he said, eyes fixed on the papers in his hands. "I know what set Earl off. These papers are all stock certificates. A hundred, two hundred shares per page. Shares in the Pennsylvania Railroad, the New York Central Railroad, and Transcontinental and Western Air—I think that became TWA." He picked up the papers Earl left on the table. "Damn, shares of the Packard Motor Car Company and Pan American Airlines."

He put the papers down and turned to Wilbur. "Every one of these companies was a giant of the 1930s, and all were bankrupt by the 1990s. From what I remember, their investors lost everything." Throckmorton flipped through the papers in his hands. "These stocks must have been worth thousands back in '35, but unless there's something else in the papers you have, they aren't worth ten cents today."

Wilbur brought the papers he'd picked up to the table. "Shit. You're right. Unless I can sell 'em to somebody as antiques, there ain't nothin' here worth spit. No wonder Earl went berserk." He chuckled. "After all the sorry suckers who bought overpriced crap from me, a guy who's been dead for eighty-two years has stuck it to me." He laughed again. "I've been screwed by a dead man."

Throckmorton sat in Otto's chair. "You think you've been screwed? Two old ladies were murdered for this worthless paper. We'll have to divvy up the expenses between ourselves."

Wilbur nodded. "Earl would grab one of his AR-15s and come gunning for me if I sent him a bill for his share." He motioned to Johnny. "You and Adam pick up the papers on the floor. Gather up the others in the safe and on the shelves too. Pack 'em up in a cardboard box and put it in Throckmorton's new office. We'll look at 'em later." He tapped Throckmorton in the ribs. "It's kinda early, but I think I need a drink. Want to come along?"

Johnny looked at the paper spread around the floor. "Where should we get a box, Wilbur? You got one around? I—"

"Johnny, for once, think. Shut up and figure it out by yourself. It ain't that hard to come up with a couple of cardboard boxes in Rockburg." He turned to Throckmorton. "Come on, Chris. I'm thirsty."

CHAPTER 33

Millie's Tavern was only a block from the brewery lot. A wood-frame building built in the late 1940s, it abutted the town's only mortuary, which many mourners found handy. Its location and two ancient television sets made it a sad excuse for a sports bar. Wilbur held the door for Throckmorton. "Handy thing about Rockburg," Wilbur said. "You never have far to walk if you feel thirsty."

Throckmorton had never been in Millie's before. The polished wood of the bar was dull with age but new enough that it lacked the carving and detail of the bars in the older taverns in town. The scarred hardwood floor needed to be refinished. Four other mismatched tables straddled the line in style between late bad taste and early Halloween.

"I'll bet the television sets are the only things that weren't here in 1955."

They took a Formica and chrome table from the 1950s sitting in a corner next to a window. Wilbur gave the table a thump. "He could'a bought this at my place last week, but I think his dad bought it new. Funny what godawful eyesores people used to think looked good."

"Maybe he bought it because it was ugly enough to drive his patrons to drink."

"That'd be more foresight than usual in Rockburg," Wilbur said.

The bartender, a once-white apron tied around his waist,

asked for their orders. Throckmorton ordered a ham sandwich and a beer. Wilbur followed suit.

Throckmorton waited until the bartender was out of earshot. "There still might be documents of monetary or historical value among the papers," he said.

Wilbur slouched back in his chair. "Yeah, but they don't look promising. I don't want to spend hours going through them. I suspect you got better ways to spend your time too."

"You've got that right," Throckmorton said, "but do you think our competition will try to steal the papers again?"

"I wouldn't worry. Before we finish lunch, Earl will tell everybody in town that what we found was worthless."

Throckmorton stroked his chin and agreed. "At least we'll get that much good out of Earl. I'll put the papers in my safety deposit box and go through them again to make sure we didn't overlook anything, but I don't want to sort through a bunch of ninety-year-old orders and invoices. Those might have value to the historical society. We need someone with an interest in history to collate all that stuff. Know anybody like that who'd work cheap?"

"Ya don't have to look far," Wilbur said. "You've already paid her to do work like that."

Throckmorton tried to think of anyone he'd hired as the waiter set a beer in front of each of them. "Who have I paid to go through papers?"

"Doncha remember Alice? Or Mrs. Jones, as I called her in seventh grade. Feisty old broad, but she's honest, sharp, and will work cheap if we donate stuff to the historical society. We can promise her the safe, for now, and maybe some of the papers later. Use those as a lure."

Throckmorton nodded. "Good idea. I'd better be the one to talk to her. I don't think she's fond of you."

"Ya don't say," Wilbur leaned back in his chair and laughed. "I kept her on her toes back then. I'm surprised she didn't kill me after some of the stuff I pulled. Probably wanted to a few times. Alice and I aren't friends, but we understand each other better'n most people in town." He winked at Throckmorton. "Besides, I wouldn't want to miss the expression on her face when I invite her down to look at the cavern and the tunnels and offer to give the historical society that safe." Wilbur sat upright, slapped the table with his hand, and laughed. "She'll want what we have, but the old girl will be too suspicious to agree right away. It'll be fun dickering with her."

Throckmorton had trouble picturing Wilbur and Alice in an amicable discussion. "That's counterintuitive, but you've known her longer than I have."

The waiter brought their sandwiches, and Wilbur ordered another round of beer.

"Mind if I show Nancy the office? She'll get a kick out of seeing where Earl lost it, and she's interested in antique furniture."

Wilbur shrugged. "Okay by me. Ask her if she'd like that old chair and table down there. They might be a family heirloom for ya. I ain't got room for 'em in the store, and I don't want to take the time to clean 'em up."

A shadow crossed their table. Throckmorton glanced out the window next to them. "Look who's here." He nodded toward the glass front door.

Johnny and Adam burst in. They spotted Wilbur and hustled to the corner table, a cloud of dust billowing behind them. They interrupted each other until Adam jabbed Johnny in the ribs. "Wilbur, look what we found."

"Lord, what now?" Wilbur muttered. He looked at Throckmorton and rolled his eyes toward the ceiling.

"One of the boxes fell apart when we got those papers to Mr. Throckmorton's office," Johnny said.

Adam glared at Johnny. "Wouldn't've happened if ya hadn't dropped it on the floor like a ton—"

"It slipped. 'Sides, that ain't what we came here to tell 'em."

"What *I* came here to tell 'em, ya mean. You was just gonna tag along. Ya said it weren't nothing, and then ya start flappin' your jaws and talkin' about stuff ya don't know nothin' about."

Johnny looked wounded. "What's there to know? They was just—"

"Quiet," Wilbur barked. He closed his eyes and took a deep breath. "Adam, what did you think was so important ya had to interrupt Mr. Throckmorton and me?"

"Well, I found it, that's what. When I picked up all them papers, I found it." Adam glared at Johnny again.

Wilbur drummed the fingers of one hand on the table. "What did ya find?"

"Only what ya was lookin' for. Here." Adam shoved several typewritten pages in front of Wilbur. "That's what ya wanted, wasn't it? The recipe?"

Wilbur stared blankly at Adam. "What the hell are ya talking about?"

"Only the recipe for the best damned dill pickles ever made. My grandma used to talk about Kessler's dill pickles all the time. What else would ya be lookin' for?"

Wilbur choked. "Pickles?"

"Dumb shit." Johnny stepped in front of Adam. "These was what ya wanted, wasn't they, Wilbur?" Johnny dropped a thick packet of yellowed typewritten papers on top of those Adam had placed on the table.

Dust boiled up from the table. Throckmorton turned away, coughed, and waved his hands to clear the air. Wilbur moved his chair back from the table out of the dust. "What . . . what is this?" He looked as though he couldn't decide whether he was angry or bewildered.

"Recipes for beer, the old Kessler beers. There's a pilsner, a wheat, a bock beer, and another one I couldn't make out. That's what ya was lookin' for, wasn't it, Wilbur?"

Wilbur's expression changed to one of pleasant expectation. "Kessler beer recipes, you say?"

Johnny looked down his nose at Adam. "See, I told ya that's what he was lookin' for."

Adam sulked, but only momentarily. His expression implied that this conversation was just beginning. "Yeah, but what about the keys I found?"

"Keys?" Throckmorton asked, as Wilbur paged through the top recipe in Johnny's stack of papers.

"Johnny's right," Wilbur said. "This is something I hoped to find." He turned to Throckmorton. "If'n ya don't mind, I'd like to hold onto these beer recipes and that compact tractor another few days. I'll pick up the extra cost on the tractor."

Throckmorton had given up asking Wilbur what plans he had for the cavern. "Okay with me, but what about the keys?"

Wilbur and Throckmorton turned to Adam. He shot a satisfied glance at Johnny. With a little flourish, he brought a pair of small keys out of his pocket and held them up for examination. "These are the keys, Mr. Throckmorton. I found 'em on one of the shelves on the wall. They was so covered with dirt an' dust I almost missed 'em."

Throckmorton reached for the keys. "I'll take these. Best to keep them with the key to Otto's office." He pocketed the keys and turned to Wilbur. "Will the sheriff's deputies keep the office under surveillance until we've had a chance to remove everything and do a careful search of the room?"

"Two murders," Wilbur said. "They'll keep an eye on it for another week. They'll probably search the room themselves."

CHAPTER 34

T he next evening Nancy and Throckmorton were seated in Bill's Place, a cozy country restaurant, after only a ten-minute wait. Throckmorton nodded toward the waiter's station. "We got here just in time. The line is out the door now. Everybody in the county old enough to vote must be here."

"Did you have a reservation?" Nancy asked.

"Bill's Place doesn't take reservations for Friday." Throckmorton looked over his shoulder. "Look at that line. If we'd been ten minutes later, we'd have had to wait another forty-five minutes."

A waitress dropped off menus and promised to be back shortly. The Friday night fish fry was an institution in the area. The kitchen turned out batter-fried or broiled cod, haddock, and walleye as fast as it could, and the waitresses were almost running with trays loaded with fish.

The restaurant was large for a tiny hamlet nestled between farms. It was on a flat plain where a coulee, the local term for a narrow valley, opened onto the larger La Crosse River valley. Two county roads crossed a hundred yards to the east of the settlement, one paralleling the brook for which Fish Creek coulee was named, the other at right angles to it. The restaurant crowd came from four towns and the county seat, all within twelve miles of the crossroads.

Tall maples and oaks around the restaurant shaded the place in the summer. That was only a memory now. All but a few of the leaves had fallen, leaving only a hint of the fall colors of a few weeks earlier. Dead leaves covered the grass like a bad hairpiece.

Throckmorton's hands felt warm and comfortable as he held Nancy's across the table. "I've looked forward to being with you tonight," he said, "but this place is so busy. We should have gone to a quieter restaurant. On Friday nights, Bill's is like a McDonald's with linen and crystal." He looked toward the line of waiting people. "Our waitress is glancing this way already. I'm having the battered cod. What about you?"

"Sounds good to me. Should we order a white wine?"

"If you'd like, but to my taste, beer or ale goes best with fried fish."

"By the way, I'm saving the bottle of burgundy you brought for us last week," Nancy said.

He turned to signal their waitress. Nancy glanced over his shoulder as he did. "Don't look, but Agnes Throttlebottom is waiting in line with her daughter and granddaughters. She's staring at me."

"What?" he asked.

"She's been nasty when I've waited on her at the drugstore. Ed said I should leave Agnes to him in the future." Nancy peeked at Agnes again. "I think she's complained about me to Ed." She shifted her gaze to Throckmorton and around the room again. "She's still staring at me."

"Maybe it's her last name. Living with a name like Throttle-bottom could warp anyone."

"She's warped, all right. I got the impression she has something against me personally. Debbie's pointing me out to her sister Gloria now. There's a man standing next to Gloria talking to Agnes."

Throckmorton pretended to turn to find a waiter. "The six-footer, receding hairline, tanned, looks like an expensive suit?"

Nancy pretended to read the menu. "That's the one. He must be ten years older than Gloria. Agnes was smiling at him. I've never seen her smile before. I overheard Agnes tell Ed that Gloria's fiancé is from upstate New York. Gloria's working on a master's degree in nursing at a college in Utica."

"He's from Utica? There was a theft of Kessler letters from the 1890s in Utica. If that guy is Gloria's fiancé, it's a strange pairing." Throckmorton snuck another peek. "He's overdressed for Bill's. He must know it, but he looks comfortable. Something about him—his gestures, the way he stands—he's a lot more sophisticated than Gloria."

"We don't know Gloria," Nancy said, "so don't judge her by her grandmother. Just don't look their way again."

"Okay. How long has that guy been in Rockburg?"

"Several months, I think."

Throckmorton took another look at Gloria and her boyfriend. "Has Debbie asked you about me or what I'm doing at the Kessler office or the excavation?"

"A few times. Debbie gossips about everything. Why do you ask?"

Throckmorton put his elbows on the table, rested his chin in his hands, and frowned. *So that's the guy who Suzy said photographed Maude's house. Six foot and fit—he could easily kill an elderly woman. That makes him a prime suspect.* "This is an excess of caution, but let me know if she asks more questions. Everybody in town must know we found a safe with nothing but worthless stock in it."

The line moved, and Agnes and family were obscured by the crowd until they were seated two tables away from Nancy and Throckmorton.

Their plates of fish arrived moments after they'd ordered. "Agnes is still glaring at me," Nancy said. "Oh my God. I think she's writing something down. She's taking notes! I hate to do this, but can we make this a quick dinner and go somewhere else?"

"Any place in mind?"

"We could pick up cheese and bread at Riverside, go back to my place, and have the burgundy." As Nancy spoke, the waitress delivered the bill.

"I think our server agrees," Throckmorton said.

———

The highway back to Rockburg took them past Riverside, a grocery store known for its cheese selection. "Grocery store" didn't approach an adequate description. It was a temple to the delectable, a cathedral of cuisine. Ceilings were high, lighting perfect, aisles wide, the presentations tasteful, and the selection of viands seemingly unlimited. Those who ate to live were admitted, but it was an emporium built for those who lived to eat.

The display of imported and domestic cheeses took up four coolers. Nancy selected white Stilton with mangos and ginger for a dessert. It was one of her favorites. Throckmorton picked up a wedge of Wisconsin aged brick and another of Gorgonzola. Last, they selected a loaf of crusty French bread.

On the drive back to Nancy's house, she peeled some of the plastic wrap from the aged brick, sniffed, and quickly rewrapped the cheese. "Pity we didn't have this the last time we went out. The eau de wet dog wouldn't have registered."

Throckmorton sniffed. "Oh, that is good. It's said to have a mild and fruity aroma at moderate distances, say fifty to a hundred yards. Closer than that, I'm told, and horses bolt. How would you describe it?"

Nancy had no intention of opening that cheese in the car

again. She described the aroma from memory. "Clearly an acquired taste." She lowered her window and took a breath of fresh air. "I'm at a loss for words to do it justice. Eye-watering, with subtle hints of assorted carrion comes close."

"Yeah. Don't you love it?"

Throckmorton pulled into her driveway before Nancy could think of a polite way to tell him that she'd select the cheese in the future.

A godawful squawk and "Son of a bitch, screw you, you bastards," and, "Fuck it. I paid that bill," greeted them as they stepped through the front door. She hurried to a hanging birdcage in which a green parrot hopped from one side of a perch to the other. "Sylvester, be quiet!" She covered the cage. "I'll put him in my room. He sleeps best there. Won't be a minute."

Banished to the bedroom, Sylvester was warned to be good or he'd be given guard duty over the aged brick.

"That bird could teach profanity to stevedores," Throckmorton said when Nancy returned. "Where did he learn that?"

"He was twenty when I adopted him. His vocabulary was . . . extensive. Exposure to my ex-husband made it worse. I can't teach him a word, but he picks up obscenities on a single hearing. He seems to know what will get a reaction."

"I'll have to watch my mouth around him."

"He rips off a string like that when I haven't spent enough time with him."

Back in the living room, she turned on a CD of Verdi favorites while he opened the burgundy to let it breathe. The opening note of "Va, pensiero" from *Nabucco* was repeated softly three times as Nancy sliced the bread; she poured crackers into a bowl as the chorus swelled to *"traggi un suono di crudo lamento.*

Throckmorton sliced the white Stilton. "That's one of my favorite melodies. I heard it for the first time a week after Jen walked out. I don't speak a word of Italian, but I felt as though Verdi had written the melody for me."

Nancy put a hand on his arm. "I read the translation. 'Let me cry out with sad lamentation.'" She waited a moment and asked the big question. "How was Jen last weekend?"

"She hasn't changed. We had a few unpleasant words when she arrived, but after that, nothing." He paused, listening to the music. "Looking back, giving me custody of Ben and demanding a divorce were the nicest things she ever did for me, but it was like a death in the family when she left."

He sliced the brick cheese. Nancy handed him a bowl to cover it. She wouldn't be able to smell the other cheeses or wine if it wasn't covered. *This stuff doesn't cross the threshold again. He can eat it outside if he's determined to get it.*

She glanced at Throckmorton happily chewing and tried to think of a way to get out of tasting the brick cheese. *He'll be insulted if I don't, but my God . . .* Holding her breath and scrunching her nose, she took a small bite of the cheese. It had a strong, pleasantly tangy flavor.

As they nibbled, they listened to Sutherland and Pavarotti singing the drinking toast from *La Traviata*. Throckmorton kissed her as Alfredo sang, "We'll drink to kisses inflamed by wine."

She liked the taste of the aged brick, but she couldn't imagine anyone serving it in a restaurant—or for a romantic evening. She tried not to giggle at the thought of patrons fleeing their tables when an aged brick was sliced. And a date? *If we weren't both eating it, the evening would be over with the first kiss and there'd never be a second.*

Nancy loved the duet and Alfredo's lyrics. She glanced at

the burgundy, as yet untouched, and leaned against Throckmorton. *Those lyrics might fit our evening if we go through the whole bottle.* He nuzzled her neck. Maybe a passionate night was what she needed.

They moved on to the white Stilton. A young cheese, its tangy flavor, tamed and sweetened by mangos, fit the lovers' duet perfectly. Throckmorton objected to serving the burgundy with the Stilton. "It'll overpower it."

"I might have something that'll go with it. Back in a minute." Nancy brought a bottle of white wine from the kitchen, a chilled California Viognier. Condensation formed on the cold bottle as she uncorked it. "I bought this on impulse months ago. I put it in the fridge this morning hoping we might try it." The cork came out of the bottle with a pop, and she poured the wine.

Throckmorton sniffed his glass, took a sip. "It's perfect with the Stilton." He sniffed again and took another sip of wine, rolled it over his tongue, and exhaled through his nose. "Floral bouquet, fruity taste—I'm impressed."

He poured the burgundy when they moved on to the Gorgonzola. The Gorgonzola was firm, even crumbly. Fine veins of blue and green radiated through the cream-colored wedge.

Nancy caught a whiff of its pungent aroma. Oddly, she thought she could learn to like it. She'd heard that among the *cognoscenti* it was agreed that two people attracted to that smell deserved each other. Perhaps this romance had a chance.

She brought taller glasses to the table for the burgundy, layered the Gorgonzola on slices of bread, and nibbled a sample. "Oh, marvelous! The crusty bread is perfect with it." She took another bite and held a finger in front of her mouth until she could speak. "We should have skipped dinner and just had this."

The wine label read, "2010 *Fixin, Clos de la Perrière, Premier Cru, Domaine Joliet.*" Glad she'd looked it up on the internet that afternoon, she looked at Throckmorton. "Sounds impressive."

"Should be. It's the vintner's promise that his wine is worth its ridiculous price. Let's see if he was lying." He swirled his glass and held the vibrant red wine up to the light before putting it under his nose. "Fruitier than I expected for a six-year-old wine." He sniffed again. "With just a hint of spice." He sipped tentatively and rolled it around his tongue, swallowed, and inhaled through his mouth. He looked at the glass thoughtfully. "Savory, juicy—tastes a bit like hazelnuts and raspberries."

Nancy was prepared for this one. "You Googled it, too, huh?"

Throckmorton laughed and leaned back on the couch. He slipped his arm around her, pulled her toward him, and gave her a kiss. "Can't fool you, can I? It is good, though."

As Throckmorton poured her a second glass of burgundy, Nancy rested her head against his shoulder. "When do you have to relieve Ben's sitter?"

"He'll be with Mrs. Heath until tomorrow. He loves the breakfasts she makes for him, and she likes fussing over a little boy again."

Nancy couldn't believe she heard herself say, "Amanda is having an overnight playdate with Emma. Frieda will bring her home tomorrow." *That was way too forward—almost asking him to spend the night. But I feel warm and comfortable when he puts his arms around me.*

Throckmorton poured another half-glass for each of them.

"You're rationing the wine now?" Nancy raised a saucy eyebrow. "Afraid I'll misbehave?"

"Nope. Bottle's empty. Would you misbehave with another half-glass?" He kissed her again.

Get a grip girl! But it was too late. She heard herself saying, "We could find out." She nuzzled Throckmorton's neck. "I've got a bottle of port in the kitchen. It'll be great with the Gorgonzola."

———

Consciousness eased its way into Throckmorton's throbbing head, slithered under his eyelids, and crept toward his brain. *Go away*, he thought. He cuddled closer to the warmth.

A bird whistled softly.

Where did that come from? Throckmorton's eyelids flickered open. Even light filtered through closed drapes felt like hot needles in his eyes. Whatever made the noise, looking for a bird wasn't worth the pain. *Nope. Not going to do that again.* It was morning. He could get his mind around that, yet he couldn't remember driving home the night before.

He tugged the sheet over his head. It was Saturday; he could stay where he was if he wanted to. He snuggled further under the covers and wrapped his arms around the warmth next to him. He slipped back into sleep, oblivious to anything but warmth, comfort, softness, and a floral scent.

With the fragrance, a question, like a thin wafer, entered his mind. An alarm buzzed in a distant recess of his brain. He ignored it, burying his head deeper under the covers where he nuzzled a subtly perfumed neck. The wafer transformed into a wedge that prized his mind open, and awareness shouldered its way in.

He was pretty sure he was naked and aroused. Just to make sure, he brushed a hand from his crotch to his chest. It didn't feel right. Stuff was missing. He couldn't feel his hand on his chest, but his hand felt plenty. *Oh, that feels nice . . . soft breasts, nipples, firm tummy, and—*

"Mmm," the neck responded, and the warmth closed what little space there'd been between them.

He tried brushing his hand over the chest again. It seemed like the polite thing to do. The sleeping body next to him pressed firmly to his. He sighed with satisfaction.

He had never wanted anyone as he'd wanted Nancy last night—and now.

Holy smokes! We . . .

He sat bolt upright. Nancy stirred, rolled over, smiled in her sleep, and snuggled against him. That felt good, and she looked lovely lying next to him.

A stray beam of morning light reflected off an alarm clock on a nightstand. He looked at the clock. Adrenaline replaced the memory of the endorphins of last night. *Frieda will drop Amanda off soon, and I have to pick up Ben.*

He looked around the room. His shirt was on a chair next to Nancy's dresser. He vaguely remembered putting it there. *Where are my shoes? My briefs? My pants? I have to pick up Ben in fifteen minutes, and I don't know where my damned pants are.*

Nancy tried to put her arms around his waist as he scrambled out of bed. She yawned. "What's your rush, lover?"

Throckmorton pointed at the clock. The doorbell rang.

Nancy looked at the clock and back at him. He was standing naked by her bed, holding the sock he'd found. The doorbell rang again. Her eyes opened wide. "Oh my God, Amanda!"

Throckmorton winced at the sound and pointed at his head. "Shhh."

She jumped out of bed, ran to her closet, tossed on a robe, and turned to Throckmorton. "That must be Frieda with Amanda. For Pete's sake, get dressed!"

Sylvester let out a squawk.

"I can't find my clothes," he whispered.

"I'll get the door. You keep looking." At the bedroom door, she turned toward him. "Look under the bed."

———

Nancy thumped down the stairs in her robe and slippers. A sledgehammer hit her brain with every step. She opened the door as Frieda gave the doorbell a long ring. She steadied herself with a hand on the doorframe. "For God's sake, stop it. I'm here."

Frieda walked into the living room with Emma and Amanda. "Good morning, Sunshine. You look terrible. Must have had a great time last night."

Nancy rubbed her face with her hands. "I'm sorry. I was—"

"Can Emma have breakfast and stay for the morning? John's office girl called in sick—hungover if you ask me. I have to cover the phones for her, and I'm already late."

"On Saturday?"

"Dairy farmers don't know Friday from Saturday. They're lucky to take a Sunday afternoon off. Gotta run." Frieda was out the door and halfway to her car. She turned and waved. "I'll pick her up at one. Thanks."

"But, I . . ."

Nancy couldn't organize her thoughts or words. Frieda roared away before she could put a sentence together. Dazed, she turned toward the kitchen. Flanked by a wall of empty wine bottles at the sink, she splashed cold water on her face to wake up. She had a long drink of water and marshaled her thoughts. She had to focus the girls on breakfast and keep them busy until Throckmorton found his skivvies and left the house.

Eyes closed, Nancy was dozing standing by the sink when she heard Emma say, "Oh, those are a daddy's underpants."

"What's this?" Amanda asked. "A pocket?"

"Don't you know anything? That's how daddies go pee."

Nancy's eye's popped open. She whirled around. The girls were kneeling on chairs at the kitchen table, waiting for breakfast, and examining Throckmorton's briefs.

"Fruit . . . of the . . . Loom," Amanda sounded out the words. "What does that mean?"

With effort, Nancy controlled her voice. "Where . . . did you find those?"

"On the floor near the stairs," Amanda offered.

"My mommy uses daddy's old ones to dust. Is that what you do, Mrs. Twittle?"

The bedroom door was open last night. "No. Rolf must have dragged them in from somewhere." It wasn't a complete lie. Rolf dragged shoes, underwear, and socks all over the house if he had the chance.

She made batter for French toast. Normally she'd have given the girls cold cereal, but preparing a hot breakfast would give Throckmorton more time and keep the girls focused. She let them fry the first slices of egg-dipped bread by themselves. Once they were eating, she grabbed the underwear and returned it to Throckmorton.

"The girls are busy with breakfast," she said as she handed him his briefs. "Better find the clothes you can, get dressed, and leave."

"*Girls?*"

Nancy explained she had Emma for the morning, and Rolf had probably dragged his shoes off somewhere quiet to have a nice chew. She kissed him and patted his bare butt. "I'd hoped we'd have more time together this morning. Pick up Ben, take a nap, and bring him back with you this afternoon."

Half an hour later, she saw Throckmorton tiptoe down the

stairs barefoot. He eased his way out of the front door, closing it and the storm door silently.

—•—

Frieda came back at one, as promised. "Thanks for taking care of Emma on short notice." She followed Nancy into the kitchen. Emma and Amanda were at the table finishing their peanut butter and jelly sandwiches. "It was a lifesaver today. Thanks for feeding her lunch. I didn't expect you to do that."

"We're just finishing. Grab a chair. Girls, rinse your plates if you're done eating. Put them in the sink and wash your hands and faces in the bathroom."

Frieda watched the girls until they were out of earshot while Nancy poured coffee. "Well? Did things go better than last time?"

Nancy's mind was clearer, but she wasn't ready for an interrogation. "We had a good time—left the restaurant earlier than we'd planned. Agnes was there with her family."

"Lord. She always reminds me of an angry wasp. So, what happened after you left the restaurant?"

"We came back here for a little wine and cheese."

"Did you really have a good time, or did he talk all night?"

"I had a marvelous time. We kissed goodnight, and that's all. I couldn't be happier with how the evening went." Nancy cocked her head to one side. "Is that enough for you?"

Sylvester stirred to life. He hopped back and forth across his perch as the women and girls walked to the front door. "Sorry, I didn't mean to pry," Frieda said, "but I know how much you like him. I'm glad you had—"

Sylvester cut in with a high decibel screech. "Pretty boy, pretty boy." He flapped his wings and whistled. "Ooh, oh, yes, faster, faster, faster," he squawked, made panting noises, and polished off his performance with an ear-piercing shriek and another flap of his wings.

Frieda stared at Sylvester, then at Nancy. "Sylvester learn some new words last night?"

CHAPTER 35

As Throckmorton left Nancy's house, he saw an older woman walking her dog across the street. She stopped and watched him. Although she looked vaguely familiar, he couldn't place her. He strolled casually to his car and tried to look as though he never wore shoes with a sports jacket and always had a necktie trailing from his back pocket.

On the drive home, the brake and gas pedals felt weird under his bare foot. Tiny pieces of gravel embedded in the rubber treads of the pedals grated against his foot when he accelerated or braked. He stopped by his house to change into jeans, a sweatshirt, and athletic shoes, and downed two glasses of water and Alka-Seltzer before driving to Mrs. Heath's to pick up Ben.

Ben was waiting for him. That wasn't normal. He usually had to prod Ben to leave the Saturday morning cartoons and Mrs. Heath's endless supply of milk and homemade cookies. "Mom's not coming back, is she," he said as they walked to the car.

It was a statement, not a question, but a topic Throckmorton had hoped to avoid for a while. "She may come back to visit you. We have to give her time to solve her problems." Throckmorton glanced at Ben. He seemed to take it well.

"What about Mrs. Twittle? Did you like her, Dad? Will she be living with us?"

Boy, the kid doesn't waste time. At least he isn't heartbroken over his mother, but she's never given him much reason for loyalty, either.

"We went out to dinner because we like each other. Don't get your hopes up for a new mother right away. This takes time."

Ben turned sullen as he got into the booster seat behind his father. "Why?"

"People want to be sure they love each other before they get married." Throckmorton was prepared for the next question. He could almost hear the wheels turning in Ben's mind. Was a mother—any mother—more important to him than Jen?

"Can we visit Mrs. Twittle this afternoon?" Ben asked.

"Yes. Why are you so eager to see Mrs. Twittle?" *How honest will he be?*

"I had fun playing with Amanda and teaching her Connect Four last week."

Throckmorton smiled. "It wasn't because you wanted me to spend more time with Mrs. Twittle, was it?"

"That would be okay. You could decide to marry her sooner, then, couldn't you?"

"Don't get your hopes up. We are just . . ." Throckmorton took a deep breath, "we are friends, very close friends."

———

His head felt better after more fluids and a nap. He took Ben to Nancy's at four o'clock. Ben ran to the porch and rang the doorbell. Nancy took Ben's jacket and sent him to the living room to play with Amanda. She held the door open for Throckmorton, put her arms around his neck, leaned into him, and gave him a kiss. "I had to put Sylvester in my room before you came. He learned some new words last night."

"New words? I thought his vocabulary was already impressive."

In hushed tones, Nancy told him about her conversation with Frieda and what Sylvester said. Throckmorton laughed.

"An older woman was walking her dog across the street when I left this morning. I couldn't place her, but she stared at me all the way from your house to my car," Throckmorton said.

Nancy looked at the kids playing Chutes and Ladders on the floor in front of the television. "We need to talk without little ears around the corner."

She walked into the living room and suggested the kids take their game upstairs to the spare bedroom. When the kids were safely upstairs, the adults sat in the chairs across from each other at the kitchen table. Nancy poured a cup of coffee for Throckmorton. "The woman you described was probably Agnes. She lives on the next block."

"She's the one who stared at you while we ate at Bill's last night?"

"Yup. I think she's been stalking me. She finds excuses to walk or drive past my house every evening. I've seen her car parked on the street where she can watch my front door. She must think my neighbor's trees and shrubbery screen her."

"Why would the old bat do that?"

"I overheard her in the store arguing with Ed. She wants him to fire me because I'm a loose woman and a bad influence on her granddaughter Debbie. Gert told me not to worry. She said Ed respects me, and he can't stand Agnes."

"How long has this been going on?"

"Ever since I got the job at Ed's."

Which would be the day after I got Otto's letter. Agnes also has a potential son-in-law from Utica. "Shoot. I've just handed her more ammunition," Throckmorton said. "I'm sorry about last night. I didn't mean for things to go that fast."

"Don't apologize. Being able to talk to someone who's interested in more than 'making good money,' football, and conspiracy-theory politics has saved my sanity. You're the best thing that's happened to me in years. That's why this is so hard."

Throckmorton reached across the table and held Nancy's hand. "I feel the same way about you. I've had Marlowe's line about love at first sight looping through my mind ever since I woke up this morning. We've only known each other for a couple of months, but I've been falling for you ever since the dinner at Frieda and John's."

Tears glistened in Nancy's eyes. "Are we friends who got carried away, or are we going to give this relationship a chance? I don't want to rush into a relationship that will lead to nowhere. I did that with Gary, and it was the worst mistake of my life."

She made a half-hearted attempt to take her hand away from Throckmorton's, but he wouldn't let go. He'd been cautious all his life and married Jen. So much for caution. He had been pushed into teaming up with Wilbur—something he said he'd never do—which had injected excitement and hope into his life. In two months of work on Otto's letter, he'd learned to seize opportunities, not watch them slide away. "I'm not Gary. I want you more than any woman I've ever met. Marry me. If you don't want to get married, move in with me. Move in today if you'd like."

Nancy sniffled and wiped her nose. "Let's take it slowly. Amanda and I will stay with you a few nights a week. Let's see how that works out for a little while."

Throckmorton gathered Nancy in his arms and kissed her. It wasn't everything he'd hoped for, but it at least they were moving in the right direction.

CHAPTER 36

N ancy clutched her jacket around her and wished she'd worn gloves as she followed Throckmorton along a path to the excavation. A sky the color of pewter seemed to press in on them. The roar of an engine echoed from inside the cave as they reached the top of the dirt ramp. Throckmorton pushed her gently to the side of the entrance; the tractor passed only a foot away from them and dumped a load of sand outside.

"That was close," she said. "Why are they still cleaning the sand out?"

Throckmorton shrugged. "No idea. That's Wilbur's project. It's okay with me as long as he picks up the tab for the work."

Throckmorton grabbed a lantern from a group recharging on a clean part of the cavern floor.

Nancy looked at the wide pillars, the low arches, and vaulted ceiling of the cavern. "This reminds me of the Rathskeller in Madison or a set for *The Student Prince*."

"Yup. Both are replicas of German beer halls—low, thick arches, heavy wooden furniture, lots of beer. Fitting, really. We're under the site of a brewery."

Nancy followed Throckmorton through the cavern to the first tunnel. They had to wait there for the tractor to back out with a load of sand before they could walk up the gentle slope of the tunnels to the office.

"Here it is—the great disappointment." Holding a lantern above his head, Throckmorton led her into the office and described the dust and masses of cobwebs they'd encountered behind the door. He unzipped his coat—deep in the tunnels, it was a constant fifty-five degrees.

Nancy took the step up from the tunnel floor and entered the room. She was wearing lace-up insulated boots, and their bulbous toes reminded her of clown shoes. "There wasn't any sand or water in here?"

"Nope. We're about eight inches above the tunnel floor and a couple of feet above the cavern floor. The door and the slope of the tunnel must have kept the water from getting in."

He led her to the safe and swung the heavy outer doors open, revealing the ornately decorated interior doors. An inch-wide strip of gold leaf shone in the lantern light and framed a romanticized landscape on the upper third of the inner doors. In the foreground, grass and birch trees in a mountain meadow bent in the wind. A fog-filled valley beside the meadow looked still and mysterious. In the distance, a mountain cliff shone in the morning sunlight. Painted rose vines tangled around the lower third of the seam between the doors.

"Strange, isn't it, to have such a romantic scene painted on a steel hulk?" she asked. "It's like painting flowers on a bulldozer."

Throckmorton admitted he hadn't paid attention to the paintings the first time he opened the safe. "I was tense. Earl was hanging over my shoulder, and we were focused on finding Otto's treasure. Then Earl dumped Otto's stock certificates all over the floor."

He opened the inner doors, stepped aside, and held the lantern for Nancy to inspect the safe. A smaller version of the landscape painting covered the door of the wooden box in the center of the safe.

"Did you open this little cupboard?" Nancy asked.

Throckmorton shook his head. "Didn't pay any attention to it once Earl scattered the papers."

Men! She opened the cupboard and reached in. There was something soft and pliable toward the back. Bringing it into the light, she saw a small leather pouch. She held it up for Throckmorton to see. "Should we open it now or call Wilbur?"

"Now. I'm not sure where Wilbur is. We can show him what's in it later." He put the lantern on the table.

She emptied the pouch on the table. Small diamonds, pearls, and emeralds set in two antique broaches and a sea-star-shaped dinner ring sparkled in the light. "Nice," Nancy said. "The stones are small, but the effect is lovely. I'm not sure if they're valuable. Women don't wear these things anymore, at least not in small towns." She smiled at him. "I'll never wear them, unless you were planning to take me to a swank restaurant in Chicago, maybe stay in a famous old hotel?"

Throckmorton looked up from the jewelry. "Huh?"

"The Palmer House is nice, I've heard."

Brows furrowed, he looked lost. He must not have paid attention to what she'd said.

"I take it that's a 'no.'" She replaced the jewelry in the pouch and handed it to Throckmorton.

"What are we talking about?"

She kissed him on the cheek. He was fun to tease, so wonderfully different than Gary. "It was a test. You flunked."

He looked so confused she told him it wasn't important. Her eyes fell on a tall piece of furniture against the wall to the left of the safe. Heavy and covered in cobwebs and dust, it didn't look promising. She turned her attention to the table, took a tissue from her jacket pocket, and wiped the dust from a small square of the tabletop near the lantern.

"Have you looked closely at this?" she asked.

Throckmorton bent over the area she'd cleaned but didn't answer.

"Honey, did you look at the table?"

"Ah, not really," he said.

"Then you didn't notice the brass ornamentation on the corners, the wood veneer inlays, or the leather inset in the top?"

"Brass?"

Nancy shot him a glance. He looked befuddled. She picked up the lantern and examined both sides of the table. "Have you opened the drawers?"

"Drawers?"

Her shoulders sagged. She shook her head and sighed. *Men and their one-track minds.*

"The three drawers. What did you think was attached to the brass pulls on the front?"

"I tugged on one and nothing moved. I thought they were ornaments."

"They are, on one side. On the other, I got one drawer to jiggle a little, so I know it's a drawer, probably locked." She grinned, turned to him, and gestured toward the table. "This is a very formal desk." She picked up the lantern and lowered it to examine the table's legs. Kneeling beside it, she ran the tissue over the upper third of the closest leg. "Cabriole, and, oh my gosh, they have beautiful brass ornamentation too." She looked up at Throckmorton. "The dust was so thick I didn't see it before." She stood and ran her hand along the top of the chair and felt the angled planes of hand-carved wood. "Oh, Chris. It's hand carved, and it has brass edging that matches the desk."

She chuckled and covered her mouth with a hand. "Chris, we *really* need to get these out of here."

"What's so funny?"

Nancy stood back, held the lantern up, and considered the

desk as a whole. "I don't want to say until I've had a good look at the desk and the chair after they've been cleaned. I'll have to do research on the internet too." She continued to examine the desk. "We'll have to have them appraised. We may have to get a locksmith to open the drawers."

Throckmorton dug into a pocket and brought out a key. "See if this fits. Adam found it on a shelf here."

She glanced at the key and stared at Throckmorton. "You had a key? Is there anything else you have that you and Wilbur didn't follow up on?"

Throckmorton looked uncomfortable. "Adam found two keys."

Nancy was about to make a comment, but he changed the subject. "You're right about getting the furniture out of here," he said. "We should do that before we open anything. I'll have Johnny and Adam—"

She whirled to face him. "Don't even think that! They're good-hearted, but don't let those nitwits touch this furniture. Get someone you can trust. We might be able to carry the desk and chair out, but that other thing is a monster." She considered what it would take to move the furniture safely. "Don't move anything until you have a professional moving crew and plenty of furniture pads to get these back to our garage."

"You think the furniture is valuable?" he asked.

She chuckled again and let her eyes sweep over the table. "I'm sure of it."

"If they are, we have to tell Wilbur."

"Really? You said he'd already given them to us."

Throckmorton shook his head. "These are pieces I want to keep, but Wilbur didn't have any inkling they might be valuable when he gave them to us."

"True, but would he tell you if your positions were reversed?"

"Absolutely. He isn't the person I thought he was, but that's not the point. I promised Wilbur I'd be honest with him. He caught me in a silly lie once. That's not going to happen again."

It took Nancy a moment to absorb that. It was getting late, and they prepared to leave. They took the jewelry with them.

"Is it safe to leave things here?" Nancy asked.

"Yeah. Everybody in town knows the safe held nothing of value, and the sheriff's department still has the cavern under surveillance."

———

Alice was behind the counter sorting old papers when Wilbur strolled into the historical society on Tuesday. "Well, how's my favorite teacher today?"

She gave him a baleful glare and went back to her work. "What sorry excuse brings you here today?"

Wilbur tried to look offended, but this was too much fun. "Did I tell ya we opened an old safe in an underground office of the brewery? Big, old two-door Yale safe. Thought you'd like to have a look at that, maybe the office, and bunch of old papers we found."

He watched for a reaction but didn't get any. "Throckmorton's got a letter that says the last time the safe was opened was 1935. The office hasn't been used since Prohibition. That would be . . . 1919 or 1920, wouldn't it?" Wilbur looked over Alice's head, rubbed his chin, and pretended to calculate. "That'd be damned near a hundred years, give or take a few."

She stopped working and looked at him. "A safe and documents?"

She's hooked. He assumed his aw-shucks expression. "Quite a few papers: invoices, letters, stock certificates. Probably nothin' to interest you, though. I'll let ya get back to work." He paused. "Pity though. We was going to donate the safe and most of the papers to the society, but if you're not interested—"

Alice held up one hand. "Wilbur, you're just as slippery and manipulative as you were when I had you in class. I didn't say we weren't interested. I'll examine the papers, and I'll look at pictures of the office and safe for you, but I'm not traipsing through tunnels and mud to see them."

Alice agreed to open the historical society when Wilbur could bring her the documents and pictures. Wilbur answered his cell phone as he walked to his car. Nancy said Throckmorton had something to show him at Throckmorton's home. Five minutes later the three of them gathered around Throckmorton's desk.

"What ya got here?" Wilbur asked.

"This." Throckmorton hefted the pouch in one hand in front of Wilbur and gently shook the jewelry out onto his desktop. "Nancy found it in a cupboard in the safe. I wanted you to see the pieces before we send them out for an appraisal."

"Kinda pretty, ain't they?" He picked up a brooch and examined it under the desk lamp. "Stones are small. A lot of 'em, though. Cuts will be old-fashioned. May not be worth much, but ya better get a couple of appraisals to be safe. Better put 'em in the bank for tonight. We still got somebody out there nosing around, dodging the sheriff."

"And what we thought was a table is a desk. Nancy thinks both the desk and chair are valuable. We'd like to get the furniture out before the sheriff's department loses interest and takes out their surveillance cameras. Clean them up someplace secure."

Wilbur snorted. "That's what I wanted to avoid—cleaning

old furniture to make it purrty." He turned to Nancy. "You got time to do that? I stuck a bottle of tung oil and a package of dust cloths in the tunnels before I came here. Shouldn't take more than a couple hours to wipe down the table and stuff."

"We can do that," Nancy said. "The tall piece is heavy. We should have professionals move the furniture to Chris's garage. It'll be easier for me to give them a thorough cleaning there. Safer, too."

Wilbur closed his eyes and stuffed his hands in his back pockets. "Throckmorton, would ya explain to Nancy that I ain't a Rockefeller. It'll cost three, four hundred to get regular movers to haul that stuff out."

"The table is antique," Nancy said. "So is the chair. I'm certain they're valuable. Chances are the big piece, whatever it is, is worth a lot too. If you don't want to pay professionals to move them, Wilbur," she smiled at Throckmorton, "Chris will. Won't you, honey?"

Throckmorton was examining one of the brooches in the sunlight striking his desk. He looked up with a jerk when Nancy said his name. He looked from Nancy to Wilbur.

"Just nod, Chris," she said. "I'll explain later."

Nancy and Throckmorton walked Wilbur out. At the door, Throckmorton asked Wilbur if he'd heard anything new about Earl.

"The greedy bastard's got his hands full. The folks he sold on that offshore scheme got a lawyer and are dragging his ass to court. 'Cause there was fraud involved, they've sued him for triple damages, a tad over a million dollars."

"Ouch! How much of his money did he get out before the fund collapsed?"

"Did better'n I thought he would. Got about eight hundred thousand out, around two-thirds of what he put in. From what

I hear, he ain't got a chance in court." Wilbur looked at the floor and shook his head. "It's hard to feel sorry for Earl, but what he's got himself into ain't pretty. He's gonna be picked cleaner than roadkill at a buzzard convention."

Throckmorton wiped cobwebs and dust from the table in the underground office by lantern light Wednesday morning. Although it was only thirty degrees outside, he was comfortable working in his shirt sleeves in the office. Wilbur strolled in as he worked.

"Nancy got you doing the worst part before the movers get here?"

"Yeah. Ever meet a woman who didn't clean ahead of the movers, electrician, or cleaning lady? It must be a side effect of estrogen. Plus, she doesn't want a load of dirt moved in along with the furniture."

"I forgot to tell ya, Alice wants the safe delivered before she'll sort the papers." Wilbur shrugged and looked innocent. "You'd think she didn't trust me."

Imagine that. Throckmorton almost said it out loud. He picked up a clean rag and tossed the dirty one into an empty five-gallon pail. He closed the doors of the safe, stood back, and tried to appraise its weight. "It would have been cheaper to pay Alice by the hour. At least whatever we spend will be tax deductible. You can hire professionals to get it from here to the arch, but how are you going to move it from there?"

"How are *we* going to move it, partner?" Wilbur pushed on the side of the safe. "Might as well try to shove the Kessler building. This damned thing's a ballbreaker. Let's go look at the ramp."

Throckmorton grabbed his jacket and followed Wilbur to

the cavern entrance and out onto the top of the earthen ramp. Wilbur looked the ramp over, gauged the slope, and shook his head. "I don't want to move that thing over this. The ramp ain't long, but it's cobbled together. I don't trust it for that kind of weight."

Throckmorton heard rocks and sand sliding above them. He glanced toward the brewery lot over their heads and threw himself at Wilbur. They fell to the side in a tangle of legs and arms as a concrete block smashed into the ramp where Wilbur had been standing. The heavy construction block buried itself six inches into the hard-packed sand and rock.

Red-faced, Wilbur scrambled to his feet. He looked ready to take a swing at Throckmorton. "What the hell do ya think—"

Throckmorton pointed at the chunk of concrete.

Wilbur turned pale. "Christ! Where'd that come from?"

Throckmorton looked up toward the edge of the brewery lot. "Maybe it was knocked loose?"

Wilbur shook his head. "By what? About as likely for Alice to throw it from the historical society. Only a couple of these blocks was up there, and they was sittin' on the level."

"Could some kids have shoved it?"

"Those blocks weigh over sixty pounds. Any kids big enough to toss that thing are in school. That weren't no accident, and so far, our competition has only worked at night."

They turned toward each other and spoke at the same time. "Earl?"

Throckmorton looked at the block and its path from the brewery lot to where it lay. His knees felt weak, and his pulse was pounding. "Is there still a deputy in the van?"

"Don't even think about letting the sheriff know about this. We've been lucky, had the deputies here, and she hasn't gotten involved."

"The county sheriff is a woman?"

"That's right. Interim sheriff. Got appointed last winter. You've been lucky so far. Never had to talk to the big cheese, always talked to a deputy. She's been decent about everything so far 'cause she wants to get credit for solving the murders, and ain't nothing illegal been done in our dig." He pointed toward the block. "We tell her about that, and she'll close this excavation as a crime scene. It could be weeks before we can move anything outta here. After that, she'll call her mother, and then I'll have her nattering in my ear."

Throckmorton did a double take. "You know the sheriff's mother?"

"Married to her for forty-five years. Most stubborn woman you'll ever meet. Sheriff's been that way, too, since kindergarten. I have to sit through her bellyaching about my business deals at Thanksgiving and Christmas dinner. I'm sure as hell not going to give her an excuse to gnaw on my ass two weeks early."

"The sheriff is your daughter?"

"She doesn't talk about me, and I don't talk about her. Typical politician. Lies for a living, then bitches at me for tryin' to put food on the table." Wilbur paused for a moment, and his expression relaxed. "My other kids turned out okay, though."

Throckmorton felt dizzy. "You're saying the county sheriff is your daughter?" he repeated.

"So?" Wilbur responded.

Wilbur's daughter was in law enforcement? Throckmorton put his hand against the ravine wall to stabilize himself. He couldn't imagine how the county had survived, but it had. She must not have been anything like Wilbur. "But we can't ignore this, Wilbur. Earl, or whoever it was, could kill you next time, or miss you and hit me."

"You call the movers and get a date for 'em to move the

safe and furniture. I'll ask around. The surveillance cameras are aimed at the entrance—wouldn't have caught who threw it. It might've been a spur-of-the-moment thing if it was Earl. Probably never try it again."

"I don't care. I don't like the idea of another person out for my scalp. Get this taken care of before we move the safe." Throckmorton's eyes followed the trail from the ramp to the county road. "How do you plan to get the safe and antiques from here down to a truck?"

"Up to a truck."

"Huh?"

"For a smart man, you sure don't catch on fast. Nancy will nail your balls to the front door if we put those antiques on a truck down here and bounce 'em over this dirt road. We'll crate everything and lift 'em outta here with a tow truck's winch, load 'em on a truck up top where it's level."

Wilbur pulled out his cell phone and made a call. Throckmorton looked up toward the brewery lot and visualized the path of the concrete block again. Unless Wilbur took care of this pronto, standing anywhere near him at the excavation could be fatal.

———

Johnny waved to a tow truck driver Thursday morning, beckoning him back toward the edge of the brewery lot above the cavern entrance and ravine. Wilbur saw Johnny's motions as he drove up. He laid on the horn and jumped out of his car. "Stop, stop! Are you nuts?"

Wilbur ran to the back of the truck and estimated the space between its back tires and the edge of the lot. "Another foot," he muttered as he leaned on the truck and caught his breath. "I'm getting too old for this nonsense." He turned and saw Johnny. "Go down and see if they need help gettin' the safe outta the office," he told Johnny. "If they don't need help, take a break and stay outta their way."

Johnny headed to the cavern entrance, and Wilbur stalked to the cab of the truck. Cigar in his mouth, the driver opened the truck door, ignored Wilbur, and looked at the ground by Wilbur's feet. That was too much. "Frank, I shoulda known. You tryin' to give me a heart attack? You're only a foot from collapsing the bank and going over the edge."

Frank shut the door, took the cigar out of his mouth, leaned out of the cab window, and smiled. "Hi, Wilbur. How's your day going?"

Too much had gone wrong on this project already, and now this jerk risked plunging his truck into the gully. "What in hell possessed you to have Johnny guide ya back to the edge? You tryin' to get yourself killed?"

"Don't you trust him?" Frank cocked an eyebrow and puffed on his cigar.

"Goddammit, Frank. You know Johnny. He woulda had ya back up until your wheels were right on the edge. You're already as far back as ya dare go."

Frank took another pull on his cigar and blew a smoke ring. "Before you blow a gasket, look at your feet. That yellow stake between 'em? That's my marker."

Wilbur looked at the top of a yellow stake stuck in the ground between his feet. "You son of a bitch. You'd give me a stroke just for a laugh."

"Your expression as you jumped out of your car was worth it. Anybody ever tell you to relax a little, Wilbur?"

Wilbur felt his face flush. He had a lot more he'd like to say, but the tow truck was working by the hour. "Set your breaks and drop the hook," he growled. "I'll wave when it's low enough. The safe will come up first. It's the only thing heavy enough to be a problem."

Wilbur watched eight muscular men carry a large plywood crate out of the cavern and onto the ramp fifteen feet below him. Four guys were on each side of the crate, straining as they shuffled out of the cavern. They carried the weight on their shoulders with two poles. It was a cold day, but all the men were sweating. His face in a grimace, the guy in charge called out, "Put 'er down on three and take five."

The crates with furniture were moved out easily after the break. Wilbur supervised raising the crates and loading them into the movers' truck. He'd asked Alice to have the historical society open. The movers bellyached nonstop about the weight of the safe and grumbled about Wilbur's supervision as they moved the steel monster into the society.

Before they left the historical society for Throckmorton's garage, the crew foreman gave Wilbur the phone number and address of their chief competitor in case he ever wanted something moved again.

Snow flurries and a fine coating of ice made roads slippery by noon. Wilbur was driving to meet a guy about a horse and a truckload of hay when his cell phone rang. It was Johnny.

"Wilbur, we found some things in the office. Do you want me to bring 'em to you?"

"What are they?"

"They was under the safe. That's why we missed 'em before."

Wilbur pulled to the curb. Talking to Johnny could drive a man crazy when you were face to face. Trying to make sense of his ramblings on a cell phone while driving could be suicidal.

"What did you find?"

"The stuff under the safe."

"Johnny, what are we talking about? What was under the safe?"

"What fell there. They must've fallen there 'cause we didn't see 'em until they took the safe out."

Wilbur resisted the urge to pound his head against the steering wheel. "What fell under the safe? What did you find?"

"Papers. That's what ya been lookin' at since we got in the office, ain't it?"

Wilbur put his cell aside, closed his eyes, and counted to twenty. Ten was never enough for these idiots. "What kind of papers? Are they more stock certificates?"

"One has 'invoice' written on top. Can't read the handwriting. It's too faded. The other one's somethin' about machines."

Wilbur looked at the time on his cell phone. He was already late for his meeting. "Hustle up to the historical society and give them to Alice. Tell her they belong in the box I brought her."

"What if she isn't there?"

"Oh, for God's sake." Wilbur took a deep breath and tried to get his temper under control. "If she isn't there, take the papers to Throckmorton's home. Give them to Nancy or Throckmorton." He turned his cell phone off and pulled onto the road.

Jen turned to the naked guy lying next to her that evening. Tall, dark, muscular—so much sexier than Steve or Throckmorton. She ran fingers through the hair on his chest. "What do you plan to do now?"

"I'm trying to decide," Carl said. He thought for a moment and asked, "You said they opened the safe and found nothing but worthless stock certificates?"

"Yeah. My friend said Earl whined about it all over town for most of the week. Today they moved the safe to the historical society and took the furniture to Throckmorton's garage."

"Furniture?"

"Office furniture, a desk, a chair, and a big bureau of some sort. They must be antiques." She leaned closer and nibbled his earlobe. "Want to do it again?"

He moved his head away from her. "Cool it. I'm trying to think. Oscar Kessler had the coin last. According to the letters, few in the next generation knew anything about it, and you said your ex and his buddies didn't even know what they were looking for."

She watched him get out of bed and move to the desk next to the dresser. A nice motel room and his broad shoulders, narrow waist, and flat butt weren't doing her any good because of an old coin.

He sorted through the pile of stolen letters. "Here it is. Oscar's 1903 letter to Joseph Kessler."

She rolled her eyes toward the ceiling. The best-looking hunk to ever pay attention to her and all he did was read those darn letters. What a waste.

He read, "'As we agreed, I'll hold the 1804 Liberty for now. I've entrusted it to my secretary.' The old fool didn't have a . . .'" His eyes lit up. "Wait. What furniture did you say they moved?"

Jen turned and glared at him. *What do I have to do to get his attention? Sit on his lap and shove a boob in his face?* She filed a nail until she got her emotions under control. "It was a tall thing, a chest of drawers. Weird, because it has one huge drawer about waist high. They said it didn't belong in an office."

"A big drawer about three, four feet off the floor?" Carl

thought about it, grabbed Jen around the waist, and swung her around in a circle. "Oh, man. That's it! I know where the coin is."

Bewildered, Jen looked at Carl.

"That tall chest you described. That big drawer isn't a drawer at all. It's a flat surface that drops down to make a desk. That chest is an antique writing desk, also called a secretary. Damn Oscar, that sly, old bastard was making a joke." He laughed, threw the letter on the desk, and pulled Jen toward the bed. "Come here, sweetheart. Let's celebrate. I'm free until we scout out Throckmorton's security system tomorrow."

CHAPTER 37

The snow flurries continued into the late afternoon. A gray cube, an electric space heater known as a milk-house heater, took the chill off Throckmorton's garage. He walked in, stomped the snow off his shoes, and took off his coat. Nancy, wearing dusty jeans and a filthy old sweatshirt, removed the towel she'd wrapped her hair in, and used it to wipe off the last bit of dust on the chair from Otto's office. Throckmorton looked over the polished wood of the writing desk, chair, and big secretary. At least he thought it was a secretary. Six feet tall, four feet wide, with little ornamentation, it looked like an armoire or an oversized dresser except for a large panel in the middle. The panel was too big to be a drawer but the right size for a drop-down writing desk.

"How's the work going?" he asked Nancy.

"I spent part of the morning and most of the afternoon going over the furniture with a vacuum cleaner, dust cloths, and tung oil. I'm bushed."

The writing desk and chair glowed with a reddish tint, the secretary with a light amber gleam. Nancy took pictures of each with her cell phone and emailed them to herself, Throckmorton, and Wilbur. "There," she said. "Now we each have pictures of these things cleaned up."

"You've done an incredible job." He ran his hands over the large front panel of the secretary. "You've turned crap into beauty."

"Thanks." Nancy pointed to a lower rear corner of the

secretary. "The veneer will need some work. It's pulling away from the wood near the back on both sides."

"Can you repair it?"

Nancy gave him an odd look. "Not a chance. These are too valuable to turn over to an amateur. I looked up similar pieces on the internet this morning."

"And?"

She grinned and gestured toward the table. "Writing tables like this were priced around fifteen thousand. The one I found that looked the most like it had rosewood and tulipwood veneers. None had a matching chair. The chair by itself might be worth one or two thousand, but the table and chair together could be worth twenty thousand or more."

Shaken, Throckmorton plopped into the chair. "Good Lord! What about the secretary?"

Nancy showed him a page with a picture on it. "I printed this from a website selling antiques. It's a 'rare Biedermeier walnut secretary'"

Throckmorton pointed at the piece. "That thing, is a Biedermeier secretary?"

Nancy nodded. "If, behind the fold-down writing desk, there are four small drawers on each side of a larger cabinet, like the one in this picture, it would be valued at sixteen to eighteen thousand. Got the keys with you?"

Throckmorton fished the keys from his pocket and handed them to her. "Thirty-eight thousand? Wow. Still, though, that doesn't seem valuable enough for murders and thefts from here to Utica, does it? A thief would get a hernia trying to steal the secretary."

Nancy agreed with him, and added, "but they have drawers." Taking the keys, she said, "Let's see what they hold. Writing desk first."

She inserted the key in the middle drawer of the desk. The key turned after she wiggled it back and forth and applied gentle pressure. She had to jiggle the drawer from side to side a little, but with finesse, it slid out. It was empty.

The key wouldn't turn in the other drawers. Throckmorton handed her a spray can of WD-40. She gave the locks a squirt and tried again. The far-left drawer opened smoothly. It held nothing but pre-1920 correspondence.

Throckmorton plucked a few letters from the drawer. "Old mail. Most are addressed to Mr. and Mrs. Otto Kessler and family." He held the envelopes up to the light. "Mailed in October 1904. Others addressed to Otto were postmarked later." Throckmorton looked at the letters and thought a moment. "I wonder if these were condolence letters. People rarely address things to Mr and Mrs. and family except for Christmas and funerals."

"Could be," Nancy said. "Who's funeral?"

"Probably Oscar's, Otto's father. Alice told me Oscar went into decline in the late 1890s and died in 1904."

Nancy opened the last drawer and removed yellowed business envelopes. Both sides were blank. "Never used." She was about to close the drawer when Throckmorton noticed a patch of color and scraps of paper in the back. He pointed to them and she fished them out.

"Stamps! Individual stamps, not on a roll or sheet." She set them on the table where they examined them. There were a dozen stamps—one, two, and four cents—with pictures of Washington, Benjamin Franklin, and Lincoln. None had dates. Turning to Throckmorton, she asked, "Any idea if these are valuable?"

"I know nothing about stamps." He looked at his watch and felt sick. "The bank is closed for today. It's open Saturday morning until noon. We'll have to get the stamps into the safety deposit box tomorrow, early. We can look them up on Google or send photos to a philatelist later."

She kissed him. "Ooh, that sounds risqué."

Throckmorton slipped his hand around her waist and gave her a kiss. "Work first. Let's get the secretary next." He tried the second key in a hole in the large center panel of the secretary. "I can't understand why this piece was in the office. It should have been in a home, in the parlor or library."

The key turned. They heard a click near the top of the upper panel. He gripped it, tugged, and it moved outward half an inch. Another tug, and the panel swung down and out with the drawn-out squeak of hinges that hadn't moved since Prohibition. Once in place, the panel became a writing desk. Above and behind the desk were eight narrow drawers and a central cupboard.

"Just like the picture on the website. The wood is beautiful." Nancy ran a cloth over the drawer fronts. She grinned at the secretary and turned to Throckmorton. "We *have* to find a place for it in the house."

"We can if we can afford to pay Wilbur for his share." Throckmorton tried to pull out the top-left drawer. It moved a bit but wouldn't open. "Feels like it's locked." He tried three of the other drawers with the same results. "Locked. Can you see a place the key might fit?"

They examined the interior of the secretary, ran their hands over the wood, and checked joints to see if anything would release. Throckmorton opened the center cabinet and felt around the inside. He put his finger in a space behind the frame around the door and gave a gentle tug. A panel—the bottom of the cabinet's frame—popped open. Behind it was a keyhole.

"Great thinking," Nancy said. They heard a metallic snick

when he turned the key, and the top-left drawer opened smoothly this time when he pulled it out.

The drawer was stuffed with wadded paper. With that removed, something in the drawer glinted in the fluorescent lights of the garage. He edged the drawer out and saw a flash of gold. As the drawer opened, and he removed the paper, he saw a layer of quarter-sized gold discs covering the bottom of the drawer. Throckmorton held two of them to the light. "Twenty-dollar pieces, minted in . . ." He angled the coin back and forth in the light. "Minted in 1885 and in 1869."

He inspected the older coin, put it down and reexamined the other. He turned the coin in the light as he examined it. "Not a scratch or sign of wear on either of them. They look as though they've come fresh from the mint."

Excitedly, he opened another drawer and found more wadded paper, which he tossed out. For the first time since he'd opened the safe, he thought there might be hope for Ben. "More coins, again in a single layer." He collected three from that drawer and examined them. "Twenty-dollar, ten-dollar, and five-dollar coins from 1870 to 1900." He turned one back and forth and held it at several angles to the light. "No scratches or blemishes that I can see." He turned to Nancy. "I'll bet that's why they were put in two drawers with all that paper."

"What do you mean?"

"These may have belonged to a collector. They were put in single layers so they wouldn't scratch each other. The wadded-up paper was added for the same reason. Perhaps there weren't individual envelopes for them back then." Throckmorton counted the coins in the two drawers. His eyebrows rose higher the more he counted. "Bullion value alone must be nearly twenty-five thousand. To collectors, they could be worth . . . I don't know, maybe thirty to fifty thousand if the coins are uncirculated. Let's assume thirty thousand to be conserv-ative." He turned to Nancy. "These may have been what our competitor is after."

He opened the bottom two drawers. Twenty silver-dollar pieces, dated from 1804 to 1880, covered the bottoms of the drawers. He turned to her and winked. "Should I open another drawer?"

The value of the furniture had unfolded over a few days, but this? He felt as though he'd stumbled into Aladdin's cave. From presumably empty drawers to tens of thousands of dollars in gold and silver in mere minutes was a challenge to absorb.

He opened the top-right drawer and found more gold coins. The gold flashed in the light when he took a few out and inspected them. "There's a bust of a woman on this one," he said, holding it so Nancy could see it. "She looks like somebody's grumpy grandmother. Minted in 1765, 1774, and 1892." He squinted and read the print on the coin. "M. THERESA. D.G.R. IMP. GE.HU.BO.REG. Maybe IMP stands for 'imperator.'"

"Is that Latin?" she asked.

"Not sure it's a word. I just added a Latin-sounding ending to 'imperial.'" His jaw dropped open as he realized what the words stood for. "These are Austro-Hungarian coins. The initials stand for Empress Maria Theresa.

The old girl is on both eighteenth-century coins. The last initials would stand for 'Empress of Germany, Hungary, and Bohemia.'" He looked at the other coin. "FRANCVS JOSEPHVS. His title is spelled out, IMPERATOR ET REX. If the *V* is a *U*, it would be Emperor Franz Joseph."

He handed two of the coins to Nancy. She examined them and asked, "Your mother's family was from—"

"Prague, part of the Austro-Hungarian Empire back then."

"And the Biedermeier secretary," she said. "I looked it up.

Biedermeier was a style popular in central Europe from the fall of Napoleon to the 1850s. Your family must have brought this furniture with them when they emigrated."

"An article I found mentioned the Kessler family coming to Wisconsin in 1847. I'd guess this is the work of a coin collector or collectors. Otto's father died in 1903 or 1904. The newest coin was collected in 1900. Oscar was thus the last collector."

"Otto's letter didn't mention the secretary or desk, did it?" Nancy asked.

"Nope. He only mentioned the safe." Throckmorton looked at the coins, the Biedermeier secretary, and had a flash of insight. "I don't think Otto knew about the coins. He never would have put a fortune in gold and silver where any clerk could help himself to it."

Nancy stepped back to look at the secretary at a distance. "The last collector died. No one else in the house had paid any attention to the collection, and Otto's wife didn't like the old-fashioned style of this secretary. She wanted it out of the house."

"I think you're right," Throckmorton said. "If Otto didn't like a piece of furniture, he would have had it hauled away. If his wife didn't like it, but it was something his father had loved, he'd store it somewhere where his wife wouldn't have to look at it."

Nancy nodded. "You're right. Nothing of value we've found had anything to do with Otto's letter."

Throckmorton's knees felt weak. "The letters stolen from the historical society and the museum in Utica were from the last years of the old man's life. It all fits. The coins are what the murderer is after, and we are in deep shit. The bank is closed. If the thief has been watching, he knows we have the secretary in our garage. Tonight is his last good chance at them."

He called the sheriff's office. The conversation was brief.

"They're shorthanded," he said. "The best they can do is have a cruiser drive past the house every few hours." He looked at Rolf hopefully. "Maybe Rolf will provide some protection."

"Rolf is a golden retriever, not a guard dog. He'll lick an intruder."

"I'll call Mrs. Heath and have her pick up the kids. They can stay with her overnight. You take care of the house. The security system makes that the safest. I'll handle the garage."

CHAPTER 38

Nancy turned on the security system while Throckmorton downed a can of Red Bull—it was going to be a long night. He dug through the guest room closet and returned to the kitchen with a baseball bat in one hand and a thirty-year-old camera with a flash bar in the other. The bar held four flashbulbs.

"Let me guess," Nancy said. "You want me to take pictures of the fight tonight?"

Throckmorton grimaced. "Oh, ye of little faith. Do you know why the cops say no one has seen this guy moving around houses or buildings at night, smarty?"

"I'll bet I'm about to learn."

"They watched on infrared cameras as he explored the cavern one night. It was pitch-black in there, but he moved fast and didn't stumble or feel his way around. They didn't detect an infrared illuminator, so infrared goggles wouldn't have helped him. He must have had night-vision goggles and a special illuminator, one that puts out as much light as you have on a starlit night."

"So?"

"Turn on bright lights when someone is wearing those and kablam. If flashbulbs in a dark room leave you blind for a second, it should be exponentially worse for a guy wearing ultra-sensitive goggles. When he's staggering around blind, that's when I use the bat."

"Do you know anything about those goggles? They must have an instant shutoff for bright lights."

"I think the good ones do, but they cost close to a thousand bucks. I figure this guy's cheap."

"What if this guy isn't stupid or cheap? Does caffeine always affect you this way, or did you get this idea from Johnny and Adam?" she asked. "Didn't you say the deputy told you not to mess with this guy?"

Throckmorton took a practice swing. "The house is secure. The only place he can get in is the garage, and that's where the secretary and coins are. I won't touch him unless he comes into the garage."

"With his fancy goggles, how will you know he's here before he sees you?"

Crestfallen, Throckmorton put the bat down, looked around, and pointed at Rolf. "Rolf will be with me. He'll growl an alert."

Nancy looked at Rolf, seventy pounds of drool and cowardice snoozing by his water dish. "Rolf is more likely to run and hide." She sat at the kitchen table and cradled her head in her hands. "I'd so hoped you were smarter than Gary. Is there anything special you want done for your funeral?"

Nancy locked the deadbolts and regular locks on the doors to the house. With the house secured, Throckmorton wedged wooden blocks between the garage doors and ceiling. Nothing was going to lift those doors with the blocks in place. Only the side entrance to the garage bay could be opened. Throckmorton locked it, but it was a cheap lock. He leaned a chair against the door and draped it with Christmas decorations—leather straps with sleigh bells attached. They'd be as good as an alarm. He unplugged the milk-house heater and put it in a corner to reduce the chance he'd trip over the cord. His preparations complete, he grabbed a stool from the kitchen and sat just inside the doorway from the house to the attached garage, close to the light switch for the garage. He turned off the lights.

The caffeine from the Red Bull made him jittery. The stygian darkness disoriented him, and he had to touch the wall periodically to ground himself; he couldn't even tell whether his eyes were closed or open.

His breath in the garage had turned to a frozen mist every time he exhaled. Judging by that, the outside temperature must have dropped to the low twenties. He regretted unplugging the electric heater in the garage. The only heat Throckmorton had was Rolf leaning against him, and that wasn't enough. Without a hat, gloves, and coat—a guy couldn't think of everything—his sweatshirt and corduroys weren't enough to keep him warm. Capillaries in his skin closed, shunting blood from his skin and increasing the circulation to his kidneys. His feet were numb, his fingers couldn't feel the camera and flash bar, and his bladder begged for relief. He was squirming on his seat when he heard a garage door creak.

Rolf growled softly beside him. He heard one of the garage doors rise an inch and settle back down. *The blocks worked, asshole. Try the lock on the door.*

A low, almost imperceptible growl rumbled in Rolf's throat. As though he'd had second thoughts, it turned into a whine. Rolf snuggled so close against Throckmorton he wasn't sure he could move. *Great. I'm protecting the darn dog.*

A latch clicked. Throckmorton moved the camera and flash bar into position, or at least what he thought was the right position. Rolf stuck his nose between Throckmorton's hands, licked his face, and tried to crawl onto his lap. That twisted him around enough he couldn't tell which direction he was pointing the camera. He'd leaned his bat against the wall. Where the hell was that now?

Rolf squirmed further onto his lap. Throckmorton lost control of the camera and it swung by two fingers of his left hand. Chair legs scraped against the concrete floor of the garage and the chair toppled. Sleigh bells jingled. *Christmas decorations announcing the entrance of a murderer and thief. Talk about incongruous.* A blast of cold air froze his ears.

He got the camera under control but wasn't sure whether he was pointing it at himself or the garage bay. He felt a couple buttons on the camera. In the dark, he couldn't tell which one would set off the flash.

God, he felt stupid. *No wonder the country is in trouble. People like me vote.*

He leaned forward, squeezed his eyes tight in case he was aiming the flashbulbs at himself, and repeatedly punched all the buttons he could find on the camera.

Bright crimson flashed before his eyes; the light took on the color of blood as it passed through his eyelids. He dropped the camera and swiped a hand toward the light switches. Rolf tried to crawl inside his sweatshirt with him, throwing his aim off.

The third swipe turned on the lights. They blinded him momentarily, but he knew they must have done that to the intruder. He felt his bat, grabbed it, and held it in front of him like a spear. Rolf fell to the floor as Throckmorton stumbled forward, almost in a dive—he always forgot that damned second step.

He felt the bat hit something. His eyes adjusted to the light as he scrambled to his feet. A figure dressed in black lay on the floor, clutching his abdomen, straps of sleigh bells tangling his feet. Small binoculars hooked to a headset lay on the floor in front of the guy. The burglar held his gut and gasped something. Throckmorton couldn't make out what it was because some idiot was screaming, "Call the cops, call the cops," and the darn fool wouldn't shut up.

The intruder rolled onto his knees and braced his arms under himself to get up. Throckmorton swung the bat as though he were splitting wood and came down on the guy's right shoulder.

Another scream joined the "call the cops" chorus. They weren't in tune.

Nancy's voice came from behind him. "Chris, stop screaming. I heard you. I called the sheriff's department."

Throckmorton stopped yelling. His throat was sore, anyway. The would-be thief was flat on the floor, his head down. Throckmorton poked him in the back with the end of his bat. "Don't move. I've got you covered with a twelve-gauge. I pull this trigger and you'll be in so many pieces you could start your own ball team."

Nancy tapped him on the shoulder and whispered in his ear, "You do know you're holding a bat, don't you?"

He glared at her. "Of course."

She shrugged. "Well, I didn't know. The way you were screaming and jumping up and down—"

"You broke my shoulder," the figure said. "You're holding a stupid bat, you dumb son of a bitch. Do you think I'm blind?"

Nancy shrugged and looked at Throckmorton, "Well, actually he'd hoped—"

"No fast movements or you're dead," Throckmorton growled and waggled the bat as though getting ready for a pitch.

Nancy rolled her eyes. "You've watched too many cop

shows."

Red and blue flashing lights shone through the windows in the garage door. The police cruiser had arrived. Throckmorton handed Nancy the bat. "Hold this. I really have to go."

———

A second police cruiser was pulling up to Throckmorton's house when the officer spotted movement in a hedge on the edge of Throckmorton's lawn. He slammed on the brakes, shoved the shift lever into park, and jumped out of the car. Turning on his flashlight as he ran to the hedge, he swept the bright beam over the area where he'd seen movement. Bushes moved, he pulled out his gun, and demanded, "I see you. Come out with your hands up. Now! Move it!"

A woman in a dark purple coat, black pants, and black gloves sputtered, stood with her hands up, and called out, "Don't shoot. I was . . . I was just trying to find . . ."

The officer's flashlight beam caught her eyes, and she turned her head away. "I was trying to find . . . um . . . a ball my son lost earlier."

The officer had her step forward and provide identification. She claimed she didn't have her billfold with her. Another officer arrived, conferred with the first, and did a pat-down of the woman. His hand dipped into her back pocket and pulled forth a billfold. He showed it to the woman. She glanced at it, looked away, and said, "Oh, I forgot I put it there."

The officer examined the woman's driver's license and compared the photo to her face. "You live in Milwaukee? Care to tell me how your son lost his ball this far from home?"

He put her hands behind her and slapped on handcuffs. The officers marched her to Throckmorton's garage—the only area with lights on—and shoved her inside. Throckmorton had just

returned from the bathroom. He looked at the officer's prison-
er and exclaimed, "Jen?"

"You know this lady?" the second officer asked
Throckmorton.

He nodded and pointed at the would-be thief. "She's my ex-
wife. I think she's that creep's partner and girlfriend."

Plaintively, Jen said, "Chris, how can you say that about me?
I came by to see you and Ben, and there was such a commotion
around the house, I got scared. I ducked behind the hedge.
That's when these brutes—" and she melodramatically pointed
at the officer behind her—"drew a gun on me and marched me
in here in handcuffs."

Throckmorton turned to the closest officer. "Like I said,
she's my ex. She's been pumping me for information for her
boyfriend. I wouldn't believe a word she says." He turned and
walked into the house.

CHAPTER 39

ilbur, Nancy, and Throckmorton relaxed on old chairs in a back room at Wilbur's store on Saturday. "So, you didn't blind him with the flashbulbs?" Wilbur asked.

"No," Throckmorton said. "He was right in front of me when I tripped on Rolf and the steps going into the garage. I stumbled into him, and the bat caught him in his solar plexus, knocked the wind out of him. I broke his shoulder with the bat when he tried to stand."

"Man, you were lucky. If ya hadn't blundered into him just right, he coulda wrestled the bat away from ya and bashed your skull in."

"Chris wasn't worried," Nancy said. "He counted on Rolf to protect him."

Throckmorton looked at her, and she broke into giggles.

"Who the hell is the guy you clobbered?" Wilbur asked.

"He's a Kessler, a distant relative of mine from Utica and Jen's latest boyfriend. He'd heard about the Kessler 1804 Liberty Bust silver dollar from his grandfather, did a little research on his own, and decided to track it down. I don't know how he met Jen, but she pumped me for information every time she visited. She was his lookout that night. The cops caught her hiding in my neighbor's shrubbery and found her car a block away. Her partner is being held on two charges of murder, which makes her an accessory to murder. Ben won't be talking to his mother for a long time."

"What about Gloria's fiancé?" Nancy asked. "Alice said he was interested in the Kessler family."

"He called me before lunch. He's a writer and became interested in the Kessler family when Adele was murdered. Says he'd like to write a book about Otto, the safe, and the murders. I'll talk to him in a couple weeks when I have a better picture of what happened."

"What do you mean?" asked Nancy.

"We don't know the whole story. Something is missing. Would a guy commit two murders, travel halfway across the country, and suck up to Jen for maybe fifty-thousand dollars in coins? What about you, Wilbur? Did you find out anything about that concrete block?"

"Earl admitted it when I pressed him a little," Wilbur grunted.

"What are you going to do about it? He could kill one of us next time."

Nancy looked from Wilbur to Throckmorton. "Chris? What are you talking about? What concrete block?"

Throckmorton started to answer, but Wilbur cut him off. "It weren't nothing, and I took care of it."

"Took care of what?" she asked.

Wilbur looked around the room as though searching for a safer topic. "A guy I did some work with a while back was one of Earl's investors. I told his boys the fund was a scam and Earl got his money out before it collapsed. The boy's folks lost all their savings, and the boys are kinda hotheaded." Wilbur adopted an innocent expression. "I talked to the boys, tried to calm them down. Earl heard the boys wanted to talk to him about that stupid fund. Earl claimed he'd love to talk to them, but his wife had planned a vacation."

Wilbur lapsed into silence until Nancy asked, "And?"

"I suspect that there vacation will be a long one," Wilbur said with a smile. He turned to Throckmorton. "Any guess about the value of the coin collection and furniture?"

Throckmorton glanced at his notebook. "From my research, the furniture is worth over thirty thousand. The stamps could be worth a couple thousand, and the coins could be worth forty thousand and up. Selling wholesale, we'll probably get half to two-thirds of that."

"Not what we hoped, but better'n nothing. At least we aren't in the red anymore," Wilbur said. "What kind of value do you want to put on the beer and pickle recipes?"

"They have value?" Throckmorton asked.

Nancy raised her eyebrows. "What are you talking about?"

"Johnny and Adam found Kessler beer and pickle recipes," Wilbur said. "They're worth somethin' to me. I've decided to take a job with less dust, bird crap, an' cobwebs. Thought I'd start a little restaurant and microbrewery."

Nancy and Throckmorton looked at each other, then at Wilbur. "Where?" they asked as one.

"The old brewery site. I'm gonna put a bar in the cavern and a restaurant on top. Call it The Cave or something. Chat a reporter up about the history, the buried office, the murders, all that stuff. With free advertising, I figure I can build the business quick and sell out at a profit in a couple of years."

Throckmorton wasn't sure what to say.

Wilbur continued, "Why don't we figure the beer recipes at a thousand a piece, the pickle recipe at two hundred? We sell off the coins, you buy my half of the furniture and jewelry, and I'll buy your share of the recipes. We each chip in five hundred for the historical society, keep old Alice happy. Deal?"

"Sounds fair," Throckmorton said. "What brought about this sudden generosity?"

"I want to see Alice's face when I hand her the check."
Wilbur chuckled. "Might have to have the paramedics standing
by in case she has a heart attack. Watching her expression will
be more fun than I've had in years."

That afternoon, Nancy inventoried the stamps and coins,
took pictures of them, and emailed the pictures to four stamp
and coin dealers. She copied Wilbur on the email. Within hours,
three of the dealers called to make appointments to inspect the
collection.

CHAPTER 40

T hrockmorton was standing behind his desk in his home office early in December wondering if he'd be able to pay for the Biotherapeutic treatments for Ben when his phone rang. It was Mr. Albert, the first dealer they'd talked to.

"Mr. Throckmorton, I'd like to make an offer on one of your coins. We can discuss the other coins later, but I'd like to concentrate on your most valuable coin."

"Which coin is that?"

"The 1804 draped Liberty Bust silver dollar. My company is willing to offer you seven hundred fifty."

Throckmorton's heart sank. His estimates looked wildly optimistic. "Surely some of the gold coins are worth more than that."

"Oh, several are quite valuable, but nothing like the 1804 silver Liberty Bust. I think you'll find that $750,000 is a very generous offer. We can offer you twenty-five thousand for the rest of the collection."

Thousand? Seven hundred fifty thousand? Throckmorton pulled out his chair and sat down before his knees gave out. Stunned, he remained silent.

"Mr. Throckmorton, are you still there?"

"Yes. I . . . um . . . I was just thinking." He didn't admit he was trying to catch his breath.

The silence continued until Mr. Albert coughed and cleared his throat. "You drive a hard bargain, sir. I can go up to $760,000 for the 1804, but that leaves me little room for profit."

"I should talk to my partner," Throckmorton said. He remembered Earl's sales pitch, the time pressure he'd applied, and decided to wing it. "Wilbur—that's my partner—he said we should wait until all the bids are in. A week isn't that long to wait." Throckmorton quickly Googled "1804 Liberty Bust silver dollar" as he talked.

"Well, I—I'd hate to wait too long. Would it help if I raised our offer to $775,00 for the 1804 and $30,000 for the rest? I'm on thin ice at that price, but I believe my associates will take the chance. I can't guarantee how long the offer will stand. These things can change rapidly."

Another version of the "don't wait too long or it won't be available" ploy. Throckmorton had always hated that, but this time, he could do the squeezing. "I want to be fair to the other dealers, Mr. Albert. They were kind enough to visit and look at the collection. Don't you think it only decent to give them a chance to bid?"

"Well, that is, I mean, I can understand your reluctance, but—"

"Just a second, Mr. Albert, I've got a call on another line." Throckmorton relaxed, leaned back in his office chair. Toying with Albert was fun, but it could collapse if he sounded eager or pushed too hard. "Why don't I call you back tomorrow, and—"

"Really, Mr. Throckmorton, I think it best if we conclude the sale today. My final offer is $795,000 for the 1804 and $31,000 for the rest. That is a take it or leave it offer."

Throckmorton checked the bid prices on the screen and decided he'd pushed Albert as far as he could. "We accept your offer. When do you want to pick the coins up?"

Throckmorton put the phone down after they'd set a date. He stared at a bookcase on the wall opposite his desk, afraid he would wake up. He shook his head and pinched himself.

Nope. Not a dream. The conversation replayed in his mind.
I'll never have a moment like this again. The money will pay for
Ben's next treatments with plenty left over for college, but it
was extracting the extra $40,000 from Albert's hide that sent
adrenaline through his veins. *So, this is Wilbur's game. I could
learn to enjoy this way too much.*

He barely registered Nancy's presence when she walked in.
She shook him by his shoulder, and he reluctantly came back to
the present. "Sorry, hon. Lost in thought."

"Are you all right?" She put a hand on his forehead. "I
asked you what you wanted for dinner tonight, and you didn't
answer. You just stared at the wall."

"I'm in shock. Mr. Albert called. His final offer was $826,000.
One coin, the Kessler 1804 Liberty Bust silver dollar, was worth
$795,000. It's been lost for over a century. Kessler cousins in
Utica, La Crosse, and Rockburg were coin collectors. Together
they purchased an 1804 draped Liberty Bust silver dollar. The
last of the coin collectors died in 1904. Other family members
weren't interested in coins and knew little about them. When
they started to look, no one knew which of the deceased cousins
had held the 1804 Liberty."

"That explains the theft in New York, the murders, and the
ransacked houses. What about the stamps?"

"He'll pay $2,500 for those." Throckmorton stood, and
Nancy threw her arms around him.

"Your share will be almost $500,000."

He hugged her. "I've been afraid that with the new office,
and the excavation, that I wouldn't have enough for Ben's new
treatments."

Nancy asked him if he'd told Wilbur. He shook his head.
"He went to the historical society to see if Alice was finished
with the papers. I thought I'd go there and tell him in person."

"I'll come with you. I want to get a picture of his face when you tell him."

———

Wilbur ambled into the Rockburg Historical Society and spotted Alice in front of the Kessler safe. Her back to him, she was taking pictures of the open safe with her cell phone. He walked cautiously, afraid the floor might squeak. When he was two feet behind her, he asked, "Well, how's my favorite teacher?"

Alice whirled around, her hand over her heart. "Wilbur, don't ever do that to me again. I almost dropped my phone. I could have had a heart attack."

Wilbur grinned. This was more fun than he'd thought it would be. "Mrs. Jones, you're too tough an old bird to do that." He motioned toward the safe with one hand. "How d'ya like it?"

She admitted she was pleased with it and asked him if he'd come for the collated papers.

"Yup. You done with 'em yet?"

"It was a bigger job than I'd expected, but I finished this morning. You're lucky I didn't charge you by the hour. If you'll wait a minute, I'll get them. I think you'll be pleasantly surprised with—"

The door opened. Throckmorton called to Wilbur as he and Nancy entered, both grinning. "Wilbur, I got a bid on the coins and stamps. You won't believe what it is."

"Try me."

Nancy took pictures of Wilbur as Throckmorton told him of Mr. Albert's final offer. "Your share for sale of the coins will be $331,000, plus $13,000 for your share of the furniture."

Wilbur's jaw dropped. He leaned against a display counter for support.

Alice butted in before he could recover. "I'm sure you'll be excited with what I found in—"

Wilbur gestured for quiet. He wanted to make sure he'd understood Throckmorton, and he couldn't do that with her jabbering in his ear. "Where'd all that come from? I thought ya said it would only be around $40,000?"

"It was the 1804 draped Liberty Bust silver dollar. He offered me $725,000 to start. I was speechless. He thought I was bargaining and kept raising his offer. He finally got to $795,000 just for the Liberty Bust."

Alice started yapping again. "If you've got a moment, Wilbur, I'll tell you about the—"

Wilbur gestured again. "Shhh. Can't ya see that Throckmorton and I got serious stuff to talk about?" He turned to Throckmorton. "Which coin is the Liberty Bust, and why'd they call it that?"

Wilbur glanced at Alice to see if she was going to interrupt again. Her face looked like a thundercloud. She glared at him, feet wide apart, her hands on her hips. He hadn't seen the old girl that pissed off since he hid the grass snake in her desk drawer in seventh grade. He shifted his attention back to Throckmorton when he mentioned "1804 coin."

". . . bust of Lady Liberty," Throckmorton said. "You know, a picture from the breasts up."

Alice stalked from the room. She returned with a library cart holding two white cardboard boxes of paper in file folders. Green and yellow Post-It notes stuck up from the folders like dandelions. She parked the cart next to the display case beside Wilbur and commenced to butt in again. "I worked my tail off on your damned papers. Don't you even—?"

Wilbur was trying to digest the news of Albert's offer. "For one coin, $795,000?"

Alice started in again. He waved absently toward her to get a little peace and quiet. *Damn, how can a man think with everybody yapping?* He stared at the wall. "Albert? Was he that little hunched-over guy, white hair, black suit? Kinda looked like a walking prune?"

"Yeah, that's him."

Alice commenced again, louder this time. "Do you want me to show you—"

Wilbur glared at her, demanded quiet, and rolled his eyes when he looked back at Throckmorton. He saw Nancy look at Alice. Nancy looked worried, tapped Throckmorton on the shoulder, and whispered in his ear. It didn't get a response from him.

Wilbur scratched his chin and frowned. "Albert, I never figured him for a guy who'd move fast, unless he thought it was a deal or he already had somebody who wanted to buy it."

Throckmorton still had a grin plastered on his face—looked like a kid left to himself in a candy factory. "For whatever reason," he said, "it's a bonanza for us. How would you like to celebrate? Dinner and drinks?" He turned to Alice. "Alice, would you like to join us?"

All heads swiveled toward Alice. *Still looks pissed,* Wilbur thought.

"I gave up drinking when I quit smoking," she growled. "What do you want me to do with your papers?" She enunciated each word distinctly.

Throckmorton looked at Wilbur. "Nothing of monetary value in there," he said. "Want to donate them to the historical society?"

That sounded good to Wilbur—maybe that'd put a smile on Alice. "How about ya give us a receipt for tax purposes, Alice?

Take a guess at what they're worth and put it in the receipt somewhere. Mail it to us when you got time."

Alice smiled. Something about the smile made Wilbur uneasy. He'd seen it before, a long time ago. Nothing good had ever happened to him when she'd done that.

"Certainly, if that's what you want." She sounded so friendly she might've been flirting. She turned to a desk behind her and pulled papers from a file. "We have a standard form for you to sign for donations. I'll fill in the top blank with . . . oh, what should we call them? 'Assorted Kessler papers?' Would that do?"

Throckmorton looked at Wilbur and shrugged. "That should cover it. Wilbur?"

"Okay by me. Where should we eat?"

Alice handed Wilbur a pen before he could head toward the door. "Each of you should sign and date the second page and initial and date the first page. The contract includes a clause stating that you'll get ten percent of the proceeds if we sell any donated material. It was added to discourage the sale of donations by the society. I'll mail you copies and a receipt."

There it is again, Wilbur thought. *If I didn't know better, I'd swear she was talkin' sweet to me. She sure must like those papers.* "Seems like there's always more paperwork than there ought to be," he said as he signed on the second page.

"I know, Wilbur," Alice said as though commiserating with him. "Life would be so much easier if it weren't for the paperwork. Just sign and date. I'll take care of the rest."

Wilbur and Throckmorton got the signatures out of the way and headed for the door with Nancy. They chatted about their luck, as well as their hard work, and speculated about what Earl would say if he ever returned from his "vacation."

Wilbur glanced back at Alice through the front window of the historical society. She was in her favorite chair, feet on an old ottoman, maybe from the Kessler mansion, looking at the signed papers. Damned near looked like she was laughing.

———

Throckmorton put the letters from the brewery office away and strolled out to the kitchen. "We were right," he said to Nancy.

"About what?"

"The letters from 1904. Otto's father did die that year. He was the last collector."

Nancy smiled. "That's what you thought earlier."

"There were later letters about a gym and a ballpark Otto built for the town. The gym was across the street from Otto's house. It became the Catholic church in the late 1930s. He built a bandstand and bought instruments for a city band too. It played at the bandstand on Main Street next to the train station. Otto's son played in the band until he left Rockburg."

"Rockburg had a train station and bandstand?"

"Yup. The station was demolished in the mid-1950s, and the bandstand was torn down about the same time. Otto was quite the civic booster. That ended with Prohibition. I'll have to check with Alice and her newspaper archives."

"Does it make you feel better knowing about Otto and your family?"

"Yeah. Kind of proud of the old boy."

CHAPTER 41

The receipt from Alice arrived at Throckmorton's new office in the Kessler building in mid-December. He filed it, unopened. Christmas and New Year's passed. Ben started the biotherapeutic treatments. There were minimal side reactions—no oral ulcers, no days too sick to eat, and no bouts with septicemia. Spending the holidays with Nancy, Amanda, and Ben was wonderful. Throckmorton hadn't enjoyed the holidays that much since his college days.

He had little spare time after New Year's Day because of the tax work he did. Nancy spent her spare time at home paging through glossy brochures from Caribbean resorts. She called him at his new office on a frigid morning in early January.

"Chris, are you busy? There's something odd in the mail today."

"I've got a minute. What's the problem?"

"There's a letter from the Rockburg Historical Society in the mail. It's an embossed invitation to a banquet on February seventeenth, and I quote, 'In honor of Mr. and Mrs. Wilbur Woodside, Mr. Christopher Throckmorton, and Ms. Nancy Twittle.'"

"What? It must be a joke. Who signed it?" Throckmorton pushed himself away from his desk and looked at his watch. It was too early to break for lunch or run home to look at the letter.

"Mrs. Alice Jones. The printing is beautiful. Any idea what this is about?"

"None. Is the dinner at Gert's? She and Alice are buddies. This could be their idea of a practical joke."

"I don't think so," Nancy said. "This letter doesn't look like a prank. It's on expensive stationery, and the dinner is at the country club. A blurb she enclosed says the dinner is for members and supporters of the Rockburg Historical Society."

"Half of those people couldn't afford to eat at the country club, and the other half are too cheap to go there. Do we have to pay for our dinners?"

Throckmorton's cell phone buzzed in his pocket. He looked at the caller's name. "I'll call you back, hon. Wilbur's calling on my cell."

Throckmorton hung up and answered his cell phone. Wilbur asked him if he'd received a strange invitation.

"You got the invitation too?" Throckmorton asked.

"Yeah, just opened it. That's what I called about."

"Any idea what Alice is up to?" Throckmorton asked. "The historical society couldn't pay the rent on their building if it wasn't almost free. How can they throw a banquet, and why on earth would they do it in our honor?"

"How the hell would I know?" Wilbur asked. "Did you read the receipt she sent us for the papers?"

Throckmorton shrugged. "Didn't even open it. Figured I'd get around to it when I do my taxes."

"Same here. We didn't look at all those papers from the office, either."

"I checked all the stock certificates. I didn't spend a lot of time on them. None were worth anything."

Wilbur hemmed and hawed a moment. "Well, that ain't quite right. There were a few neither of us saw. Johnny called me on my cell the day we moved the furniture. He got ahold of me on my way to a meeting—said they'd found a couple've papers that slipped under the safe. I had to pry that much out of him. He said they were invoices and something about machines. I told him to drop 'em off with Alice and tell her to add 'em to the rest of the papers."

"It doesn't sound like they were anything of value," Throckmorton said cautiously.

"Well, it was Johnny, though. He wouldn't recognize a stock certificate if you shoved it down his throat."

Throckmorton felt queasy. "I'll take your word for it."

"And remember when Alice tried to talk to us about the papers she organized? We were all excited about the money we got from those coins. Neither one of us listened to her, and I tried to shut her up a couple times. That pissed her off."

Throckmorton strained to recall the day they'd donated the papers. He remembered Wilbur cutting Alice short. She'd looked angry, darn near spitting nails, but she'd been solicitous when Wilbur had complained about all the paperwork and signatures for the donation.

A band tightened around Throckmorton's forehead. He'd never had a migraine before. "And she had us sign a contract transferring ownership to the society." Nervous, he opened a file and searched through it for the receipt from Alice.

"This dinner, it ain't no fish fry, either," Wilbur said. "There's a note here under Alice's signature says it's black tie." The line was silent for a moment. "Is that what I think it is: tuxedos and that nonsense?"

Throckmorton's mouth was dry. "Yeah." He slit the envelope open with a letter opener. "Just a sec. I've got the receipt here." He scanned through the paper looking for the critical lines. "Assorted papers from a buried safe once owned by Otto Kessler, value to be determined."

"That's helpful as shit," Wilbur said. "I got a bad feeling about this."

———

The Rockburg Historical Society Gala was held on the coldest Friday night in February. Throckmorton thought it suited his apprehensions of the evening. A waiter in tails and white tie showed Nancy and Throckmorton to the head table at the Maple Grove Country Club. Wilbur and his wife Florence were already seated near the center of the table. Nancy found Throckmorton's name on a place card between the card for Nancy and one labeled Mrs. A. Jones. Alice joined them moments later. Throckmorton, already wary as he took his seat, developed an ache in his gut when he saw Alice wink at Gert sitting at a table in front of them. The old girls were both dressed in evening gowns and smiling way too much whenever they looked at Wilbur or him.

Throckmorton thought the audience appropriate for a historical society banquet. Most of those in attendance were more than thirty years his senior. None of them would see sixty again.

When the beef Wellington was served—with salad, potatoes, asparagus, and an excellent California burgundy—he heard Wilbur's wife, Florence, snarl, "Your donation paid for a spread like this, but we couldn't afford a vacation at the lake last summer?"

A podium and microphone were placed on the center of the head table as the waiters cleared the dessert dishes. Alice stepped behind the podium, tapped a glass with a fork, and asked for silence.

"Allow me to introduce our guests of honor, the people who made our feast possible, Mr. and Mrs. Wilbur Woodside . . ." Alice nodded toward Wilbur and Florence, "Ms. Nancy Twittle, and Mr. Christopher Throckmorton. Please stand and join me in showing our appreciation."

Throckmorton could almost hear the arthritic knees and backs creak as the audience rose and Alice led them in a standing ovation. Throckmorton held Nancy's hand under the tablecloth. She looked at him, eyebrows raised in a silent question. He shrugged and mouthed, "Darned if I know." Throckmorton glanced at Wilbur. Slumped in his chair, he looked pale and nervous under a withering glare from Florence.

At a few tables, one or more of the diners pointed at Wilbur. Hoots, laughter, and even louder applause followed. *Former customers of Wilbur's*, Throckmorton thought.

Alice asked the crowd to be seated and gave a brief history of Otto Kessler's 1935 letter, the safe, and the generous gift of the papers. "All of Otto Kessler's investments were worthless by 1995," Alice said. She let the words hang in the air for a moment and gave Wilbur a smile before she continued. "Save only one."

She savored every syllable of that last sentence, Throckmorton thought. He and Wilbur looked at each other. Feeling as though he were in a fishbowl, Throckmorton turned his eyes back to the audience.

Alice continued. "After the stock market collapse of 1929 and up to his death in 1935, Otto Kessler slowly acquired the discounted stocks of several great companies, a hundred to two hundred shares at a time. By 1935, he had between five hundred and a thousand shares each of Packard Motor Car Company, the Pennsylvania and New York Central railroads, TWA, and Pan American Airways" Alice paused and looked over the audience. The clatter of forks on dessert plates ceased, and a hush came over the room.

Throckmorton peeked at Wilbur. Under the lights on the

head table, beads of sweat were sprinkled across his brow. Occasional glares from Florence might have had something to do with that.

Alice continued, "Otto also had shares of International Business Machines, better known today as Big Blue, or IBM." She dragged out the letters *I, B, M*, reciting each as though it were a separate word.

The crowd, Wilbur, and Throckmorton gasped. Florence, her jaw set, her brow deeply furrowed, glared at Wilbur. He put a finger under his collar as though it was too tight.

Alice again smiled graciously at Wilbur and Throckmorton and gestured for them to stand. Throckmorton didn't think his knees were up to the task. He had difficulty organizing his thoughts through the second standing ovation. He looked at Wilbur to see how he'd taken it. He hadn't stood, either. He'd faded from pale to white. Frequent side glances toward Florence made him look shifty. Her face was contorted into a grimace, her black eyebrows a threatening V, she looked like a Wagnerian harpy as she glared at Wilbur.

"Purchased at two dollars a share, Otto bought five hundred shares of IBM for one thousand dollars. The five hundred shares, purchased from 1929 to 1933, after multiple splits and reinvestment of dividends, had become forty-nine thousand, seven hundred ninety-five shares by December of last year—truly a mind-boggling and beneficent gift from our guests of honor."

Wilbur buried his face in his hands at the start of the third standing ovation. Throckmorton would have mistaken it for humble embarrassment if he hadn't known Wilbur. From the applause, laughter, and whistles, it sounded as though no one else in Rockburg made that mistake, either.

Throckmorton estimated the current value of the stock

they'd given away. He couldn't handle that many zeros in his head. He saw Wilbur jerk and look at Florence. *Probably kicked him in the shins under the table. What'll she do when Alice announces what it was worth?*

Throckmorton nudged Nancy and nodded toward Wilbur. She wouldn't want to miss the drama taking place three chairs away.

"The stock price, only two dollars at the beginning of the Great Depression, was over $161 a share when the society sold the shares last month."

Wilbur buried his head in his hands again. Throckmorton heard him moan softly and saw him flinch twice. *Yup, Florence is giving it to him. Wonder if he'll need help getting to his car.*

"As per our usual contract for donations of monetary value," Alice continued, "Mr. Throckmorton and Mr. Woodside will each receive a cashier's check for $362,000. The remainder, over $7 million, will be used by the society to establish several foundations and grants. These will include the Throckmorton-Woodside Educational Foundation to assist Rockburg High graduates enrolled in college; the Woodside-Throckmorton Foundation, a foundation for the preservation and maintenance of Rockburg's historic Main Street; substantial grants to four state universities; and $500,000 to found the Woodside Foundation for Ethics in Business."

Laughter and applause erupted without a prompt from Alice. She resumed her seat between Nancy and Wilbur after the fourth standing ovation. Beaming, she leaned toward Wilbur. She spoke barely loud enough for Throckmorton to eavesdrop. "Never shush a teacher, Wilbur. Never."

As the banquet broke up, people came up to Throckmorton to shake his hand. Between well-wishers, he looked toward Wilbur and Florence, also shaking hands with people. He whispered in Nancy's ear, "We may have to give Wilbur a bed for the night."

Nancy asked Throckmorton how he felt about the accidental donation as they drove home.

"We have more money than I'd hoped to find, enough for Ben's treatments, enough to guarantee he'll have health insurance until he's in college, and there'll be enough for a few vacations."

"What about the foundations Alice set up?"

"I can't sit on the board of directors without jeopardizing the tax write-off for the gift, but she said she'd keep me in the loop on the grants they make. I think we'll have fun seeing how it's doled out, and Otto will get his wish too."

"How so?"

Throckmorton smiled. "If Wilbur builds a microbrewery and restaurant—and he can afford to now—Otto's beer and pickles will be sold in Rockburg again."

Nancy snickered. "But still, you gave away millions. No regrets?"

He reached across the car and took Nancy's hand. "None. Searching for Otto's assets was quite a trip, and Alice and Gert put them to a use Otto would have been proud of. We have each other. What's to regret?"

Nancy squeezed his hand. He glanced at her again and asked, "So how about getting married? Do you think I'm a keeper?"

"Oh, you're a keeper all right."

ABOUT THE AUTHOR

Raised on a Wisconsin dairy farm, Jones went to high school in a small town dominated by the old, brick brewery built by his great-grandfather and grandfather. He grew up hearing stories of the tunnels and caverns under the brewery and the town's main streets. The brewery, used since prohibition as a canning factory and later a feed mill, was demolished in 2015. The lot is still empty, though the old brewery office building and bottling plant are still standing.

Jones practiced veterinary medicine, primarily treating dairy cattle, in rural Wisconsin before returning to graduate school and earning a PhD in microbiology at the University of Minnesota. He has written fiction since retiring from working in the research and development of animal vaccines.

Gary lives in Omaha, Nebraska.

OTHER BOOKS BY
GARY F. JONES

When Wisconsin veterinarian Doc dies, his family learns that to inherit his fortune, they must decipher the cryptic codicil he added to his will: "Take Doofus squirrel-fishing." They can only do that by talking to Doc's friends, reading the memoir Doc wrote of a Christmas season decades earlier, and searching through Doc's correspondences. Humor abounds as this mismatched lot tries to find time in their hectic lives to work together to solve the puzzle. In the end, will they realize that fortune comes in many guises?

Doc's Codicil is a mystery told with abundant humor where a veterinarian teaches his heirs a lesson from the grave.

Doc's Codicil was the winner of the bronze medal for Humor in the INDIEFAB Book of the Year Awards, 2015.

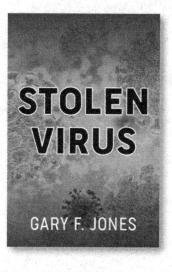

"A medical thriller and satire that will keep you guessing and engaged while offering subtle humor as the good guys triumph."

Veterinary virologist Jason Mitchell can't keep his mouth shut, can't lie convincingly, and can't follow orders. He's an unlikely candidate to help the CIA locate and destroy a deadly hybrid virus stolen from Jason's lab at the University of Minnesota. From Washington to Djibouti, From Minneapolis to Yemen, Marines cringe, Senators turn livid, and CIA agents shudder as Jason struggles to prevent the virus from becoming a biological weapon in the hands of insurgents.

Jason and Ann Hartman, veterinarians, lovers, and graduate students, conduct a study of BCV in calves, a common virus that causes diarrhea in cattle. A recently arrived Chinese student accidentally exposes the calves to the SARS virus, a close relative of BCV. The calves and the Chinese student develop a severe and puzzling pneumonia. The Center for Disease Control (CDC) isolates a hybrid BCV-SARS virus from the Chinese student and the calves. The FBI is notified of the new and dangerous virus.

Meanwhile, Ahmed, more con man than graduate student, discovers samples of Jason's that contain the virus. He steals them and flees to Yemen where he pretends to be a devout Muslim to get funding from a terrorist group that believes the virus will be valuable as a biological weapon and as bait to lure the CIA into military action that will kill innocent civilians and increase hatred of the US. In a perilous situation with a bumbling hero and unexpected situations, Jason and an unconventional CIA agent redefine "thinking outside the box" as they con Ahmed, dodge bullets, and thwart the bad guys.

Nature, climate, and stupidity produce a pandemic

Grant Farnsworth, a post-doc student, veterinarian, and virologist at the University of Minnesota is upset when his professor tells him to prepare to work on tissue samples from the Iceman, a 1,200-year-old corpse discovered in the Swiss Alps.

Grant is already working seven days a week and his wife is eight months pregnant with their second child.

The situation becomes dangerous when a Swiss professor, to avoid regulations, smuggles the samples into the United States, putting Grant and his professor in legal jeopardy. A blizzard diverts the professor's flight to Chicago, Customs is hectic, and the professor mistakenly swaps his suitcase with Frank, a drug mule. Frank discovers the error and follows the professor north on I-94 to recover the missing drugs. Snow forces the professor to stop at a motel in the hamlet of Kirby, Wisconsin; he has no idea that he's carrying drugs and that his life is in jeopardy

The Swiss government confidentially informs the CDC that those who handled Iceman samples are ill, and one has died. Grant is sent to Kirby to find the Swiss professor and isolate the samples. The CDC learns of the samples in Kirby and dispatches Dr. Sybil Erypet to Fort McCoy, a nearby Army base, to get the samples under control. Between dangerous drug mules, eccentric locals, and infected tissue samples, many lives in the snow-bound village and surrounding area are in jeopardy.

"... This cinematic-style caper is perfect for readers who have also loved movies such as *Fargo* and *Weekend at Bernie's*. Gary Jones's novel is a triumph. If you haven't read his work yet, put *The Iceman's Curse* on your list. Highly recommended."

- Christine DeSmet, mystery novelist, writing coach, member of Mystery Writers of America and Sisters in Crime